THIN ICE

QUENTIN BATES

LARGE
PRINT

First published in Great Britain 2016
by
Constable
an imprint of Little, Brown Book Group

First Isis Edition
published 2018
by arrangement with
Little, Brown Book Group
An Hachette UK Company

A catalogue record for this book is available
from the British Library.

ISBN 978–1–78541–521–0 (hb)
ISBN 978–1–78541–527–2 (pb)

Published by
F. A. Thorpe (Publishing)
Anstey, Leicestershire

Set by Words & Graphics Ltd.
Anstey, Leicestershire
Printed and bound in Great Britain by
T. J. International Ltd., Padstow, Cornwall

This book is printed on acid-free paper

THIN ICE

When two ...ll-time crooks rob Reykjavík's premier drug ...ler, their plans start to unravel after their ge... ...y driver fails to show. Tensions mount betwee... ...e pair and the two women they grabbed as h... ...es, when they find themselves holed up in ... isolated hotel that has been mothballed fc... ...he season. Back in the capital, police officers... ...nhildur, Eiríkur and Helgi find themselves at... ...d end investigating what appears to be the unre... ...f disappearance of a mother, her daughter and t... ...ar, and the death of a thief. But Gunna and h...r ...eam soon realise that all these unrelated incide... ...are, in fact, linked — while at the same time ...o increasingly desperate lowlifes have no choice... ...to make some big decisions on how to get rid ... ...eir accidental hostages . . .

0138595579

For the two Sylvias

CHAPTER ONE

Thursday

The hard guy in the leather jacket was big, with bulky shoulders and knotted forearms, and his jaw jutted forward as if asking to be punched.

So Magni obliged, swatting the tough guy aside with an effortless backhander. He never could resist an invitation; the big man stumbled back, emitting a high-pitched keening sound as he hit the wall, his dinnerplate hands held to his face as blood seeped through his fingers.

Magni felt no animosity towards the meathead who had been stupid enough to be in the wrong place at the right time. Or was that the wrong time, he wondered? Whatever, the guy was spitting teeth into his cupped hands and whimpering, so he only needed a casual eye to be kept on him. Nothing to worry about, Magni decided with satisfaction. At any rate, the ugly black pistol in Össur's nervous hand was far more persuasive than mere muscles.

The old man's face went pale, paler than it normally was, and Alli the Cornershop didn't look like a man who spent much time in the sun. He looked sick as he handed over a carrier bag that Össur glanced into before tucking it under one arm.

"You must know you don't have a chance in hell of getting away with this," Alli snarled. "I'll have the pair of you bastards brought back here trussed up in barbed wire."

"Good luck, grandpa."

Even from behind the black balaclava, Össur's nasal voice was enough to identify him. He was sweating, though he had promised himself that he would stay calm. At last he had the cash in his hands. Maybe it wasn't, enough to retire on, but it would keep him in comfort for a good few years somewhere warm and cheap, especially if he could lose the thick-headed halfwit looking sorrowfully at the big guy who was now counting his remaining teeth.

"Come on. We're out of here," Össur snapped and Magni emerged from his reverie, pushing open the door. "Sit yourself down, grandpa, and don't even think of trying to come after us. All right?" The pistol in his outstretched hand pointed at Alli's face.

With an apologetic glance at the big man, now spluttering through the blood in his mouth, Magni followed Össur out and down the stairs, emerging into the quiet residential street of well-tended gardens in front of houses built fifty years ago. Nobody was moving and nothing was happening on this quiet afternoon with a chill in the still air. A dog barked in the distance and children could be heard playing in a garden somewhere in the tangle of old houses that made up this dog-leg street leading downhill to the town centre.

"Where the fuck is Árni?" Össur pulled the balaclava off his face and thrust the pistol into the pocket of his jacket, casting about for a glimpse of the souped-up Land Cruiser that should have been waiting for them, its engine idling and Árni behind the wheel, ready to roll to the end of the street, then a burst of power up the hill and they'd be on the main road and out of sight of a livid Alli the Cornershop and whatever goons he could summon at short notice.

"He's not here, is he?" Magni said, stating the obvious to Össur's irritation.

"I can fucking see that. So where is he?"

"I don't know. Call him," Magni shrugged. "But I reckon we'd be best off out of here pretty quick," he said, setting off downhill at a smart pace and without a backward glance at the house they had just left.

Össur had to admit that for once Magni had a point and set off after him, one hand on the 9mm pistol in his pocket and the other hugging the shopping bag full of euros, with the smaller bag of Alli the Cornershop's finest merchandize stuffed inside his jacket.

They burst through the shopping centre's doors to find comforting but slightly distorted Christmas muzak burbling inside, even though it wasn't yet December. It was only two minutes from the quiet street where Alli the Cornershop lived in his flat above a boarded-up shop that had been closed for years, but it seemed to be a different world to this one of families browsing through shops and teenagers cruising aimlessly between the hot-dog stand and a shop selling computer games.

3

"Where the fuck is Árni?" Össur snarled as he sat himself down in a corner of the coffee shop, glancing out of the windows as if expecting the police or worse to arrive at any moment. He stabbed at his phone and listened in frustration as the ring tone echoed from the loudspeaker until a warm voice politely informed him that the user must be out of range and invited him to try again later.

Össur tried again immediately and the result was the same.

"Shit, shit, shit!" Össur swore, dropping the phone on the table. "Fucking hell!" he added in a savage afterthought.

"Hey, you mind your language," Magni reminded him gently. "There are children about."

"Don't you tell me what to do," Össur snapped back, furious that the seriousness of the situation was not making an impression on Magni, who sat with his beefy hands in his lap.

"You want a coffee?"

"Of course I don't want a fucking coffee."

"You sure?" Magni asked. "I think it looks a little suspicious, two guys sat in a coffee shop with no coffee."

Össur had to admit that the big man, who normally seemed slow on the uptake, was quite right.

"Go on, then."

Össur tried his phone once more while Magni queued patiently, calling Árni's number again before trying another.

"Hey, man," he said, trying to sound as relaxed as he could when the phone was finally answered by a sleepy voice. "You seen Árni Sigurvins today?"

4

"Who?" The voice queried.

"Árni Sig. Drives a Land Cruiser. You know."

"No, pal. Sorry."

The same conversation was repeated twice with minor variations until Magni returned with two coffees and a sticky Danish pastry.

"You want half?" he asked, making to break it in two.

"Fuck, no."

Össur's fingers drummed frantically on the table.

"Don't swear. I told you already."

"Yeah, yeah. Look, we need to get out of here, and quick."

"How about we get a taxi?"

"Are you insane?" Össur stared at him. "A taxi? Fuck, no. Alli's going to be searching for us high and low soon. That's if he hasn't put a price on our heads already."

Magni stuffed half of the pastry into his mouth and chewed, grinning amiably at Össur. "Like he's going to be searching for us in a shopping centre, right? No sign of Árni?"

"Come on."

"Already? Why don't we wait until dark?"

Össur's teeth chattered in agitation. "Because we have to get away from here before someone notices us."

"And that old guy finds us?"

"That's it. We need a car."

Magni shrugged. "Árni?"

"That useless bastard," Össur snarled. "When I see him, I'll twist his fucking head off. We need a car," he repeated, looking desperately across the car park outside where people were coming and going with bags of shopping, some of them laughing as if they didn't have a care in the world. Össur wanted to kick and punch them.

"Come on."

He pushed his chair back so hard that it banged against another table and people looked up to see what the commotion was.

"Calm down, man," Magni urged him, but Össur was already heading for the door, practically at a run, while Magni loped after him.

Outside he cast about urgently and Magni wondered what he might be looking for.

"Hey, slow down, will you?"

"Come on," Össur said decisively, and hurried across the car park towards the more sparsely filled area furthest from the shops. It was almost dark and the street lights flickered into life, casting their orange glow.

A large white car stood with doors open as Össur scurried towards it with Magni trailing behind. Magni saw the driver's door close and the headlights come on as the car rolled slowly across the car park. He wondered what Össur was doing as he saw him break into a run, heading to intercept the car, and then catch hold of the rear passenger door handle, yank the door open and yell something at the occupants.

By the time Magni caught up, Össur was in the car, hunched on the back seat, the door still open behind him.

"Just who are you and what do you want? Get out or I'll call the police."

The woman in the driver's seat had the sort of determined voice that carried, but her jaw dropped and she sat in shocked silence as Össur pulled the pistol from his pocket and jammed it low and hard into the ribs of the young woman in the passenger seat. The girl started and stared, her mouth hanging open.

"You're going to shut the fuck up and drive. Understand?" Össur said, his voice hoarse. He shuffled across the broad back seat and snapped at Magni. "Get in, will you? This lady's going to give us a lift. Now go."

"Where are you going?"

"Be quiet, will you?" Össur pushed the muzzle of the pistol hard into the girl's ribs, making her cry out.

"Mum, please," she pleaded.

"But where?" the woman asked. "Which way?"

"She means which turn-off," Magni explained patiently. "Calm down, will you?"

"OK, the main road," Össur decided, gnawing at the fingernails of the hand that didn't hold the gun pressed into the girl's side.

"Where are we going, Össi?" Magni asked in an undertone. "I mean . . ."

"We'll just get away from town and have them drop us somewhere. Or we can take the car and leave them, maybe?"

"The police will be looking for it the moment these two are on their own," Magni pointed out.

"Hey, you," Össur said, jabbing the girl with the pistol. "Give me your phone."

"I forgot it. Left it at home," she replied, her voice both surly and frightened as she edged across the seat as far as she could from the gun.

"Hers, then," Össur ordered. "And don't try and tell me you both came out without a phone."

"Where is it, Mum?"

"In my bag. On the seat."

"This one?" Össur demanded, lifting up a bag made of soft leather. The girl nodded and Össur stuffed the pistol back in his pocket as he went through the bag, throwing the contents on the seat. Lipstick, a makeup compact, a pack of tampons and a bunch of keys were all shaken out in a pile on the plush white seat before Össur triumphantly put a smartphone into his pocket. "And your phone?" he snapped at the girl. "Where is it?"

"Really. I didn't bring it. It's on the table at home. The battery was flat so I left it there to recharge."

"If I find out you're lying . . ." Össur said, eyes narrow.

The woman in the driving seat looked around. "Listen —"

"You watch the road."

"Look, where do you want to go? Take the car if you want, as long as you don't hurt us. We won't say anything to the police. We'll just say the car was stolen, honestly."

The fear in the woman's voice was clear. Magni could see that her hands were sweating on the wheel and he wondered what Össur had planned, if he had anything planned now that their flight would certainly have left without them. He could see that Össur was terrified that his plans had fallen through and Árni had failed to be there just at the critical moment they needed him.

"Go that way," Össur said suddenly.

"Where?" The woman asked, baffled.

"That way over there, you stupid bitch, take the turn-off there," Össur yelled and the woman quailed as she hauled the car off the main road and up the slip road.

"Now what?" she screeched as a roundabout approached.

"Over there, that way, go on." Now it was fully dark and they could only see the woman's features in the glow of the dashboard. "Faster," Össur ordered.

"Össi, where the fuck are we going?" Magni demanded, and the brooding lack of a reply convinced him that Össur had no idea.

"Look," Össur said in an urgent whisper, "we'll find some place up in the country where there's no phone or anything, dump these two there and we can take the car. By the time they're found, we'll be clear away. All right?"

Magni nodded in dubious agreement.

"All right," he said, wondering where they would find somewhere safe to dump two city women in the middle of a winter's night.

"What the hell is this place? Magni?"

Össur's voice trembled. A large white building loomed out of the darkness in front of them. Every window was black and a padlock hung from the front door.

"It used to be a community centre years ago," Magni said. "Then it was a hotel for a while. Don't know what it is now, though."

"Shit. We can't stop here. We need somewhere nobody's going to see us."

The two women still sat in the front seats of the car, hugged by the deep upholstery, and staring at the building lit up in the glare of the headlights. They sat in silence until the engine stopped and the silence deepened.

"What happened?"

"I think we ran out of petrol," the older woman said, her hands still gripping the wheel. "I tried to tell you, but you wouldn't listen."

"Shut the fuck up, will you?" Össur snapped.

"Well, we'll have to stay here now, won't we?" Magni said with a laugh that set Össur's teeth on edge with frustration.

Magni made short work of the padlock and the door swung open. Össur scowled and went in last, shepherding the two women ahead of him. He flicked a light switch and swore when nothing happened.

"Hold on," Magni said, looking around him in the faint beam of light that the torch in his phone emitted. "There must be a fuse board here somewhere. There's power because there are lights over there."

His voice echoed and the vapour of his breath gathered in the beam of light. Then there was darkness as he vanished around a corner and into another room, his footsteps slapping on the tiled floor.

"In here," he called, and the two women looked at each other.

"Go on," Össur ordered. "You. Give me the car keys."

"I told you, it's out of petrol," the older woman said in rising panic, her arms wrapped around herself. "Why are you doing this? What's wrong with you people? Why have you brought us to this place?"

"Keys," Össur said, standing close to her and glaring into her eyes until she looked away and dropped them into his outstretched hand.

They stood in the kitchen doorway to see Magni standing on a stool looking at a fuse box high on the wall. He clicked one of the switches and looked over his shoulder.

"Try the light."

The girl switched on the light and the long kitchen with its steel tables was flooded with fluorescent brightness as the tubes in the ceiling flickered into life. Magni jumped down from the stool.

"The lighting circuit must have been switched off," he said, looking around the kitchen with a grin on his face, "but the power wasn't off." He opened a chest freezer in the corner and his grin widened as he lifted up a frozen leg of lamb. "Roast lamb for breakfast?"

Magni turned up the heating that had been set just high enough to ensure that nothing froze and the place gradually began to warm up enough for him to discard his coat, while the two women remained huddled in theirs as they perched on kitchen chairs. Össur sat with his hands deep in his coat pockets, angry at the usually thick-headed Magni's practical nature.

"Hey, you," Magni called over to the older of the two women. "Come here and stir this, will you?"

A saucepan of soup was starting to simmer on the vast stove, filling the kitchen with its aroma.

11

"Me?" the older woman asked.

"No, Father Christmas. Who do you think I mean?"

She took the wooden spoon uncertainly while the girl smiled to herself.

"You," Magni said, pointing at her and the smirk disappeared. "Have a look in those cupboards and see if you can find some bowls or something."

Magni ladled soup into four bowls and handed them round. Össur spooned his up quickly, the two women exchanging glances and wrinkled their noses as he slurped. Magni drank his soup straight from the bowl in long draughts, and belched.

"Fuck me, that's better," he said. "I'd forgotten how hungry I was. Who's washing up?" He looked at everyone in turn. "Well, I'm not doing it."

"Nor am I. Wash up, for fuck's sake?" Össur dropped his empty bowl with a bang on the table.

"Looks like one of you ladies, I reckon." Magni scratched his head and yawned. "We ought to get to know each other considering we might be here a while. What's your name?"

The older woman pointed her nose in the air.

"I'm Tinna Lind," the younger one said, a spark of amusement in her dark eyes. "This is my mum and her name's Erna."

"You didn't have to tell them, did you?" Erna snapped. "How long is this ridiculous charade going to go on?"

"I'm Magni and that's Össur over there," Magni said slowly, picking his teeth with the nail of his little finger while Össur scowled at the mention of his own name.

12

"And we don't want to be here any more than you do. I wonder if there's any coffee here?"

After the long drive in the dark, it was a release to sit back and relax. Össur brooded to himself, while Magni took the opportunity to examine the two women they had managed to abduct. The older one was stylish, blonde hair smartly and simply cut, her soft leather jacket zipped to the neck, designer jeans and boots made from what looked to be the same expensive leather as her jacket. The daughter was very different, a slight young woman with an impish button nose and an air of suppressed energy about her, wearing jeans that looked more bargain basement than designer and with hair in braided cornrows, tied in a loose knot at the back of her head.

Tinna Lind looked back at him with a curiosity that contrasted with Erna's frosty aloofness. She saw a raw-boned young man with red stubble and shoulders as wide as a wardrobe sitting opposite her, with no apparent concern on his face, while the sinister of the two, the older man with the air of desperation about him, had disappeared down the hall.

Össur came back to the table and sat down, his hands still deep in his jacket pockets. He glared at the two women and finally took his hands out of his pockets, holding a packet of cigarettes in one hand. He clicked his Zippo and blew a cloud of grey smoke.

"So what do we do now, Magni?"

Magni rattled the contents of a cupboard and came up with a vacuum pack of coffee. "I don't rightly know. This was supposed to be an easy job for me. Stand there, look a bit heavy and cash on the nail afterwards. Now I'm stuck out here in the arsehole of beyond."

"What have you guys done?" Tinna Lind asked, looking from one to the other. "I won't tell anyone."

"Mind your own business if you know what's good for you," Össur snarled.

"I want to go home right now," Erna broke in, her voice shrill and angry. "I demand to go home immediately." She pushed her chair back so that it clattered on the floor behind her. Össur stood up slowly, the smoke from the cigarette curling past his eyes and into his hair.

"Shut your mouth," he said with quiet menace.

"No. I won't be quiet. I refuse to be quiet. I've been abducted and I'll see you spend years in prison for this, you . . ."

Her words were cut short as Össur's short, sharp punch slammed into her belly and Erna fell to the floor, doubled up and gasping for breath. Tinna Lind knelt by her mother and cradled her as Össur stepped back, the cigarette still between his lips.

"Hey, man, what d'you do that for? No call for that, was there?" Magni said, standing up and towering over Össur. "The lady's upset but even you can see she might have a reason to be pissed off, so there's no need to smack her." He folded his arms, the muscles of his forearms bunching and straining the sleeves of his hooded sweater.

"Don't you give me that. I don't need lessons from the fucking hired help," Össur spat and stalked out into

14

the lobby of the echoing hotel, clicking off lights as he went.

The man with the deeply unfashionable mullet was face down on the floor. He craned his neck, twisting around to try and see what was happening behind him, until a sharp cuff to the back of the head discouraged him. His hands were secured behind his back and one foot had been tied to the leg of the table with many bindings of thin blue rope.

He could hear the old man wheeze as he pulled up a chair and sat next to him, leaning down close enough that he could feel as well as smell the brandy fumes on his breath.

"Árni, I'm disappointed in you. I never thought you'd let me down like that."

Árni wriggled on the floor and tried to reply, but the rag tied around his face and filling his mouth simply turned his protests into an unintelligible mumble.

Alli leaned down and picked up something from the table. He tapped it on the floor and Árni's eyes widened in disbelief. "Now listen to me, Árni," he said, and there was a furious desperation in his voice. "You're going to tell me where Össi and that other idiot went, aren't you? Because Baldvin's not a happy boy these days, had his beauty spoilt. So if you don't sing like a bird, then I'm going to give these to Baldvin to play with."

He snapped shut the pair of garden clippers, and two short, curved blades meshed neatly together as the long handles closed.

15

"Understand?"

Árni nodded furiously.

Alli nodded to Baldvin, lips swollen from the casual backhand swipe he had received. The big man pressed a button and the CD player burst into life.

"Ah," Alli said with approval. "Good old Black Sabbath, you've gotta love 'em." His voice hardened suddenly. "Where's Össi?" he demanded, yelling over the music, leaning forward and loosening the rag tied around Árni's face.

"I don't know where they went. They asked me to meet them here and that's all I know."

"Bullshit!" Alli screamed and slapped Árni's face. "You were part of it. Where did they go?"

"Honest, Alli. I don't know. Össi just said meet him here at three to give him a lift somewhere and that's all there was to it. I thought it was a job."

"It was a fucking job," Alli yelled, his face going red.

"No! I meant I thought it was a job for you."

Alli nodded to Baldvin, who sat on the floor to untie the lace of Árni's scuffed training shoe and pull it off. He wrinkled his nose at the smell and glanced at Alli.

"Get the fuck on with it."

Baldvin pulled off the sock and threw it behind him.

"Last chance," Alli said, his eyes bulging in fury.

"I'm telling the truth!" Árni screeched. "Össi said he needed a lift and to be here at three! I won't be late again!"

Alli handed the clippers to Baldvin. Árni could feel the cold metal hook around his little toe. Even now he

16

could not believe that Alli could be so brutal as to carry out his threat.

"Where. Did. They. Go?" Alli said, pausing between each word. "What was the plan, Árni?"

"I told you, I don't know any plan."

"Shit, you're too stupid to live," Alli said, and pointed at the foot tied to the table as Árni twisted round to see the two handles come smartly together. There was no pain at first but his eyes bulged as he saw his little toe roll across the carpet while Baldvin stood up and hurried from the room with his hand to his mouth. It took a few seconds before the full realization hit him, followed by the pain. Alli stood up and went to the CD player, turning up the volume to drown out Árni's disbelieving sobs.

The place seemed warmer. Magni boiled water in a pot on the stove and used it to make coffee, which he gulped with obvious pleasure.

"No milk, I'm afraid," he said to Erna, who sat pale and drawn opposite him, a cup in front of her.

"What's going to happen to us?"

"What? Oh, you'll be all right. I expect we'll drop you off somewhere tomorrow."

"Where?" Her eyes widened in confusion. "Why? Who are you two?

"Eh? I shouldn't tell you. You know, you'll tell the police and everything."

Erna's face softened as she looked him in the eyes, arms wrapped around herself. "Help us get away. I won't say anything to the police," she whispered. "But don't hurt us, will you?"

"What?" Magni looked surprised at the suggestion. "Why should I want to hurt you?"

"Your friend?"

"Össi?" He laughed. "He won't hurt you."

"He already did. Didn't you see?"

A tear crept down Erna's cheek.

"He gave you a bit of a tap, but you were screaming at him," Magni said. "And Össur's a nervous type. Know what I mean?"

"This place is called Hotel Hraun," Tinna Lind announced, marching into the kitchen and dropping some brochures on the table. "See? Hotel Hraun offers peace and seclusion in its selection of twelve luxury rooms, all with full en suite facilities. Guests have the opportunity of sampling some of the finest Icelandic cuisine in our exclusive restaurant," she read out. "That's the big room out there, I guess. Anyway, the place is open seven months a year, but closes from November to April. So nobody's going to come here until April. That's cheerful, isn't it?"

"We won't be here long, just you see," Magni said.

"We have a car and no petrol and we're stuck in an empty hotel miles from anywhere. Oh, and I already checked, the phone's not working. So how do you propose getting back to civilization, or even have any ideas on what we eat once the freezer's empty?"

"I . . . er. That's for Össur to decide. He's the man," Magni said as Össur appeared in the doorway. "I'm just the hired help."

Erna looked up, lifting her eyes from the floor.

"Where do we sleep?" she asked, eyes darting around the room.

"Up to you, I guess," Magni said. "There's plenty of rooms to choose from."

The house was the cheapest place Gísli and Drífa had been able to find, a ramshackle building dating back to a time before building regulations had been anything more than a loose set of guidelines. In the intervening years a string of owners had put their stamp on the place one by one, adding an extension here and a bathroom there, as well as a couple of sheds outside.

There was a front door that was rarely used, while the parking spaces at the back of the house meant the back door was the entrance that everyone used. Gísli and Drífa were living in the kitchen and the room at the rear of the back-to-front building, while the living room had become a workshop while the new floor was being laid on old joists. For Gunna it was a relief to escape the city and spend a couple of hours with young Kjartan Gíslason on her lap while Gísli, Laufey and Steini hammered and sawed in the next room.

"You look tired, Drífa," Gunna said when there was a lull in the hammering.

"Yeah, a bit."

"Keeping you awake, is he?"

"Twice last night," Drífa yawned. "Which is a good night."

"The house looks good. Or it will do once the living room's done."

"I hope so. I don't know how Gísli would have managed without Steini to give him a hand. He's such a lovely man. Where did you find him, Gunna?"

"Floating in the harbour at Sandgerdi a few years ago."

Drífa looked sideways at Gunna, unsure if this were a joke of some kind. "But you knew him before, didn't you?"

The question gave Gunna an awkward stab of recollection. "Sort of. I knew who he was and that he had been at sea with Laufey's father. Steini was on board when Raggi was lost and took part in the search. I know he was at the memorial service, but to be quite honest, I was such a wreck that day that it all passed in a daze."

She shivered at the recollection of those weeks, first the call from the command centre to tell her that Ragnar was not accounted for, a phrase that she found ridiculous at the time, the visit from the ship's commanding officer, ill at ease and formal in his dress uniform, and the difficult calls and visits from others he had sailed with. The part that she found hardest to accept was that there had been no body, no remains, nothing to pack in a box and bury where she and the children could visit it. There had been a formal inquiry that placed no particular blame anywhere and culminated in an open verdict. There had been no discernible reason why Ragnar should have vanished under the hull of the disabled coaster the Coast Guard vessel had towed clear of the bay where it had grounded, and his dive partner at the time had not been able to account for his disappearance.

The memorial service had been packed and Gunna had sat through it numb as uniformed figures filled the church behind her. What had stayed in her mind as the defining image of that grim day was ten-year-old Gísli in his best clothes with a look of confusion on his face, wondering where his stepfather had disappeared to while baby Laufey laughed and chattered to herself.

"Gunna?"

It seemed suddenly unreal that the young boy and the girl who had been a baby in her arms on that long, cold day were now busily nailing down floorboards in the next room.

"Gunna?"

She shook her head and hugged Kjartan as he gurgled on her lap.

"Sorry, Drífa. I was miles away."

"You want me to take him?"

"No, he's fine here. I'm sure you don't mind a break, do you?"

"Not at all." Drífa laughed, and looked at the kitchen clock. "Do you want to eat here, or are you and Steini and Laufey going home?"

"I'm happy to eat here. Shall we get a takeaway?"

Drífa fetched a menu pinned to the corkboard and they quickly selected.

"Half an hour," Drífa said, putting the phone down. "Will you go, or shall I?"

"I'll go," Gunna decided. "After all, it's granny's treat. The place just down from the church, is it?"

"That's the one. It'll be great not to have to cook for a change."

Gunna poured herself half a mug of coffee and sipped. Kjartan sat with his hands on the table in front of her, playing with a spoon that tinkled every time he dropped it on the table top.

"Gunna, I'm a bit concerned about Gísli," Drífa said quietly, peering through the open door at the three of them laughing and working in the other room.

"What's the matter?" Gunna asked, her antennae immediately alert.

"It's his father," Drífa said haltingly and Gunna felt a chill for a second time. "I don't know if I should tell you, really."

"Why? What's the problem?"

"I'm not sure. You know they were in touch for a while when Gísli went and found him? It was when he was having a really bad time, you know . . .?"

"Yeah, I know," Gunna said. Gísli fathering two children six weeks apart had hit her hard, but she could not avoid seeing that guilt had eaten him up during those awkward months after Soffía had given birth to Ari Gíslason and Drífa had produced Kjartan Gíslason only a few weeks later.

"Well, you know his dad didn't want to know? Wasn't interested?"

"Yeah, and I wasn't exactly surprised."

"He's been in touch again. A couple of weeks ago his dad called and then came out here to see him. He's not well and I think Gísli's a bit screwed up about it. But you know what he's like. If he has a problem, he keeps it bottled up inside."

"Tell me about it," Gunna said with a shudder at being reminded within the space of a few minutes of both the man in her life she would rather forget about and the one whose loss was still deeply painful. "I'll have a quiet word if you like."

CHAPTER
TWO

Friday

Smoke belched from the upstairs window in a thick black column into the cold morning air. Eiríkur stood back, his nose wrinkled against the smell of burning plastic as he and two uniformed officers kept back the line of vaguely interested spectators.

"Anyone in there?" a voice behind him asked.

"We don't know yet."

"Because that's my cousin's place."

The voice sounded worried and Eiríkur looked round to see a woman in a raincoat with its hood protecting her head from the drizzling rain.

"In that case, you'd better come with me," he said.

In the shelter of a shop doorway she folded her arms and looked disappointed, as if she had always known that her cousin Árni would one day come to a bad end.

"Árni, you say his name is? Whose son?"

"Sigurvinsson. His dad was Sigurvin Jónsson. We're related."

Helgi was tempted to tell her that the man's genealogy didn't need to be traced, but he kept quiet.

"He lives there alone?"

"I'm not sure. He's married to a woman called Inga Jóna Steinsdóttir, but sometimes they're together and sometimes they're not, if you understand what I mean."

"Children? I mean, any children who might be in the property?"

"Inga Jóna has kids of her own, but they're grown up and they don't think much of Árni, so there's not much chance of any of them being in there."

"A stormy relationship? Do either of them drink?"

The woman pursed her lips. "Let's say that Árni wouldn't knock your hand away."

"Drugs? Anything like that? Where does Árni work?"

"He's never done a lot of that, but he used to work at a garage up at Hellnahraun and he drives a taxi sometimes as well." The woman sniffed. "When he's sober enough, that is."

"Your name?"

"Hulda Benediktsdóttir."

Eiríkur wrote everything down and added the woman's phone number.

"I'll give you a call when we know anything," he said, handing her a card. "That's my number, so if you hear from either Árni or Inga Jóna, I'd appreciate it if you could let me know they're safe."

The nighttime wind had howled, shaking the roof as they lay in their stiffly laundered hotel beds. Towards morning the wind had dropped, and when Magni rubbed his eyes and looked out of the front door in the daylight, he could see the slopes of the bowl of hills that surrounded Hotel Hraun on three sides white with snow. The yard and Erna's pearly white Ford Explorer were also covered with a thick layer of snow, heaped into drifts around the car and anywhere there was a lee from the wind that brought the dry powder snow down from slopes higher up.

The yard, enclosed on two sides by the hotel's wide L-shape, was dotted with the meandering track of a fox, but what attracted Magni's attention were parallel lines that ran along the edge of the yard, into it and around the Ford, before snaking back down the hill alongside the road. He pulled on his shoes and went outside, examining the trails and noticing that the snow had been roughly dusted off the car's registration plate.

"So we've had a visitor," he muttered to himself, before going back into the relative warmth of the echoing lobby and Wondering whether or not to tell Össur.

Steini had left early, his pickup loaded with toolboxes, for a job that Gunna guessed would keep him happily deep in the bowels of a boat somewhere for the rest of the day. She was sitting on the sofa, revelling in being home alone with her shift not due to start until midday, when she realized that Laufey was at home as well.

She turned up the radio and took the hated vacuum cleaner from its place in the cupboard by the door to run over the floor of the living room, expecting the noise to flush Laufey from sleep if she could keep it up long enough. But her dislike of anything more than the most essential housework won, and by the time Laufey emerged from her room, Gunna had retreated to the sofa with Steini's iPad.

"Cleaning up, Mum?" Laufey asked, eyeing the vacuum cleaner propped against the wall.

"Just the essentials, sweetheart. No more than that. Speaking of which, shouldn't you be at school today?"

"Not until this afternoon. Can I get a lift with you?"

"You can, but it means going early. I'm meeting Soffía this morning. That means I'm going at ten, not a moment later."

Laufey yawned again and nodded, vanishing into her room, and a moment later an insistent beat made its way through the thin panel, not loud enough to be worth complaining about, but not low enough to be easily ignored. Gunna dropped the iPad back on the table and returned to the vacuum cleaner, determined to at least make a dent in the housework.

Erna dragged herself unwillingly from sleep, wondering why there was an unfamiliar duvet on the bed, then wondering why she was still wearing her clothes, before the previous day's events came flooding back and she wanted to scream. The room's other bed was empty, the covers thrown back, so Tinna Lind had to be up already. She sat on the bed and stared blankly at the wall, as if it might provide her with the answers she was desperate for.

In the bathroom she found a tiny tube of toothpaste and scrubbed her teeth with a fingertip to get rid of the stale taste in her mouth. Her hair was a mess, she saw with dismay, and there was no brush or comb to be seen anywhere. There had been a hairbrush in her bag, but that had to be in the back of the car now.

It was the smell of roasting meat coming up the stairs that reminded her how hungry she was. There had been brunch yesterday with Sunna on the 19th Floor, then they had gone to Hafnarfjördur to check out that new antique shop she had heard about, and after that there had been nothing but the awful drive in the dark with those two men. She shuddered at the thought of it.

She went down the broad staircase with trepidation and her footsteps clicked on the tiles of the kitchen floor as the aroma of cooked meat drew her there. Tinna Lind and Magni sat at the table peeling potatoes and giggling at a joke.

"Good morning."

"G'day, sleepyhead," Magni said with a grin. "The day's half gone and you're still snoring."

"I do not snore," Erna said in a tone that was intended to be cold but came across as hurt.

"You know what I mean. Anyhow, there's a roast dinner for breakfast, once the spuds are done. We had a little hunt around earlier and it looks like we could camp out here until the spring."

"I do hope not," Erna said, elbow on the table and the back of her hand to her forehead.

"Not feeling well?" Tinna Lind asked.

"I have a headache." She sighed. "But I don't suppose there are any painkillers anywhere?"

"Don't know," Magni said, forehead furrowed.

"I had some in my bag, but it's in the car. Magni, could you get the keys from your friend and fetch my bag, do you think?"

"Sure."

As soon as Magni had gone, Erna hissed at Tinna Lind. "You still have your phone, don't you?"

"Yeah. But there's no signal here."

"Shit. Shit. Tinna, what the hell are we going to do?"

"I don't know, mother. I really don't know. But so far I'm enjoying the ride."

Össur hadn't slept late, woken by his jangling nerves and an unwelcome dream of Alli the Cornershop snarling at him. He'd spent the night in Hotel Hraun's bridal suite in the biggest bed he'd ever slept in, but still found himself in the morning along a narrow strip at one edge instead of spreadeagled as he'd intended to be, making the most of the downy expanse of it.

He counted the money and, to make sure, he counted it again. Two hundred and eighty thousand euros in mixed, mostly two- and five-hundred denominations, left him with a warm feeling of satisfaction that evaporated when he remembered that if their plans had gone as intended, he would be on a beach in Spain now, with Magni lost somewhere along the way.

The heist had been timed to perfection. They had just enough time for Árni to drop them off outside the airport at Keflavík for the charter holiday in Spain that Össur had no intention of returning from for a long time. As the leader, he naturally kept hold of the cash, which he was going to stow in his baggage, not that either of them had planned on taking much. His own plan was to disappear among the throng of rowdy British and German holidaymakers at the airport in

Alicante before making his way down the coast to somewhere he could enjoy the cash by himself. Company wouldn't be a problem for a man with a quarter of a million euros in his pocket.

He cursed Árni once again and wondered what had happened to him. Something must have come up, or else he had simply been late and missed them? It wasn't easy to tell with Árni. It was different with Magni, who wasn't really a criminal. The big guy had no qualms about squashing someone's nose when it was needed, but he'd have been just as happy grafting for a living if the trawler he'd worked on hadn't been sold to a Russian company, leaving the crew redundant and the less prudent among them flat broke.

Instead of lounging in the Mediterranean sunshine next to a blonde beauty with expensive tits and cheekbones you could cut yourself on, without a care in the world, for a few months at least, Össur ground his teeth that he was now stranded in an empty hotel miles from anywhere, wondering if the police were looking for him; or worse still, if both the police and a furious dealer with a score to settle might be searching for him. He brooded that Alli the Cornershop's boys would undoubtedly be hunting for him and, given the choice, he'd prefer to take his chances with the law, although that would end with a year or two in Litla Hraun, where Alli was certain to have friends keen to do the skinny old man a favour. Punishment had merely been deferred, he decided, unless there was a way of getting on another flight to somewhere warm. Hell, he decided, it didn't have to be anywhere warm, just somewhere

30

nobody knew him. Were there still flights from Akureyri? Surely Alli the Cornershop wouldn't have heavies looking for him up north?

Then there was the thought of what to do with the baggage downstairs, slow-witted Magni and those two women. The girl seemed all right, and something of a looker in a grungy kind of way, but he shuddered and told himself he wouldn't climb over the girl to get to her sour-faced mother. A neat enough figure and the good bits in all the right places, but definitely a snobbish bitch, used to getting her own way and the best of everything. He might have to give her another slap, he decided, but he'd wait until the moment was right. There was no point in letting the damned woman get too full of herself and start bossing him around.

He yawned, stretched and tossed the useless TV remote back on the bed. No phone coverage, no TV and only boring old steam radio. A cable coming down the wall told him that the hotel usually had cable TV, but with the place closed down for the winter, it had presumably been switched off. Well, maybe they could find a way to switch it on again. At least that way they could stay indefinitely, or at any rate as long as the contents of the freezer lasted, and by that time Alli the Cornershop might have given up looking for him, although he reminded himself with discomfort that the two women would be missed soon, if they hadn't already been reported missing by a husband or a father. He'd have to ask them, he decided as he reached for his trousers, noticing the bag of Alli's best quality grass and deciding to roll himself a joint to settle his nerves.

It was almost like a family dinner. Magni effortlessly disposed of half the leg of lamb that came out of the oven, fragrant and studded with garlic, surrounded on his plate with potatoes mashed with butter and flooded with thick gravy.

"You cooked this?" Erna asked, surprise in her voice.

"Yep," Magni said with his mouth full. "It's not difficult, this cooking stuff. Used to cook on a boat," he explained.

Erna picked delicately at her food, pushing morsels onto the back of her fork. Tinna Lind shovelled meat and potatoes down with enthusiasm, while Össur ate the meat and left everything else.

"You won't grow up to have curly hair if you don't eat your spuds," Magni told him, leaning back in his chair and belching. Erna blanched.

"How much food is there here?"

"Enough for a few days, I reckon. But not enough to waste," he added, nodding towards the potatoes and peas left on Össur's plate.

"I don't eat green shit."

Magni shrugged. "Depends how hungry we get, doesn't it?" He grinned. "Who's washing up then?"

"Up to you. I don't eat green shit and I don't do dishes," Össur announced, tapping a cigarette from its packet and lighting up.

"Do you have to?" Erna coughed and waved a hand as smoke stole across the table towards her. "And how long are we going to have to stay here?"

"As long as I say," Össur said quietly, meeting her look.

Erna held his eyes and then faltered, dropping her gaze to the floor. "And how long's that?"

"I haven't decided yet."

"A day? A week?"

Her voice was becoming shrill and Tinna Lind laid a hand on her arm.

"Mum . . ."

"I mean," Erna said, standing up, an accusing finger pointed at Össur. "It's intolerable. We've been kidnapped on the street. Abducted and brought to this . . . this place," she said in disgust. "With two common criminals."

"Sit down," Össur said, his voice dropping almost to a whisper and his mouth hardening into a thin line.

"I will not. It's a disgrace. We live in a democracy. Not some stupid banana place in Africa or somewhere. I demand to know what's going to happen to us."

Her voice had risen to a shriek, and Tinna Lind stood up and put an arm around her shoulders.

"Mum, please. Calm down. You're not doing yourself any good."

Össur glared. "Sit the fuck down, will you?" He took the pistol from his pocket and weighed it in his hand, clicking the safety catch on and off with his thumb. Magni went pale and looked from Össur to Erna and back.

"Hey, man. Calm down. The lady's upset, all right? She'll get over it."

"I will not get over it!" Erna yelled at the top of her voice. "What's going on? Why are we here? I don't even believe that's a real gun and I've a good mind to just walk out the door this minute."

"Go on," Össur hissed, "try it. See what happens."

Erna stood up and stalked towards him, her hands on her hips, glaring down at him from the extra height two inches of heels gave her while Össur sat still, looking up at her from under heavy lids.

"I don't believe you. I think you're a petty, thieving conman, and I don't believe for a second that you'd dare carry a gun if it was real. I've half a mind to give you a slap and go to that phone in the lobby and call the police."

The report was deafening, and as the smoke cleared there was a rattling of metal from one of the cupboards. Össur had fired without taking his eyes from Erna's face and he watched her expression dissolve from fury into disbelief as her hands went to her mouth.

"God . . ." she whispered.

They looked to see a hole punched neatly in the cupboard door while Erna gradually sank to the floor on her knees.

"I think the lady . . ." Össur said with a sneer. "The lady has had a shock. So maybe she'd feel better if she went to lie down for a while?"

Gunna scooped Ari Gíslason up from the floor and the little boy squealed with excitement as she tickled him.

"He's a big lad now."

"He is," Soffía agreed, and the smile on her face beneath the pile of red curls made Gunna stop for a second and think of what could have been if Soffía and

Gísli had stayed together. "Getting bigger all the time, and he looks more like Gísli every day."

Ari sat on Gunna's lap, his plump feet splayed wide as he played with a set of coloured blocks on the table in front of him.

"Talking yet?"

"He's trying to. There are a few words coming through, along with the teeth."

"How are things? You're doing all right?"

"I'm fine, Gunna," Soffía assured her. "We're doing just fine and there's nothing to worry about. How's Gísli?"

Gunna pursed her lips and helped Ari place a red block on top of a blue one. "I'm not really sure. We're not communicating as well as we used to. In fact, I seem to speak to you more than I do to Gísli these days."

"He probably thinks you're pissed off with him."

"And he'd be right."

"How's Drífa? It must be tough for her."

"She's all right. She's a sweet enough girl and she'll be fine when she's done a little more growing up. It's a shame she's been pitched into it all a little too young."

Soffía smiled sadly. "I couldn't say. I only met her once, and that was just for a minute when they collected Ari a few weeks ago, but she seems to be a sensible enough type."

Gunna rearranged Ari, who was fiddling with the buttons on her jacket, the bricks on the table forgotten, and sat him on one thigh as he yawned and rubbed his eyes.

"Are you tired, little man?" Gunna cooed and suddenly had an uncomfortable vision of her own mother saying the same thing to Gísli as a baby. "Hell, I'm really slipping into the granny stereotype, aren't I?" she asked ruefully.

"You?" Soffía laughed. "Never!"

"Anyhow, it's a delight to see my little grandson, but unfortunately I have to go and catch villains for the rest of the day."

She planted a kiss on the little boy's cheek and he squirmed in her grasp as she lifted and passed him to Soffía.

"Gísli's collecting him for the weekend tomorrow morning, so you'll see him again soon enough."

"I know, but you know what we grandmothers are like."

Soffía looked suddenly awkward and Gunna sensed a change in her.

"What's up?"

"Well, we might be moving away."

"Ah. Far?"

"I'm not sure yet," Soffía said, and Gunna could see her chewing her lip uncertainly.

"Go on."

"You know I'm graduating this year? Well, I've applied to do a master's at Lund."

"In Sweden?"

"Yep. Two years, I expect. You look dubious," Soffía said, trying to gauge the expression on Gunna's face.

"I couldn't stop you, and I wouldn't want to," Gunna said. "Even though it means you're taking this little man away for a while. Does Gísli know?"

"No. That's what I'm worried about. He might not agree to me taking Ari out of the country. He doesn't have to."

Gunna nodded. "Want me to have a word with the boy?"

"Please. If you would."

"What the fuck did you do that for?" Magni demanded once Erna had gone upstairs with Tinna Lind supporting her.

"You saw what was happening. I don't take that shit from anyone."

"You didn't have to make the bloody woman piss herself with fright, did you?"

Össur shrugged.

"Look, what the hell are we going to do? Are you planning on staying here for days or weeks, or what?"

"I'll tell you when I've made up my mind."

"OK, you do what you like. Hand over my share and I'll walk it."

"And get picked up in five minutes flat? I don't think so."

"What do you mean? I can walk to the main road and hitch a lift from there. What makes you think the law's looking for me?"

Össur stalked to the window, his hand deep in his pockets, and Magni could hear the safety catch of the Baikal clicking on and off, muffled by the jacket that Össur never seemed to take off.

"They'll be looking for someone right now." He jerked his chin upwards. "You reckon nobody's missed those two yet? Someone's wondering where they are and why they haven't come home. One of them might go off for a bit of fun, but both of them together? No."

"You think so?"

"I know so," Össur snapped. "By tonight those two are going to be missing and the filth will be searching for them and whoever they were last seen with."

"Which was us."

Össur spread his hands.

"Who knows? Did anyone see them and us together? Did some nosy bastard notice the car?"

"It didn't take two minutes, did it?"

"No. But what do you think the coppers are going to be looking for first?"

"Well, two women, I guess," Magni hazarded.

"Shit, you've so much to learn." Össur shook his head. "That thing outside. The car. A white car, and whatever the registration is. That's what they'll be looking for first of all."

"So we get rid of the car? But there's no petrol in it."

"Lose it or hide it."

"Yeah. But where?"

"Good question." Össur rummaged in his pockets and tossed the keys in the air. He caught them and lobbed them to Magni. "That had better be your task for the afternoon. It needs to be out of sight or gone. I don't care what you do with it as long as it disappears."

Eiríkur knew the reek of smoke on his clothes would stay with him for the rest of the day as he arrived at the police station on Hverfisgata. He poured a himself a

38

coffee and sat in the detectives' coffee room to look through his notes.

"G'day, Eiríkur."

"*Hæ*, Gunna." Eiríkur looked up from deciphering his own bad handwriting. "How goes it?"

She sniffed. "You had a barbecue for breakfast?"

"Nothing that great. There was a house on fire in Hafnarfjördur and there was an F1 just as I was on the way past, so I put in an appearance."

"Early in the day for a house fire, isn't it? Anything suspicious?"

Eiríkur stood still in silent thought for a moment. "One middle-aged man dead in his bed, almost certainly smoke inhalation. Hard to say if it's suspicious or just some stupid fatal mistake. But it doesn't feel right, if you know what I mean. The fire was by the door, not in the living room or the bedroom. I've had a look on the system and both the occupants have records. The woman has convictions for fraud — selling a couple of cars that weren't hers to sell — and the deceased has a couple of minor drugs convictions, as well as an impressive string of motoring infringements."

"Name?"

"Árni Sigurvinsson."

Gunna shook her head. "Doesn't ring any bells. Age?"

"Forty-five."

"Fair enough. It should be a job for uniform, but as you're on it already, you may as well follow it up."

Her phone buzzed and she peered at the number on the screen.

"Gunnhildur," she announced as Eiríkur poured himself a coffee, listening to one side of the conversation and watching as the frown on Gunna's face deepen while she took notes. "All right. Let me know, will you? I'll be with you in twenty minutes. No problem, thanks for letting me know."

She put the phone down.

"Doesn't look pretty," she said.

"Go on."

"A disappearance. Mother and daughter. Uniform have been to the address and now it's our turn, or rather my turn, as you're busy with this fire. Treat it as suspicious," Gunna decided. "Helgi's not in today so it's up to you to start tracking down the deceased's wife and checking his movements. I'll go and see this man about his missing wife and daughter and I'll check with you later today. OK?"

"Understood, chief," Eiríkur said.

"You'll need to establish if there's a crime here or if it's a stupid accident of some kind, but start with the next of kin. I don't have to tell you what to do, you know the drill."

Magni was enjoying exploring. The hotel was bigger than he had imagined from the front. Admittedly, he had been there before, but it was a few years ago and he had been far from sober, back when Hotel Hraun had been less upmarket and hosted country hops in what had since become the hotel's restaurant. The place had been smartened up a lot since then, although he could tell that most of it was cosmetic. The weatherboards were still rotting gradually under their fresh coats of paint and the rooms he had taken a look at had been furnished nicely, with the stuff that needed to be fixed hidden behind curtains and more paint.

The back of the building looked the same from the outside, but the old dance floor had become the restaurant laid out with tables and chairs that nobody would sit at until winter was over. The room had a ghostly quality to it, with its high ceiling and a chandelier that wouldn't have looked out of place in a venue four times the size. A thin film of dust covered everything and made Magni cough, the dust rising in the cold air as he began shifting tables and chairs, stacking them up to make a space in the middle of the floor.

Outside he ransacked the workshop at the bottom of the grounds behind the hotel, rooting through tools that had seen better days or which had been left to rust in peace. Eventually he found a jerry can containing a couple of litres of petrol. Magni turned his attention to the couple of old lawn mowers and a hedge trimmer, upending them over a tin tray and decanting the petrol they yielded into the can. With a triumphant grin, he banged shut the shed door behind him and set off for the front of the hotel, keys in one hand and the can of scavenged petrol in the other.

The florid man in his expensive but crumpled suit looked tired and his patience was stretched.

"I already told the other guy, the one in uniform," he said. "You really want me to tell the whole story all over again?"

"I do," Gunna said. "When did it occur to you that your wife and daughter were missing?"

"Stepdaughter," Bogi Sveinsson said absently. "Erna and I have been together about fifteen years and Tinna Lind came as part of the package."

"Fine. What happened? When were they expected home?"

"Erna and Tinna Lind went shopping yesterday. I don't know when they went out or where they were going; that's all I know. Erna told me when I called her at breakfast time that they were going out, but as Tinna Lind doesn't like to be up earlier than midday without a good reason, I don't suppose they left the house before twelve at the earliest."

"So where might they have gone? Smáralind? Kringlan? Downtown?"

"I have no idea. If there's one thing Erna's good at, it's shopping, so they could be anywhere. Maybe Laugarvegur, or maybe Smáralind. Jewellery, clothes, furniture, it's all grist to her mill," he said, looking up and around the overfurnished room, with its shelves full of figurines and ornaments.

"Where have you been?"

"Where have I been?" he asked with a blank look.

"That's right. What were your movements over the last forty-eight hours?"

"I drove to Akureyri on Wednesday. I was there all day yesterday and had two meetings. I spoke to Erna at breakfast time yesterday and again some time in the afternoon between meetings. I left at five this morning because I wanted to be home in good time, got back

42

here soon after twelve. I stayed both nights in Akureyri at Hotel Kea."

"And I suppose there are people who will vouch for that?"

"The staff at the hotel, I'd guess, and the people I was with yesterday will confirm I was there. I stopped and bought diesel at Blönduós on the way and that'll show up on my bank statement, if that's what you're after," he said stiffly, stung that Gunna could even consider he might have something to hide.

"You've tried to call their phones?"

"Of course I have. I thought they'd be out shopping somewhere still, but never this late in the evening, and neither of them are answering their phones. That never happens. Erna might lose her phone in the bottom of her bag and not notice it was ringing, but not Tinna Lind. She practically always answers, and if she doesn't she'll call back within half an hour."

"You think they're together?"

"I —" Bogi stopped. "I don't know. I just assumed they'd be together."

Gunna nodded and made notes.

"How's your relationship with your wife? Any disagreements? Arguments?"

"No more than any other couple, I suppose."

"And at the moment? Does she have a reason to be pissed off with you? No recent disagreements?"

"Not at all. We had two weeks in Thailand and if anything things have been smoother and happier than for quite a while."

"And your stepdaughter," Gunna said, looking at her notes. "Tinna Lind? What kind of a relationship do you have with her? Do you get on well or do you clash?"

"We used to clash when she was a rebellious teenager, but even then she was more at loggerheads with her mother than with me."

"And her father?"

Bogi Sveinsson hesitated. "He's never been in the picture. In any case, he died some years ago."

"So you've been married to her mother for how long?"

"Fifteen years." He said it as if it was a prison sentence. "And Tinna Lind is twenty-four now."

"And still living at home?"

"She left and then came back after a year or so."

"You're happy about that? No tension there?"

"None at all. Not on my part, anyway. Like I said, she clashes more with her mother than with me."

"So you have a fairly close relationship?"

"We have a good relationship." Bogi bridled. "Listen, are you trying to insinuate something? Because if you are, I don't appreciate it."

"Where is my car?"

Erna sounded just as shrill as she had that morning when she'd harangued Össur. Magni could see her lip quiver and the finger she pointed at him trembled.

Magni grinned. "It's in the restaurant."

"What are you talking about?" Erna's brow furrowed in confusion.

44

"Like I said. It's in the restaurant."

Erna shook her head and closed her eyes. "Where is it?"

"In the restaurant," Magni repeated. "Go through that door there and the double doors at the end. "That's where it is."

Erna marched along the unlit passage and pushed open the doors at the end. She peered into the gloom and moaned quietly to herself as she approached the car. It had been driven into the restaurant through a pair of wide double doors that opened out into what, in summertime, would be a garden area of sorts. But the doors had not been quite wide enough and a line of scratches had been left along the passenger side of the car by its encounter with the door frame.

She looked round to see Magni standing behind her, clearly proud of his achievement.

"How . . .?" she muttered, shaking her head, her voice laden with anger. "Why . . .?"

"Össi said the car had to be out of sight, so I put it in here so it's out of the rain and snow as well."

"But you've scratched it!" Erna screeched. "It's a new car. I've only had it two weeks and you've fucking scratched it, you clumsy, selfish bastard. Look at it! Look what you've done!"

"Don't worry about it," Magni assured her placidly. A bit of polish and that'll come out easy enough."

"But it's a brand-new car!" Erna yelled, her face turning an unhealthy red as she stalked past him and back into the hotel.

His eyes glazed, Össur appeared once she had gone, although her sobs of fury could still be heard echoing along the corridor.

"Looks all right to me. At least it's out of sight. How did you get it in here?"

"There were a few old lawn mowers out the back in the workshop," Magni waved a hand in the general direction of the garden behind the hotel. "So I drained the fuel out of them and put it in the Explorer's tank. Easy."

"Was there much?" Össur asked, his interest quickening.

"Enough to get us out of here, you mean?"

"How far to the nearest filling station?"

Magni thought. "Forty-odd kilometres? I don't reckon it'd get us that far."

"Shit. Anything else we could use?"

"Instead of petrol? No. Össi, are you going to take them with us?"

"Hell, no. They can look after themselves here. But we need to make a move. Someone must keep an eye on this place, and sooner or later they'll come and have a look. Then what?"

Magni thought of the ski tracks in the morning snow, but said nothing, merely nodding sagely.

"We need to sneak off. We leave them here and hope that it's a couple of days before anyone comes snooping around and finds them. By then, I'd hope we'd be long gone."

"And if nobody comes here until the spring and they starve?"

Össur shrugged his shoulders. "Their problem."

"And what if they try to get away and raise the alarm somewhere?"

"That's why we need to be out of here." He jerked his head towards the Explorer, the lumps of compacted snow stuck to its underside now dripping onto the dance floor. "So the sooner you figure out how to get that thing as far as a filling station, the better."

"My name's Grímur Halldórsson from Holt." The visitor stood in the lobby and looked around. "I saw the car that was here has gone, so I thought there was nobody about, but then there was a light last night. So I thought I'd check that everything's in order here."

"Everything's fine," Össur assured him. "We're just here for a few days."

The man had a lined face under grey hair that stood up at angles as he took off his hat. He patted his hair down with one hand as his eyes flickered over the lobby and he replaced the hat.

"Ársæll didn't say anything to me about visitors," he said. The doubt in his voice was plain. "But I'm sure it's all right and he just forgot to let me know."

"Probably," Össur said, wondering who Ársæll might be. "You live near here?"

"Just down in the valley at Holt. Normally Ársæll lets me know when someone's going to be here and asks them to drop by at Holt to pick up the keys."

"Oh, he gave me the keys himself before we came up here, said he didn't want to disturb you."

47

Grímur Halldórsson nodded and walked around the lobby. His shoes with their square toes made to fit cross-country skis clicked on the tiles.

"How many of you are there here?"

"Just the two of us," Össur said, moving to stand in the doorway leading along the corridor to the kitchen, awkwardly blocking their visitor's path.

"Really? I was sure I saw at least two other people when I passed by earlier."

"No." Össur laughed unconvincingly. "There's just me and Magni here. The girls went back to town and they'll be back in a while."

"Ah, that's why the car's gone, I suppose. A nice enough truck to be driving around town, but not a lot of use in a bit of snow. Am I right?"

Magni nodded and grinned, not knowing what to say and painfully aware that the car was dripping black water all over the restaurant floor on the other side of the building.

"So where's the place you live, then?" Össur asked, keen to change the subject.

"Down the road about twenty minutes."

"You don't know if there's a shop anywhere near here, do you? It was dark when we drove up here and it'd be handy if we could go and get a few essentials."

"What do you need? I can get you a few things if I run down to Selfoss later."

"Selfoss?"

"Well, you don't think I'm going to go all the way to Reykjavík without a damned good reason, do you?"

Össur looked nonplussed for a moment. "Well, no. I don't suppose so."

"City types, are you? Never been further than Mosfellsbær before?"

"Not me," Magni said. "I'm no city boy."

"Oh, right? Where might you be from?"

"I'm an islander, me. Westmann Islands, that is."

"Ah." The old man nodded sagely. "Did a few seasons there myself. Before you were born, I'd guess. I'll be off, I reckon. There's work to be done and it won't do itself. You want me to get anything from Selfoss for you?"

"Don't think so," Magni said before Össur had time to say anything. "But how far's the nearest petrol station?"

"Petrol?" The old man looked at him quizzically.

"I'm trying to get the lawn mowers running so they're ready for the summer, but I could do with a can or two of petrol so I can fuel them up. It keeps condensation from forming in the tanks."

"Wise man. There's a filling station a way south of here. Go that way," he said, jerking his head in roughly the right direction. "Take the Selfoss road at the fork and it's not far after that. They close at four in the winter, although you can buy fuel any time if you have a plastic card to pay with. Otherwise I guess you'll have to wait for your girlfriends to come back, won't you?"

The apartment overlooked the sea and Esja behind it, its fifth-floor location giving it a view above the slow-moving stream of lights of the traffic on Sæbraut far below. Unlike Erna's house with its clutter of ornaments and trinkets, Gunna felt this place was so minimal as to be virtually uninhabited.

Erna's friend Sunna ushered Gunna to a sofa in the echoing living room with its back to the window and sat herself in a deep chair, crossing her legs and looking expectant.

"What can I do for you, officer?"

"Erna Björg Brandsen's husband gave me your name as you were one of the people she might have met for lunch yesterday. Is that right?"

"That I met Erna for lunch?" Sunna asked with a flicker of a smile. "That's right, I did. There were four of us."

"Including Erna's daughter Tinna Lind?"

"Tinna Lind was with us. What is this about?"

"Erna and Tinna Lind have disappeared. Bogi reported them missing. I'm trying to trace their movements and it seems that the 19th Floor restaurant was the last confirmed sighting we have of them. Did Erna say where she was going after that?"

"Not that I recall."

"She didn't say anything about returning home, or going shopping somewhere?"

"Not that I recall," Sunna repeated.

"So what was your last sighting of them? In the restaurant?"

"In the car park. Erna and Tinna Lind got into Erna's car and I got into mine. Our friend Dúa was with us and she went with me in my car."

"You didn't see which direction Erna was going as she left the car park?"

"No. What do you think has happened to her?"

Gunna paused before answering, trying to work out if there might be any concern behind the woman's outward display of indifference.

"I'm keeping an open mind at the moment. It's too early to speculate. You knew Erna well?"

Sunna extended a hand, palm down, and rocked it from side to side.

"Well, but not intimately."

"She didn't share secrets?"

"If Erna had secrets, which I somehow doubt. I don't get the feeling she lived dangerously these days."

"Meaning she did at one time?"

"Maybe. A long time ago. I gather she had a wild past, but that was long before I got to know her."

"In what way?"

"Tinna Lind isn't Bogi's daughter. Nobody seems to know who the real father is."

"And you haven't asked?"

For the first time there was a change in Sunna's expression and she looked shocked.

"Of course not! That would be so inappropriate."

"Can you give me an impression of Erna's character? And how long have you known her?"

"Fifteen years or so, I suppose. Actually I knew Bogi first; at the time he and my husband were members of the same golf club, probably still are. Then Bogi met Erna and we'd all meet occasionally. Sometimes all of us together, sometimes I meet Erna for lunch or for a drink. We see each other at parties and receptions."

"And your take on Erna?"

Sunna's face unbent into a stiff smile and. Gunna wondered if she'd been botoxed.

"Erna's harmless. She wouldn't hurt a fly, but she doesn't venture outside her own little circle. If you think she might have gone off on some adventurous fling with a toyboy, think again. Erna knows how well off she is with Bogi and she wouldn't do anything to jeopardize that, not in a million years."

Gunna nodded as Sunna's assessment tied in with the picture of Erna that she had begun to piece together.

"And Tinna Lind?"

Sunna sniggered. "Drives her mother wild. Those two are so unalike in so many ways it's hard to imagine that they're related, but they both have that same stubborn streak inside. Erna knows she's well off holding Bogi's hand and I guess she can't understand why Tinna Lind hasn't even tried to find herself a wealthy husband yet when she has boys falling over her."

"So you know Tinna Lind well?"

"No, not at all. I don't know the girl all that well and what I know is what Erna tells me, normally through gritted teeth."

"Go on."

Sunna took a deep breath. "Erna lives for the future, security is paramount to her. She has to have money, and preferably plenty of it, which is why Bogi suits her

52

so well. He works like a slave, buys her whatever toys she asks for and worships her."

"You don't imagine he would do her any harm?"

Sunna's eyes widened in astonishment. "Bogi? Good grief, no. He'd be lost without her."

"And Tinna Lind?"

"Ah, she's the opposite of Erna. Tinna Lind lives for the moment. She has a good degree and could easily have a well-paid job. Instead she lives at home, does low-paid work and every time she's saved something up, she disappears abroad. She comes back when she's broke and goes back to work. Erna and I used to meet in Borgarkaffi sometimes, but since Tinna Lind has been waitressing there, she can't bear to go in any more."

"Are you all right, Mum?"

"Of course I'm not all right," Erna snapped back tearfully. "What the hell's going on? What are these two thugs going to do to us?"

"I don't expect they're going to do anything to us. The big guy seems all right, but the little one looks like he might be dangerous. They're probably as desperate to get rid of us as we are to get away from them."

"And I haven't had a shower. I don't have any clean underwear. My hair's in a mess and I don't have a toothbrush. My car's been wrecked by that oaf, and I don't know when I'm going to get home."

"All right," Tinna Lind said, backing away and wrapping her arms around herself. "Just trying to help, that's all."

"Aw," Erna crooned, leaning forward to touch Tinna Lind's cheek. "I didn't mean it like that."

Tinna Lind drew away with a frown.

"You didn't say anything about Bogi. Don't you think he's worried. He should be home by now, shouldn't he?"

"You're right. It's Friday."

"Do you think he'll go to the police?"

"I'm sure he will," Erna said. "Sure of it. And they'll come and get us."

"You mean they might if they knew where we were," Tinna Lind muttered. "How is anyone going to know where we are?"

"Somebody must see us sooner or later, surely?" Erna's eyes were red-rimmed with tears of frustration and wide with fear. "I'm not sure I can stand this for much longer."

Tinna Lind shrugged. "So what other options are there? Walk off into the snow when the guys aren't looking?"

"Don't be stupid, girl. There must be a farm or something near here somewhere."

"Yeah, but where? Do you want to go looking for the nearest farm on foot? You know, it's cold out there and you're not going to get very far in those heels. And what if you don't find somewhere before it gets dark? We wouldn't survive a night outside, even if it's fine."

"You think so?" Erna said, her voice laden with doubt. "Surely there must be farmers around here?"

Tinna Lind tapped her toe on the floor in irritation. "Mother, when did you last go outside Reykjavík? I mean, other than to go to the airport?"

"Don't be silly. I went to Hvolsvöllur only a few weeks ago with Bogi to see his aunt and uncle."

"OK, so you must have seen what the rest of Iceland looks like? Lots of rocks with only a long way between everything? Well, we're right out in the middle of that long way between everything and it's a long walk to Selfoss from here."

"Selfoss? Erna looked blank. "Why Selfoss?"

"Because that's the nearest town."

Erna shook her head. "How do you know?"

"Because there's a box of leaflets in the lobby behind the reception desk for Hotel Hraun, which is this place, and according to the map on the leaflet, Selfoss is about thirty kilometres that way." She smiled slowly. "Besides, I think they had a visitor today, so it might not be long before somebody finds out that there's something going on up here."

Gunna switched off the unmarked Golf's engine in the car park behind the Hverfisgata police station as her phone rang.

"Gunnhildur."

"Hæ. Siggi. You wanted some info, didn't you?"

"I did indeed, and as there's no warrant needed, then you should have it all at your fingertips."

"For you, sweet thing, anything," Siggi said with exaggerated courtesy. "The two numbers you wanted, one ending one-seven-five, the other nine-nine-six."

"That's the two missing persons, yes."

"OK, what we can gather from the phone company is that both are out of range."

"Not just switched off?"

"No," Siggi said. "It seems that they both dropped off the network within a few minutes of each other on Thursday evening, around seven-thirty. The last contact was through a mast near Thingvellir."

"Right," Gunna said, thinking through the implications. "So what should that tell me? This is taking into account that Iceland has virtually complete GSM coverage these days."

"That's right. There aren't many places where there's no coverage at all nowadays, but there are nooks and corners here and there where there's no signal and plenty of areas with poorish coverage, so if it's an old phone or just a lousy one, then it might not get a connection."

"Would that explain why they didn't disappear at precisely the same time?"

"It could," Siggi said. "You don't know what types of phones these are?"

"No, but I'm going to find out in a minute."

"Cool. Let me know and we'll see if that could be something to do with it."

"That's it? No phone traffic up to when they vanished?"

"There's a list of calls to and from both phones earlier in the day and I'll email you that. Nothing after four that afternoon on either of them."

"Thingvellir, you said?"

"That's it."

"So they went through Reykjavík, onto Highway One, towards Mosfellsbær, took the Thingvellir road and then dropped off the radar somewhere there?"

"Yep, I think you have it."

"So they're in Thingvellir or Grímsnes, somewhere around there?"

"Well, the phones are. That's all we can say at the moment. But as soon as one or the other pops up, I'll let you know right away."

Magni hummed as he peeled an onion and sliced it. The slices sizzled in the pan and the smell spread quickly. He turned down the heat under the pan to let them fry gently and sharpened a kitchen knife on a steel, using quick, sure movements.

"I thought you were going to cut your fingers off," Tinna Lind said as Magni used the now fiendishly sharp knife to dice beef into chunks.

"Nah. Comes with practice."

"Where did you learn to do that, then?" she asked, sitting on the worktop opposite and swinging her legs.

"What? Sharpen a knife? I thought everyone could do that."

Tinna Lind giggled. "Don't be silly. Mum has some kind of electric thing in the kitchen that sharpens her carving knife."

"Fair enough," Magni shrugged. "I just use a steel like I always have. You work in the fish when you're a kid and it just comes as part of the work. Everyone learns that sort of thing."

"Yeah, in the Westmann Islands, maybe."

Magni dropped pieces of beef into a bowl, rolling them in flour a few at a time.

"All right, so where did you learn to cook?"

"On a boat."

"A fishing boat?"

"What other kind of boat is there?"

"I don't know. Yachts. Merchant ships. Cruise ships. The Coastguard has boats."

"All right. But there are only fishing boats where I come from."

Tinna Lind nodded and watched as he adjusted the heat under the pan.

"Magni?"

"Yeah?"

"How long are we going to be here?"

He tipped the onions into a deep dish and replaced them in the pan with some of the beef. "Hell, I don't know. Long gone before anyone turns up here in the spring, I hope."

"You know, I don't think it's going to be long before there's company."

"What?" He looked up sharply. "What do you mean?"

"It stands to reason, doesn't it? Look, I've worked in cafés and restaurants. If you're closing down for a while, you clear everything out, don't you? How come there are onions and garlic and potatoes in the cupboards? I reckon it won't be long before whoever runs this place comes back to finish closing up for the winter," she said, her head on one side as she watched him. "Just a thought."

"I guess you're right. I don't know what my mate has planned, but I don't reckon we'll be here more than a day or two," Magni said thoughtfully, pushing the pieces of beef around the pan with a spatula as they spat and sizzled.

"What are you making?"

"A beef casserole, like a stew."

"For tonight?"

"Yep."

"Don't you like me, Magni?" Tinna Lind asked, her voice dropping an octave.

"What?" Magni asked, taken by surprise. "Well, to be honest, I hadn't thought about it."

"I thought you liked me, the way you stopped your friend being so aggressive this morning."

"Oh, that." He laughed. "Don't worry about Össur. He can be a bit of a fucking idiot sometimes."

"Idiot? He has a gun, a real one! He scared my mother half to death."

"Well, he had me a bit worried as well," Magni admitted, scratching his head.

"Have you known him long?"

"Össur? Yeah, a while."

"You've been friends for a long time?"

"Not really. I used to see him with all the deadbeats around the Emperor sometimes, but it was only after I got laid off that I sort of got to know him."

"Laid off, how?"

"Lost my job a few months ago."

"Wow. Can't you get another one?"

"D'you think I'd be running around the countryside in the middle of winter with a nutcase like Össur if I could get a proper job?" Magni said, and for the first time there was a note of irritation in his voice.

"I'm sorry," Tinna Lind said, backing off and sounding contrite. "How did you lose your job? Were you sacked for something?"

"We all lost our jobs. I was working on a factory boat and earning some damned good money, but the old bastard who owned it died and his heirs sold the lot."

"What, the ship?"

"Yep. They sold the quotas to other companies and the ship to someone in Russia. So we all lost our jobs, forty of us, all at once."

"What? That's terrible!" Tinna Lind sounded shocked. "You must have got something out of it, didn't you?"

"A bit of redundancy money and we finished the trip with a decent load of fillets. But there's not a lot of that left now."

He poured water from a jug into the pan and put the lid on it. "That'll do for an hour or so," he decided, turning the heat down to a simmer.

"Magni?"

"Yeah?"

"There's something I'd really like to do?"

"Oh, yeah?"

"Can you turn on the hot water so I can have a shower?"

60

"That's my next job," Magni said, scratching his chin so his fingers rasped on the stubble. "I've put your mum's car inside, I've got the telly to work so Össur can see the motor racing, I've cooked the dinner and next I'll see if I can get the hot water routed to the rooms." He sighed, turning on the kitchen tap and waiting for the steam to rise in the sink as the hot water rushed into it. "There's hot water here, so there must be a valve or something to divert it upstairs."

"I'd be really grateful, Magni, if you would," Tinna Lind assured him.

Össur lay in the bed with half a dozen pillows banked behind him and an ashtray at his side as he looked at his mobile phone for the hundredth time and threw it down on the bedspread in disgust; no signal. On top of that it didn't help that he was also going to run out of cigarettes in the next day or so.

The cars whizzing around a track somewhere far away in Europe on the TV were ignored as his thoughts drifted again to how to extricate himself from the hotel, preferably leaving his companions behind, and ideally taking himself away somewhere warm, although he would happily settle for somewhere cold if it were out of the reach of Alli the Cornershop and the Reykjavík police.

The whining of racing cars brought him back to reality and reminded him how much he would have to rely on Magni. Twenty years had passed since he had last sat behind the wheel of a car, cut free of the three-way smash that had left him with a broken arm, a jail term for reckless driving under the influence and a lifetime ban, as well as shattered nerves that never failed to bring on an anxiety attack when he sat in the front of a car. He could probably get Erna's Explorer to the edge of the car park, but he knew that by the time he reached the road his legs would be like jelly and he'd be sweating with nervous tension.

Össur shivered at the thought. Could the police pin a kidnapping charge on him? Was that a crime, as the snooty woman seemed to think, he wondered? It was unlikely that Alli would have gone to the police to complain that someone had relieved him of a few hundred thousand euros of used notes that should have been on their way to Amsterdam to finance a heavy shipment of marching powder. He nodded to himself and decided that the police and Alli would be looking for some very different things if they were to catch up with him and wondered if there might be something like a drink to be found in this godforsaken dump in the middle of nowhere.

The motor racing came to an end without him noticing and he was surprised to look up and see football on the screen. Had he not been watching, or had the channel changed without him noticing it? He shook his head and decided that it must be him, and it wasn't like him to miss Formula One when it was on. It must have been the smell of food that had brought him round, as a meaty, fragrant aroma wormed its way through the building. It had been a surprise that Magni was so practical. Was he cooking again? Or maybe it was the girl? Össur had no doubt that the older woman wouldn't dirty her hands with food. After all, Magni had hidden the car, got the TV to work and even cooked a damned decent meal, in spite of all the green stuff he'd served up with it. It was just a shame he'd have to rely on him to get him out of their present mess.

Inga Jóna Steinsdóttir stood at the till and looked at Eiríkur's warrant card with confusion.

"My Árni?" she asked.

"We believe so. Can we talk somewhere private?" The queue for the till was tapping its impatient collective feet. Eiríkur turned to the line of people. "I'm sorry, ladies and gentlemen, but this till is closed," he said firmly. "Try the next one. The manager will be along in just a minute."

By the time Inga Jóna led him to the canteen there were tears streaking her makeup. The manager looked up at her with questions all over his round face.

"Good morning. My name's Eiríkur Thór Jónsson and I'm a police officer. I'm sorry for the interruption but I need to speak to this lady in private. Can we use this room?"

"Er . . . yes, of course," the manager squeaked as he saw Eiríkur's card. He hastily gathered together the paperwork he'd been studying and made for the door.

"There's a long queue waiting for you at till three," Eiríkur added as the man vanished through the door.

"What's happened to my Árni?"

"Sit down, please," Eiríkur said and pulled out a chair for her.

"So what's all this then? Is he badly hurt?"

"I'm sorry to tell you that Árni Sigurvinsson is dead. There was a fire in his flat early this morning and we believe that the body of a middle-aged man firefighters found in the apartment is probably his."

"Christ . . ."

"And the body will have to be identified."

"God . . ."

"I'd like to offer my sympathy for your loss, and I understand completely that this must be a terribly difficult time for you. But there are questions we really need to have answered as quickly as possible."

Inga Jóna sniffed. "Yeah, of course. Go ahead."

"Where had Árni been working? I mean, had he been working?"

"He'd been doing taxi shifts a few nights a week. That's all."

"And had he been doing any other work? Anything that might not have been strictly legal?"

"Why? What makes you think he'd been up to anything?"

Eiríkur sighed, knowing this wasn't going to be easy. "I know you both have criminal records, so I have to ask, and the circumstances of the fire are suspicious."

"That was years ago! And what are you saying? That someone murdered my Árni?"

"I'm sorry, but we have to look at every angle," Eiríkur said. "And yes, I'm sorry to say so, but it seems that someone may have helped him on his way. We can't tell yet for certain, but it seems the fire may have been started deliberately."

64

"Christ," she muttered and buried her face in her hands and then lifted her head, clear-eyed. "I should have known. I should have fucking known."

"Known what?"

"Those friends of his, nothing but trouble the lot of them. It's why I moved out."

"You weren't living together?"

"We haven't . . ." she said, then gulped and corrected herself. "We hadn't for a few months. All right, Árni was doing taxi work, but he was also doing something that stinks, and I never really found out what. He was out most nights and he had more money than usual, so I knew he had to be doing something a bit more than just driving drunks around."

"So what do you think he was doing?"

"My daughter told me he was delivering stuff."

"What sort of stuff?"

"You know. Stuff. Snort."

"Ah, who for? Or was this on his own account?"

Inga Jóna laughed mirthlessly. "On his own account? Hell, no. Árni didn't do anything on his own account. He did what other people asked him to do."

"Go on. Like what?"

"Like what I said. He was delivering snort to people who ordered it from somewhere. I don't know where, and from what Bogga told me, he was delivering girls as well."

"Girls? Prostitutes?"

"Call it what you like, but yeah, something like that."

"Sounds like I need to talk to your daughter."

"Go ahead. She lives at the end of Strandvangur. Number nineteen. Second floor. Borghildur Sævarsdóttir her name is."

"Who had Árni been working with, or going around with, who was enough to make you move out?"

"His miserable pals. The worst one's a guy called Össi. I could never stand him. Anyway, it seems that Össi was bringing Árni the work, and that's all I know."

"You know Össi's proper name?"

Inga Jóna shrugged. "Össur, maybe. I don't know. A mean little bastard with a sharp nose. I'll bet anything you like he's in your files somewhere."

"You're prepared to identify him?"

"If it means that little shit gets locked away in Litla Hraun for a few years? Hell, yeah."

Magni looked around the kitchen and wondered where he'd left the knife, shrugged and decided to worry about it later.

"Hey!" he yelled through the kitchen door. "Come and get it!"

He threw cutlery on the table, set the water to run from the cold tap and put a jug next to it as he gave the pot a stir for the last time, letting the fragrant aromas of onions and the few dried herbs he'd been able to find in half-empty jars well up from it. He breathed deep and looked around as Erna came into the kitchen, her eyes red, and sat at the table.

"Smells good," Tinna Lind said as she took four plates from the draining board and Magni drained the potatoes over the sink.

Without a word, Össur planted himself on a chair at the end of the table and wrinkled his nose. "It's not spicy, is it?"

"That's for you to find out," Magni said.

"I don't do spicy shit."

"What the fuck do you eat?" Magni demanded, banging the pot of potatoes on the table harder than he had intended to. "You don't eat vegetables. You don't eat fish, and now you don't eat anything spicy either. It's no surprise you're as skinny as a starved cat."

Össur scowled and ladled stew from the casserole dish onto his plate. He flicked half-moons of onion aside with his fork, leaving meat on one side of his plate, which he scooped up quickly.

"Any bread?"

"Sorry, haven't had time to get to the shops today," Magni snapped back. "Of course there's no fucking bread. There's no milk either, not many spuds or onions, and there's only enough chops and fish and stuff in the freezer to keep us going into next week. After tomorrow we're down to one meal a day."

Tinna Lind's and Erna's eyes swivelled back and forth between them during the exchange.

"So we find some way to get out of here by next week or we starve?" Tinna Lind said in a soft voice. "Is that what you're saying?"

Össur sat back, the meat on his plate eaten. He lifted the plate and scraped the remainder back into the pot.

"We'll see," he snarled over his shoulder as he stalked from the room. "We might just have to eat one of you two bitches if we don't find a way out of here before the food runs out."

Magni speared a potato and started to peel it with his knife, quickly lifting the skin from it and placing it on the edge of his plate. Tinna Lind followed suit, dropping alternate potatoes on her plate and Erna's.

"You don't get on very well with your friend, do you?" Tinna Lind asked.

"He's no friend of mine," Magni said. "He's a proper miserable fucker."

Erna quailed at the savagery of his tone and pushed food around her plate.

"Eat, Mum," Tinna Lind ordered, and Erna forked up some of the meat nervously, then faster as it turned out to taste better than she'd expected. "So why are you hanging around with him?"

"Needed the money, simple as that."

"Can't you just get a job, like everyone else?" Erna said in a tone that was close to hysteria.

"I had a fucking job until it was sold out from under my feet, and a good job it was too."

"Magni used to work on a trawler and then it was sold," Tinna Lind explained.

"Oh, I'm sorry," Erna said. "I thought you were . . ."

"Thought I was what?" Magni asked, mashing potatoes into his gravy.

"I thought you were some kind of scrounger or a criminal."

"Like him?" Magni jerked his head to one side, indicating the door Össur had exited through. "No chance. Össur's never had a proper job in his life, and until a month ago I'd never been without one."

For the first time, Tinna Lind saw Magni looking frustrated.

"Is he a real criminal?" Erna asked.

Magni shrugged. "Össi? He's a chancer. He's done bits and pieces of work here and there, but he can't stay off the piss and he's never held down a job."

"So how does he live?" she asked, perplexed, her eyes wide in confusion.

"Össur sells a little dope, does a little enforcement. That keeps him going," Magni replied and pushed his practically clean plate aside. "I gather he knows enough about a few people to call in a favour when he's properly in the shit."

Magni put his finger to his lips.

"Your old lady's gone to sleep, hasn't she?"

Tinna Lind looked up suspiciously from where she lay on the sofa in the hotel's lounge, a duvet from the bedroom wrapped around her. She put aside the book she had found in the office and sat up.

"Yeah. Why?

Magni winked. "You look like a girl who appreciates a drink. Or am I wrong?"

"I think you could be right."

Magni lifted the hand that had been behind his back. "How's this?"

Tinna Lind's face broke into a slow grin as he placed the bottle on the table and produced a couple of glasses from behind his back.

"And where did you get that from?"

"The bar's empty, so I thought I'd have a snoop around. Found this in the manager's office at the back of the filing cabinet."

He glugged two fingers of whisky into each glass and offered her one. Tinna Lind put the glass to her nose and breathed deep.

"A pretty decent single malt," she said.

"Yep. Good, isn't it?" Magni raised his glass and admired the deep amber tone of the fluid. "Cheers."

They clinked glasses and settled back on the sofa.

"What do you do when you're not running round the country with a bunch of criminals?" he asked.

Tinna Lind giggled. "I don't make a habit of this."

"You a student, or what?"

"Do I look like a student?"

"Hell, I don't know. The combat trousers and the weird hair make you look like a student to me."

Tinna Lind sighed. "Well, I guess you're right. I'm a sort of student at the moment."

"Which means what?"

She sipped, holding the whisky in her mouth and letting it roll over her tongue.

"It means I'm a student as far as university and my parents are concerned, but in reality I don't do a lot."

"No job?"

"Not really."

"So how do you earn a few shekels to keep yourself in clothes and whatnot?"

"A bit of this and a bit of that."

70

"Which means what?" he asked, topping up both glasses and then reaching behind the sofa to drop the bottle out of sight. He left his arm draped along the back of the sofa.

"Hiding the booze, are you?"

"Fuck, yeah. If Össur knew it was there he'd neck the lot in two seconds flat. Haven't you seen him start to get the shakes yet?"

"No. Does he get it bad?"

"Yeah. Tomorrow night, I reckon."

"So, tell me about yourself," Tinna Lind said, cradling her glass in her hands and leaning slightly into the arm that had dropped casually off the sofa onto her shoulders.

"Me? You know all about me already."

"No wife, no family?"

"Not at the moment."

"But there was?"

"Two so far," Magni said, and looked up at the ceiling. Something creaked overhead. "Someone creeping about?"

"Might be the old lady going to the toilet."

Tinna Lind leaned into Magni's side and rested her head on his shoulder.

"So what do you do to keep yourself busy? A lady of leisure?"

She gurgled with laughter. "I worked for a travel agent for a couple of summers while I was a student and now I do some waitressing at Borgarkaffi. That's about it at the moment."

"I'll come and have a meal at Borgarkaffi one day and be waited on hand and foot."

"Not after some kind of special service are you?"

"Depends what you mean by special service, doesn't it?"

"Play your cards right, big man, and we'll see," she said in a husky voice and huddled deeper into the crook of Magni's arm.

Ívar Laxdal was in the car park about to disappear into the dark recesses of his Volvo when Gunna parked the unmarked Golf next to him.

"Finished for the day?"

"I am, and so should you be," he replied. "What's the story with your disappeared women?"

"No sign of them," Gunna said, shutting the car door and shivering in the cold wind. "I have alerts out all over the country, checked flights, passed the word to the taxi companies for their drivers to look out for Erna Björg Brandsen's car, and I've had patrols scour the roads around Thingvellir and beyond in case they've just broken down somewhere or are stuck in a ditch."

"Everything short of a full-scale search, you mean?"

"Yep, ads on TV and radio, and a missing persons announcement on Facebook."

Gunna nodded and zipped up her coat. She looked upwards at the low cloud that appeared to be lurking just beyond rooftop height.

"I'd have an air search if I could."

"Not in this visibility, I'm afraid."

72

"And I'm not convinced by the Thingvellir location," she said and watched Ívar Laxdal think over her remark.

"Really?"

"It's too neat. I get the feeling we might be being lead astray. My feeling is to concentrate on the family for the moment."

"Something close to home?" Ívar Laxdal asked. "Domestic violence, possibly?"

"I'm not sure. I need to push the husband a little harder, and I'm meeting another of Erna's acquaintances in the morning, as well as some of the daughter's friends. I need to get a better picture of them and their relationship. If there's nothing that rings alarm bells, then I'll be more inclined to look harder up-country."

Ívar Laxdal rolled his shoulders, lifting his collar higher around his neck as he settled deeper into his coat.

"Up to you, Gunnhildur. I'll leave it to your discretion," he said, getting into his car. "Let me know tomorrow, will you?"

She shivered and had to force her teeth to stop chattering with fear. Every step was an ordeal. The floor creaked and she tried to step as slowly and lightly as possible, placing her feet toes first, then heel, then moving her weight forward as gradually as she could. She could hear the indistinct burble of noise from the television in the room and a band of light slashed across the wall at the end of the corridor.

Erna inched closer, fists clenched, breath held as long as she could as she took each step, exhaling and taking a few deep, slow breaths before taking the next step. The television became louder the closer she got to the half-open door. Finally close enough to peer inside, she fought back the urge to walk smartly back down the corridor to the room she had taken as hers and bury herself under the duvet. Erna told herself that whatever happened, sooner or later she would have to confront these men and make sure that something happened, while Tinna Lind seemed happy enough to go with the flow, apparently unafraid of the two thugs. The beefy young man with the muscles and the reddish hair was all right, she had decided, probably a decent enough lad and not too proud to make himself busy in the kitchen. But the skinny man with the eyes that never stayed still was another matter. There was something about him that sent shivers of fear coursing up and down her spine every time he opened his mouth. He was a man with no values and no morals other than making a quick buck and unconcerned at whatever the cost might be to anyone else.

She eased her head around the door frame and looked inside, then breathed a sigh of relief. The television was blaring out some foreign music programme in a language she didn't recognize, with pneumatic young women bouncing to a band playing some smooth seventies-style rock, punctuated by squealing guitar solos. Össur was spreadeagled across the bed, his chin pointing at the ceiling. She could see the grey stubble sprouting on his chin and the top of an old, blurred tattoo that snaked up past the neckline of his grubby shirt and into the hair behind one ear.

She stood for a moment, transfixed at the sight of the man, then reached slowly behind to pluck the knife she had lifted from the kitchen from the waistband of her trousers. It scared her. The young man had sharpened it with slow, easy strokes on the steel until it was sharp enough to carve meat with virtually no effort, and she imagined it plunging into the skinny man's neck.

Erna leaned forward and lifted the knife, then gasped as one angry eye opened and glared at her. Össur's hand shot out and grabbed her wrist. The other hand snatched a handful of hair close to the scalp and hauled her face to within an inch of his, eyes smouldering with fury.

"Going to give me a surprise, were you?" he hissed, and the stench of his breath made her want to retch. The hand buried deep in her hair held her head secure so that she was unable to move away; she didn't dare close her eyes. The other hand was firmly around her wrist, keeping it locked as he forced her arm behind her until she could feel the point of the knife pricking her back.

"Please . . ."

"Please, what, you fucking evil bitch? You were going to stab me, weren't you?"

"No, of course not."

"What, then? You don't carry a blade unless you're going to use it."

The little man's sheer strength took her by surprise. She had not imagined that someone so thin and small would be able to exert such a powerful grip and she could feel her wrist going numb. At the same time, she was bent over him where he lay on the bed, her nose almost touching his.

"Or after something else, were you?"

"No, not at all. Definitely not."

"Drop the blade. Throw it on the floor. So I can hear it fall."

"I can't," Erna gasped. "You're holding my hand too tight."

His grip relaxed for a moment. She let the knife clatter to the floor by the bed and Össur jerked her head forward, hauling her bodily onto the bed on top of him.

"That's what you need, is it?" he mocked. "You didn't want to do me any harm, did you? Just wanted a man for a bit of fun, didn't you?"

"No, absolutely not. Not in a million years!"

Erna writhed and one knee caught Össur sharply inside the thigh, making him hiss with pain.

"You're nasty bitch, you are," he winced, sitting upright and pushing her away as he did so, but still holding onto the handful of hair so hard that tears began to blind her.

"Let me go, please. I didn't mean it."

"Didn't mean it? Came in here with a blade and you didn't mean it?"

"I . . . I just wanted to talk, and you scare me. That's why I brought the knife."

"Like fuck you did," he hissed, and dropped her wrist, lifting his hand to deliver a slap across her face that made her shriek.

Gísli looked flustered as he let Gunna in. His clothes were spattered with paint and there was a streak of blue in his hair.

"*Hæ*, Mum. What brings you this way?"

Kjartan Gíslason wailed from the next room and Gunna could hear Drífa cooing to him.

"Simple enough. I'm on the way home and I have to drive right past, so it seemed a good idea to see my grandson. All right, is he?"

"Yeah, he's fine. Drífa was just feeding him and he doesn't want to burp." There were pots of paint on the kitchen table and brushes were soaking in a jar in the sink. "The living room's painted, so when it's dry and I've been round the edges, we, can move downstairs while I smarten up the rooms upstairs."

"You don't know how long you have the place?"

Gísli shrugged. "Haven't a clue. Old Bryngeir said we could stay as long as we wanted it."

"Fair enough. You're not tempted to buy it?"

"I would be if it was for sale, but I'm not sure it is, and anyway, we couldn't afford it right now. The only thing that worries me is if Bryngeir pops off. I'm sure his children would have the place on the market before he's even cold."

Gunna nodded and poured herself a coffee. "And is he on his last legs?"

"Not as far as I can see. He was here this afternoon and he seemed lively enough."

"Think about it in the new year when you're back at sea. You'd get the loans easily enough, wouldn't you?"

"Well, yeah," Gísli said, his mind elsewhere and a thumbnail rasping the stubble along the line of his jaw. "At the moment I'm just happy to be renting something that isn't breaking the bank. It's a nightmare out there, you know, Mum. It really is."

"Spoken to Soffía recently?" Gunna asked, dropping her voice.

"Yesterday. Why? Have you?"

"I have. She's worried."

"About what? Maintenance? Come on, I'm looking after my end of things and she can't complain I'm not having Ari as often as I can, but it's not easy." His chin lifted and his eyes went to the ceiling and the sound of Drífa's footsteps pacing back and forth. "It's sensitive. You know?"

"I know. Of course it's sensitive."

"So what, then?"

Gunna took a breath. "Soffía has applied to do a master's degree in Sweden. She's concerned that you might not agree to her taking Ari out of the country."

Gísli shook his head. "For crying out loud, Mum. Why would I object?"

"That's what I said."

"If she was talking about moving to Argentina permanently, then I might have something to say about it. But a year or two in Sweden's not going to hurt

78

anyone, and I guess she'd be running back and forth anyway."

Gunna patted Gísli's hand. "It's all right, sweetheart. That's what I told her as well."

"So what's she worried about?" Gísli's voice had risen and Gunna noticed that the sound of Drífa's footsteps upstairs had stopped. "That I'll bite her head off and stop her taking the boy to Sweden because she threw me over?"

"With reason, maybe? And calm down, I'm just delivering a message."

"She can speak to me herself, can't she? Shit!" Gísli swore and shook his head. "We were together for three years and now it's like I'm some kind of stranger."

"You're not the same person you were during those three years any more than Soffía is. You're not the easy-going character you used to be, you know."

"I know," Gísli admitted, deflating, his shoulders slumping. "Tell her it's fine by me, and she can speak to me about more than just who's picking Ari up and when."

"No, Gísli," Gunna said, squeezing his hand. "You tell her."

Tinna Lind's lips parted and presented themselves for a kiss. Her hand had already curled under Magni's shirt and he had half lifted her to lie across his lap. Magni felt his excitement growing and knew that she had to be feeling the bulge in his trousers, which he was confident wouldn't disappoint her. Their lips touched; she pulled back for a second and then lifted her head, seeking him out. Her tongue explored his lips just as the shriek from upstairs pulled them from each other.

"What the fuck . . .?"

Magni was on his feet in a second and pounding up the stairs. Tinna Lind was close behind as Magni shoved the door aside and glared at Össur sitting calmly on the bed, cleaning under his fingernails with the razor-sharp kitchen knife. Erna was huddled on the floor, her back to the wall and her face streaked with tears. A red wheal covered half of her face.

Tinna Lind crouched next to her and wrapped her arms around her as Erna sobbed.

Magni glared. "What happened, Össi?"

Össur looked past him at the bikini-clad girls bopping on the television. He shrugged and held the knife up, the point against the tip of his left forefinger.

"The old bag pulled a knife on me, that's all." He yawned. "So I had to show her why it wasn't a good idea."

Magni scowled and looked at Erna. "Is that right?"

"I just wanted to talk to him," she said between the sobs that welled up from deep inside. "We need to get out of here. I can't stay here. It's driving me mad."

"Tinna Lind, will you take your mother to her room and look after her?" Magni said. "You don't smack women like that, Össur. You hear me?"

Össur looked away from the television for the first time.

"Says who? The hired help?

There was a snick as the Baikal appeared and the safety catch was clicked off.

"Sweet on the girl, aren't you, Magni?" Össur's voice was so low that Magni struggled to hear what he said. "Listen, meathead. There's a stack of cash to split between us when we get out of this place tomorrow, the next day, whenever. *If* we get out of here. So stop thinking with your balls and start thinking about how to get out of here."

Magni backed away. The vicious fury in Össur's eyes was unmistakable and the barrel of the Baikal loomed huge as Össur trained the weapon on him. Magni wondered for a second if he could step to one side and grab Össur's hand before he had time to fire, but he knew there would be no hesitation on Össur's part, no second chances would be given. He backed slowly out of the door and breathed a sigh of relief as he closed it behind him. A second later he heard the door lock from the inside.

Downstairs he took a pull at the whisky bottle and hid it back in the manager's office with three more that he'd found in the same place. Erna's shuddering sobs could be heard through the ceiling, but they had slowed, and the interval between howls became steadily longer until Magni fell asleep on the sofa, huddled under the purloined duvet.

It was late when Tinna Lind crept downstairs and under the duvet. Magni raised an arm and laid it on her back as she rested her head on his shoulder and closed her eyes.

"How's the old lady?" he muttered.

"Exhausted. And so am I."

"Go to sleep," Magni said. "We'll see what happens in the morning."

CHAPTER
THREE

Saturday

Magni's arm was numb as he opened his eyes, surprised to see Tinna Lind's feet in their thick socks in his armpit, while at the far end of the sofa he could see a thoughtful frown on her sleeping face, as if something serious were happening in her dreams. He eased himself gently off the sofa from under her and drew the duvet up to her chin before padding to the kitchen. He spooned up a few mouthfuls of the cold stew left over from the day before and washed it down with a mug of water. In the shower he felt himself wake up properly under the hot water. He wrapped himself in one of the hotel's fleecy towels and laid his threadbare socks on a radiator to dry.

In the kitchen he put some water on to boil for coffee, noting with dismay that the coffee would also start to run short soon.

"Morning," Tinna Lind said as she appeared behind him. "Why did you let me sleep so long?"

"Didn't want to disturb you. Have you checked on Erna?"

"I will in a minute. Is there any breakfast?"

"Just last night's leftovers. Warm some of it up in the microwave."

"Beef stew for breakfast. That's really decadent, isn't it?"

"Decadent?"

"You know, unusual. A bit random."

"Oh, right. I'll warm it up if you want to go and check on the old lady."

He pulled on his trousers and shirt, and turned on the hot plate under the saucepan, which was still half-full of stew. By the time Tinna Lind returned, the kitchen felt warmer and alive with the fragrance of food.

"She's still asleep," Tinna Lind yawned. "Look, I'm sorry about last night. I got a little carried away, and then all that shit happened."

Magni ladled stew into bowls and put them on the table. "That's all right. These things happen."

"Your friend, Össur. He's dangerous, right?"

"He's not exactly my friend."

"Yeah, but you know him well enough, don't you?"

"Along with all the other pissheads at the Emperor."

"How did you get tangled up with him, and us, if you don't mind me asking?" Tinna Lind blew on a spoonful of stew. "I mean, you can tell me, can't you?"

Magni growled. "I suppose so. Like I told you, I've been out of work for a while and berths don't pop up out of nowhere any more. Someone asked me if I could do with some easy money and I said yes. Like you do."

Tinna Lind looked up at him and nodded. She swept a lock of hair back over her shoulder. "Go on."

"Someone said Össur was looking for a bit of muscle to help him out with a problem. All I had to do was go

84

with him and keep the other guy's minder quiet. So that's what I did."

"And how did you end up here with us?"

Magni sighed. "That's where it all went wrong. There were two tickets to Spain waiting for us at the airport. We were going to go straight to Keflavík and get on a flight to London, and another one from there to Alicante the same day, so there wouldn't be a direct trail?"

"Yeah. Understood."

"But the driver who was going to run us out to the airport didn't show up. We came out of this old guy's place and there was nobody there to pick us up. So we had to run downtown, and by the time it was getting dark we knew Árni wasn't going to show."

"Árni? That's the getaway driver?"

"That's him. We tried to call him but couldn't get a reply. Then Össur started to get a bit jumpy and he hopped in the back of your car, and by that time we'd already missed our flight."

"So instead of being in the sunshine in Spain, you're holed up in a deserted hotel in the back of beyond?"

"That's about it."

Tinna Lind finished the last of her stew and pushed her bowl away.

"So what did you go and see this old guy about?"

Magni grimaced. "He owed Össur some money, or so Össur says."

"And did Össur get it?"

"Yeah. There's a bagful of money upstairs that Össur's sitting on."

Tinna Land's eyes glinted. "How much money?"

"A couple of hundred thousand, I think."

"Icelandic money? That's not that much to be on the run for."

"No, euros."

Tinna Lind sat back and whistled. "And my guess is this old guy will want it back, won't he?"

"Table for one?" the waiter asked, without waiting for an answer as he swept past with a tray in his hands.

Gunna waited by Borgarkaffi's counter and tried to recall what the place had looked like the last time she had been there. Then it had been modern, with plastic furniture and a severe utilitarian look. All that had been swept away now and the place looked like an interior designer's vision of a European coffee house — all dark wood, clattering crockery and bustling staff in understated dark uniforms with aprons wrapped around them.

Even at this early hour on a Saturday, it was evident that the brand-new look that made Borgarkaffi appear as if nothing had changed in the last five decades was paying off, and she had plenty of time to examine the place before the waiter returned.

"Table for one, was it?"

"I'm not a customer. It's the manager I'm looking for."

The waiter shrugged. "Come back at twelve. She might be here by then."

"So who's in charge until then?"

"Me, I guess, until Eydís finally shows up. Why, are you from environmental health? There's an official sort of look about you," he said with a sly smile.

"Nothing so glamorous," Gunna told him, showing her identification as the young man's eyes widened in surprise. "CID."

"Ah. Then I guess Eydís is the one you need to speak to." His eyes flashed suspiciously past her as he checked the tables and the handful of staff attending to them. "But I can find a few minutes."

"Ten minutes," Gunna said, jerking a thumb at an unoccupied table. "I'll have a cappuccino."

"Take a seat and I'll be right with you," he instructed, waving to a waitress as she approached with a tray in her hand. "Thóra, would you look after the till for me, sweetheart? This lady needs a few minutes of my valuable time. Could you bring us two cappuccinos, please?"

The seat in the window gave her a view over the street outside, where a blustery wind nagged at the coats and scarves of people hurrying through the city centre.

"So tell me," the waiter said with a grin once two cappuccinos had been delivered. "You're from the Special Prosecutor's office and you're investigating Eydís's shady business affairs?"

"What makes you think that, Leo?" Gunna asked, making a point of looking at the man's name badge.

"Just wondering. Her husband is tied up in all kinds of financial shit and we reckon this place is a tax dodge."

"Interesting. I'll pass that on. But no," Gunna said and sipped her coffee. "I'm interested in Tinna Lind Bogadóttir. I understand she works here."

"She's worked here on and off for the last couple of years, and she's a real grafter when she's here. Works like a slave."

"When she's here, you said."

"Yeah. Haven't seen her for a few days and she should have been at work here today, so I had to call someone to fill in for her. Why? What's she done?"

"I'm not sure she's done anything. You haven't seen the ads? She's been reported missing. Tell me about her. Has she worked here long?"

Leó's cup stopped halfway to his lips. "She's disappeared? Again?"

"She's done this before?"

Leó nodded. "That's just it. Like you said, when she's here. Tinna Lind likes to travel and once she has enough saved up for a flight to somewhere warm, she's off. There'll be a day's notice and she'll disappear for a week or a month, or more."

"You know where she likes to go?"

"Anywhere, I reckon. She likes Portugal, Italy, Greece. She had one trip to the Caribbean but said she didn't like it a lot, too many fake zillionaires."

"And she travels alone? Does she tell you what she does on these trips?"

"Normally alone. I gather there might be an on-off boyfriend somewhere a long way south of here."

"But you've been here for a while, and so has Tinna Lind. How well do you know her?"

Leó shrugged and sat back with his arms folded as he gazed out of the window as an empty carrier bag was caught by the wind, which swept it high into the air and twisting as it flew, until it was caught in the bare branches of a tree.

"I don't know her well at all. She keeps to herself, doesn't say too much. I don't know much about her personal life, although I get the feeling she can be very focused if she has something to focus on. I know I can rely on her completely once she's here, but I can't always be sure she'll turn up. Tinna Lind could have been the manager here if she wasn't always running off to the sunshine. She knows that but I guess she's not interested."

"Something of an enigma, then? Any boyfriends in Iceland? Does she socialize with colleagues here?"

"Not that I know of. There's not a lot of socializing that goes on here. The staff turnover is pretty high, so people don't really get to know one another well before they move on."

Leó looked uncomfortable for a moment and dropped his eyes.

"What?" Gunna asked.

"Well," he said and fidgeted with the strings of the apron around his waist. "Tinna Lind doesn't do boyfriends. If she wants to . . . you know . . . then she does. But she doesn't have boyfriends, doesn't do relationships, not as such."

"Meaning?"

"If she wants to, then she'll grab a guy for the night. But she can't be doing with men hanging around her all the time."

"Ah, and you have personal experience of this?"

Leó nodded and looked embarrassed. "We . . . a couple of times. I wanted to take it further. She didn't.

Not interested in commitment. Tinna Lind does her own thing."

It was a cold morning outside as Magni trudged through the snow around the building. At the back of the hotel the tyre tracks that he had left getting the Explorer into the restaurant had been half-filled with fresh snow. He looked around the surrounding hills at the bowl in the landscape that Hotel Hraun occupied. A gentle hill with a long slope leading to a round top sat to the south while two other sides of the little valley were made up of sheer sides leading to jagged escarpments high above. To the south the land sloped gradually away to the flat land beyond and the road leading away to Reykjavik or Selfoss. He rooted through the cupboards in the shed, more out of curiosity than because he was looking for anything in particular, but at the back of his mind was the thought that there might be a can of petrol somewhere.

He pushed through a door at the back of the shed and found himself in a wide lean-to built against the end. He clicked the switch a couple of times but wasn't surprised when the light didn't come on. At the far side was another door, which he finally persuaded to open and let in some light, then he wiped down a grimy window with a rag to let in some more. A quad bike squatted in the corner of the lean-to, with two wheels missing and its front end resting on heavy wooden blocks. He could see the battery on the bench.

Magni put his weight to the bike, gently rocked it from side to side and was rewarded by the sound of something sloshing in the tank. He grinned to himself and started hunting through the junk under the workbench for a hose to siphon the fuel out.

As he knocked at the door of the flat the noise behind it reminded Eiríkur of a zoo and the sound blasted out at him as the door opened.

"Yes?"

"Borghildur Sævarsdóttir?"

The tired-looking young woman swept a strand of hair behind one ear as she looked him in the eye.

"Who's asking?"

"Eiríkur Thór Jónsson, city CID."

"You got any ID?"

After having checked his warrant card, she let him in, leading him past a living room in which five toddlers were sat in front of a DVD.

"Not all yours, are they?"

"Hell, no. Two of them are mine and the rest are my neighbours'. This is the Strandvangur childcare co-operative at the moment. We all take turns so we can do a few mornings' work every week. You want a coffee?"

"The co-operative works at weekends as well?"

"Oh, yes. Half of us work in shops and hotels, and these days shops open every day of the week and you don't turn down a weekend shift if you want to stay in work." She handed Eiríkur a mug. "So what can I do for you? My mum said I might hear from you."

"Tell me about Árni Sigurvinsson. Your stepfather, right?"

"Yeah, sort of. He appeared on the scene when I was seven or eight. That's when I guess he and my mum got together, so he's been about, on and off, for as long as I remember."

"I gather he and your mother had parted company not long ago? I spoke to her yesterday and she was pretty upset."

"More upset than she should be," she snorted.

"Bogga —"

Her voice skipped from harsh disdain to concern as a small boy looked up at her with big eyes.

"Yes, sweetheart? What's the problem, Hannes?"

"Can I have a biscuit? I'm hungry."

"Not now, darling. I need to talk to this gentleman for a little while and then I'll give everyone a drink and a biscuit. All right?"

"All right," he said doubtfully, as if concerned that he was being fobbed off with the bad end of a deal.

"Go on, Hannes. Go and watch Donald Duck with the others. I'll call you in ten minutes." She looked up as the boy ran back to the living room and the crashes and bangs coming from the television.

"Árni. What was I saying?"

"That your mother needn't be too upset?"

"He was a decent enough guy most of the time. If he'd got his head down and just worked for a living, everything would probably have been fine, but he was always screwing around with little scams here and there, like a kid, really."

"How so?"

"Árni's friends were always his downfall. If he'd kept clear of those deadbeats, he'd have been all right. But this last year or so things started to get worse."

Eiríkur sipped his coffee and nodded, confident that the story would unfold, hoping it would happen before the small boy returned.

"So what happened?"

"He used to work at a garage up on Hellnahraun, but they had less work after the Crash so he was laid off and he started doing taxi work all the time instead of just occasionally. I don't tell Mum everything I hear because it would only upset her more." She opened the window next to the kitchen table and lit a cigarette, blowing smoke outside. "Árni had been doing work for Alli the Cornershop and Össi Óskars."

"Ah. There's a familiar name."

She nodded and puffed. "Isn't it just? And you didn't hear any of this from me and I won't go to court. It's too . . . you know."

"That's unfortunate," Eiríkur said. "But I can understand. I'm not making notes, as you can see."

"Everyone knows who Alli is and what he does. He sells dope and he's been supplying girls as well. I reckon Mum knew about that and that's what made her finally move out."

"Because Árni was doing the deliveries?"

"Exactly. Árni was on the rank every evening as usual, and he'd do a few fares, but after about ten every night he'd be doing deliveries for Alli. Mostly bags of white stuff and driving young women to punters. He has a couple of them living in Hafnarfjördur and they

93

seem to rotate every few weeks. They go back to wherever he gets them from and then a couple of fresh ones take their places."

"How do you know all this?"

Borghildur twisted her face in distaste.

"Because one of them was here. She rented the spare room for a while last year. She was a sweet enough girl, but very young, and it was heartbreaking to think what she was having to do every night. If she had to do it, I don't know. After two months she moved on and Árni asked if I could put another one up, but I said I needed the room for someone else."

"Yes, yes, Tinna Lind worked here."

The sign on the travel agent's desk proclaimed that Sigvaldi Tómas Hauksson was a senior travel adviser, and the heavy beard that Gunna guessed was intended to make him look like an experienced explorer contrasted with his salmon-pink shirt. The sight of Gunna's identification clearly took him by surprise.

"What's the matter? Has she done something?"

"Why do you think that?"

"Well, there was a little unpleasantness when she left here," he said reluctantly.

"Go on," Gunna prodded. "How long ago was this?"

"She left here about a year and a half ago. The middle of last year, I think it was."

"How long had she worked here?"

"Two years, on and off. She was studying as well, or so she said, so I guess she wanted to work around university."

94

"And she was good at her job?"

"Very good," he said ruefully. "She could sell sand to Arabia. I was sorry to see her go."

"So tell me what happened."

Sigvaldi sat back and Gunna could see him running things over in his mind.

"We run competitions every few months, normally on Facebook; we get people to like or share our page and one lucky person who shares the page wins a trip somewhere. Normally it's something cheap, nothing fantastic. But there was a trip to Egypt that we put on there that time . . . He fell silent.

"And? What happened?"

He sighed.

"It was a trip for two, four days in Cairo and four days on the Red Sea coast, flights, transfers, hotels and full board for two. Tinna Lind rigged it. She made sure one of her friends won the trip, and guess which friend was invited along with her?"

"Ah, I see."

"The boss was furious. But by then there wasn't much we could do about it without a whole load of ill-feeling and a stack of bad publicity, so eventually we let it go. Tinna Lind got her eight days in the sun, and when she came back she'd been replaced."

Össur looked worried, Magni thought, slumped in a chair and gnawing at his fingernails.

"Össi, we need to sort something out here," Magni said. Össur ignored him and stared into the distance.

Magni poured himself coffee into a mug and sat down opposite him.

"Sweet on that hippie chick, aren't you?" Össur sneered.

"She's all right. What business is it of yours?"

"It's my business while we're stuck here."

"If you say so. Look, Össi, what the fuck's going on? Who was the old bastard you robbed?"

"You're better off not knowing, believe me."

"Come on, don't give me that."

Össur grinned a humourless smile that showed his damaged teeth. "That was Alli the Cornershop."

"Him? The famous one?"

"The very one, in person."

"Why's he called that?"

"You saw the place he lives in, didn't you?" Össur asked. "That weird little house? Years ago it really was a corner shop with a flat upstairs. Now it's still a sort of corner shop, except not just anyone can walk in and go shopping there. Alli's particular about his clientele and he likes customers to call in advance."

"So I guess there are people out there who won't be all that happy with you?"

"Too right. And they won't be happy with you either."

"Fair enough," Magni said. "So what do you want to do about this? Are you planning on staying in this place until the search dies down, or do you reckon your friends are going to come and find you here? Come on, tell me what the fuck's going on, will you? I know you've got a stack of cash, and a chunk, of it's mine, don't forget."

"It's yours when we're clear. Payment when the job's done. You're the handyman, not the brains."

"If you say so. What fantastic scheme has the brains come up with to get us out of here? It won't be long before someone comes to check on the place."

Össur gnawed at a fingernail. "I'm wondering if we can risk a week or so here," he said finally. "Alli will be going crazy for the next few days, but I don't think he'll search for long. He has other stuff to deal with and he'll be concentrating on business."

"If you want to stay here a week, then there's stuff we're going to need."

"Like what?"

"Food, to start with," Magni said. "And you'll be out of smokes sooner or later."

A nerve twitched under Össur's eye. Magni could hear the click of the Baikal's safety catch deep in his pocket.

"All right, then, smartarse. Let's have your ideas."

"I can get the Explorer to a petrol station and fill the tank, so it's ready for when we need it, stock up on supplies, smokes for you and get back here."

Össur glared at him in suspicion. "It's out of fuel, isn't it?"

"I can deal with that."

"How?"

"Never you mind. But I can get it to a petrol pump."

"So what's to stop you just disappearing into the beyond, leaving me here to starve with the hippie chick and that sour-faced old bitch?"

"How much cash do you have hidden away upstairs?" Magni asked. "Come on, how much did you lift off that dealer?"

"About two hundred thousand."

"Euros."

"Euros. Used notes, fifties and hundreds."

"So I guess I have about a hundred thousand reasons not to disappear, wouldn't you say?"

Össur's eyes bulged. He opened his mouth and closed it again. "Fifty," he said finally.

"That's about eight million krónur, am I right?"

"It's a damned good payday for an afternoon's work, I'd say."

"But it's more than an afternoon's work now, isn't it?"

"What the fuck? All you did was stand there for five minutes."

"Yeah, but I also broke that big bastard's nose and knocked his teeth out for him, I've spent three days so far hanging out up here in the arsehole of beyond with you, and there's an angry gangster in Reykjavík who wants my balls on a plate, along with yours, so I reckon that adds up to something close to a fifty-fifty split."

Össur glared and chewed a nail.

"So I'm wondering if I need to be on the way to Spain for a few years like you."

"Who says I'm coming back?"

Magni shrugged. "Speaks for itself, doesn't it? But if we're going to be here for longer than a few more days, we need some supplies to keep us going. Whatever happens, we're going to need fuel in the tank."

"I still don't trust you not to come back."

"It's up to you. But if I wanted to walk away, I could do it any time."

"What?"

Magni leaned forward and placed his folded arms on the table in front of him. "Look, Össi, you thought you were getting shit-for-brains hired muscle, which is all I thought the job needed. But I'm no idiot. If I wanted to I could have had Erna's Explorer down the road yesterday, instead of going to the trouble of putting it inside and going through all this shit with you now."

Össur quailed at Magni's frown. "All right. Go on, then. If you think you can do it. When? Now?" he asked. "I might consider adjusting your percentage once we're clear."

"Yeah, right. Let's leave it until it starts to get dark, shall we? No point in drawing attention to ourselves. But I'll need some cash."

Össur laughed for the first time. "Don't think you're going to spend a handful of euros in a country petrol station without anyone noticing."

"Krónur, obviously."

"I don't have any cash."

"Or a card?"

"Don't be stupid. I deal in cash."

"Well, my card's maxed out until next week, so I guess we need to persuade the lady upstairs to part with her security numbers. So maybe you had better be a bit nicer to her. An apology might be in order."

Alli the Cornershop rarely felt nervous, but the robbery the other day had left him feeling vulnerable, as well as a lot poorer than he wanted to be. It didn't help that Baldvin, who was supposed to be there to keep nutjobs like Össi Óskars out of his hair when their presence wasn't required, was out of the picture while some wealthy dentist was making himself even more wealthy trying to patch up the mess that Össur's tame gorilla had made of Baldvin's teeth.

"A shame about your friend Árni the other day," Rafn commiserated.

Alli shrugged. "It's a dangerous habit, smoking in bed."

The young man never failed to make even Alli the Cornershop's blood run a little colder. The impassive expression and chilled blue eyes were unnerving enough, but Rafn had a reputation for brains as well as ruthlessness. Alli hated having to involve a bunch like the Undertakers, who were not only his competition but also people who would gladly take every shred of his business if they thought they could.

"What's the problem, Alli?"

"It's a problem with someone who's been making a nuisance of himself. It's a job I'd like to contract out rather than deal with myself."

"Why?" Rafn's gaze remained completely impassive as he took stock of Alli. "I'd have thought you'd want to keep something like that in-house?"

The words "something like that" made Alli shudder as he wondered how much of his business was common knowledge.

100

"Logistics and discretion," he said smoothly. "It calls for someone who isn't going to be traced back to me, and if there's no trail of footprints, it won't lead back to you either."

"You're not thinking of the law here, are you?" Rafn asked, and Alli saw the faintest glimmer of sardonic amusement at the corner of the young man's mouth.

"I don't have your manpower," Alli said.

"The famous little black book doesn't have all the right contacts in it?"

"Not this time."

"What's the problem and what are you after?"

Alli shifted uncomfortably. He didn't much like going out, and he certainly didn't like this gloomy cavern hung with motorcycle memorabilia that the Undertakers described as their world headquarters. This wasn't his style. Old-school, he preferred to keep things quiet and operate from his own place, but felt that he would have to accept that times were changing and so was the business.

"Someone has done me a bad turn. All I'm looking for is some eyes. This guy has vanished, and either he's hiding away somewhere or he's skipped town."

"Össi Óskars?" Rafn asked. "Is that the man you're looking for?"

Alli felt a rush of anger and wondered who might have been spreading rumours.

"That's the guy," he said finally.

"I had a feeling you two would fall out eventually," Rafn said, defusing the situation. "What would you like us to do?"

"Just find him. I'll deal with Össi in-house, but I need some eyes and ears to find out where the little bastard has hidden himself away."

Erna's friend Dúa was so different from Sunna that it was difficult to imagine any common ground between them. Gunna's reception was one of emotion and tears, unlike Sunna's initially reserved manner the day before.

A cat was shooed from a chair to make room for Gunna in the cramped kitchen and Dúa clattered cups and plates as she cleared the table and brewed coffee, before disappearing and returning with her greying hair in order and her dressing gown replaced by jogging bottoms and a sweater. She chirruped and clucked, talking almost ceaselessly as she pottered with the coffee pot.

"You take milk, do you, dear?" she asked, speaking half to herself and half to Gunna, as if she were a child, even though she guessed there could hardly be more than a few years between them.

"A drop of milk, please," Gunna confirmed and waited for Dúa to settle.

"Oh, I do hope they come back soon," Dúa twittered. "I can't imagine what could have happened to them. I just can't understand it."

"You know Erna well?"

"I've known Erna since we were at school together."

"So you've known Tinna Lind all her life?"

"Of course. I'm her godmother. Such a sweet girl. Headstrong, but sweet."

"I gather the two of them don't get on all that well. Is that right?"

Dúa poured milk into her coffee, forgetting that she had already done so once.

"Well, they're so different in so many ways, but then they're so alike as well, not that either of them would admit it."

"How so?"

"Erna was just as headstrong and stubborn as Tinna Lind when she was younger, although when Erna was her age, she already had Tinna Lind. She had her at nineteen. Too young, I always thought," Dúa said, shaking her head. "You have children, do you, dear?"

"And grandchildren," Gunna said. "So it wouldn't be usual for them to go somewhere together if they get on each other's nerves, would it. Or is it just Erna who is easily irritated?" she asked, anxious to nip giving any personal details in the bud.

"You know what it's like, surely? Erna can't understand why Tinna Lind won't settle into a good job. Because she could, you know," she added with emphasis. "And Tinna Lind can't see what all the fuss is about because she's having a good time, has no ties and is able to travel whenever she can afford it. She's been all over, you know."

"So why were they together with you and Sunna on Thursday, if they don't get on?"

"They bicker but they still get on, and I think Erna wanted to start on some early Christmas shopping. You know, before the rush starts next month."

"As Tinna Lind travels frequently, would it be out of character for her to disappear with no notice?"

"At short notice, yes. But I don't believe she'd just go without a word."

"And Erna?"

"Not at all, never. She's always been in control, knows where she's going to be and what she'll be doing this time next week."

"And the marriage is stable? As her childhood friend, I guess you'd know if there was anything wrong there? No infidelities?"

Dúa shook her head vehemently. "Absolutely not. Erna and Bogi are a lovely couple, and he's devoted to her."

"This is what puzzles me most," Gunna admitted. "I can understand one of them disappearing for a day or two for whatever reason, a fling or something else. But they've gone together. That's what's so odd about this, because from what I've heard from you and others, I can't see Erna running away from Bogi, and I can't see Erna and Tinna Lind wanting to spend so much time together without good reason."

Dúa looked blank. "I know. We can't understand it either."

"Tell me about Tinna Lind. Do you know anything of her private life?"

This time there was a sly smile. "I probably know more than Erna does, or maybe what Erna guesses."

"Nothing between Tinna Lind and Bogi?" Gunna asked and Dúa looked shocked, her jaw dropping.

"How can you say such a thing?"

"I have to say things like that. I have to look at every angle, and that means the least palatable options have to be examined as well. Have you noticed anything between Tinna Lind and her stepfather? Domestic violence? Abuse?"

"Absolutely not!"

"And would you know? Would you recognize the signs?"

"I think so! Believe me, Tinna Lind is a very self-possessed young woman, and if there were anything like that going on, she would have shouted from the rooftops."

"You said she's headstrong? Likes her own way?"

Dúa paused with her coffee cup halfway to her lips and nodded slowly. "Headstrong's not the word. She just goes her own way, always has done."

Magni coaxed the scratched Explorer along the track towards the main road. He knew the few litres of petrol he had extracted from the lawnmowers and the wrecked quad bike should be enough to take him the thirty kilometres to the nearest filling station, but he still nursed the car as best he could, keeping to a steady fifty with the economy indicator smiling happily at him. It coughed and spluttered a couple of times and he gritted his teeth, wondering if the old fuel he'd had no option but to put in the tank might have gone stale, or if the fuel filters were starting to clog up with whatever muck had been in the quad bike's tank. He revved the engine hard a few times and was relieved when it settled down, but the car still felt sluggish.

His real dilemma was the card in his pocket. Erna had been persuaded to part with both her credit card and the PIN to go with it. Tinna Lind had made the case for refuelling the car and stocking up on provisions, arguing that they may as well be comfortable if they had to be prisoners. Magni had promised faithfully to buy nothing more than petrol and food, and he wondered if she expected him to go on some kind of spree in the little town of Selfoss with her credit card. He had his own card in his pocket, but he knew that it was close to its limit and that there was every chance it would be declined. Snowflakes spun away into the darkness as the headlights caught them fleetingly in their beams, and he pondered whether or not to try his own card, but decided that while using Erna's card might flag up an alert for her, with his own clean record he was reluctant to pin himself down as having bought fuel.

Magni drove with care. He had no wish to be stuck by the side of the road in this ridiculous girl's car that drove like it was made of rubber. He even kept the radio and the heater switched off to conserve fuel, keeping the window open a crack as he drove.

At last the filling station appeared by the crossroads, exactly as the old man had said it would. The windows were in complete darkness but the two pumps under a plastic roof were floodlit, and he guessed they would be covered by security cameras. In any case, he rolled up his collar as far as he could and pulled a wool hat low to his eyebrows before he punched the numbers into the self-service machine.

"Thank fuck," he muttered to himself as the pump began to dispense petrol into the Explorer's tank, and he filled all three of the petrol cans he had found in the sheds behind the hotel.

He had timed the trip carefully. He wanted to be on the road in the dark when there was little chance of the car being noticed on the quiet country roads, but he wanted to be in Selfoss when the town was at its busiest, as he would less noticeable in a busy shop.

The branch of Samkaup wasn't huge, but it would do. It was hot inside and Magni stuffed the wool hat into his pocket as he pushed a trolley around, filling it with everything he had on a list in his head. He took tinned vegetables, bags of frozen chicken and pork, and packets of biscuits. He added catering-sized packets of coffee and tea to the top of the growing pile and wondered what else he would need. Next to the biscuits he took half a dozen loaves of bread, reckoning that he would be able to freeze some of them for later.

"*Hæ!* Magni? Is that you?"

He spun round to see a young woman with a batch of freckles across her flushed face and a wide smile.

"Svava, my sweetheart! Wow, fancy seeing you here. What brings you to Selfoss?"

She punched him gently on the arm, her slender fist sinking into the thick padding of his jacket.

"Silly! I moved back here after I split up with Hjalti. Don't you remember? You said you'd come and see us, didn't you? And you never did."

A mock pout accompanied her words and Magni ruffled the hair of a yawning child in a push chair in front of her.

"He's growing quickly, isn't he? Last time I saw him he was only the size of a sixteen-ounce cod fillet."

"I know" Svava sighed. "Before I know it he'll be a sulky teenager wanting tattoos and piercings."

"Like his dad, you mean?"

"Shit, I hope not. Anyway, what brings you out this way? Last I heard you were on *Hafthór?*"

"I was until they sold the quota and the ship," Magni said. "The company made a killing, put the money into property and left forty families without an income. You've got to love the quota system, haven't you?"

"Aw, shit. I'm really sorry to hear it. But what are you doing out here?"

Magni stopped with his mouth half open, wondering what lie he could tell that might be vaguely convincing. "I'm, er . . . I'm helping a guy up-country here for a few days."

"Yeah." Svava grinned at him and winked. "Got a special friend around here somewhere, have you? I know what you're like. And now you're anxious to get away, aren't you?"

Magni nodded, embarrassed but relieved all the same. "I'm really sorry, Svava, but I'm in a proper hurry and I've a long way to go yet tonight. Heading eastwards."

"Oh, right. Thorlákshöfn?"

"No, Vík."

"Vík? Hell, you'd best be on your way. That's going to take you a couple of hours on a night like this." She winked again. "And I guess there's a lucky lady waiting for you at the other end?"

A clock on the shelf ticked so loudly that Gunna wondered if it could be heard in the street outside or if it was just because the house seemed deserted. Bogi Sveinsson seemed to have shrunk since the day before.

"No news?" Gunna asked.

He looked at her in belligerent surprise. "You think I wouldn't have told you?"

"You'd be amazed the number of people who report someone missing, they turn up and nobody bothers to say anything to the police."

"What have you found out? Anything?"

"Yes, but I obviously can't say too much until things are confirmed. What types of phones do Erna and Tinna Lind use?"

"What difference does that make?"

"It does, believe me."

"All right. Tinna Lind has my old iPhone 4. Erna has a Samsung."

"You know what model?"

"No idea. She bought it herself and I know for a fact that the box was thrown away, so I can't tell you offhand."

"You know where she bought it?"

"Smáralind, I expect. She seems to spend half her life in there."

"We tracked both phones and the last communications were on yesterday around midday. That would have been you?"

"Probably. I spoke to her at some time during the day, but I couldn't tell you when. I can check my phone if you like."

"Don't worry. I have the phone records on my desk at Hverfisgata. I'm more interested right now in bank records. We have already checked with the bank to see if there's any movement on Erna's account and we'll get an alert as soon as one of her cards is used."

"I checked the account online a couple of hours ago and her debit cards haven't been used. I can't tell if she's used her Visa but I can call the bank on Monday."

"I can get someone to badger the bank. Don't worry, we'll get a notification as soon as her card is used."

Bogi Sveinsson sat in his own living room as if lost, not knowing what to do with himself in the echoing house decorated with too many ornaments and statues. His fingers moved constantly in his lap, fidgeting as he gazed around the room as though he were taking a good look at it for the first time.

"We've already been through security tapes at Smáralind, and Erna's Ford Explorer was there earlier in the day on Thursday," Gunna said, breaking the uncomfortable silence.

"And they were all right then?"

"So it seems. We're still looking through more footage to check if we can see where they went inside the shopping centre. There's plenty to search through."

"I see." Bogi Sveinsson's fingers twined together, untangled themselves again and then he placed his hands flat on his thighs, as if irritated by his own impatient fidgeting. "Do you know if Tinna Lind was with her?"

"So it seems. There's an image of a girl who resembles your stepdaughter by the vehicle at Smáralind, so we're working on the assumption that the two of them are together," Gunna said. "Bogi, do you have any connections with the region around Thingvellir, or Grímsnes? Hrunamannahreppur, maybe?"

"No, why?"

"You don't have a summer house out that way or anything like that?"

"We have a flat in Tenerife that we share with another couple. We're golfers, you see. We go there to play a couple of times a year."

"But nothing in this country? No connections with that district? No family farm or anything like that?"

"I was brought up in Kópavogur and both my parents were from around there. Erna's a hundred and five per cent Reykjavík, never goes further than Mosfellsbær. She was brought up in the city and her family's all from Reykjavík."

"So no rural connections at all? How about Tinna Lind? She's not your biological daughter, is she? What about her natural father's family?"

Bogi's face twisted into a scowl of discomfort. "It's sensitive," he said, and looked at the floor.

"Maybe so," Gunna said gently, "but any piece of background information could lead us to them. And I can assure you that anything you say is confidential."

"Erna never told me who Tinna Lind's real father is," he said and sighed, looking at the overstuffed room as if it might give him inspiration. "Erna was a pretty wild youngster by all accounts. Look, you're sure this won't go any further?"

"Between you and me. Unless it becomes essential as evidence, in which case it would have to come out."

"All right, it's not going to be relevant to the investigation. When Erna was a teenager she had an affair with her older sister's husband, who was six or seven years older than she was. I know because Agla, that's her sister, told me herself; said she'd caught them at it. There was a huge row and the family smoothed it all over so there was no gossip. I'm certain that he's Tinna Lind's natural father. You understand that this all happened before I appeared on the scene? Anyway, Tinna Lind was registered at birth as having no known father, and when Erna and I got together and had been married a few years, I adopted her formally, so she's Tinna Lind Bogadóttir," he said in a rush and took a deep breath. "And that's the first time I've ever told anyone about that or mentioned it outside Erna's immediate family. I'm not even sure Tinna Lind knows. It's not something any of us have ever talked about."

The clock seemed to tick even more loudly once Bogi stopped speaking.

"I see," Gunna said, impressed by the effort he had made to tell her the family secret. A tiny bead of perspiration had rolled down his forehead and his fingers were again twisted together in a knot. "In that case, do Erna and her sister get on today? How about the brother-in-law?"

"He died two years ago. Erna and Agla had a difficult relationship for a long time, but since Gautur died they have been a lot closer."

"Is there any enmity there?"

"Are you suggesting that Agla might have an axe to grind? Come on, this was all put to bed years ago. In any case, Agla's not well herself these days."

"Friends, acquaintances? Who does Erna associate with?"

"Women who shop and do lunch, mostly."

Magni pushed his trolley to the checkout and stacked everything on the conveyor. A girl who bounced a wad of gum from cheek to cheek scanned everything and the total appeared on the screen as Magni put the goods in two cardboard boxes.

"Cash or card?"

"Card."

He swiped the card through the machine and prayed. The card machine chattered and the girl looked at the strip of paper it ejected.

"It's refused."

"What? Try it again, can you?" Magni said, hoping that the girl didn't take it into her head to look at the name on the card or the photo of Erna on the back of it.

The girl sighed, rubbed the card energetically against her sleeve and ran it through the machine a second time. This time it chattered again but Magni breathed as the girl spun a receipt towards him.

"Sign here."

He took the offered ballpoint and scribbled an indecipherable scrawl instead of a signature on the slip, then looked up to see the girl looking at him strangely.

"Erna Björg Brandsen?" she said, a plucked eyebrow lifted in question at the beefy ginger-haired man standing in front of boxes stacked with groceries.

"What?" Magni asked, trying to be convincing and taking the card. He looked at it and shook his head with what he hoped was an engaging grin. "Shit, I picked up my wife's card by mistake. Ah, what the hell, nobody'll notice," he said lightly, pocketing the card and picking up a freesheet newspaper from the rack and dropping into the box.

The girl opened her mouth to say something.

"Sorry, sweetheart. It's my mistake. Happens all the time. She's probably at the hairdresser's with my card in her handbag," he said and placed his hands on the trolley. The girl looked at the queue snaking back into the shop, shrugged and started scanning the next customer's items.

Two places along the queue, Svava looked at Magni and caught his eye.

"Wife?" she mouthed at him. "Really?"

He pushed the Explorer through the darkness, furious at having been recognized in the shop and wondering if Svava having seen him there could prove to be a problem later. Realizing he was driving dangerously fast, he told himself to act rationally and slow down. There was nothing to connect him with anything illegal, he was sure of that, and he brooded all the way

114

along the long straight road. He'd even wiped down the car's interior as best he could to remove any prints and worn gloves for the journey, but he still had the nagging feeling there could be a print or two that had escaped him, and hoped they would be Össur's rather than his.

At least the Explorer was behaving better now that the tank was full of fresh petrol, and as he barrelled along he almost missed the junction by the filling station onto the unmade road northwards, and had to stop and reverse to make the turning, scolding himself for not paying attention.

Hotel Hraun was in darkness. He parked at the front and took the boxes in one by one, stacking them on the kitchen table. All but one of the loaves of bread and cartons of milk went into the freezer, as did the bags of chicken and pork, along with a bag of still-frozen fish fillets, although he pulled out a couple to defrost for the next day.

"Hello! Where is everyone?" he called out. He put water on to boil and ripped open a bag of coffee.

"How did it go?"

"Ah, not bad. The tank's full and there's food in the fridge. How's your mum?"

Tinna Lind grinned. "Going stir crazy, I think. She hasn't been shopping for two whole days. She's watching TV upstairs and fretting that you might be living the high life on her Visa card."

"In Selfoss? Yeah, sure."

"You could have gone to the booze shop, couldn't you?"

"Yeah, I could have. But I wanted to keep it discreet, so I got fuel and food, and that's it. Don't want to take too many risks with someone else's card. In fact, the girl in the shop in Selfoss looked at it strangely and I said I'd picked up my wife's card by mistake."

"And you got away with it?"

"Yeah, of course," Magni said, and thought back to Svava mouthing "wife?" at him as he left the shop.

Össur appeared in the doorway.

"It went all right?"

"It did. Food and fuel."

"You got smokes?"

Magni tossed a carton of Camels to him and Össur caught it with the first smile that any of them had seen on his face.

"Food as well?"

"Yep, stocked up with stores."

"What are we eating tonight?"

Magni delved into the last box and took out three paper bags.

"As it's Saturday night, grilled chicken and salad," he said, adding a couple of cartons to the pile on the table. "Help yourselves. The chef gets a night off tonight."

"Fucking hell . . ."

Magni turned to see Össur with the newspaper spread out on the table in front of him, an unlit cigarette in his mouth.

"What?" he asked, making his way to the other side of the table to see what had taken him by surprise.

ONE DEAD IN HAFNARFJÖRDUR HOUSE FIRE read the headline, over a picture of an old-fashioned house with smoke billowing from an upstairs window while a fire engine filled the foreground of the picture.

"Shit. That's Árni's place," Össur said in a dead voice.

"Fuck. You're sure?"

"Of course I'm fucking sure."

Magni picked the paper up, checked the date, saw it was the previous day's paper and went to an inside page for the full story.

"'A man was pronounced dead at the scene after fire crews attended an incident in the upstairs apartment of a house in Hafnarfjördur early this morning,'" he read out. "'The deceased is believed to be a man in his forties and his name has not yet been released as relatives are still being informed. A police and fire-service investigation is in progress to find the cause of the fire. Police have not ruled out that the blaze could have been started deliberately and are seeking witnesses who may have been aware of movements in and around Vitastígur between five and seven this morning.'"

"That's Árni," Össur said, lighting his cigarette with trembling fingers. "It has to be Árni. That's his place. Fuck, that evil bastard Alli must have got to him."

"You think so? It might have been an accident."

"Sure. 'Police have not ruled out that the blaze could have been started deliberately,'" he said, finger on the page. "That means they definitely think someone set fire to the place. Christ, I could do with a drink. You didn't go to the booze shop, did you?"

★ ★ ★

"OK, thanks. That's great," Gunna said. "I'll speak to you again in the morning." She put the phone down and turned to face Ívar Laxdal as he appeared silently in the detectives' office.

"Busy weekend, Gunnhildur?"

Ívar Laxdal was finding it harder to take Gunna by surprise and he decided that she must have developed an instinctive sense of when he was approaching.

"Weekends are always busy, aren't they? Eiríkur's liaising with the fire investigators on the house fire in Hafnarfjördur. He says the dead man's a taxi driver and some kind of petty criminal, so he's really waiting to find out for definite if the fire was deliberate or not."

"Was it?"

"Officially, we don't know yet."

"Unofficially?"

"According to Rúnar, who was the fire officer at the scene, it looks like a bunch of petrol-soaked rags through the letterbox and the victim died of smoke poisoning, probably without even waking up."

"So it's a murder investigation?"

"It is, or will be as soon as the fire investigator confirms their findings. But Eiríkur's on it and he'll have Helgi with him tomorrow."

"Suspects?"

"Hard to say. Working on it."

Ívar Laxdal sat down in Helgi's chair and leaned back, his hands clasped over his chest, fingers entwined in a way that reminded her of Bogi Sveinsson.

"And this missing persons inquiry? Something of a mystery?"

118

"Very much so, but a bit of information just turned up a few minutes ago."

"Explain."

"The bank where Erna Brandsen has her account. Her credit card was used a couple of hours ago to buy petrol at a filling station not far from Selfoss."

"Interesting. So the husband is no longer a suspect?"

Gunna rattled her fingernails on the desk. "To start with, I thought he could be."

"And now?"

"Now I'm not so sure. I was sitting in his living room talking to him when the card was used, so that certainly wasn't him."

"That's as good an alibi as a man could hope for."

"The woman and her daughter, who is the husband's stepdaughter, seem to have disappeared together. Their mobile phone records show they both dropped off the network at roughly the same time and place, somewhere near Thingvellir. So they're most likely together, or their phones are. The husband has a solid alibi. He was in Akureyri and didn't get home until Friday afternoon, and that's been confirmed, so he's out of the picture. Plus he's devastated, doesn't know what to do with himself. Strangely, he seems more upset about the girl than about his wife, who seems to me to be one of those women who landed herself a wealthy husband and then set about spending it all as fast as he can earn it."

"And the domestic violence angle you mentioned yesterday? Anything?"

"Nothing at all. Nothing to indicate abuse. A fairly happy and well-balanced family, by all accounts. So I'm back to square one and a wider search."

Ívar Laxdal straightened his back, clapped his hands together and nodded once.

"Good. I'll leave things in your capable hands. What's next?"

"On the missing women? I have alerts out all over the place for Erna Brandsen's white Ford Explorer, their phones are being tracked and I'll get an alert as soon as one of them pops up. I'm getting some poor droid at their bank out of bed on a Sunday morning to go through any more traffic on her debit and credit cards, and if nothing's happened by midday it could be time to mobilize rescue squads for a search, although we really need a better defined area to search than just somewhere around Thingvellir. If that confirmation hadn't come through that Erna Brandsen's card had been used today, I'd be looking at organizing the rescue squads to start a search right now."

"You think they're dead? An accident of some kind? A robbery or a kidnapping? Or some kind of personal crisis?"

Gunna spread her hands wide. "Who knows?"

"A nervous breakdown? It has been known."

"Maybe. But it seems totally out of character for Erna Brandsen, who it seems didn't like going further out of town than the outlet stores in Mosfellsbær."

"And the fire?"

"I'm leaving that to Eiríkur and Helgi. They'll shout if they need help from me."

120

"Do you need anything? Resources, bodies?"

"A search flight if you can get the Coast Guard to organize it and the Dash isn't in use elsewhere. It's the car we need to find, if the cloud lifts enough for a flight."

"A white car on a snow-covered landscape," Ívar Laxdal smiled. "That's not a problem, is it? So what now?"

"It's five o'clock on Saturday afternoon and I'm going home. "D'you know what date it is?"

Ívar Laxdal closed his eyes and thought for a moment.

"Of course," he said softly. "It was today. Fifteen years ago. How could I forget?"

The booming of the television from the room at the end where Össur had once again locked himself in could be heard as a dull bass beat. Magni reached behind the sofa in the hotel's lounge and lifted the whisky bottle out.

"It's Saturday night. Drink?"

Tinna Lind grinned. "Hell, yeah."

He handed her two fingers. They clinked glasses and sipped. Magni rolled it over his tongue and leaned his head back to savour it.

"We'd better not stay here too long or we'll be out of whisky in a few days."

"Are you planning on staying long?"

"Are you in a hurry to get away?"

"Mmm, a bit," Tinna Lind said. "I can sort of imagine how worried my dad must be by now."

"You think he'll have reported you missing?"

"Oh, yeah. He probably did that on Friday when he got home and found my mum wasn't there, or when she didn't turn up by dinner time."

"So the police are going to be searching for you?"

"Probably."

"What's your dad like?"

"He's all right. He's not my real father, though. Mum shacked up with him years ago. But he's a decent guy. A bit dull, plays golf and that, but he's a kind-hearted sort."

"What about your real dad?"

Tinna Lind giggled. "It's a big secret. The olds never talk about it and they think I don't know. Years ago Mum had an affair with her sister's husband. It's the big skeleton in the family closet and nobody's allowed to know about it." She sat next to him on the sofa and cradled the glass in her hands, then she looked up at him with a sly smile. "Now you have to tell me a secret."

Magni looked blank.

"Well, I've led a pretty boring life so far. This is about the most exciting thing I've ever done."

"But you've been to sea on big fishing boats, haven't you?"

"Yeah, but that's not exciting. Not mega-exciting, anyway. It's pretty boring a lot of the time, like working in a factory but getting paid a bunch of money for it."

"No huge storms and wrecked ships?"

"A few big storms. Quite a lot of them, really." He sipped his drink and looked at the ceiling. "All right.

122

When I was a kid there was a teacher at school who really didn't like me. He used to call me a thickhead and give me detentions all the time. So I got my own back on him."

"How?" Tinna Lind asked dubiously.

"I used to help out at one of the fish plants at weekends, and one day I managed to get hold of a catfish frame. You know, what's left when the fish has been filleted? The head and the bones, right?"

"And you put it through his letterbox or something?"

"No, I wrapped it in tin foil, and then I wrapped the tin foil in a bit of chicken wire. And when it was dark I sneaked round to his house and fixed it to his car."

"Yeah?"

"Yep, crawled under his car and fixed the whole thing to the exhaust with some fencing wire, right under the driver's seat. So he'd get in the car and drive somewhere, and the fish would start to get hot as the exhaust pipe warmed up and the car would fill up with this smell of hot, rotten fish. It drove him nuts. He had to drive everywhere with all the windows open. He couldn't understand where the foul smell was coming from. He even took it to a garage and had them strip the seats out and search inside. But they never thought to look underneath."

"How long did this go on for?"

"Oh, weeks and weeks. Months, until he gave in and scrapped the car." He reached back behind the sofa, retrieved the bottle and poured another finger each. "He couldn't sell it because it stank so bad and he couldn't figure out where the smell was coming from."

"That's the worst thing you've ever done?"

"Probably not, but it was the most fun and I've never told anyone before that it was me."

"So your teacher bought a new car. You didn't do the same to that one?"

"I thought about it, but I reckoned he'd had enough punishment."

Tinna Lind lifted her chin upwards. "Your friend. What's the worst thing he's ever done, do you think?"

Magni shuddered. "I'll tell you now, he's done plenty of nasty things, and I don't know the half of it."

He put the bottle away and left his arm draped along the back of the sofa. Tinna Lind reached up, grasped his hand and pulled the arm down to rest around her shoulder as she huddled into the hollow of his side.

Ragnar Sæmundsson looked down on them from his photograph on top of the bookcase. The camera had caught him just as he looked into the lens with a mischievous grin on his face, his Coast Guard cap pushed too far back on his head for the regulations, hair awry in the wind and with the sharp look of cheerful intelligence that Gunna had found herself bewitched by all those years ago.

The house was full to bursting and she wondered how many years it had been since quite so many people had gathered around the table. Steini sat at the end nearest the kitchen, his hand holding Gunna's under the table. Laufey's eyes shone with unshed tears and Gísli had his hands full with Ari Gíslason while Drífa held baby Kjartan.

124

Steini let go of Gunna's hand and stood up awkwardly.

"It's the first time I've done this," he said and paused. "I knew Raggi well and he was a magnificent character. A true friend and I still miss him. Glasses, everyone."

Gunna gulped and glanced sideways at Laufey, who was looking at the tablecloth.

"Ragnar," Steini said and lifted his glass.

"Ragnar."

"Ragnar."

"Raggi," Gunna said and swallowed a sob.

"Dad," Laufey said in a small voice.

They all drank and placed their glasses on the table. Laufey turned and buried her face in Gunna's neck. Gísli looked solemn as Ari tried to wriggle out of his grasp and Steini bit his lip.

"We are going to get out of this place, aren't we?"

"Sure we are. Why shouldn't we?"

Magni lay back practically horizontal, hands behind his head, his legs stretched out and his heels on a low table. Tinna Lind lay flat on her back, her head resting on Magni's leg and her cornrow hair spread out around her.

"I don't know. Össur just seems dangerous, you know."

"He's fucking nuts, that's true enough. But we're the ones who are in danger, not you and your mum."

"You think so?"

"Hell, yeah. Össur's scared shitless of what the old guy he robbed will do when he gets hold of him, and I guess he probably will sooner or later."

125

Tinna Lind looked up at Magni and he saw the concern in her eyes.

"And you?"

Magni scratched his head. "I don't really know. I don't reckon I'll ever be on his Christmas card list," he said with a gurgling laugh.

"I don't want you to get hurt, Magni."

He put out a hand and tousled the cornrows spread across his lap.

"Don't you worry, sweetie. I'm a big boy."

"I'm serious. I don't want you to get hurt because of something Össur did."

"And something I did as well. The old guy had a minder, too, but his minder was smaller than Össur's. Oh, and Össi has a gun. That helped."

"He still has a gun."

"And a knife, and he'd use either of them if he feels he needs to. I told you he's nuts."

"And you're not?"

"No, not really. Maybe just enough."

"I think you have to be. If I was you I'd be terrified."

Magni upended his glass and leaned forward to place it on the table. "I ought to be, and maybe I will be in a day or two, but right now I'm warm, I'm not hungry and there's a glass in my hand," he said. "That's to say there was a glass in my hand. I'll worry about tomorrow when it comes because there's nothing I can do about it now."

"I like you, Magni."

"Thanks. You're all right yourself."

126

"No, I mean it. You're not like the guys I know from college or around Reykjavík."

"Oh? How so? What are they like?"

Tinna Lind stretched and twisted onto one side, lifting her head and propping it up with a hand under her chin.

"Serious, artistic. Hipsters, y'know what I mean? They all play guitars and dream of being in bands."

"Oh, right."

"And you know what I really like about you, Magni?"

"No, go on."

"You're practical. You can cook and fix stuff."

"Well. You pick that sort of stuff up."

"And you haven't tried to get my knickers off. I like that."

Magni was suddenly, clear-headed.

"Oh, right," he said.

"Because you can, if you like," Tinna Lind said, lifting a hand and draping it around his neck to pull him down to her. "I think I'd like that."

CHAPTER
FOUR

Sunday

Erna's voice was as harsh as grinding gears. Magni opened one eye to see Erna staring down at him, hands on her hips, and Tinna Lind's face nestled in the thick mat of reddish hair on his chest.

"This is a hotel, you know. You could at least have found a room."

"Shit . . . what time is it?" Magni asked.

"It's almost nine," Erna said, and Magni closed his eyes again as her footsteps faded into the distance. He stroked Tinna Lind's cheek with a finger. "Hey, sleepyhead. It's daytime and your mum isn't impressed."

"So? What's new?" Tinna Lind replied, eyes firmly closed and huddling deeper into Magni's chest.

"Sorry, sweetie. You're going to have to move."

"Don't want to. I like it here."

"Yeah. I really need to pee, and I don't want to worry you but the pressure's about to go critical down there."

"I suppose I'd better let you go."

Tinna Lind opened one eye, reached up and planted a kiss on the end of his nose. She rolled off him, wrapping herself in the duvet as Magni struggled into his jeans.

He was halfway through his business at the urinal when an ear-splitting electronic alarm began wailing. Magni cursed, finished as quickly as he could and didn't bother shaking off the drops before he ran to the kitchen, passing Tinna Lind on the sofa, her eyes now open in confusion.

"What the fuck's going on?"

Erna stood in the middle of the kitchen, her eyes darting around the room in confusion. Two ink-black slices emerged guiltily from the toaster.

"I . . ."

"Yeah," Magni yelled over the squealing alarm. "I know what you did. But how the hell do we switch it off?"

In the office he ran his eyes over the flashing lights of a grey control box. A loudspeaker above it continued to wail its deafening alarm as he searched for a reset button. He tried several of the unmarked buttons until a dialogue box appeared on a screen and he selected the flashing cancel/reset option. The wailing stopped and the sudden silence was deafening.

In the kitchen Erna stood forlorn. "I was only making some toast for breakfast."

Magni saw her lower lip tremble briefly and guessed the inner turmoil was pushing her to limits she had never experienced before.

"That's OK," he said. "This stuff happens. Don't worry about it."

"What the fuck's going on?"

Össur stood in the doorway, the Baikal in his hand and fury on his face as he glared at them, taking in

Erna and the barefoot and shirtless Magni standing next to her.

"It's all right, Össi, panic's over. It was just the smoke alarm."

"Was that you?" Össur snarled at Erna.

"No, it wasn't her," Magni answered quickly. "It was me. Just trying to make a bit of toast for a change. Now put that thing away, will you? Before you hurt someone."

"For fuck's sake," Össur growled, lowering the pistol. "It's off now, right?"

"Well, it's stopped making a noise."

"So that's all right and I can go back to sleep."

Magni scratched his head and yawned. "I hope so. I'm just concerned that it might be linked to the phone system. If it is, then the fire service will have had an alert as well and we might see a fire engine bumping up the road any minute. Or as soon as it takes them to get here from wherever the nearest fire station is. That'll be Selfoss, I guess, which is an hour away."

Össur's eyes bulged for a second and he turned to leave the room, and then spun on his heel. "Check it, can you? See if it's linked to the phone line?"

In the office Magni unscrewed the fire alarm's front panel and surveyed the bundles of wires and sensors inside. He traced the phone line and followed where it went through a hole in the wall. His finger hovered over it as it went up the wall under many layers of paint and past the control box.

"The phone line's dead and I don't think it's connected," he said without a great deal of confidence.

130

"Of course, it could be wireless, but I don't think so. It's quite an old system."

"Is the car still outside? You'd better hide it away again," Össur snapped. "Just in case some nosy bastard starts looking around."

Helgi was at his desk early. He looked up and nodded as Gunna appeared, tapped at his keyboard and clicked the mouse before he sat back.

"How was the game? Did they win?"

"Slaughtered them, absolutely took them to the cleaners in the first round." Helgi grinned and rubbed the top of his head. "Then they lost in the second round, not by much, though."

"Your lad wasn't disappointed, then?"

"He was furious." Helgi laughed. "There's a hell of a competitive streak there. Don't know where he gets that from."

"That'll be his mother, surely?"

"Probably," Helgi said. "She always was good at wanting to keep up with the neighbours."

"And you weren't?"

"Not really. I never could see the point of splashing out on a new car just because Magga down the street's husband had one. Hey, ho. That's life, I suppose. Good weekend?"

"Not bad," Gunna decided. "Not that it's over yet. Today's Sunday, in case you hadn't noticed?"

"I had, and I have been given to understand that it's not a great day for a husband and father to be at work, but she'll get over it."

"I do sometimes wonder if your Halla knew what she was letting herself in for with you, Helgi."

Helgi coughed. "I sometimes wonder if I knew what I was letting myself in for, if it comes to that. You'd have thought second time around would be easy, but it's no bed of roses."

Gunna mumbled something non-committal. She knew that Helgi led a hectic life with two young children by his second wife, as well as two boys in their late teens with his first. He was constantly shuttling between the two families, much to his wife's disquiet, as he did his best to not let the two older boys disappear from his life.

"So what's new?" Helgi asked, leaning back dangerously far in his chair and stretching out his legs. "On the good news front, I can tell you that Halla and I are off for two weeks in January."

"Really? Just the two of you?"

"Yep, going to Portugal with her parents, her brother and his wife. You know Halla's family's loaded? They have a villa out there and there's room for the whole herd, and Halla and I are going to rent a car for a few days and go off on our own for a bit."

"Sounds great."

"Yeah. The only downside is that the old boy will want to drag me around the bloody golf course and make sure I lose by a decent margin."

"And will you?"

"I'll make sure I do. No point upsetting him."

"Good. Sensible man. Now, back to business. The fire in Hafnarfjördur on Thursday morning."

Helgi raised his hand in a mock salute.

"Your word is my command, dear lady," he said. "May I ask what you're up to?"

"I thought I'd go and get my hair done and then go shopping for shoes while you and Eiríkur do the hard work. Then when you two have the bad guys under lock and key, and all the paperwork's in order, I'll take the credit for it. How does that sound?"

"I'd expect nothing less of you."

"Good. Because I'm going for a drive in the country while you do all that hard work."

Össur liked having an en-suite room. He had never had as much space as this to call his own, and while he would have liked a drink to go with it, now that he had cigarettes, a bag of good grass and a television, he was as content with the door locked behind him as he could ever remember being.

He tried to swat away the recurring thought that it couldn't last. They would have to leave soon, or he would have to leave soon, regardless of what the others decided to do, and he would prefer to get away without taking them with him. The best option would be to get to Akureyri and hope to get a flight from there. It didn't really matter where to as long as it was far enough away from Alli the Cornershop. The thought of the vindictive old man sitting in his gloomy sitting room and issuing orders made him shudder.

He thought idly of taking the car, but deep inside he knew he wouldn't get far on his own. He wondered if there might be another way to get to Akureyri. The main international airport at Keflavík would be better as from there he could fly anywhere, but he had the nagging feeling that Alli the Cornershop would have his feelers out for him there, and he preferred the idea of what he hoped would be a sleepy regional airport, hopefully with a more relaxed attitude to security. Or maybe a ship? Could he get a berth on a ship going abroad? Magni would know about things like that, and he reflected with chagrin that the half-drunk beefcake he had taken on, imagining him to be fairly dull-witted, had proved to be anything but stupid.

It was time to take some emergency measures. He counted out a hundred thousand euros in the highest denomination notes and wrapped them in a towel, ripped in half to make a tight bundle, which he secured with a roll of tape taken from the office while Magni had been out the previous afternoon.

Then he wrapped the towel in a carrier bag, and then a second bag, taping both up tightly. In the bathroom he stood on the cistern and gently lifted a panel in the ceiling. It was a struggle, and by the time he'd jumped up to haul himself into the roof space, he was perspiring. The hotel was an old building and the surprisingly low roof space was deep in dust. He decided against finding a special hiding place and just placed the package between two rafters, easily reached but out of sight of anyone who might casually poke their head up through the access hatch.

He slid the panel back in place and sat on the toilet seat to get his breath back. His arms were covered in dust and he ran a hand over his head to find it was caked in cobwebs. Although it wasn't a comfortable idea, Össur decided it might be time to make use of the en-suite shower for the first time, but felt happier knowing that at least part of the cash had been hidden away for a rainy day.

The wind whistled through the partly open window as she sat in the car pool Golf and looked at the petrol station, a lonely building that had the look of having been planted in one piece in the middle of a bare plain between the sea and the mountains, hardly visible in the thick clouds that were heavy with snow ready to be scattered. The reason for its position was clear enough, placed as it was opposite a junction where an unmade road turned off to snake into the distance.

"This is the place," Lárus Erlendsson of the Selfoss police force said. "Doesn't look much at this time of year, but it's a busy enough road in the summer."

"You spoke to the manager?"

"He's waiting for us," he said, pointing to a large 4x4 that almost dwarfed the building. "His truck's over there."

"Come on, then."

The filling station's manager was almost as large as his car, a broad-shouldered character with a belly that preceded him.

"G'day, Lárus," he said, popping open a can of Coke and looking at Gunna. "You're the copper from Reykjavík, I take it?"

"That's me. You must be Ástmar?"

"That's me. We run three of these places, one in Selfoss and two out here in the country."

Gunna flipped open her folder of notes.

"This is what I'm interested in," she said, tapping the scanned transaction document the bank had sent. "Someone bought fuel here at 16:28 yesterday. Do you know who was here then?"

"There wasn't anyone here then. This time of year the place is open ten to four only, Monday to Saturday. Summertimes we're open from seven until ten at night all through the week, but there's so little traffic in winter we don't open more than we have to.

"Everything is logged here, isn't it? Can you find that in your system?'

More than my life's worth," Ástmar grumbled. "If we don't keep track of every penny and every drop of fuel, then we'd be in no end of shit. Like gold dust these days, petrol is."

The petrol station's computer whirred into life and Ástmar clicked at the screen.

"Eighty-five litres of unleaded, so something with a big tank that wasn't far off being empty, I reckon. Finished pumping at 16:28, like you said. That's the only one between . . ." He scrolled up and then down. "One at 15:05 and then there was one more at 19:49. That's it. Not much business yesterday and the margin on every litre is pennies," he grumbled.

"How do you make a living on this if it's that low?" Gunna asked.

"Cans of drink, hot dogs and that kind of shit during the summer. I'd close the place completely in the winter if I could, but the franchise stipulates we have to

136

stay open all year round, and to be honest, it's a public service as much as anything else."

"And how about CCTV?"

He took off a pair of thick glasses and polished them on a fold of his shirt.

"Well, we do have CCTV, but it's not all that reliable. Hang on, it's a stand-alone system so I'll have to go and get the memory card from the camera."

Outside a white van pulled up and a man swathed in a heavy blue padded overall with his hat pulled down to his eyebrows slotted his card into the pump and waited impatiently for the machine to accept it before he could pump fuel.

"Here it is," Ástmar said, and slotted the card into the computer. "It has a motion sensor so it's supposed to start recording when it senses something. The trouble is it's a bit too sensitive and a fox running over the forecourt or even long grass waving in the wind will set it off," he muttered as he scrolled through the files. "Ah, here we are."

Some very clear footage with the camera at an alarming angle showed a pickup truck at the pump, the driver chewing a toothpick as he gazed around before driving away.

"That was the 15:05 sale, and it keeps going for a minute or so after," Ástmar explained. "Here it is."

Gunna leaned close to the screen while Lárus Erlendsson sat back and watched with little apparent interest. This time the vehicle had pulled up on the opposite side of the pumps, so the view of the driver and the car was obscured, but Gunna could still make out the white Ford Explorer, and instead of Erna Brandsen or Tinna Lind, a bear of a man stood for a long time as the tank filled.

"Must have been almost running on fumes. Those things have a seventy-five litre tank, if I recall correctly," Lárus observed. "How come he bought eighty-five litres of fuel?"

"That's how," Gunna said, watching as the man opened the back of the car and took out three five-litre cans. "You can't see his face at all," she said.

"You can see he's clocked where the camera is. He's being careful not to look at it and his coat's pulled up over his face," Lárus added, and watched as the transaction was completed with the man standing with his back to the camera.

"Pause there, please," Gunna instructed as the car began to pull away. She peered at the screen. "That's it. That's definitely our missing person's vehicle."

"He's a cheeky bastard, isn't he?" Lárus said.

"Either cheeky or desperate. My guess is he had no choice. He had to get petrol there because he was probably already running on empty. So where did he go after that? He must have gone to Selfoss, or through Selfoss? Lárus, are there any cameras in the town that might have picked him up?"

Magni noticed that Össur had, at last, taken a shower, and that could only be an improvement. The Explorer was back in the restaurant, this time without any additional scratches to the bodywork, and Erna seemed, for the moment, mollified.

The police would soon come looking, he decided. Before long there would be a search for the two women and there had to be a trace of them somewhere providing a trail that could be followed. Then there was the old man down the valley, and Magni had no doubt that he would turn up again. Unlike the others with their city-dweller habits, Magni knew perfectly well that country people keep an eye on each others' comings and goings, and he was certain that movements would be watched even in somewhere as remote as the district around Hotel Hraun.

"Is there a radio anywhere?" he asked as a thought occurred to him.

"There's one in the lounge," Tinna Lind said, her mind elsewhere. "Why?" she asked, turning to him.

"Because I'm an idiot and ought to have more sense," he said.

"My big idiot," she said fondly.

"I ought to have figured out that there's bound to be something on the news about you and your mum. If you're reported missing, that's where there'll be an appeal or an announcement or something. Why didn't I think of that before? Shit, I can be dumb sometimes."

"Not that dumb. You've thought of it now, haven't you?"

It took a while to find the radio. Magni switched it on and the muted sound of Channel Two whispered through the speakers.

"There. Now we wait for the news, I suppose."

"You're worried, aren't you?" Tinna Lind said.

"Well . . ."

"You don't show it, but you are."

Magni chopped an onion on the kitchen table with more force than was strictly necessary.

"It's Árni. Össur's sure he's the one who died in that fire."

Tinna Lind's eyebrows knitted in puzzlement. "All right, so just who is this Árni?"

"He was supposed to be the driver. I told you before, didn't I?"

"Yeah, maybe, but I don't see how he fits in."

Magni lifted one of the two fish fillets, laid it flat and worked the knife carefully between the meat and the skin, pinching its tail with the fingers of his free hand.

"It's Össur's job. He had the idea and the inside information, so I guess he knew when the old guy was going to have all that money ready. Árni and me, we were just the hired help, independent sub-contractors, if you like."

"I get that, but he wasn't with you on Thursday? So why's he dead?"

Magni pushed the knife forward with a single smooth motion and held up the skin, leaving the fillet on the table.

"Y'see," he said, working the knife into the tail of the second fillet and repeating the operation. "You see, it was Össur's job, but with me to help out, like a minder. I was flat broke and he offered me a payday to just go with him and watch his back. Árni was supposed to be the driver. He was supposed to turn up outside the old guy's place just as we came out the door."

"Right, so what went wrong?"

140

"No idea," Magni said, slicing the fish fillet into steaks. "We came out the door. We'd left Árni round the corner and told him five minutes. I'm not sure Árni knew what it was all about, if he'd figured out what Össur was going to do. Maybe he was held up, or just didn't think he had to be there right on the dot of three. Anyway, out we came, expecting to jump straight into his truck and off to the airport, but he wasn't there, so we had to run for it."

"And you ran into us?"

"Yep. Össur was frantic."

"It could have been an accident. Nothing to do with the old guy you robbed."

"That's just it. We don't know what went wrong, and it's not as if Árni can tell us now. But if it's something to do with Alli, then we're properly screwed if he gets hold of us."

Tinna Lind watched in fascination as Magni dipped the fish pieces in egg and then breadcrumbs, laying them carefully in the pan one by one.

"Did you know how dangerous this job was going to be?"

"Hadn't a clue," Magni said with a scowl. "I thought it might be a bit hairy, but not like this. If I'd known he was going to bump the old bastard for all that cash, I'd have backed out right away. But I thought he was just collecting some small amount he was owed; never thought it was going to be this hardcore."

"Why did you take the job?"

"Because I needed the money, and because I was drunk," he said, flipping the fish in the pan. "Drain

141

those potatoes, will you? And call the others. This'll be ready in a few minutes."

Gunna plugged the memory card from the petrol station into her computer and watched the same footage half a dozen times without getting a decent view of the man's face. She was staring at it yet again when Eiríkur came in and sat down.

"Any luck?"

"The fire investigator has confirmed that the fire was started deliberately, and it seems the dead man had been working for Alli the Cornershop."

Gunna groaned. "Not that arsehole again? Why can't we put him away and lose the key?"

"Who knows? We might be able to this time if we can pin Árni Sigurvinsson's death on him."

"Post-mortem report?"

"Miss Cruz is doing the post-mortem tomorrow. She said that judging by her initial examination, the victim had been beaten badly and had lost a toe."

Gunna told herself not to be impatient, knowing that the force's only forensic pathologist was already stretched too far for comfort.

"So he had been mistreated?"

"Looks like it," Eiríkur said. "We'll find out when she's finished the post-mortem."

"You're going?"

Eiríkur grinned. "No. We drew straws for it and Helgi's going."

"But the doctor at the scene reckoned smoke inhalation, didn't he?"

"He did, and I reckon that's what the post-mortem will come up with tomorrow. How did you get on this morning?"

Gunna gestured to the screen.

"Good and bad. There's footage of the missing women's car with someone else buying a tank of petrol, but he's taken care not to let his face show."

"So, not much use then?"

"It places the car outside Selfoss and the owner not in it, so it looks like he drove into the petrol station from the north and drove away southwards, as if he was going to Selfoss. I had two hours going around the town with Lárus Erlendsson looking for anywhere with CCTV that might have picked it up, but no luck."

She turned back to the screen and the footage that she had left playing and saw a white car flash past on the screen.

"What?"

Eiríkur crouched behind her as she rewound the footage and found that it had run on for more than an hour, triggered every time something went past the filling station.

"Is that the same car?" Eiríkur asked.

"Looks the same, doesn't it?" Gunna said, slowing the replay down and noting the time, just over an hour later than when the Explorer's driver had bought fuel. They watched the car speed past on the fringes of the camera's vision, but then stop and come back, the reversing lights bright and the registration number unmistakeable.

"It's him. He drove into Selfoss, stopping to get fuel, and then drove back out the same way."

"He missed the turn-off," Eiríkur said as the Explorer turned off into the dark along the unmade road at the junction, its tail lights disappearing into the blackness.

It felt like a lazy Sunday. Össur had again retreated to the bridal suite. Erna had washed up, not particularly well, but she'd done it. Tinna Lind lounged in an armchair with a book while Magni dozed on the sofa.

As the bongs sounded the hour and the news on the radio, his eyes opened and he listened to the series of advertisements first. A dry-voiced announcer read out news of a visit by a Norwegian minister to Iceland and cut to a brief comment by the visiting politician's Icelandic counterpart on how satisfying it was to welcome his opposite number, although there were issues they still had to agree on.

His eyes started to close again as the news moved on to a judgement by the supreme court on the case of a trade union threatening to take a case against the government to a European court, and the news from Ukraine had him yawning. But then his eyes snapped open and Tinna Lind laid the book down.

"Police in Reykjavík are still seeking to establish the whereabouts of Erna Björg Brandsen and her daughter Tinna Lind Brandsen Bogadóttir who were last seen on Thursday afternoon. They were last seen travelling in the city area in a white Ford Explorer registration number . . ."

"That's us," Tinna Lind said and Erna appeared from the kitchen with a dishcloth in her hands.

"What's us?"

144

"On the radio."

"Shhh," Magni scolded.

"Anyone aware of Erna Björg or Tinna Lind is asked to call the confidential police information line on . . ."

"Shit."

"You didn't think they wouldn't be looking for us, did you?"

Magni sat up and smacked a fist into the palm of the other hand.

"Össi!" he yelled. "For fuck's sake, what's he doing up there on his own?"

He hammered on Össur's door and eventually it opened, the pistol again pointing at him.

"Put that fucking thing away," he said in frustration.

"What?"

The room was thick with smoke and Össur had a dazed look on his face.

"You're blasted, right?"

"I've had a puff. What business is it of yours?"

"Listen. There was something on the news just now."

"About us? What on the TV?"

"On the radio. Listen, they're looking for the girls and the car. It's the car that's the problem. They know the number and that's what they're looking for."

"So? It's hidden away, isn't it?"

"Yeah, but did that old guy who was here the other day see it? Do you remember?"

Össur's face was blank. "I don't know."

"It has to go," Magni decided.

"Why? Just keep it hidden away. Nobody's going to notice it in there, are they?"

"And then what? We just walk out of here? We need a car, and we need that car to get another car."

"I see," Össur said, but Magni found it difficult to be sure that he understood.

"Look, I'm taking the car as soon as it's properly dark and I'll be back with another one tonight. Got that?"

"Yeah. Reckon so."

"That means you're going to have to straighten up and be downstairs while I'm away so the old lady doesn't do anything stupid and run for it. Understood?"

"Yeah, I know. Don't give me orders."

"And tomorrow we move out of here, right?"

Alli preferred neutral ground. The last place he wanted to go near was the Undertakers' black-painted headquarters, and he didn't want to have Rafn sitting in his place with that sardonic look on his face. Instead he chose a coffee shop and they met outside.

Rafn was wearing a suit that made him look very different to the denim-jacketed character he normally dealt with, and Alli felt disturbed by the change as they took a seat in the corner, Rafn taking the seat by the wall, which gave him a view of the door and the rest of the room, while Alli sat at a disadvantage with his back to the rest of the world.

Alli ordered coffee for himself and raised an eyebrow at Rafn.

"A latte with a hazelnut shot," he said crisply.

"You're looking smart," Alli said, and Rafn nodded seriously.

146

"We have to these days. Business is changing."

Neither of them wanted to get to business until the waitress had delivered their coffees, which she did fussily, arranging cups and saucers on the little table, looking stonily at Alli and giving Rafn a smile.

"She wouldn't have smiled at you quite so sweetly if she knew what you're really like," Alli said, sounding sour.

"Appearances can be everything."

Alli looked around quickly.

"Any results?"

Rafn sipped his coffee delicately.

"Nothing," he said. "Absolutely nothing at all."

"He's disappeared?"

"That's what it looks like. Vanished. No sign of him anywhere."

Alli's brows knitted in frustration. "If Össur was about, you'd find him. He can't not flash cash around if he has it."

"And he has."

Alli's coffee suddenly tasted sour. "Somebody would know someone else who would know. Reykjavík's not that big."

"You know a guy called Magni? I don't know his patronymic. A big guy by all accounts."

Alli's mind went back to the brawny man with the red stubble who had knocked Baldvin flat with no apparent effort.

"No. But I might have seen him."

"The last we heard was that Össur was hanging about with a guy called Magni, and the sadly deceased

Árni Sigurvinsson," Rafn said, placing his tall glass delicately on the table and dropping his voice. "I don't suppose Árni told you anything before his tragic accident?"

Magni couldn't help being nervous. He had driven plenty of cars before that had been borrowed from their owners without the formality of asking permission, but this was different. The police would undoubtedly be actively searching for this one. The number would trigger an alert as soon it was noticed and Magni had no desire to spend days answering awkward questions, especially not with a hundred thousand euros waiting for him.

He turned off the main road as soon as he was able and kept to suburban roads through the city outskirts, looking around to scope out any possible replacements for the Explorer. It would either have to be something old that he could hot wire, as a modern car would be beyond his skills, or the other option would be to break in somewhere and steal the keys to a car.

On the other hand, his own car was sitting unused on the forecourt of his sister's house in Gardabær, though he immediately dismissed the idea of using that. That was his cherished car, the one he had worked hard for, rebuilt and frequently polished until it shone. He needed something anonymous that could be sacrificed if necessary, not the apple of his own eye.

He cruised through the city at a strictly legal speed until the germ of an idea emerged. He wanted to be able to take a car that wouldn't be noticed too easily, and he also wanted to park the Explorer somewhere

148

out of the way, preferably where it wouldn't be noticed for a few days.

The sight of a police vehicle in the distance made him start and he held his breath as he hauled the Explorer off the road and down a side street, where he waited for a few minutes before venturing back under the street lights. The sighting convinced him that it was far too hazardous to stay in the car, so he took it quickly past a busy junction and into a district where shops outnumbered houses. He drove into the car park of the local church, tucking the Explorer away at the far end between two other cars.

He left the key in the ignition, reasoning that with any luck someone else would steal it, which would throw the police off the trail in what he hoped would be completely the wrong direction. But before walking away, shoulders hunched and his collar turned up high, he stooped, lifted a handful of half-melted snow and mud, and smeared it over the number plate.

Magni walked fast. The place he had decided on was somewhere he had been before and he had no objection to doing the place's owner a bad turn. The parking lot was lined with cars, some for sale and some for hire, and many of them, Magni knew, with chequered histories.

The office was a temporary building and the back door was no match for the long crowbar he had brought with him from the shed behind Hotel Hraun. The lock manfully withstood his efforts, but the door frame itself splinted and parted. Inside he rifled the office space, discovering a shallow cupboard of keys on hooks that also yielded to the crowbar. Eventually he selected a clean-looking grey Skoda, which he knew would have four-wheel drive without looking out of the ordinary. Minutes later he swept from the car park, but cursed as the fuel light immediately came on. There was no choice but to buy fuel and he cast about for a filling station, preferably an unmanned one.

He didn't like having to do it. Filling the stolen Skoda up only a few kilometres from where it had been taken was a dangerous move, but he took the precaution of stopping to smear the car's registration plates with more mud before rolling up his collar and once more relying on Erna's credit card to do its work as he did his best to hide his face from the cameras he knew had to be there somewhere.

Gunna had hoped to catch Gísli alone, and the sight of a yellow Mazda that had seen better days parked outside made her wonder whether or not to drive past and go home. It had been a long day, she was tired and she didn't relish the prospect of an intense investigation, which intuition told her was probably more complex than it appeared.

The door swung open as Gunna strode up the path and Drífa stepped outside with a backward look. Gunna frowned, wondering why the girl looked so furtive, shivering outside the front door.

Her raven-black hair had made a comeback, Gunna noted, but she was relieved the black lipstick and what she thought of as personal ironmongery had gone. Not much more than a year ago, Drífa had been a radical student with a penchant for goth accoutrements, but the arrival of a child and the effort of salvaging a relationship that neither she nor Gísli had expected to embark on had called for compromises all round. Drífa had ditched her style and put university on hold, while Gísli had stopped spending most of his respectable seaman's earnings on gas-guzzling cars and had made the effort to go back to college.

"What's the matter, sweetheart?" Gunna asked, seeing how awkward Drífa looked, standing in the half-light by the front door, the skin of her bare arms turning rapidly to gooseflesh. "Are you all right?"

"We have a visitor," Drífa said. "I thought I'd warn you," she added awkwardly.

"Why's that?"

"Well. I wasn't sure." Gunna saw Drífa struggling to find the right words. "It's Gísli's father. He's here."

"Ah." It took Gunna a moment to take in what she had said, and she stifled her rising, bitter anger with a couple of long breaths. "I'm probably not the best person to turn up right now," she said finally, swinging her car keys on one finger.

"I thought so, and I reckoned I'd warn you before you came in."

"How is he?" Gunna asked, her voice strained.

"He's so frail I don't know how he managed to get here on his own. I don't know how old he is, but he looks like a very old man."

"He's not sixty," Gunna said, calculating rapidly. "Fifty-eight, maybe? Fifty-nine?"

"Whatever," Drífa said. "He looks ninety, but I guessed you'd prefer not to meet him."

"Any more than he's likely to want to meet me."

"He's asked about you a few times. Twice today."

"All right, thanks, Drífa. That was thoughtful of you. A confrontation wouldn't do any of us any good," Gunna said, spinning her keys.

"Say hi to Gísli and tell him I'll drop by tomorrow if I can get away early enough."

"I will," Drífa said, still sounding awkward but also relieved.

Gunna drove away, wondering why she was angry with a man she hadn't seen for more than twenty years, while she could see Drífa standing by the door, watching her until her view of the house in the mirror had disappeared into the darkness.

It was late when Magni arrived back at Hotel Hraun. Reykjavík had been clear, but north of the city snow had started to fall and he was forced to take it slowly. It was tempting to leave the Skoda, which he found to be a far more comfortable drive than the big but underpowered Explorer, outside overnight. But he bumped it through the hotel garden and drove it into the restaurant, where it added to the pools of water already there.

The kitchen and lobby were in silent darkness. Össur was asleep on the sofa, his hand in the pocket of his jacket, and Magni wondered if now might be the moment to try and take the Baikal off him, but he decided against it, reasoning that the pistol's safety could be off and it would be too dangerous. Besides, he

152

was tired. The nervous trip to the city and the constant fear of being noticed had exhausted him.

"Össi," he said gently, a hand on his shoulder. "Hey, man. I'm back. Where are the girls?"

"What? Asleep; I think."

"I hope they're asleep and not halfway to Reykjavík by now."

"Nah. It's snowing outside, isn't it?"

"Yeah, it is. But you might have stayed awake all the same."

"You get a car?"

"Yep, a Skoda, four-wheel drive. Decent car. And tomorrow we get out of here. I'm going to get my head down, Össi. You should do the same," he said, and saw Össur's head already beginning to nod while his right stayed firmly clasped around the pistol in his pocket.

Magni went upstairs in the dark. He listened at the door of the room Erna slept in and was satisfied to hear her snoring gently inside. In the room he had taken for himself, the one nearest the top of the stairs, he stripped off his clothes and reminded himself that he would need to wash some things in the morning. He crawled under the duvet and felt the fatigue in his aching legs. He had underestimated how stressful the trip would turn out to be, especially the last twenty kilometres over roads that were on the brink of being blocked by the deepening drifts.

He stretched his hands behind his head and felt the muscles in his back begin to relax. His neck cracked and he twisted his head as far as it would go each way to relieve the tension. His eyes closed as he was close to sleep, but he jerked awake when a cool draught caught at his feet.

"Shhh," Tinna Lind whispered. He could hear the rustle of her clothes being pulled off and she crept under the duvet to lie on top of him, resting her head on his chest. He lifted a hand and placed it on her back, pressing her against him.

"Did it go all right?"

"Yeah. It was OK. Parked the Explorer where someone will find it and left the key in it. Came back with a Skoda instead."

They lay still for a long time before she parted her legs to straddle him, lifting herself up to gaze into the glint of his eyes in the not quite complete darkness.

"Shall we?" she murmured. "How would you like it?"

CHAPTER
FIVE

Monday

Magni emerged from the shower refreshed and clean, his socks and underwear clean but also wet.

"Smart," Tinna Lind said as he came back into the bedroom. "Taking a shower and washing your undies at the same time."

She sat cross-legged on the bed, cornrows loose around her shoulders.

"Seaman's trick," he said, arranging them on the radiator to dry.

"So, going commando or coming back to bed?"

"Any preference?"

"Commando is always good."

Magni dropped the towel and climbed back on the bed, lying down and putting out an arm to caress the back of Tinna Lind's head and pull her down towards him.

"After something, are you?"

"Could be," he said, nuzzling her neck. "Why d'you ask?"

"Just wondering."

Her hands strayed across his back and down towards his thighs.

"It always pays to look after the cook, you know."

"That's just what I thought I was doing," she said, her voice dropping to a husky whisper.

"Oh, yes. That's good. The cook likes that. Don't stop."

Afterwards they lay still and entwined as weak daylight began to filter through the curtains.

"Magni? You asleep?"

"Me? No. Just savouring the moment."

"Magni?"

"Hmmm?"

"Is this a bit serious, or what?"

Magni snapped awake. "What did you say?"

Tinna Lind rolled over onto her front and rested her chin on his chest.

"I said, is there any danger of this getting serious? And before you start to get worried, I'm not being needy or clingy."

"I . . . I don't know. Hadn't thought about it," he lied.

"Look, Magni. We might not have much time together so it's not as if we'll have an opportunity to go through the boyfriend/girlfriend shit and all that picking out favourite movies and choosing curtains stuff. And I don't go in for keeping what I think to myself."

"OK," Magni said. "I'm sort of wondering where this is going."

"Straight out. I like you a lot and I have an idea the feeling's mutual. Would I be right?"

"You'd be right."

156

Tinna Lind lifted herself up and crossed her legs again, letting her hair fall about her shoulders before roughly bunching it into a bun behind her head.

"I have a proposition for you."

"You want to have my babies and live happily ever after?"

"That might come later, who knows?" she said, and her voice dropped. She reached out and walked her fingers up Magni's chest, ending up with one finger on his chin. "How much money does your friend in the bridal suite have?"

"Something around two hundred thousand euros, I think," he answered and found himself becoming slightly breathless at the thought.

She leaned forward and looked into his eyes.

"So how about you and me? We ease your friend out of the partnership, drop him somewhere with a long walk to civilization, then we drop my mother next at a bus stop somewhere."

"And?" Magni's mouth was dry.

"And we disappear. Just like you and Össur were going to do. Think about it. We could live well with that much money if we could get to somewhere warm."

"Like where?"

"Anywhere that life's cheap and people don't ask too many questions. Sicily. Morocco. A Greek island. Bulgaria."

"That's a thought," Magni admitted.

Tinna Lind winked, got off the bed and headed for the bathroom. Magni heard her pee and then the shower began to run.

"Think about it for a while," she said with a sly look around the door, and Magni lay back and did just that.

The habit of being up and about before the rest of the world was an old one and she enjoyed the tranquillity of the early part of the day. But today the morning's tranquillity had already been shattered by an argument with Laufey before she even reached the detectives' office at Hverfisgata.

"Late, Gunnhildur?" Ívar Laxdal asked in surprise. "I don't think you've been late for anything since about 1996, have you?"

"The last time I was late I'd found out I was pregnant with Laufey," she snapped back and instantly regretted it, but Ívar Laxdal's face creased into a grin in a way that wouldn't have happened had anyone else been present. "I'm sorry," she apologized. "I had a call when I was on the way this morning to tell me that Erna Brandsen's card was flagged up last night at the filling station on Fellsmúli, so that's where I've been."

She dropped a memory key on her desk and waited for her computer to start.

"CCTV?"

"Yep, and if it's as much use as last time, then it'll be about as useful as a wet fart."

The video sequence showed a car pull up at the pump and the driver using a credit card to pre-pay before filling the tank to the brim and driving away into the night.

"When was this?"

"Just before eleven last night. This place is manned until ten and it's card-only after that."

"Numbers obscured," Ívar Laxdal mused. "A grey Skoda. It's not as if there's a shortage of those about."

Gunna put on the glasses she hated using and sat with her nose a hand's breadth from the screen, intent on not missing any detail.

"It's the same man," she said finally. "I'm certain of it. That's the same coat the man buying petrol for Erna Brandsen's Explorer wore at the first filling station. That's the same hat pulled down past his ears."

"You have that footage as well?"

"On the hard drive."

"Let's see it," Ívar Laxdal said, and sat back as Gunna ran the earlier recording.

"See? Gunna said when the sequence had finished. "The shoulders are the same, the way he stands is the same. It's the same guy."

"I agree. It's not necessarily courtroom evidence, but as far as I'm concerned it confirms it's the same character. But why change to another car?"

"He's better off now as before we knew he was driving a fairly distinctive white Explorer with a known registration. Now he's driving an anonymous grey Skoda and we can't see the number."

"Send the footage to Albert upstairs. He might be able to make out some of the registration plate."

"The question is," Gunna said as if she hadn't heard Ívar Laxdal's words. "Where's Erna Brandsen's Explorer? And where are these people? Are Erna and Tinna Lind and this mystery man all together, or what? Are they still alive?"

"That's the problem," Ívar Laxdal said with an uncomfortable shift in his chair. "We need something concrete on this, preferably today, and ideally some indication that Erna Brandsen is alive. Otherwise there'll be no choice but to call out a full-scale search."

"Yes, but where? The region they would need to search is huge. We need a starting point. What about a search flight? Did you request the Dash from the Coast Guard?"

"I did, but in case you hadn't noticed, there's been virtually rooftop-level cloud cover for the last week. They'll be ready to go as soon as there's a break in visibility."

"In that case you'd better let them know we're looking for a grey Skoda as well as a white Explorer."

"I'll do that. Gunnhildur, do you need help on this?"

"I need a break on this," she said and pointed to the screen. "I need this guy to make a mistake. Until then, we'll see if anything comes in. Their pictures were in the papers again this morning."

"And the fire in Hafnarfjördur? Árni Sigurvinsson?"

"Helgi's attending the post-mortem this morning. Eiríkur's report is on the system and I need to have a look at it. I haven't seen him since Saturday."

"D'you want to shift Helgi to the Erna Brandsen inquiry? I can put Sævaldur and his team onto the Hafnarfjördur investigation with Eiríkur?"

Össur's head jerked up and he looked at Magni with his eyes full of panic.

"What was that?"

160

"That was the door."

"What do we do?"

"We see who it is," Magni said. "What else can we do?"

He stood up and went to the hotel's big front door, which had already swung open before he could touch the handle. Mentally he tried to prepare himself for the sight of a black-clad police team tumbling through the door with automatic weapons at the ready, or worse, Alli the Cornershop smiling at him from behind a squad of hired heavies.

Behind him he heard the click of the Baikal's safety catch and offered a fervent prayer that if there was any shooting, then at least Össur wouldn't be the one to start it.

A thickset man in a blue overalls with a toolbox in one hand stood there and stared at them from under a baseball cap.

"Who the hell are you?" he demanded. "I thought the place was supposed to be empty?"

"Oh, Ársæll said we could stay here for a couple of days," Magni said smoothly, sensing the tension in Össur behind him.

The visitor put his toolbox down and kicked snow from his boots, pulled off his gloves and rubbed warmth back into his hands.

"So who are you guys, then?" he asked. The suspicion in his voice was clear. "I spoke to Ársæll a couple of days ago and he said nothing about there being anyone up here. The place is supposed to be closed down for the winter."

"My mate spoke to him a couple of weeks ago and he said it was OK to come up here when we could get away, as we weren't sure when we could all get a few days off work to get out of Reykjavík. So what brings you up here? Routine visit?"

"Nah. Had an alert to say one of the alarms had gone off and then reset itself, so it's probably a fault, but I thought I'd take a look anyway. How long have you been up here?"

"We . . . we got here on Saturday afternoon."

"Must have been you setting it off, then."

"Yeah, one of the girls burned some toast. I reset the alarm and didn't realize you'd get a notification as the phone's dead."

"The phone's diverted. That's why it's not working, but the line stays live for the alarm system. I got the alert right away, but didn't worry about it immediately as it was cancelled," the man said, marching through the lobby, past the reception desk and straight to the office, as if he were at home there. Magni watched him go to the fire alarm control box and go through the menus, muttering under his breath.

"That looks about right," he mumbled to himself, and his thumb moved to the test button.

"There are people asleep —" Magni said, but his words were cut off as the alarm began to shriek.

"What d'you say?" the man yelled.

Magni shook his head and the alarm shrieked for twenty seconds before the man pressed the test button a second time and it lapsed into silence.

162

"I was just saying there are people asleep upstairs," Magni said, hoping to sound offended and frosty.

"Well, if they sleep through that, they're doing well," the man retorted, snapped shut the control box and stepped down from the stool he had needed to reach it.

"Is that all?" Magni asked, conscious that Össur was still hovering behind him and that he hadn't heard the Baikal's safety catch click for a while.

The man glared suspiciously. "Yeah. That'll do for today," he said. "I'll give Ársæll a call when I get back in phone range. It still seems odd that he didn't say anything to me," he grumbled, and as he looked over Magni's shoulder his voice faded away.

Magni turned and followed his gaze to see Erna with an expression somewhere between confusion and irritation standing in the doorway, while the man in the blue overall stared at her.

"There's something a bit damn spooky about all this," he said with a sudden burst of anger and pointed at Erna. "I know who you are. Your picture's been in the papers and on the TV; they said you'd gone missing somewhere. So what's all this about?"

He made for the door and Magni tried to head him off. "Hey, listen, man. It's not what it looks like, all right?"

The man shook Magni's hand from his shoulder. "I don't care what it looks like. There's something proper fishy happening here and the sooner I'm out of this place, the better."

Fat flakes of snow drifted lazily down through still air as the man set off across the yard.

"You fucking stop." This time it was Össur who was yelling. "I'm warning you."

"Össi, no . . ." Magni said.

The man in the blue overalls stopped and turned, staring at Össur who strode towards him, hands in his pockets, snowflakes collecting on his thin grey hair.

"And what?" the man said with a truculent look at Össur, who was shorter than him by half a head and certainly seemed less of a threat than the beefy Magni might have been. "What you going to do? You can fuck off, pal. I'm out of here."

"You stay right where you are," Össur snarled, his voice hoarse.

"And if I don't?" the big man demanded, squaring up to Össur. "I'm out of here and you're not stopping me."

"Össi, no . . ." Magni called, hurrying across the yard to where the two of them were almost nose to nose.

"If you know what's good for you, shitbag," Össur drawled.

"Well, fuck you!" The man in the blue overalls yelled in his face and placed both hands on Össur's chest, sending him staggering backwards.

"Össi, don't . . ."

The pistol appeared from Össur's pocket and Magni could see the blood drain from the man's face.

"Hey, this ain't right . . ." the man said in disbelief, the words barely out of his mouth before Össur's first slug caught him in the chest. Magni had expected the man to be thrown backwards, like he'd seen in the movies, but instead he stopped still for a moment and a

164

second shot hit him only an inch or so away from the first. The two shots were rapid, dry cracks that echoed off the surrounding hills, dulled by the damp in the air; and before the second shot's echo had faded it was joined by Erna's piercing scream bouncing off the rocks as the man sagged gradually to his knees before falling forward into the snow.

Helgi was tight-lipped and pale when he made his appearance. He went to the coffee room, poured himself a mugful and sat staring into space.

"All right?" Gunna asked. The faint smell of the autopsy room lingered around him.

"Yeah. I'll be all right in a minute."

"So? Árni Sigurvinsson?"

Helgi sipped his coffee, grimaced, squirted some long-life milk into it from a carton on the table and sipped again.

"Smoke inhalation, as we expected. Absolutely no doubt that was the cause of death, according to Miss Cruz. But there's more."

"Explain, young man."

"It'll all be in Miss Cruz's report. He'd been beaten up quite efficiently probably only a couple of hours at most before he died. There's a good bit of internal bruising, but not many outward signs of it. There's a decent amount of alcohol in his blood, and Miss Cruz reckons they'll probably identify a few other goodies as well once the tests have been done. Plus he's missing a toe on his left foot."

"Eiríkur said. A recent injury?"

"His toe was chopped off with something sharp, a chisel maybe, and very recently."

"Miss Cruz knows this is a priority?"

"I didn't have to tell her. This one goes to the front of the queue, along with everything else she was supposed to have done by last week," Helgi said bitterly. "She's trying to identify what kind of tool was used."

"The Laxdal's threatening to put Sævaldur on to this with you."

Helgi groaned. "No, please. Sæsi's fine harassing hoodlums, but we don't need bull-in-a-china-shop tactics here. Not yet, anyway."

"I'd agree with you on that. What's Eiríkur up to?"

"He was questioning anyone and everyone he could find yesterday who might have known the victim, and I think the landlord came across as suspicious. Eiríkur's in at twelve today, I think."

"And where are you taking this?"

"You know, I'm damned if I know. Doing the same as Eiríkur and hoping that somebody saw something or someone that morning. Here, Gunna?"

"Hmm?"

"You have a contact who's a taxi driver, don't you?"

"Do I? Oh, yes. I know who you mean."

"Can you put me on to him, find out if there's any gossip about Árni?"

Gunna thought. "I'm not sure he'd talk to anyone else." She checked her watch. "I'll tell you what. I know where this character goes for his lunch break. I'll go and surprise him and let you know what I find out."

Erna stood with her hands to her mouth and screeched.

"What the hell happened?"

Tinna Lind appeared behind her and looked from her mother to Magni and Össur to the corpse of the man in the blue overalls on the ground between them. The pistol in Össur's hand told the story by itself and Tinna Lind took her mother's arm to lead her inside the hotel.

Össur's teeth chattered. "What the fuck do we do now?"

"You're asking me? Christ on a bike, Össi," Magni spluttered in fury. "You're the gangster here. You're the man with the experience. How about you come up with an idea of your own?"

In the face of Magni's outburst, Össur's face reverted to its usual impassive look. "Sort it out, will you? I'm cold. I'm going inside."

Magni stood speechless and helpless in the yard as snow continued to fall around him and settle on the lifeless man in the blue overalls. He knelt by the man, rolled him onto one side and felt with two forefingers in a fold of his neck for a hint of a pulse, hoping that somehow Össur's shots had missed anything vital and that the man had merely been stunned. Flakes of snow fluttered slowly downwards, melting as they landed on the man's face and collecting in his thick dark hair. The resolute refusal of his fingers to find a pulse, the man's open eyes and the face that was surprisingly peaceful in death were enough to convince him he was wasting his time.

He laid the man in as dignified a position as he could, closed his eyes and stood for a moment before going inside. Erna sat huddled on the sofa, her legs folded beneath her, rocking in Tinna Lind's arms. Magni looked questioningly at her, wanting to ask a dozen questions. Tinna Lind looked back at him, lifted a finger to her lips and shook her head briefly without stopping her gentle rocking motion.

In the office he went to the filing cabinet, took out one of the bottles and poured himself a finger of whisky that he threw back in one, thought about another and decided against it.

He put on a coat and a pair of gloves that he had found in the shed at the back, pulled a wool hat down to his eyebrows and went back outside. The man in the blue overalls had driven from where? He wondered if the man had come from Reykjavík or Selfoss, or maybe even from Akranes? It was impossible to say and it wasn't as if he could ask him now, he reflected bitterly.

The man's car had been parked at the side of the road, further down the curving road that put the hotel out of sight, and as Magni approached it, he could see why it hadn't been driven all the way into the yard. A drift of snow snaked across the road, a little more than knee high but still enough to warrant caution. The man's car was a small van, but Magni saw it had been fitted with robust tyres with heavy treads and studded with nails, and he guessed the van was made for the terrain with four-wheel drive.

He had no idea what to do. For the first time, Magni was struck by indecision. The van was bright red and would be easily spotted. He had no idea where he could safely dispose of it, or even if he could hide it

168

effectively. The keys had been left in the ignition. The engine fired first time and the radio blared into life at the same moment, making him fumble for a button to switch it off. Unable to find one, he settled for turning the volume down low and manoeuvred the van in an awkward series of turns to spin it around and drive down the track.

He was surprised at how quickly he found a place to leave the van, thankful that there would be no overly long walk back. He realized that there were narrow tracks forking off at long intervals, each one leading to a summer house hidden among rocks and trees. Choosing one at random, he bumped the van down a track to a summer house that had conifers planted around it, their branches heavy with snow, and tucked the van underneath the largest of the trees, where he knew it would be out of sight of the road, and hoped it would be out of sight from the air as well.

He left the keys in the van, as if the owner had just got out of it, trudged back along the track to the road and towards the hotel. He found the going harder than he'd expected. The unmade road under a thick coating of hard snow was unpredictable. Several times he lost his footing, and with the thickening snow falling through still air, he could see no more than a few dozen yards ahead. He trusted that the road he was following would lead him back to the hotel.

"Looking good, Matti." Gunna leaned over to kiss his cheek. "Good to see you're looking after yourself."

"Thanks. I'm trying. It's Marika's doing really."

The lunchtime trade at Grandakaffi was brisk. Gunna and Matti sat in the glass-sided extension with a view over the dock and the handful of taxis parked opposite while their owners addressed themselves to the day's meat soup.

"Not eating, Matti?" Gunna asked, nodding at the counter.

"If you're buying, then why not?"

"Fair enough. You go and get them and I'll pay."

The soup with its heavy chunks of mutton was one of those traditional staples that she and Matti had grown up with, something that their mothers both served at least once a week.

"Not bad, is it?" Matti said appreciatively once he was halfway through his dish.

"As good as your mum's?"

"Don't talk stupid. Nothing's as good as Mum makes."

"How's Marika? Keeping you under control?"

Matti grunted. "Yeah. She's doing well. Assistant manager at that place now."

"Where's she working? Remind me?"

"Travel firm that runs coach trips. It's quiet this time of year, but she was rushed off her feet last summer. How's your brood keeping? I understand congratulations are in order?"

Gunna sighed. "Gísli has two boys now, with two different women, six weeks apart."

"Yeah. I heard that. Tough position," Matti commiserated. "So is he settled down with one of them? Your brother's girl, wasn't it?"

"Svanur's stepdaughter. That's the situation at the moment, but I guess it could all change in five minutes. He's living with Drífa, which doesn't do a lot for family harmony. But there was an episode last year with a girl from New Zealand."

"Wow! He gets about, my cousin does."

Gunna scowled. "That's as maybe, but he has two children to support now. Anyway, the girl from New Zealand didn't last long. I think she figured out pretty quickly that a guy with two small children to support was never going to be much of a prospect. A shame, a very smart young woman. It's Laufey I'm more concerned about these days."

"In what way?"

"Ach, probably worrying about nothing. She just doesn't seem able to settle. Dumped the boy she'd been knocking about with and hasn't found new friends."

"She'll be all right," Matti said unconvincingly. "You want a coffee?"

Gunna leaned forward, arms crossed. "Listen. You have your ear to the ground."

"Not as much as I used to."

"Árni Sigurvinsson," she said, and knew as she saw Matti blanch that she'd hit the target.

"Árni's dead."

"He's not just dead. He was murdered."

"Yeah. I heard that."

"And? Any thoughts? What was Árni up to?"

"I suppose I should have come and seen you, but I didn't know what to say."

"Matti, are you involved in this?" Gunna asked in alarm.

"No, not as such." Matti looked out of the window at the rain pattering into the puddles in the street outside, grey water on a greyer street. "There was a whisper going round. No names, no comebacks. Understood?"

"Understood," Gunna assured him over her mug of coffee.

"Look, there was someone looking for a driver for a job last week. Cash payout. That's all I know. I turned it down. Didn't have to think twice."

"Why? How come you turned it down?"

Matti scratched his neck and fiddled with a corner of his moustache. "It was just too . . . woolly. You know what I mean? I don't know who had the job, but the message came through someone I'd be wary of trusting. Anyway, too many unanswered questions and I guess too many things to go wrong. Anyway, I'm straight these days, keeping my nose clean, and Marika wouldn't be impressed if I were to get a year in Litla Hraun. Done that, don't want to do it again."

"Very commendable, and not before time, cousin Matti."

"Thank you, cousin Gunna."

"A changed man, I'm pleased to see. I'm sure your mother is delighted."

"You know what our mothers are like. It's not as if either of them is easily pleased."

"True enough. Any idea what this job was supposed to be? If it was last week, has it been done, and is that why Árni came out of it so badly?"

172

Matti shifted uncomfortably in his chair and glanced around to reassure himself that nobody was listening.

"Thursday afternoon last week. Somebody stitched up Alli the Cornershop good and proper."

"That old bastard? Good for whoever did it."

"I don't suppose Alli's been along to report a robbery to the police, but the word is that a couple of hundred thousand euros disappeared and Alli's on the warpath."

"Ah. Definitely not small potatoes."

"Far from it. I've no idea if Árni had anything to do with it, but to my way of thinking it's a bit too much of a coincidence. Not that I'm selling the tale any dearer than I bought it, if you get my drift."

"How about a name?"

Matti scowled as if he'd felt a sudden stab of pain and Gunna wondered if she'd pushed him too far, as her phone chirped and she looked at the screen before answering.

"Gunnhildur."

"Can you hear me, chief?" Helgi said, standing somewhere outside where the wind snatched at his words. "That Ford Explorer you were looking for has turned up. Unlocked and keys in the ignition."

"Where?"

"The car park behind the Digranes Church."

"Great stuff. Get a forensic team on it right away, and I don't care how busy they are with something else. I'll be right there." She looked back at Matti and stood up. "I need to get back to work and I guess you do as well?"

"Should be back on the rank already, but it's quiet today so no harm done."

She put a hand on his shoulder and pecked him on the cheek.

"Good to see you. Look after yourself."

"And you, Gunna. Don't forget, you didn't hear anything from me," Matti said, shrugging on his thick fleece. He dropped his voice. "And you definitely didn't hear me mention anyone called Össi."

Össur locked the bridal suite's door behind him and sat on the bed. What had been a pristine white duvet was now grubby and grey, and he sat in the patch where his feet had left black marks. Moving as if in a trance, he felt numb, as if he were looking down on himself from above as he sat cross-legged on the bed where he had been for most of the last few days, surrounded by shreds of tobacco and grass scattered across the duvet. A brimming ashtray sat on a corner of the bed and a half-litre glass of water was on the bedside table. The contents of both had overflowed, leaving trails that Össur hadn't noticed.

The dead man outside was something he had to think about. How to get out of this place was something he had carefully not been thinking about, other than dreaming about a carefree existence somewhere where Alli the Cornershop would never dare venture. But he realized with a sinking feeling that now there was stuff he would have to deal with — the last few days had been a blissful idyll of non-stop television and one spliff after another, with the occasional noseful to adjust the balance.

He also noticed with regret that he could see the bottom of the bag of Alli the Cornershop's finest quality homegrown grass, probably produced in some big old house with heavyweight hydroponics, converted for the purpose and still not discovered by the filth. Not that Alli would be too worried. He never came anywhere near this stuff in person, and by the time the law caught up with the production side of things, he would have another workshop up and running somewhere else.

It was time to take charge again. These last few days he had kicked back and taken it easy. He had allowed Magni to take decisions, although he admitted to himself that the boy was no fool, contrary to what he had expected when he'd offered him an easy payday and a holiday in return for an hour's work. He found the sober and capable Magni a threat, much preferring the more amiable and compliant man he had got to know in the Emperor, the Magni who liked to take the edge off the day with a couple of cold ones.

This efficient and practical character was someone new, as far as Össur was concerned, and he didn't like it. Yes, it was definitely time to assert himself again, he decided. But first, a quick smoke to settle his nerves. It's not every day that you get to shoot someone dead, and Össur wasn't sure this was going to end happily. But the bastard had pushed him, hadn't he? Sent him flying. So that had to be self-defence. Magni and the girl with the weird hair, who he was sure Magni had been screwing these last few nights, had both seen it. Even the dried-up old bag had seen it. What was her name again? Erla? Or Erna? Not that it mattered, but dear God how that woman had screeched. He'd wanted to give her a slap, but fortunately the girl had taken her inside and Magni had hidden the guy's car away where nobody would be any the wiser.

He lay back and dragged the fragrant smoke deep, holding it there as he felt his toes and fingertips tingle and then go numb. It was definitely time to leave, but now the snow was coming down hard, and while that would stop them travelling, it would also keep unwelcome visitors away. He'd have to go downstairs and take charge soon, throw his weight about. But first he'd have a puff, he told himself. Magni and the girl were pretty capable, after all. They'd sort things out. As soon as the weather let up, they'd be away.

"Nobody's touched anything, have they?"

The white Ford Explorer was parked as far from the road as it comfortably could be.

"The patrol that checked it out opened the door and then shut it up tight," Helgi said. "It was the priest who reported it. Said it wasn't parked here yesterday but it was when he turned up here this afternoon."

Gunna looked around. "It's pretty well hidden, isn't it? Any idea when it showed up here?"

"Not yet. We're knocking on doors but nothing's turned up so far. Late last night's my guess."

"The forensic team on the way?"

"Should be here any minute."

"Good. Fingerprints to start with. I don't believe for a second that Erna Björg Brandsen and her daughter parked this thing here, so the absolute priority is to find out who did. The second there's a match, I want to know. I have to give something to the Laxdal today, and he has to be able to report something upstairs to keep all hell from descending onto his shoulders, which will in turn . . . You get the picture?"

"Vividly, thanks." Helgi looked up and screwed up his eyes. "They're here," he said.

"Good. Then I'm off. Where's Eiríkur?"

"With the fire investigation team at the house fire scene in Hafnarfjördur," he said, as the two forensics investigators got out of their van and began pulling on sterile clothing. "It's this white one," he called to them. "And it's urgent."

"It always is," one of them grumbled as he pulled on a mask and lifted the hood of his white suit.

"Leave them to it," Gunna said, taking his arm and leading him away from the parked Explorer. "You can chivvy them once they've got started. Listen. About Árni Sigurvinsson, a fairly reliable contact tells me that Alli the Cornershop got seriously rolled last week. Somebody stuck him and his goon up with a pistol, grabbed a bag of cash and ran for it. He seemed to think that Árni might have either been involved or could have known something about it."

"Shit," Helgi fretted. "A prize scumbag like that's all we needed to make things more fun. You think it might be a revenge thing?"

"No idea, and my contact didn't really want to talk about it."

"But you forced it out of him?"

"Let's say I got as much as I'm likely to out of him."

"You want to pay Alli the Cornershop a visit?"

Gunna pondered. "No. Not yet at any rate. Listen, our man left this car here and the next we see of him he's in a Skoda and on his own. So where did he go from here? Check stolen cars, all right? We know when he bought fuel, so we have a pretty good idea when the car must have been parked here, so let's knock on doors and ask questions before we turn up at the Cornershop."

As he trudged back across the hotel yard Magni saw that the man in blue overalls had been practically covered by snow. The tip of his nose was still visible but his eye sockets had been filled with the white flakes that had started to cover his body like a blanket. He guessed that in an hour or so the corpse would be completely hidden.

Magni hadn't realized just how cold he was. He pushed through the door and dropped into the first chair he found, shivering and beating the snow from his arms. He pulled off his gloves and saw that his fingers were white. He rubbed them but the feeling obstinately refused to return.

"You OK?"

He nodded in reply to Tinna Land's question, unable to speak, hunched in the chair and with each hand thrust deep into the opposite armpit.

"You're frozen stiff," she said, the concern in her voice clear as she took his arm and hauled him upright. In the lounge she made him sit on the deep sofa next to Erna, who sat there red-eyed and in shock while Tinna Lind pulled off his coat and boots. She wrapped a heavy duvet around his shoulders and he shivered next to Erna, who sat immobile, staring at the wall.

It took Magni half an hour to recover enough to stand up and stretch his legs. The feeling had returned to his fingers, and with it the pins and needles that stung as he ceaselessly rubbed his hands together, wincing at the pain and wondering if he'd done permanent damage. The walk back had taken him longer than he'd expected and he had become dangerously cold, he realized now. It scared him how close he had come to disaster so near to the warmth of the hotel.

"What are we going to do now?" Tinna Lind whispered, hugging him tightly in the kitchen once he had finally managed to get to his feet.

"I don't have a clue," he replied despairingly. "I hate to say it, but probably the best thing we can do is get in the car, drive to the nearest police station and give ourselves up, except that I'm not sure I trust myself to drive that far with the snow coming down this hard."

"Is that what you want to do?" Tinna Lind pulled her shoulders back and cocked her head to one side as she looked into his eyes. "If it is, then that's what we'll do, but you'll go to prison, won't you?"

"Probably. But not for as long as Össur will."

"I don't want you to be locked up." She disentangled a hand from behind his back and tugged at his trousers,

179

snaking a hand down and cupping the tight, cold ball of his testicles through the heavy denim. "I'd miss these."

"Me, too. So what's the best way out of here that lets us pass go and still collect our two hundred?"

"We have to be out of this place soon, don't we?"

"The sooner the better," Magni agreed. "Someone will come looking for that guy eventually and we have to be out of here as soon as the snow lets up. We might be able to get away tomorrow if there's a thaw tonight."

"Can we move him? Hide him?"

Magni stopped with his mouth half-open. The thought of moving the man in the blue overalls had not even occurred to him.

"We could," he said slowly. "But you realize we're digging a deeper hole for ourselves, don't you? Concealing a crime is only going to make things worse."

"We had to, didn't we?" Tinna Lind whispered. "Don't forget your pal Össur has a gun and he tells us what to do."

"His name's Össur Óskarsson," Gunna told Ívar Laxdal, entering his office with a perfunctory knock to find him reading through a report, an old-fashioned fountain pen in his fingers as he unhurriedly initialled the final page and closed it.

"And who is the gentleman?"

"Gentleman's not exactly the word I'd use. He's a minor criminal with a string of convictions stretching back into the last century; dope offences mostly, some drunk and disorderly, housebreaking and one assault charge a long time ago. On top of that there's a stack of

180

old motoring offences that includes one which was a massive smash that killed the poor bastard he ran into. Össur's blood-alcohol level was practically off the scale and he did time in Litla Hraun for that."

"This is in connection with the house fire that Helgi and Eiríkur are investigating?"

"Too early to say. But Össur Oskarsson is the guy whose prints are all over the back of Erna Björg Brandsen's car, which we found this afternoon tucked away behind the Digranes church in Kópavogur," Gunna said, deciding to keep some of what Matti had said her to herself until she could be certain of it. "It looks like someone made a half-hearted attempt to wipe the prints off the car, but didn't do a great job of it. We've already identified Erna's prints, her daughter's and her husband's, plus there's an unidentified set of prints in the back, over the petrol cap and the steering wheel."

Ívar Laxdal sat back in his chair and looked at the ceiling. Gunna took the opportunity to sink into a chair.

"Two missing persons, a known criminal and an unknown set of prints? Sounds interesting. What do you make of it?"

"I have no idea. It's bizarre, especially as Össur Oskarsson's prints are only in the back of the vehicle."

"The drivers are Erna Björg Brandsen and the unidentified man?"

"That's the shape of it."

"The woman picks up two hitchhikers who then steal the vehicle?"

"And what do they do with the two women?"

Ívar Laxdal lifted his shoulders in a shrug. "Who knows?"

"From what I've gathered from the husband, picking up a hitchhiker would be totally out of character for Erna Björg Brandsen."

"The daughter, maybe?"

"I need to talk to the husband again, and then try and track Össur Oskarsson's movements."

"No response from the appeal on the radio or the newspaper?"

"Nothing," Gunna said. "Not even any crank calls, which is unusual."

"Sitrep on the house fire investigation?"

"There's a lot of knocking on doors going on in Hafnarfjördur all over the district around the house. The victim had been beaten up quite recently, possibly only a few hours before the fire, plus there are indications he was intoxicated."

"You're leaving it to Eiríkur and Helgi?"

"As much as possible. They have a couple of uniformed officers with them doing the legwork. I'll tell you more tomorrow."

"Cooking again?"

"This is for tomorrow. I'm getting it ready now in case we need to move out tomorrow."

Tinna Lind helped herself to slices of onion and chewed them thoughtfully. "We could get that gun off him easily enough," she said in an undertone.

Magni shook his head. "Not yet," he said absently, turning a panful of minced beef with a spatula. "Pass me the pepper, will you?"

182

Tinna Lind jumped down from the worktop she had been sitting on. Magni gave the pepper mill a couple of twists over the sizzling meat.

"Why not?"

"Because Össur is dangerous with or without a gun. He doesn't have any brakes and he doesn't have a conscience. The pistol makes him feel safe, and I'd rather he felt safe than threatened."

"Mister psychologist, aren't you?"

"I try my best."

She leaned close to him. "Have you thought about . . ." she said, jerking her head to where Össur lay half asleep in the lounge, curled up on the sofa. "About what I said?"

"Yeah. I like the idea," he said and watched Tinna Lind's face crack into a smile. "It's a question of picking the right moment and not getting noticed."

"So what do you reckon?"

"I'm not sure at the moment. We can either try and run for it, and get a flight from Akureyri, which is what I reckon Össur has in mind. Or — this might be safer — we get hold of the dosh, stash away about two thirds of it and just give ourselves up."

Tinna Lind frowned. "You're not serious?"

"It's all right for you. You're the victim here. It's different for me. Össur will sing his heart out once the police get hold of him, and I can expect a sentence of some kind, although by the time the justice system gets round to it, it'll probably be a year's suspended sentence. If it even gets that far."

"I think we should go for it."

"You want to just leave?" Magni asked, pouring the meat into a deep saucepan and adding the contents of tins of chopped tomatoes. "Just cut yourself off completely? Walk away from family, friends, all that stuff?"

Tinna Lind's nose wrinkled. "If you're coming with me, then yeah. Let's do it."

Magni stopped stirring the pot and stared.

"You're certain of that? We've known each other for what? Four days?"

"Yeah. I'm certain. Mind's made up."

"All right . . ." he said slowly.

"And you? Is your mind made up?"

"To be honest, no it's not. I have ties that I'm not ready to walk away from just like that."

"Like what?"

"I have kids, to start with."

"And how often do you see them?"

"Well, yeah. You're right there," he conceded. "Once a year, if that. Maybe I wasn't top-quality husband material." He put the spoon down and reduced the heat under the saucepan to its lowest setting. He turned back to face her where she had resumed her seat on the worktop as she watched him cook. "So, what do you think?" he asked as he put his arms around her. Tinna Lind responded fiercely, hugging him tight and wrapping her legs around his waist.

"What is there to keep you here? No job? Kids you never see? A couple of ex-wives who hate you?"

"You're doing a great job of persuading me here."

184

"And this old bastard that you and Össur robbed. What's he going to do when he tracks you down," she whispered in his ear, her head resting on his shoulder."

"He's going to break my legs," Magni replied. "That's if he finds out who I am, and unless he gets hold of Össur first. Össi's the one he really wants. Össi worked for him, I think. I'm not part of this criminal stuff. I just used to drink with these guys in the Emperor. I didn't really hang around with them anywhere else."

"So why don't we just give the old guy what he wants?"

"What he'll want to start with is his bag of money back. The second thing he'll want is Össur. I'm probably third on the list."

"All right. Let's give him some of what he wants," Tinna Lind murmured. "How about we give him Össur to play with while we disappear with the money?"

"I'm looking for Össur Oskarsson."

"He's not there," the young woman with a toddler at her ankles and a baby on her hip said, looking around the door. "Thank God," she added with heartfelt relief.

"Any idea where he is? When did you last see him?"

The woman looked Gunna up and down. "You don't look like one of the lowlifes he hangs around with."

Gunna showed her warrant card and the woman relaxed.

"In that case, please lock him up when you find him and don't let him out," she said with feeling. "The last I saw of him was the middle of last week."

185

"You remember which day that was?"

"Wednesday, I think." She stopped to consider. "But it might have been Thursday. Hold on, I had the doctor on Thursday and I saw Össur when we were going out, so it must have been Thursday."

"Does he usually disappear for days at a time?"

"It's nothing unusual, not that I keep tabs on him."

"Somehow I get the impression that you don't get on?"

"We don't," she said with even more feeling. "I can't stand the sight of him and hate having to live in the same building. We're thinking of selling up and moving if it doesn't improve."

"Noisy, is he?"

"Sometimes. It's more the way he undresses you with his eyes every time you see him, and those vile friends of his. There were some of them here yesterday looking for him."

"Can I come in? I could do with getting some questions answered."

Gunna perched on a stool in the corner of what served as a kitchen while the woman fussed with coffee and gave the toddler an iPad playing cartoons to watch.

"How long have you lived here?"

"Two years."

"And has Össur been here all that time?"

"Yes. He rents the flat upstairs. What's he done? Anything serious?"

"I'm afraid I can't tell you, but there are concerns about his safety," Gunna said, making an effort to sound diplomatic. "All I can say is it's not trivial."

186

"No concerns here," the woman snorted.

"Does he come and go at regular times or all hours?"

"It can be him coming and going or his pals turning up at all hours. My husband works shifts and sometimes he can't get a wink of sleep all day, and the next week he'll be on days and there's endless noise at night instead. Not loud noise, you understand, but people coming and going, shouting, that sort of thing. We've complained to the police but nothing happens," she added sharply.

"Nothing regular? I take it he doesn't have a job or anything as mundane as that?"

She snorted. "Job? I don't imagine he knows what a job is."

"And his friends? Any idea who these people are?"

"Lowlifes like him. I don't know who they are, but there are plenty of drunks who find their way up there."

"And the people who came looking for him yesterday. Who were they? Bailiffs? Drunks?"

This time the woman looked dubious.

"Well, they weren't the usual crowd," she said finally. "One of them parked a motorcycle outside."

"I don't suppose you happened to get the number?"

"Well, my husband was at home yesterday and he likes motorbikes," she said and leaned down to the toddler. "Hey, darling, can Mummy use the iPad, please? Just for a moment?" She clicked and swiped with her finger. "He likes bikes and cars and stuff, and he took a picture of the bike out of the window." She turned the iPad round to show a low-slung black bike on its stand in the street outside.

Gunna took it and enlarged the picture until she could make out the licence plate.

"Thanks," Gunna said, jotting down the number. "Oh, and don't worry about selling up quite yet. I have a feeling your neighbour might not be back for a while."

Össur told himself to think straight. The door was locked. The pistol was on the bedside table. He had turned the television's volume down low and now only disjointed images on a music channel flickered past him for a few seconds at a time, pneumatic women in skimpy clothes and flashy pseudo-gangsters of the kind he inwardly despised. Alli the Cornershop had taught him long ago that it's better not to stand out in a crowd.

A vision of Erna squealing as he bent her over the back of the sofa downstairs, those designer trousers round her ankles, appeared before him and he relished the thought. Magni was clearly screwing the daughter, he decided. The loved-up sloppy grins on both their faces told the story clearly enough, and Magni looked as if he was falling for the girl in a serious way. In other circumstances, and if he'd thought about it, Össur might have been almost happy for Magni, but now the sight of them cooing to each other, their hands snaking under each others' clothes, made him feel sick.

But he recognized, to his chagrin, that he needed Magni, and their biggest mistake had been not to ditch the two women right away and just take the car. That way they would have been free of the pair of them. A hunt would have started up right away, as soon as the women reached a phone and alerted the police, but there was a hunt in progress for the two missing women anyway, which would inevitably lead to him and Magni.

Össur picked up the pistol and weighed it in his hand. He put it down, comforted by the weight and feel of it, and reached for the bag of grass, before he put that down as well and told himself to get a grip.

They would have to get rid of the girls, he decided, after suitable treatment for the vinegar-faced old bitch. Then he'd have to lose Magni, but not until Össur had been delivered to somewhere close to an airport without registering on Alli the Cornershop's radar.

He knew with a crushing certainty that the odds were heavily stacked against him, and he reflected that it had always been this way. Every time he felt he had made a little headway in life, something came along that would knock him back to where he'd started, broke and alone. He took a final toke on the spliff before crushing it out on the blonde wood of the bedside table and lay back watching the ceiling throb. Everyone was against him, even Magni. Especially Magni, he decided, and the sudden thought gripped him that the three of them would take the car while he was asleep and leave him alone in this empty building miles from anywhere to starve or until someone turned up in the spring, if he were to survive that long.

Then he remembered the depth of snow in the yard outside and reminded himself that Magni hadn't been far off dying of exposure just that afternoon. He reassured himself that nobody would be going far for a while, as he curled himself into a ball under the duvet and put a comforting thumb into his mouth.

"I need a warrant," Gunna said, without bothering to introduce herself.

"What for?" Ívar Laxdal asked.

Gunna looked up and down the quiet street, her phone at her ear. "I'm outside Össur Oskarsson's flat. He hasn't been seen for a few days and I want a look inside."

"You're concerned for his well-being?"

Gunna laughed. "Not really. I just want to know where the hell he is."

"You're concerned about his well-being," Ívar Laxdal decided. "Get yourself a locksmith and some uniformed back-up and get in there."

"On your authority?"

"On my authority," he agreed. "Get on with it. I'll fix the paperwork."

"Good. I'll let you know what happens."

She closed the connection and made a second call.

"Siggi. Communications."

"Hæ. Gunna Gísla here. Can you check out a number for me?"

She recited the motorcycle's registration number and walked a few paces along the street, listening to the muffled rattle of a keyboard down the line.

"It's registered to Jón Egill Hjörleifsson," Siggi said. "His address is Kirkjuholt forty-six."

"Good stuff, thanks," Gunna said and rang off.

★ ★ ★

Gunna arrived back at the Hverfisgata station in a black mood after spending two hours at Össur Oskarsson's dingy apartment. She was determined to share her gloom with Ívar Laxdal, but he found her first at her computer in the detectives' office.

"Busy, Gunnhildur?"

"You always ask the same question and I always give you the same answer."

"In that case you're not the only one. We have another missing person to look for now. A middle-aged man called Brandur Geirsson, last seen the day before yesterday. He lives alone so nobody worried about him until he didn't show up for work this morning. He lives in Akranes, so they're dealing with it up there for the moment."

"Good. I've enough on my plate as it is."

"The good news is that the weather's supposed to break tonight and there might be clear enough conditions for a search flight tomorrow between one weather front and the next."

"That would be great. If only we knew where to look and what to look for." She yawned. "I'm going home; it's been a long and fruitless day."

"No luck with that apartment in Hafnarfjördur?"

"It might have been interesting if someone hadn't got there before us and trashed the place. It's a disaster area. Every single drawer, shelf and cupboard has been tipped onto the floor and most of it's broken, not that there was much of interest there to start with, except a couple of 9mm rounds that looked as if they'd rolled under the bed."

"D'you think the man's armed?"

"I wouldn't rule it out."

"Prints?"

"Working on it."

"Ideas?"

"Oh, yes. It seems that a gentleman riding a motorcycle registered to Jón Egill Hjörleifsson was there looking for Össur yesterday, and it seems that Jón Egill Hjörleifsson has a record for the usual misdemeanours and is an Undertaker."

"You mean he organizes funerals or he's a member of that law-abiding and much-loved group of philanthropists in Gardabær who happen to ride souped-up motorbikes?"

"He might do both for all I know. But he's certainly a biker. He wasn't at home, so there's an alert out for him to be brought in if traffic spot him before I track him down. But it seems clear enough that Össur has upset someone badly, and I'm starting to wonder if there isn't a real connection here."

Ívar Laxdal sat down and crossed his ankles with his legs stretched out, as if waiting to be told a bedtime a story. "Explain, if you'd be so kind," he instructed.

"Someone rolled Alli the Cornershop for a pile of either money or drugs, or both, or so it seems. Össur Oskarsson has been involved with Alli for years and so has Árni Sigurvinsson. Árni came to a bad end, beaten up and then killed in a house fire. Össur has had the sense to disappear and now someone's looking for him. There aren't a lot of dots to be joined here, are there?"

"Interesting."

192

"Except for the Undertakers getting involved. They have fingers in plenty of pies and the rumour is they're aiming to become legitimate businessmen. But for the moment they're in much the same business as Alli the Cornershop and they don't like each other a lot."

"Evidence?"

"Not a lot."

"Gut feeling?"

"Overwhelming."

The whisky was almost finished, Magni noticed with sadness. The hotel was quiet as he went up the stairs. There was no blaring television from Össur's bridal suite at the end of the corridor. He padded to the end and listened at the door, but there was no sound and he guessed that Össur had probably knocked himself out for the night.

He put an ear to Erna's door and heard muffled sobs inside.

Tinna Lind turned down the sound of the television as they pushed open the door of the room he had taken.

"We were on the news again. Me, Mum and a picture of a car like ours," she said in a flat voice.

"What did they say?"

"Just a request for anyone who might have seen us."

"The only person who saw us was that guy who's under the snow in the yard."

"And the old guy who came here that first day, don't forget."

"And anyone who might have seen the car in Selfoss when I went to stock up on food," Magni added, his mind elsewhere. "Listen, your mother doesn't sound great. You want to check on her?"

"Why?"

"It sounds like she's crying in there."

Tinna Lind shrugged.

"So? She's a big girl."

"You don't sound concerned about her."

Tinna Lind stood up and looked out of the window into the blackness outside. "She's a cold-hearted character, my mother. There isn't a shred of empathy in her."

"She's had a tough time these last few days."

"She and Össur would make a fine pair, wouldn't they?"

"Did you see the weather forecast?" Magni asked, uncomfortable and anxious to change the subject.

"Yeah. Rain and a gale tonight."

"Southerly?"

"You mean with all the arrows pointing upwards? Yeah."

"That's perfect."

"Why's that?"

"Because southerly means warmer, and warm means that some of the white shit will melt and we can get out of here. I hope," he added. "Now, are you going to check on your mother or shall I?"

Tinna Lind pushed at the door and tapped at it when it refused to move.

194

"Mamma?" she called softly and the door opened a crack.

Tears has scoured their way down Erna's face and Magni was shocked to see how much older she looked than the stylish socialite of only a few days ago. Lines had appeared in a network at the corners of her eyes and her fringe looked to have a touch of grey in it.

She stepped aside and they entered the room. The bed had been made. The floor was clean and the sparse contents of her handbag were lined up around the mirror on the dressing table.

Erna looked at them enquiringly and sat down in the only chair. Magni stood and Tinna Lind half lay on the bed, an arm angled under her head as she viewed her mother sideways. Magni was surprised to see how rapidly Erna's self-composure returned as she collected herself.

"How is your friend?" she asked.

"He's not my friend."

"I hope he dies a painful and miserable death," Erna snarled. "Somewhere I can watch."

Gunna switched off the engine and sat for a moment with her eyes closed. She wanted to put it behind her and forget work, but Erna Björg Brandsen and Tinna Lind Bogadóttir kept coming back to the forefront of her mind. With a sick feeling in her stomach, she admitted to herself that the pair could be dead. Disappearances are a rarity, she told herself, especially disappearing women. She tried to think back to the last time a woman's disappearance hadn't been resolved, and found herself stumped. Women in Iceland don't just vanish, she told herself. The two of them must be out there somewhere, and it won't be long before they appear, hopefully alive and well, with some plausible reason for dropping out of sight.

The thought had plagued her all day that she could be on the wrong track, that the two women could be already dead somewhere in the countryside and that she should have called out a search immediately. She shivered to herself at the thought that their deaths could have been avoided if she had acted faster, and took a deep breath before getting out of the car, telling herself that she had done the right things and a high-profile search could have driven the women and whoever they were with even further into hiding.

The lights were on, although Steini's car was nowhere to be seen, and she wondered where he was as she opened the front door, sat down to pull off her boots and called out to an empty house. The radio was on and there was coffee in the percolator, but the place was deserted. Gunna told herself to stop being a detective. She poured a mug of coffee and sniffed at it to find that it was very fresh. She stretched herself out on the sofa with the mug close to hand and picked up the thriller Steini had left on the table.

When she woke up, the book was open on her chest and the mug of coffee was hardly more than lukewarm, but faint laughter and voices came from beyond the door, which burst open as Laufey appeared with Kjartan Gíslason in her arms and a grin on her face.

196

"Look, Granny's taking it easy," she crooned, loping forward, placing the little boy on Gunna's chest and going to shake off her coat while Kjartan gurgled and took in the room around him.

"Hey, little man," Gunna said softly, as he gripped her thumbs in his hands and looked at her with clear eyes. "Who's a handsome little man?"

"The description can only apply to me," Steini said, blowing water off his moustache and carrying a couple of carrier bags, which he deposited on the table. Drífa followed him into the room, dropping her own bag full of baby stuff by the door.

"No Gísli?" Gunna asked rubbing her eyes.

"Gísli's a bit busy tonight," Drífa said, sweeping Kjartan up and pulling off his tiny boots, unzipping his padded snow suit and unpacking him like a Christmas parcel. "He needs a change," she said, wrinkling her nose. "Can I use your bed?"

"Yeah, go ahead," Gunna said. "Laufey, what's going on?"

Laufey was rattling plates and throwing cutlery on the table. "Æi, a bit of a situation over there at the moment. So Steini and I took an executive decision, in your absence, to collect Drífa and Kjartan, and I talked Steini into getting a takeaway at the same time."

"I'm sure he needed plenty of persuasion," Gunna said, getting to her feet as Laufey opened the cartons and the smell of Chinese food filled the room. "You've been to Hungry House?"

Laufey grinned. "We couldn't just drive past, could we? Come on, it's ready."

There was little talking as they ate. Steini used chopsticks with aplomb, Drífa stuck to a fork and Gunna ate with one hand and with Kjartan, now fresh and sweet-smelling, perched on one knee as she fed him noodles.

"So where's my son tonight?" Gunna asked finally, chasing the last of her food around her plate. "What's the crisis?"

Drífa flashed a glance at Laufey.

"It's his father," she said and waited for Gunna's face to set like stone. "Gísli took him to hospital."

"Ah. Problem?"

"He's not well," Drífa said. Laufey and Steini stood up and started to clear the table, leaving Gunna and Drífa with their heads together.

"What's the matter with the old rogue?"

"Well, you know Gísli looked him up a while ago and he wasn't interested?"

"Yeah. Gísli told me that. I could have told him that Thorvaldur probably wouldn't want to know," Gunna grunted, shifting Kjartan to the other knee. She looked up at the picture of Ragnar Sæmundsson on the bookcase and nodded towards it. "Raggi was much more of a father to Gísli than that old reprobate ever was."

"I know." Drífa sighed. "Gísli was devastated when he found him and the interest didn't seem to be mutual. But then Thorvaldur called him and wanted to meet, and they've being seeing a bit of each other ever since."

"Anything serious?"

"I think he's very ill," Drífa said. "Thorvaldur comes to see him occasionally and they sit there and talk. Gísli doesn't say much to me, though."

"But he has other children," Gunna said, conscious of the anger within her that she knew she could not properly justify. "All right, I know he treated Gísli and me badly, and I can't feel charitable towards him, especially as things weren't easy when Gísli was little. But he never wanted anything to do with him as a child, and now all of a sudden he does."

"From what Gísli has told me, his other children aren't interested, and some of them live abroad. I gather he didn't go out of his way to support any of them."

Gunna lifted Kjartan up and turned him around to sit him on the table in front of her, each of his hands wrapped around one of her fingers.

"Well, it's up to Gísli," she said. "He's a man now and I wouldn't dream of telling him what to do. If he'd wanted to make contact with his half-brothers and half-sisters, and I gather there's quite a brood here and there, then I could have understood. But I don't understand what he expects to get out of trying to forge some kind of a relationship with Thorvaldur."

"I think that's just it," Drífa said. "Gísli's such a soft-hearted character underneath. It's partly because none of the others want to know; it's as if there's some kind of guilt there."

"Thorvaldur's the one who ought to have a guilty conscience," Gunna snapped.

199

"I think he does, and I suppose because he doesn't have long to live, that's why he wants to establish some kind of contact."

"Doesn't have long to live? What's wrong with him? He's certainly left it a little late in the day, hasn't he?"

CHAPTER
SIX

Tuesday

With his eyes half closed, Magni swung his legs out of bed and padded to the bathroom to find Tinna Lind sitting naked on the edge of the bath with a pair of scissors in her hand, snipping off the beads, holding the end of each thin plait and sending them tinkling into the bathtub one by one.

"Hæ," he said blearily. "What are you doing?"

"Taking my braids out."

"Shame. I liked them."

"Yeah. But they're distinctive. I'll bet there's a description out there for a girl with cornrow hair. I don't want to stand out."

"You can get it done again," he said, twisting the end of a braid in his fingers.

"You'd better give me a hand unbraiding them, otherwise it'll take all day."

It took an hour of painstaking unpicking to unplait all the narrow braids and Tinna Lind finally shook out a flood of thick brown hair over her shoulders.

"That feels so much better," she said, sweeping the beads and tufts of hair out of the tub and setting the shower to run. She stood under the hot water and let it course through her hair, feeling it loose for the first time in weeks. Magni watched in admiration.

"Coming to join me?" she asked, sweeping her hair back over her head and down her back. "Or shall we fill the tub and try it in the bath?"

"There's food in the pan. Eat up. It might be a while before we have another chance," Magni said. "Help yourselves. Tinna Lind, would you be so kind as to give Össur some?"

Erna picked at the mince and pushed the onions to one side, while for once Össur ate every scrap on his plate.

Magni pushed his plate to one side. "Now we're all here and, for a change, none of us are wasted," he said, looking at Össur. "We need to discuss what the next step is."

"You want to talk about this in front of these two?" Össur demanded.

"I reckon we owe them that."

"Why?"

Erna opened her mouth to speak but Tinna Lind laid a hand on her arm.

"Like it or not, they're involved, and we have screwed up their lives these last few days."

"Yeah. All the same," Össur grumbled, "they're not part of the job."

"We need to get away from here and we need to do it soon. Today. Now," he said, the determination giving urgency to his voice as his words became clipped. "The wind's in the south. It's been raining hard all night and

202

the snow's melting already. If it keeps raining and the forecast's right, then I'll bet the road down the track from here should be clear. It won't be easy, but we should be able to get out of here."

"Sounds good to me," Össur said, though he sounded uncertain at the prospect of venturing beyond the little circle of hills surrounding the hotel. "What about these two? They'll drop us deep in the shit the first chance they get."

"Not if Tinna Lind comes with us."

Erna's mouth dropped open and she squawked. "What? No way!"

"I'm sorry, but we'll have to," Magni said. "Össur here has everything to lose. There's no way he can afford to be caught. So we part company with you today and Tinna Lind comes with us."

"That's . . ."

"There's no choice here," Magni said with decision. "We get out safe and sound, she comes to no harm."

"But . . ."

"That's all there is to it."

Breakfast was a hurried affair before they made for the car in the darkness outside. The Pajero was buffeted by a gusting wind and the road was slick with water. Driving through Grindavík, Laufey peered out of the window.

"Gísli's awake," she said.

Gunna wanted to grind her teeth. "And is that shitty old Mazda there?"

"No, Mum. Gísli's dad's not there."

It wasn't until they reached the street lights of Reykjanesbraut that Laufey cleared her throat and spoke again.

"Mum. Have you spoken to Gísli these last few days?"

"No, I haven't."

"Maybe you should?"

"Why?" Gunna asked, surprised how Laufey had inherited Ragnar's firm intonation, which invited agreement but promised an argument if any opposition were aired.

"Because it's driving the rest of us nuts. All right, you don't like Gísli looking up his father after all these years, and we can accept that, but you've been sulking for days and Steini and I are fed up with it."

"Excuse me?" Gunna said, glancing sideways to see a look of determination on Laufey's face that reminded her instantly of Ragnar when he had a point to prove, normally rightly so, she told herself. Their few years together had been virtually argument-free, but on the occasions they had not agreed, it had generally been on something mundane, not worth an argument. It was still a source of lasting regret, even all these years later, that some of these petty squabbles had taken place. "Are you reading the old bag the riot act, young lady?"

"No. I'm just pointing out the truth. You've been wrapped up in this silly frustration for the last few days and I don't know if you've noticed or not, but you've been taking it out on me and Steini."

"Is that so?" Gunna said with iron in her voice, and they were silent as the lights of Reykjanesbraut flashed past.

204

The rain had begun to lift by the time Gunna pulled up outside the college. Laufey was an hour early for her first class of the day.

"Going to the library for an hour are you?" Gunna asked, hoping a truce would be forthcoming.

"Maybe," Laufey said, opening the door and letting in a blast of cold air.

"Call me later in the day and let me know if you need collecting. All right?"

"Sure you won't be busy somewhere?"

Gunna opened her mouth to deliver the sharp comment that had been on the tip of her tongue. "No, I can't be sure that I won't be busy somewhere else," she said finally. "That's the way the job is. You know that as well as I do."

"Sorry, Mum," Laufey said. "I didn't mean it like that."

"What, then?"

"Mum, talk to Gísli, will you? He's having a proper rough time of it at the moment and the last thing he needs is you being all hurt and offended."

"Maybe I am hurt and offended."

"I know. But your quarrel shouldn't be with Gísli. He's only doing what's natural and you can't blame him for that. It's different for me. I know Ragnar Sæmundsson isn't out there somewhere waiting to reappear, unfortunately. But Gísli's had this big question mark there all these years and he doesn't have long to get all his questions answered."

Gunna sighed. "You're probably right, young lady," she said, startled again at how similar to her father

Laufey sounded. "Text me when you know what you're doing later."

"All right. If you're not about I can get a lift with Gísli."

"He's in Reykjavík today?"

"Mum, Gísli's in Reykjavík every day until Christmas. I thought you knew that."

"Össi, talk to me," Magni said as Erna went upstairs and Tinna Lind started clearing up the kitchen.

In the restaurant the Skoda, and before it the Explorer, had dripped meltwater all over the floor. The parquet was soaked in places and Magni could see that the floor was starting to warp.

"I feel sorry for the owners of this place," he said. "There's a lot of damage been done here."

"Fuck that!" Össur growled. "They'll get it off the insurance."

"Or from us if they catch up with us."

"Which they won't. I reckon we leave those two here."

"Listen, Össi," Magni said. "They're both coming with us. We drop Erna somewhere safe and Tinna Lind stays with me."

"Yeah, yeah. Like you said."

Magni folded his arms, knowing that the sight of those bulky forearms had settled more than one argument in the past.

"No, she's coming with us, all the way. We split the dosh down the middle. We take half, you take half, and when we get to an airport or a ferry or whatever, we go our separate ways."

"Seventy-thirty," Össur said instantly. "That's what we agreed."

"That was when we were going to go straight to the sunshine, not spending days or weeks holed up in the back of beyond."

"It's my job. I fixed it up. I take the risk. I take seven tenths."

"I'm taking risks here as well. You reckon that old bastard isn't after me, too? Fifty-fifty or I'm out of here."

Össur grinned. "Yeah, but I've got the car key, and a gun." The Baikal's safety catch clicked off and on in his pocket.

Magni glared at him, and a look inside the car proved that the key had vanished from the ignition.

"Yeah, you've got a car that you can't drive. Are you going to get to Keflavík or somewhere like that on your own?"

"There are people here who can drive, like you. You're not going to get out of here either without the car."

"That's where you're wrong. Don't forget the guy you shot? Forgotten that, have you?" Magni saw the corner of Össur's mouth twitch in anger and his hand start to lift out of his pocket. "I know where his truck's parked. All I have to do is slip out of the door and I'm away while you're still here."

Össur snarled. "You wouldn't fucking dare."

"You better believe I would. But you don't have to worry about that. We go fifty-fifty and we all get somewhere safe together."

Össur sagged. "All right. We split it down the middle."

"Cool. I'd shake your hand if it didn't have a gun in it. We split the cash before we leave, count it out together. No mistakes. Straight down the middle."

"Yeah. Don't rub it in."

"And we leave here soon. It gets dark around four and I want to get to the main road in daylight. I'm going north. You?"

"Yeah. North. I don't want to go anywhere near Alli the Cornershop's territory."

The tension crackled in the air as Össur dumped the bag of money on the table.

"That's it?"

"All of it," he agreed.

"Right," Magni said with disbelief. The bag looked smaller than it had when they'd run out of Alli the Cornershop's house and down the street into the twilight.

Össur emptied the bag and bundles of notes tumbled out. "You really want to count all of it?"

"Just make two equal piles? Yeah, of course I want to count it."

Össur shrugged. They each began counting, Össur counting under his breath, Tinna Lind flicking smartly through each wad of notes and Magni counting

208

carefully as they each made bundles of a thousand euros, then combined these into stacks often thousand.

Half an hour later they looked at one another and Magni counted the nineteen piles and leftover piles of fifties.

"A hundred and ninety-four thousand euros. That makes ninety-seven thousand each."

He moved piles across the table deliberately, making sure Össur imagined no false moves, and split the last pile, counting it out until there were two piles of equal value.

"Happy with that?" he asked. "Fair?"

"It's not fair and no, I'm not happy with that," Össur retorted. "I still say it should be seventy-thirty, but I guess I don't have a choice."

Magni stacked the cash into neat piles of notes, snapping a rubber band around each one. Össur swept his pile back into the bag and stood up.

"I'm going to get ready," he said. "It's going to be a long day."

"Do you think he's swindling us?" Tinna Lind asked when Össur had gone upstairs.

"I'm damn sure of it. That bag was a lot thicker before, so I'd bet anything you like that he's skimmed a stack off the top and stashed it away somewhere."

"It'll be in his room?"

"In the bridal suite? Probably. He's hardly been out of there for days. I think his bag of grass must be pretty much finished by now."

"His hands are shaking."

"And he's a lot sharper. He probably hasn't been without a spliff for a whole day for years and I suppose it might be a shock to his system. But now . . ."

Jón Egill Hjörleifsson was far from overawed by the interview room and met Gunna's gaze.

"My name's Gunnhildur Gísladóttir and I'm a detective with the city CID," she said, sitting down.

"And I'm Jón Egill Hjörleifsson, but I reckon you know that already," he said in a deep voice that seemed out of place from someone so stocky. He barely reached Gunna's shoulder, but the barrel chest and thick arms encased in a worn leather jacket indicated this was no weakling. "Why am I here? Haven't been speeding, have I?" He grinned, showing a flash of gold set among pearl-white teeth.

"On Monday a vehicle registered to you was identified in Vesturbraut at 13:45. I'd like you to account for your movements."

"I was looking for a friend."

"Really?"

"Yeah. But he wasn't home."

"Your friend's name?"

"Össi. I can't remember whose son he is. He drinks in the Emperor some nights."

The man's manner was confident and the answers were plausible enough, but the underlying tone of mockery convinced Gunna that Jón Egill Hjörleifsson was too experienced to lie outright, but not too clever to stop himself showing off.

"Why?"

"Why what?"

"Why did you decide to go and see your friend at that particular time? You don't have a job?"

"I have a job, officer. And I pay my taxes like a decent citizen."

"Where do you work?"

"I'm self-employed. I run a couple of kiosks. One in Hafnarfjördur, one in Keflavík, one in Mosfellsbær. Lunchtime trade, mostly."

"And you weren't busy with the lunchtime trade at 13:45 on Monday?"

Jón Egill Hjörleifsson looked at her pityingly. "I don't flip fucking burgers myself. I have people to do that."

"Why does a successful businessman show an interest in a small-time dealer like Össur?"

"He's a dealer?"

"Why did you go to look for him that afternoon?"

"We were short-staffed. I was going to offer him a couple of shifts in the kiosk as it's round the corner from where he lives."

"I suppose you had checked that Össur has all the required hygiene certificates?"

"No, but if he hadn't I'd have put him through the course."

Gunna placed a photograph on the desk. "Recognize this character?"

"I've seen the face but couldn't put a name to it," he said finally, after examining Árni Sigurvinsson's driving licence photo.

"And this one?"

He blanched at the sight of the same face in death, its eyes half open and lips parted as if about to speak.

"Who's that?"

"The same guy after someone set fire to his flat early on Friday morning. Where were you between five and seven that morning?"

"At home. Asleep, I expect."

Gunna could see that he was uncomfortable. "And will anyone confirm that?" she asked softly.

"Is this really necessary?" he demanded. "I can have my lawyer here in five minutes, you know."

"Feel free," Gunna replied, watching his composure disintegrate. "You're not under arrest, but you have a right to a lawyer if that's what you want. However, you still haven't answered my question. Is there anyone who can vouch for your presence at home between five and seven on Saturday morning?"

Magni pulled on his trousers. He watched Tinna Lind dressing, gazing as the trim dark triangle between her legs disappeared into her clothes, hoping this wasn't the last he'd see of it. He took a deep breath.

"Ready?"

"As ready as I'll ever be. And you? No second thoughts?"

"None."

"You know, if you give yourself up, we can pin every single thing on your friend," she said in a low voice. "He held us at gunpoint the whole time."

"True," Magni agreed. "But I'm not keen to hang around where Össur's friend Alli might decide he wants to ask me a few awkward questions. So let's go for it, shall we?"

Tinna Lind hugged him, laying her head on his shoulder and squeezing him tight. He laid a hand on her head, stroking the long brown hair, the crinkles from its long imprisonment in braids starting to disappear.

"Come on. We'd better check on the others," she said.

Alli got into Rafn's car, having first made sure there was nobody in the back seat.

This time it was a blue-collar Avensis of the kind that nobody would look at twice rather than the sleek black van with its tinted windows.

Rafn drove in silence in a circuit around the town and back to the centre, stopping outside the shopping mall.

"Coffee, Alli?"

"Yeah. Why not."

Inside, Alli pointed to a table. "There."

They both knew and accepted the subtext. It was a place chosen as randomly as could be arranged and outside each of their normal stamping grounds, so there was no chance of a wire being under the table. Alli remembered with discomfort that Rafn could be wearing a recording device of some kind, but told himself not to be paranoid as the younger man, this time back in his habitual denims, collected two white mugs of ink-black coffee.

He could see Rafn was perturbed.

"Still no sign of them, Alli," he said. "Not a whisper."

"That's strange. Össi's a city boy. He's never been one for going much out of town."

"It's not just that." Rafn stirred his coffee with a slow, deliberate motion and looked up. "I'm not sure this is worth the effort. I've had the police sniffing around."

Alli sat silent and waited for Rafn to continue.

"One of my associates has been picked up and questioned by the police, and it certainly isn't some kind of routine thing."

"What were they after?"

"I reckon it's your gopher. The one who's dead."

"Árni? That was an accident," Alli said quickly.

"Was it? I wonder. It looks like the law have connected Árni's untimely demise with Össur's sudden disappearance, which is no surprise. The problem is that anyone looking for Össur becomes someone who might be involved in Árni's death, as far as the law is concerned, and we can do without the attention."

"So you're telling me you're backing off?"

Rafn sipped his coffee. "Not at all. We haven't stopped looking for Össur." He looked up and smiled in a way that made Alli shiver. "We're just having to be a little more discreet about it, and casting the net wider means it becomes a more expensive operation."

Össur opened the hatch in the bathroom ceiling and felt between the rafters for the package he knew was there. He retrieved it and blew off a thin layer of dust. Grinning to himself, he opened the bag and unwound the towel. A hundred and ten notes, each worth five hundred euros. He took off his jacket and carefully secreted

214

the thick wad of notes, with his passport, deep in the lining via a tear in the inside pocket, then wondered if that was a safe hiding place. He thought briefly about hiding the money in his trousers or shoes, but realized that would never work. He'd keep the money behind the Baikal, he decided. Anyone wanting to get to his nest egg would have to get past the gun first.

The rest of the money, his half of what they had shared out the night before, he kept in the bag it had come in. He promised himself that the first thing he would do when they got to anywhere with a shop would be to buy himself a decent pair of shoes, some smarter clothes and some luggage to travel with.

He looked regretfully at the now filthy bridal suite where he had spent most of the last week sitting on the bed working his way through the bag of grass. He upended the bag on the table, shook it out and decided there was enough there for one final spliff before they hit the road.

The kiosk was empty and the wind blew under the clear plastic panels of the shelter attached to it, where customers could bolt down a microwaved burger and a can of something fizzy while sheltering from the rain, if not the wind that whistled around their ankles.

"What can I get you?" The young man with dark curls and mid-night eyes glanced at Eiríkur without taking any notice of him.

Eiríkur took in the smell and the sight of hot dogs in their bath of hot water that didn't look as fresh as they might have been.

"I'm looking for Julio."

"Who's looking for him?"

The young man's accent was unmistakeable as he tried to get his tongue around Icelandic vowels.

"Reykjavík CID," Eiríkur said, presenting his warrant card in its wallet.

"He was here just now," the man said vaguely. "I think he come back later."

"You have his number?" Eiríkur asked. "Give him a call, can you?"

"I don't think he have a phone."

The accent had become thicker and more nervous as the man edged away from Eiríkur.

"And you are? What's your name?"

The man's mouth opened for a second and Eiríkur could see him thinking hard before he spoke.

"I'm Manuel," he said finally and smiled unconvincingly.

"And do you have some identification?"

"Yeah. Just a moment." Eiríkur noticed the shifty look, peered into the kiosk's preparation area to see what the man was doing and saw the door swinging open.

He took a couple of steps out of the plastic shelter and looked behind the kiosk to see the man walking fast along the street, pulling on a hooded sweater as he went. Rather than give chase and lose him to a long head start, Eiríkur walked after him, jogging when he was sure he would not be seen by a backward glance. In a few minutes he had the lanky figure in sight but well beyond easy reach.

Eiríkur clicked his communicator. "Control, zero-four-fifty-one."

216

"Zero-four-fifty-one, control. What's the problem, Eiríkur?"

"I'm in Hafnarfjördur, walking south along Strandgata, following a suspect. One metre eighty, dark curly hair, wearing a dark grey hoodie. He's coming up to Fjörukráinn, as far as I can see. I'm about two hundred metres behind him. Can I get a patrol to head him off?"

"Two minutes. Let me know if he changes route."

"Will do, thanks."

Eiríkur let himself drop back, hunching his shoulders with his hands deep in his pockets as he walked, trying to look as if he were walking to work but keeping his gaze fixed on the distant figure hurrying through the puddles. He saw the man stop, glance behind him and look around in panic, then saw the patrol car come to a halt by the side of the road. Two officers got out and one of them gently took the young man's arm.

"This is the guy, is it, Eiríkur?" one of them asked as he approached

"This is the gentleman," he replied, turning to the young man. "Manuel, or is it Julio?"

"All right, where are we going?" the first officer asked. "The station?"

"No, I'm not sure he's done anything wrong, so we just need a chat," he decided. "Drop us at the kiosk by the bank, will you?"

Jón Egill Hjörleifsson's bluster had evaporated and he was sweating heavily. Gunna brought him a cup of coffee and sat opposite him.

"Still nothing you want to tell me?"

217

"No. Speak to Julio. He'll confirm where I was on Saturday."

"We're trying to find him right now."

"What! The little shit ought to be at work by now."

Jón Egill cracked his knuckles and his eyes flashed around the room.

"So Julio is one of your employees?"

"He's casual staff, does a few shifts when he's not busy somewhere else."

"Where's he from? Julio isn't exactly an Icelandic name, is it?"

"Portugal, I think. I'm not sure."

"And his work and residence permits are in order, I presume?" Gunna asked.

"I have no idea. I expect so," he retorted and started as there was a knock.

Eiríkur put his face, complete with a broad grin, around the door. "Chief, can I have a moment?"

Gunna nodded and looked at Jón Egill. "Two minutes and I'll be back." Outside in the corridor Gunna wanted to ask Eiríkur what was so amusing, but knew she wouldn't have to. "You found him?"

"I did. He tried to do a runner, but I rustled up a patrol car to head him off."

"And?"

He confirms he was with Jón Egill Hjörleifsson on Saturday morning. In fact, he was cuddled up with him all night, until about eleven on Saturday."

Gunna hooted. "Our tough biker leans to the lavender?"

"He clearly has a sensitive feminine side, if that's what you mean."

"Fair enough, so he has an alibi. I'd better let him go, in that case. I had a feeling he wasn't our man when it came to the fire at Árni Sigurvinsson's place, but he's still tied up in all this somehow." She put a hand on the interview room door handle. "Listen, Eiríkur. I want as much pressure as possible put on this guy, so can you have a word with the immigration department and the food hygiene authorities, and ask them to have a close look at Jón Egill Hjörleifsson and his businesses?"

"Will do. Oh, by the way, there's an old boy downstairs who wants a word with you."

"What does he want? Not another talent scout for a modelling agency, is he?"

"No, says he's Johnny Depp's agent and can you fly to the Caribbean to look after him for a couple of weeks as his personal trainer is on holiday?" Eiríkur said, and there was a moment's silence.

Gunna's eyes widened in surprise. Her jaw dropped and she struggled for words as she realized that the usually reserved Eiríkur was making a joke; she was pleasantly surprised.

"Why, you cheeky young bastard," she guffawed. "Get away with you."

Eiríkur's face showed his immediate relief that the remark hadn't been taken badly. "He asked specifically to speak to the officer in charge of the missing persons inquiry. That's you."

"OK. Give him a cup of coffee and tell him I'll be along in a few minutes. I just need to tell our tough biker that his boyfriend's confirmed his alibi and he's free to go."

Magni backed the grey Skoda out through the restaurant doors and drove it round to the front of the building. He left the engine running by the front door. There was no luggage to carry out to the car.

"Come on, then," he announced. "Time to go."

Erna went outside, blinking in the brightness of the day as a band of sunlight fought its way between the towering clouds, and stood uncertainly by the car.

"Going in the front, Össi?" Magni asked.

Össur shook his head. "No. I'll sit in the back with one of the ladies." He sat in the car, making himself comfortable behind the passenger seat. "You," he said, pointing at Erna. "Get in the other side."

Erna looked imploringly at Tinna Lind, who shrugged and looked quickly at the mound of snow in the middle of the yard, which she knew the stranger was still under. "Don't argue, Mum. He has a gun," she muttered.

Magni took the driver's seat. Tinna Lind closed the hotel's door for the last time and looked around. A few stray drops of rain strafed the yard, rattling on the car's roof as she got in.

"Belts, everyone," Magni instructed. "It's going to be bumpy."

The Skoda slalomed down the slope to the road, its wheels fighting to grip the surface under a foot of snow, momentum alone keeping it from coming to an undignified halt. Erna closed her eyes and Magni whooped with relief as the wheels finally found a purchase on the rutted single-track road, thankfully under a thinner layer of slush than on the slope leading

220

from the hotel's yard. He kept the speed steady, taking the corners gently and knowing that if they were to get stuck, nobody would be likely to pull them out. In the back of the car, the couple of shovels rattled next to two jerry cans of petrol and a bag of sand he had taken from the hotel, just in case they were to hit problems.

He glanced sideways at the track leading downhill from the road to the summer house where he had hidden the dead man's van. To his relief there were no footsteps or tyre tracks to be seen in the snow.

At a junction he slowed and took the right-hand fork onto a main road that was virtually clear and looked as if a snowplough had been past only that morning. The landscape was flat and featureless beneath distant hills that were white higher up while there were signs of rapid thawing closer to ground level. At another junction Magni again slowed down and looked at the Selfoss sign that proclaimed only thirty-two kilometres, but instead put his foot down and carried on westwards instead of going south.

Össur sat still in the back, showing no apparent interest in the route or anything outside the car, one hand in his pocket where Magni had no doubt he was clasping the pistol.

"Where are we going?" Erna asked when the lake at Thingvellir appeared, its surface gunmetal grey in the flat light and rippled by the stiff wind.

"That way," Magni said as he slowed at yet another junction, wondering whether to stick to the safer but more visible main road north of the lake or the less frequently used road by the water's edge. He decided to

221

keep to the sensible route, reasoning that the other road would probably not have been cleared and he had no desire to be forced to seek help.

"My name's Gunnhildur Gísladóttir and I'm overseeing the missing persons inquiry for Erna Björg Brandsen and Tinna Lind Bogadóttir. What can I do for you?"

The man sat upright in his seat. He was a handsome character, Gunna decided. He looked to be in his seventies but his hair was thick and combed straight back, while the lines on his face around deep-set blue eyes told her that this was a practical man who liked to spend his days outside.

"My name's Grímur Halldórsson and I live at a place called Holt. It's between the Thingvellir and Apavatn lakes," he said and gave her a moment to draw a mental image of where the place might be.

"I see. I know roughly where that is."

"Well, the weather's been lousy recently and I haven't been out a great deal. I don't often watch the television and as I hadn't been out anywhere for a week or so, I hadn't seen the newspapers." He pulled a folded-up newspaper from his pocket and opened it on his knee. "So when I got to Mosfellsbær this morning I stopped for a coffee and a read of the papers at the shop there, and I saw this."

Gunna recognized the page from one of the weekend papers, with pictures of Erna Björg and Tinna Lind, as well as one of a Ford Explorer like the one owned by Erna.

"You've seen these people?"

222

"No. I haven't. But I've seen this car."

Gunna's eyebrows lifted. A search through the vehicle registry showed that there were relatively few cars of the same model in the country.

"Where?"

"Outside Hotel Hraun."

"Which is where?"

"About eight kilometres from my place at Holt. I ski that way sometimes when the weather's reasonable. The hotel's closed during the winter, so I go past there and check on the place now and again," he added.

"And have you seen these people?"

"No, I haven't. There were two men there. Spoke to one of them and he said that they were there for a break and that Ársæll, that's the owner, had said they could use the place for a few days. I thought it was odd — two men — but the man I spoke to said their girlfriends or wives or whatever had gone somewhere that day and would be back that night."

"Are they still there?"

"I've no idea. They were there last week, I'm sure enough of that. I know when I'm poking my nose in and when I'm not wanted, so I left them to it. Then the weather kicked up at the weekend and, like I said, it hasn't been travelling weather for a few days."

"Wait a moment," Gunna said and got to her feet.

"Helgi? Eiríkur?" she yelled, elbowing open the detectives' office door and glaring at them. She snatched a file from her desk. "Helgi, with me, right now. Grab a map."

"Map of where?"

"Thingvellir. Eiríkur, go and find the Laxdal and bring him to the interview room right now."

The door banged behind her and a moment later she was showing the old man Össur Oskarsson's mugshot.

"Is this one of the men?" she asked, as Helgi appeared and sat next to her.

"We can do this the easy way or we can do it the hard way," Magni warned. "And I reckon we're going to be doing it the hard way."

"Why?" Össur demanded. "You're not going that way, are you?" He shivered as he looked at the road that trailed off into the distance next to a signpost, beyond which the white landscape at some point merged into the pale sky.

"Because everything that goes through the tunnel gets filmed and the number recorded, that's why. Sooner or later they'll be on our trail and that's one of the things that'll be checked."

"So the law will think we're still in the south and not up north somewhere?"

"Precisely."

"But is the road passable?" Tinna Lind asked dubiously.

Magni beat an impatient tattoo on the steering wheel with his thumbs. "That's what we're about to find out."

The Skoda bumped down the shallow incline and Magni was relieved to see that the snow was no more than ankle deep. He kept to third gear and a moderate speed, his eyes glued to the road ahead and aware that even a shallow drift of snow could be enough to bog them down in spite of the Skoda's four-wheel drive.

A couple of times the car grounded, but its momentum was enough to keep it going through shallow drifts that meandered deceptively across the road. In places the wind had stripped the road surface bare, down to the deep potholes and long pools of dark water that Magni tried to steer around whenever he could. There was no other traffic to be seen other than a couple of roadworks vehicles parked by the side of the road in the lee of a metal shed, and Magni was thankful that nobody was likely to have noticed them.

With the junction to join the Hvalfjördur road practically in sight, the Skoda finally crunched to a halt in a drift that was a little too deep and wide for the car's speed to carry it across.

"Now we're going to have to dig," he said. He handed a pair of gloves to Tinna Lind. "Ready?"

The chill of the wind was a shock after the warmth inside the car, cutting through their coats and biting at their cheeks. Magni set to with a will, first pacing through the drift to see how far they needed to go and then scooping away snow from around the front of the car. Tinna Lind shovelled snow from underneath, trying to clear the depth of snow the car had grounded on, while Magni cleared a path in front until he reckoned they should make it.

"Everyone out," he ordered. Össur scowled and Erna's face displayed how perplexed she was.

"Why?" she asked.

"Because the lighter we can make the car, the easier it'll be to get through this lot," Magni said, clapping his hands together to restore the circulation. "And I'll need you all to push."

"Push?"

"Or you can just stay in the car until the fuel runs out and then we can all freeze to death together. Up to you," he said, getting into the driver's seat and holding the door open as he put it into gear. "All of you, line up at the back, and when I shout, lift and push. Now!"

The car inched forward, the front wheels gripping intermittently and hauling the car forward while Erna, Tinna Lind and Össur bumped the car up and down.

"Harder!" Magni yelled from the driver's seat. "Almost there! Go on, push!"

For a long moment the car seemed to sit still in the pit it had dug for itself as Magni dropped the engine revolutions as low as he could until all four wheels finally found a purchase. He sighed with relief as it gradually picked up speed out of the drift, leaving the three of them sprawling in the snow. Tinna Lind helped Erna to her feet and took her arm to help her totter through the tracks the Skoda had left, and Össur struggled to his feet, panting with exertion.

"Good stuff," Magni said when they reached where he had stopped in a clear patch of road. "With luck we won't have to do that more than a couple of times."

The Special Unit went in first and it wasn't long before six black-clad figures emerged.

226

"The place is empty," Steingrímur said with clear disappointment in his voice. "And it's a hell of a pigsty."

"Eiríkur, go round the back and check the rest of the building, take pictures of everything, including those tyre tracks," Gunna instructed. "As soon as the forensic team show up we need to get the place swept for prints so we can find out just who has been here."

The hotel's yard was full. Two squad cars had come from Selfoss and Lárus Erlendsson had brought every available officer with him. The Special Unit had been delighted to be mobilized after a quiet few months, and as well as Gunna, Eiríkur and Helgi, six more officers in two squad cars had been dispatched on the hour's drive to where Hotel Hraun occupied its quiet niche in the hills beyond Thingvellir.

Even Ívar Laxdal had arrived in his sinister black Volvo, the forensic unit following behind him. He emerged from his car and walked over to the door where Gunna and Helgi waited.

"Situation, Gunnhildur?"

"The place is deserted. The Special Unit has swept it and we'll go in and have a quick look behind the forensic team," she said, unable to hide her chagrin. "They're not long gone."

"How do you know?"

Gunna looked at the sky. "There was a bit of snowfall last night, I think; there's been some rain this morning and the snow's melting, but those tyre tracks are very fresh. Too crisp to be more than a few hours old, I'd say."

"New tyres as well," Ívar Laxdal said.

"And a mobile phone black spot, too, I see," Gunna said, looking at her phone. "If it's them, it's no surprise their phones dropped off the networks out here. It looks like four people, judging by the footprints in the snow, and you can see where the car was parked when they all got into it."

"Hell and damnation. We could have had the lot of them if we'd been a couple of hours earlier."

They watched as the two forensic technicians in their white overalls trooped in through the hotel's front door.

"Four sets of footprints tell me that Erna Björg and Tinna Lind are alive and that they're all together."

"Which is certainly something to be thankful for. D'you want to do a press conference?"

Gunna groaned. "Do we have to?"

"I think so," Ívar Laxdal decided. "If this man is armed, we ought to warn people not to approach him."

"Fair enough. Will you do it or do you want to get someone higher up the food chain to talk to the press?"

"I think I'm far enough up the pecking order to be able to take that kind of decision." Ívar Laxdal's smile was as wintry as the terrain around them. "Although I'm wondering if the officer in charge of the investigation shouldn't be the one who meets the press?"

Gunna blanched. "Really? You look so much better than I do in front of the cameras."

"We'll do it together. I'll see if I can get RÚV and Channel Two to send camera crews up here right away. If this man is dangerous, as you say, then we ought to get the warning out on tonight's evening news." He looked around at the hotel in its sheltered position with hills on three sides. "A lovely spot in the summer, but damned desolate at this time of the year," he commented.

"You've been here before?"

"A few times, dinners and the like. It used to be quite an exclusive place, but it's years since I was here last. What's that heap over there by the forensic van?"

Darkness was approaching by the time the deserted whaling station hove into view, its pier a shadow against the water, glittering in intermittent moonlight beneath ragged clouds. The Skoda's headlights swept the road ahead and Magni found himself relying on the reflective marker posts along the sides of the road. The road was mercifully clear of snow and he told himself that he had underestimated the power of the Gulf Stream that flowed around Iceland and the warm south wind to keep the coastal regions clear of snow. There had been no more need to get out and shovel the car clear of drifts, but he fretted about being late. He had wanted to be clear of the winding road around Hvalfjördur and to have completed this leg of the trip in daylight, but the long Kjós road had been a slow drive, even with just that one nervous patch they had been forced to struggle their way through.

He was already regretting not choosing the easier route that would have taken them through the tunnel. By now they would have been close to Borgarnes, and he reminded himself that soon they would have to get fuel and eat, and sooner or later they would need a place to sleep. He wondered where they could safely leave Erna without her being able to raise the alarm immediately.

The Skoda growled through the evening darkness at a steady speed, its radio burbling beside him. Every time there was a news report, Tinna Lind turned the volume up, but so far there had been nothing they needed to worry about. On the north side of the long fjord, Magni found a lay-by off the road; he pulled up and switched off the engine as he pushed open the driver's door.

"Break, everyone," he said.

He walked a few steps from the car and found that his feet were numb and his shoulders ached. The hours of concentration had taken their toll and his bladder was set to burst as, with relief, he found a tree to pee behind, wondering as he did so why he'd bothered finding privacy. Tinna Lind squatted in the bushes not far away while Erna had gone, with nervous distaste, deeper into the dark undergrowth. Össur was still in the car, lounging in the seat with the door open, his eyes half closed and a cigarette hanging from his lips.

"We have to ditch the bitch," Össur said. "Leave her here."

"You must be out of your fucking mind."

"She can walk."

"She'll die of exposure."

"It's not that far, is it?"

"When did you last go anywhere further north than Grafarholt? It's a good hour's drive from here to

Borgarnes. Leave her here and she'll be dead in a few hours. D'you want another death on your conscience?" Magni asked, and then reflected that Össur probably didn't have a conscience to trouble him.

Össur laughed a dry cackle that descended into a hacking cough. "You think I care?"

"She stays in the car," Magni said and walked away to end the argument. He rolled his shoulders and winced at the tension in them.

Tinna Lind appeared from the silent blackness of the clump of trees surrounding the lay-by and put an arm around him.

"Tired?"

"A bit."

"How far to go?"

"To where?" Magni asked. "Borgarnes is another hour at least. Akureyri five or six hours, depending on the state of the roads."

"Where do we stop tonight?"

"I've no idea. But we ought to get going."

"Listen," Tinna Lind said. "What do you plan to do with my mother?"

"Össur wanted to dump her here."

"We couldn't do that, surely?"

"That's what I said. She has to go all the way, or at least as far as Borgarnes with us. Look, we're going to have to stop and fuel up and eat somewhere. That's what worries me about your mum. Is she going to start shouting and yelling as soon as we get to somewhere there are people about?"

"There aren't any more lying about anywhere are there?" asked the bemused forensic technician, called from the hotel itself to examine the body under the snow. As the man's wallet was in his pocket, it was a mere minute's work to decide that the corpse under the snow pile was the missing Brandur Geirsson.

"This is just carnage," Gunna said, shaking her head. She put her phone back in her pocket, having walked to the far end of the yard to get a signal and demand that more equipment and the force's forensic pathologist be dispatched from Reykjavík. The few available lights were rigged up over the scene in the yard and a makeshift shelter had been erected by two officers from the Selfoss force over Brandur Geirsson's body.

"We need a search," Ívar Laxdal decided. "Checkpoints, roadblocks."

"Agreed," Gunna said. "Össur Oskarsson, Erna Björg Brandsen and Tinna Lind Bogadóttir, plus one mystery man in a grey Skoda. But where? Which way did they go? My guess is they're headed back to town."

"You're probably right, and wherever they've gone they have at least two, three hours' start, I'd reckon, maybe more."

"If they've headed for Reykjavík, then they'll be there by now, although I notice I haven't had a notification from communications to let me know that either of the phone numbers we're tracking has popped up, which should have happened very quickly after leaving here. So were their phones left behind, or dumped somewhere? Or just switched off?"

232

"Do they have any cash?" Ívar Laxdal mused.

"Probably not. Both times the man who definitely isn't Össur Oskarsson bought fuel, Erna Björg Brandsen's debit card was used. We asked Bogi Sveinsson and the bank not to cancel her cards so that we could at least see what they are buying and where."

Ívar Laxdal shaded his eyes from the glare of the lights that had been switched on by the shelter over Brandur Geirsson's body.

"They're here," he said, looking down the track leading to the road. "Come on, we'd better welcome them."

"But . . ." Gunna said, eyes on the hotel.

"Come on, Gunnhildur. Sometimes the public relations stuff has to take precedence, and the building is off-limits until forensics have finished anyway. Now we need to head the gentlemen of the press off before they get too close to the dead guy in the yard. Ready?"

Magni could feel the exhaustion in his bones. He knew that he would have to take a break some time soon if they were to avoid having an accident. He was taking care to drive at a sensible speed, knowing there were traffic cameras along the road approaching Borgarnes.

"Listen," he eventually called to the others in the dark. "We'll be in Borgarnes in a little while. We'll fuel up and we all need to eat, right?"

Erna sat silent in the back, and in the mirror Magni could see the glint of the dashboard lights reflected in her eyes.

Össur yawned. "Suits me."

233

The reflective road markers flashed past them, the headlights hitting three or four at a time on the straight sections of road, and before long the lights of Borgarnes could be seen in the distance. Magni pondered simply going straight to the motel that sat by itself on the southern side of the fjord opposite the town, but decided against it. It had to be food and fuel.

He stopped the Skoda by the furthest pump at the least busy filling station and took Erna's card from his pocket. He turned around in the seat and looked behind with the card between his fingers.

"This is going to work, right?"

Erna stared back at him. "How should I know? For all I know my husband has had the card cancelled by now."

"Try it," Össur said.

"You're sure? The police might be able to track the card when it gets used. That was all right in Reykjavík, but this is going to point a finger right at us in Borgarnes, isn't it? Does anyone have any cash? Erna?"

"I don't carry cash."

Magni grinned. "Like the Queen of England, I guess. OK, card it'll have to be, I suppose. If it doesn't work, then we're fucked." He pulled his hat down low over his eyes and turned his collar up. "Faces away from the windows, please, people. There are bound to be cameras everywhere."

He thought fast. His own card, or Erna's? Should he place himself at Borgarnes or leave a trail for the police to follow? He slotted his own card into the self-service machine and punched in numbers. Lights flashed and

234

Magni pumped fuel, carefully replaced the nozzle and twisted the filler cap shut, thankful that there had been enough credit on his card to fill the tank.

"Easy. Now, where do we eat?"

"Up to you."

He eased the car off the filling station's forecourt and a short distance back the way they had come to pull up between a handful of other cars outside a cafeteria-style eaterie.

"We go in like one big happy family, right?" he said, twisting round to look at the pair in the back. "That goes for you as well, Össi. Best behaviour. No arguments, nothing offensive, nothing that's going to attract any attention. Understood?" Össur grunted his unwilling agreement. "Erna? I'm not saying this as a threat, but you know what Össur has in his pocket and he's a desperate man. As long as nobody moves or shouts out of turn, then we'll all be out of here safe and sound with a meal inside us."

Erna scowled and nodded, her eyes narrowed with anger in the half-light.

"So. We go in. We get a table and we eat. Like I said, one big happy family, and I'm fucking starving."

As Ívar Laxdal spoke easily to the camera, Gunna envied his confidence and wished there had at least been a chance to brush her hair.

"We are naturally devoting every available resource to this," she heard him say in urbane, measured tones. "This is certainly a complex investigation that's going to require a great deal of manpower to ensure that we reach the right conclusions and apprehend those responsible," he said and paused. "Will that do?"

"Perfectly, thanks," replied the sharp-faced television presenter wearing a skirt and heels that were as far from practical for the terrain as could be imagined, and turned to Gunna. "You're next. I'll do a quick piece to camera and then ask a couple of questions. OK? You want to mention a suspect, right?"

"That was the whole point of dragging you up here," Gunna said. "The man's armed and it's important that people know about him."

"Good, good," the presenter said absently, touching up her lipstick and checking her face in a compact. She looked at the cameraman, swathed in a bulky parka. "Ready?"

"Ready when you are," he said, head cocked on one side as he looked down at the camera's screen and gave her a thumbs up.

Gunna noticed that a few yards away Ívar Laxdal was giving a second, virtually identical interview to a rival TV station's cameras.

"I'm standing in front of Hotel Hraun, a well-known name for the lavish parties, weddings and music events held here over the years, but today this household name for wholesome enjoyment has been tarnished by a series of brutal crimes that have taken place here while the hotel was closed for the winter," she said as the cameraman panned away from the presenter to the building in the distance, with the line of police vehicles parked outside.

236

"I'm speaking to detective chief inspector Gunnhildur Gísladóttir who is in charge of the investigation here today," she said, and Gunna wondered whether or not to correct the presenter, before deciding that she liked the promotion, even if it was a fictional one. "Can you confirm that the incident you're investigating here today is linked to the disappearance last week of Erna Björg Brandsen and Tinna Lind Bogadóttir?"

"I can confirm that there are links between their disappearance and what has happened here," Gunna said stiffly.

"And that a body has been found here? Have you found Erna Björg Brandsen?"

"All I can say is that the body of an adult has been located. I can't confirm anything about the person's identity or the cause of death until the forensic investigation has been completed and relatives have been informed."

"Was this person the victim of a crime?"

"As I said, I can't comment at this point and this part of the investigation is at a very sensitive stage. However, we are anxious to trace a particular individual in connection with the investigation. He is Össur Óskarsson, forty-six years of age, one seventy-four in height, short greying hair, slim build. We ask members of the public to report any sightings of him on four-four-four-one-thousand, and not to approach or challenge him. We believe he may have a firearm in his possession."

"Gunnhildur Gísladóttir, thank you. This is Arna Perla Arnarsdóttir reporting from Hotel Hraun," she finished.

237

"Can you get that out on tonight's news?" Gunna asked.

"Yep, should be able to," the presenter said. "If we get back in time we might make the seven o'clock news, otherwise definitely the bulletin at ten, and the radio news desk will get it as well." She jerked her head to the other news team at work not far away. "A shame they had to be here as well."

"Maybe, but we need to reach as many people as possible with this. D'you need a mugshot of Össur Oskarsson?"

"We could use one, I suppose."

"This guy has a gun in his pocket. Believe me, people have a right to know what he looks like. If you call the station as soon as you're in phone range, ask for the duty inspector at communications. Tell him I asked you to call and he'll email you our bad guy's mugshot. All right?" Gunna said, looking impatiently at the scene in the hotel yard. "I'm sorry, but I have to go."

Erna ate with her knife held in her hand like a pen and stacked everything on the back of her fork. She was still only halfway through her steak when Magni pushed his plate away with satisfaction and belched. Tinna Lind smiled at him fondly and dug him in the ribs with her elbow.

"I thought you said not to attract attention," she said.

They sat close together on one side of the table while Össur and Erna sat opposite them and as far away from each other as possible.

238

"Shit," Magni said, looking over the top of Erna's head.

"What?"

"Look at the TV."

They craned their necks to see the screen high on the wall and a woman wearing a police uniform and a grim expression talking to the camera with Hotel Hraun in the background behind her. Magni strained to hear what was being said but the sound was just a low mutter that he couldn't make out. A police mugshot appeared suddenly on the screen and Össur jerked his head as if someone had hit him. He looked around the room and was relieved to see that none of the few diners appeared to be taking any notice of it. Only a bored young man at the counter appeared to be watching the TV in between checking his phone.

"That's you, man," Magni said as the picture of a younger, slimmer and meaner-looking Össur left the screen to be replaced by a young woman holding a microphone in her hand and saying something serious — if the expression on her face were anything to go by — before a phone number flashed up across the bottom edge of the screen.

"Fucking hell," Össur said savagely. "Fucking bastard hell."

"It's getting on for eight o'clock now," Magni said. "It was still just about daylight in that interview, so they must have got there before four. It looks like we moved out just in time."

"There'll be cops everywhere now."

"I'm not so sure. I reckon they expect us to have gone to Reykjavík, not up here."

"Yeah. But they'll still be checking. What now?" Össur asked. He looked despondent, while Erna had the most cheerful expression Magni had yet seen on her face; not quite a smile, he decided, but close.

"We have enough fuel now to get pretty much all the way to Akureyri, I reckon."

"So we go all the way now?"

Magni glanced at Erna, and Össur quickly shut his mouth. "I don't think so. I think our best option's to hunker down somewhere for the night and get moving early when things are quiet."

"Where?"

"No idea yet, but at this time of year there must be plenty of empty summerhouses and chalets. It shouldn't be hard to borrow one for the night, and it'll probably be months before anyone notices we've been there."

Erna's slightly more cheerful, expression vanished. "I need the bathroom," she said, her voice flat.

Magni and Össur looked at each other.

"Go on," Magni said, nodding at the door. "Don't be long."

"We need to get out of here," Össur said, fretting and looking around, imagining people recognizing him from the few seconds that his picture had been on the screen. He pushed away his plate, his burger only half-eaten and his appetite gone.

"Sit still, will you?" Magni told him. "Nobody's looking at you. Nobody's noticed you. Anyway, I'm going to get a coffee."

240

He took his time, poured himself a coffee at the counter and picked up a newspaper discarded on another table. He sat down and sipped his coffee, the newspaper open in front of him.

"Good likeness. Very smart," he said, finding a page with a picture of Erna looking glamorous. "'Missing women still unaccounted for,'" he read out. "'Erna Björg Brandsen and Tinna Lind Bogadóttir were last seen leaving the Smáralind car park on Thursday last week. In spite of an intensive search, there has been no sign of them. A search has been carried out in an area where their mobile phones are believed to last have been identified. Police have confirmed that Erna Björg Brandsen's white Ford Explorer has been located and they are seeking several individuals in connection with the disappearance.' That's us, I suppose. Or rather, that's you, Össi."

Össur looked up from his fingernails and glared at the toilet door. "If she doesn't get back in here quick, I'm going to go and get her," he rasped.

Tinna Lind stood up. "I'll go," she said, and was gone before Össur had a chance to say anything.

Gunna remembered that her phone had buzzed in her pocket while she'd been trying to look serious and authoritative for the TV camera, and she squinted at its screen. The forensic team had finished sweeping the ground floor of the hotel, so she and Eiríkur gingerly made their way through the kitchen and lounge to the restaurant.

241

"That's why nobody saw a car from the air," Eiríkur said, waving at the tyre tracks across the restaurant floor. "They've made a proper mess of the place."

"Shit, hell and damnation," Gunna cursed and Eiríkur looked over at her in surprise.

"Anything the matter?"

"No, just that I forgot to let Laufey know I wouldn't be able to pick her up."

She read the message on her phone a second time.

"*Hæ, Mum. Saw you on the TV so I guess you must be busy. Got a ride home with Gísli. PS. You really should go and see him. xL*"

"Anything serious?" Eiríkur asked.

"Not really. She got a lift home with her brother, so nothing to panic over. I should have remembered, but we were in something of a hurry to get up here."

Tinna Lind's voice echoed among the empty stalls.

"Where are you?"

She checked every one, pushing open the doors and finding nothing. Sighing, she made use of one of them herself, flushed and was washing her hands when she started.

"Tinna Lind!"

"What? Where are you?"

Erna stood behind her, eyes full of doubt and distrust. "Are you coming with me?"

"Where to?"

"Anywhere. Out of here. Home."

Tinna Lind dried her hands. "No. I'm going with Magni."

242

"Why? What for?"

"Do I need to tell you?"

Erna's blank gaze illustrated her disbelief. "You're really going with these lowlifes?"

"Össur's a lowlife, I'll grant you that, but Magni is a good guy."

"For God's sake, girl. He's a criminal," Erna hissed.

"All right, he's been down on his luck. But he's no more of a criminal than I am. He's a far more decent guy than any of those braindead cockblankets in cheap suits that you keep trying to pair me off with."

"Don't you speak to me like that."

"Are you coming back out there with me?"

"No, no. Tell them I've escaped. Tell them I crawled out through a window, or something. I don't care. I can just imagine what your poor father's going through. I can't stand this any longer, Tinna Lind. I tell you that horrible man is going to drive me to distraction and one of us is going to kill the other."

"And he's the one with the gun, for the moment."

"What do you mean?"

"Nothing," Tinna Lind said, looking around. "There isn't a window in here. Look, come with me, before Össur comes in here looking for us. Mum, if anything happens, you want it to be in front of witnesses, not hidden away in here. Listen, I'm going with them and don't try to persuade me not to. But I'll be back soon. Can you at least give me and Magni a headstart? I promise we'll dump Össur in the deepest shit we can find. All right?"

"No, it's not all right. You should come with me."

"Sorry. Mind's made up," Tinna Lind said, moving awkwardly towards Erna and extending her arms. "Are you going to give me a hug before I tell the boys we need to get out of here quick?"

Össur glared as Erna and Tinna Lind returned, sensing that something had changed as they sat down. Erna's lips were pursed.

"You took your time."

"Girl talk," Tinna Lind said. "Listen, boys. We have to go, and my mum's not coming with us."

"What the fuck?"

"Shut up, will you, Össi?" Magni snapped. "We have company."

"What's going on?" Össur grated, staring at Erna, who met his eyes without flinching. "What's all this about."

"I'm staying here," Erna said. "Try and force me, and I'll howl the place down. There's a police station round the corner so you won't get far."

Össur's eyes flashed from Erna to Tinna Lind and back to Magni. "What does the hired help reckon? You cooked this up between you, did you?"

"Not at all," Magni told him. "We were going to drop the lady off somewhere safe anyway."

"She's not going to call the law the moment our backs are turned?"

"Not while I'm with you," Tinna Lind said. "We have a head start."

"When you're out of here, I'm going to have another cup of coffee," Erna said, ignoring Össur and

244

addressing Tinna Lind. "Then I'll get someone to call your father and ask him to come and get me. Tomorrow morning I'll ask him to call the police and let them know I'm safe. I just wish you weren't going with these —" Her voice cracked. "With these lowlifes."

Tinna Lind squeezed Erna's hand. "I'll be fine, Mum. Don't you worry." She pushed her chair back. "Come on, boys. It's late and we'd better go."

The forensic team had done its work and returned to Reykjavík, leaving Gunna and her team with Ívar Laxdal at the hotel. Two uniformed officers from the Selfoss force remained outside with their cars and had gently fended off a number of interested visitors from the surrounding countryside who had found reasons to be passing. Làrus Erlendsson had gone back to Selfoss with his other officers and a hearse had braved the long drive to collect Brandur Geirsson's remains to be taken to the National Hospital in Reykjavík.

"We have a ton of prints everywhere," Gunna said, yawning. "There are Össur's, Erna's and Tinna Lind's prints all over the place, plus the mystery man who doesn't have a record, and a few more that are presumably staff, which we'll have to eliminate. We'll get a lot more from forensics tomorrow, I hope, once they've started going through everything properly, but it seems that Össur was living in the bridal suite upstairs and it's a proper pigsty, with roach ends everywhere and I don't know what. Helgi, did you get hold of the owner?"

"Yep, Ársæll Jónasson. He's in Spain and I gather it was a bit of a shock to get a call from the police. He said he'd get the next flight back, although that might not be until tomorrow or the next day. He also said that they closed on the twentieth of October, and he was going to be up here next week to finish cleaning the place up before it's mothballed for the winter. Around the beginning of March they start getting things ready for the summer and they open in April."

"In that case, this was a perfect refuge. The question is, did these people know about this place or did they end up here by chance?"

"Ársæll said there are a few people with keys, including Grímur, the old boy who came to the station this morning, and the dead fire alarm guy."

"Who probably came out here to check something and was just unlucky, do you think?" Ívar Laxdal asked.

"I would guess so. Eiríkur, did you get hold of any next of kin?"

"I did. Brandur Geirsson had a sister and one of the Akranes officers has gone to see her. I reckon she'd be the best candidate to identify him."

"We know it's him. That can wait until Miss Cruz has done her stuff."

Now Helgi was yawning as well.

"It's been a long day and there's not much more we can do here tonight," Gunna decided. "Tomorrow, gentlemen. Start with Alli the Cornershop, early for preference. I want him thoroughly shaken down. Be as heavy as you like — within the rules, of course — if you think that's going to frighten the shit out of him, although he's an old lag and he's probably seen more police interview rooms than the rest of us put together."

"I remember seeing Alli the Cornershop in a cell in the old Múlin station, and that's been gone a good few years," Ívar Laxdal mused. "It was a pleasure to lock up someone like that, even if his lawyer had him out first thing the next morning."

"Happy days, and long before our time."

"Only just, Gunnhildur. Only just."

"I take it there won't be any overtime problems while this case lasts, Ívar?"

"No, just get on with it. But all of you go home now. Who needs a lift back to town?"

"Don't hurry. You'll attract attention."

They walked across the car park, expecting to hear a call or see a blue flashing light come around the corner at any moment. Magni started the engine and drove carefully out of the car park and back onto the road, turning towards the little town.

"Which way are we going?" Össur sat in the back, hunched in his coat. Magni could hear the nervous clicking of the Baikal's safety catch in Össur's pocket and hoped that when he finally fired the thing, Össur's only casualty would be himself.

"North, at least for the moment," Magni decided. "If she gets to the police, we want to be out of here before they start asking her questions."

"Are you sure, guys?" Tinna Lind said as the Skoda left the town behind and headed into the night.

"Why? What do you mean?" Össur said, leaning forward.

"What I mean is that you won't be able to get a flight out of the country from Akureyri."

"Sure you can," Össur insisted. "There are flights all the time."

"No. That's where you're wrong. There are flights only in the summer. June to September."

"You're sure?" Magni asked, glancing sideways at her.

"Absolutely. I used to work for a travel agent. Believe me, there are flights from Akureyri, but they all connect at Keflavík."

"Shit."

"Why the fuck didn't you say so before?" Össur yelled, the Baikal out of his pocket.

"Why the hell should I?" Tinna Lind yelled back. "You kidnap me and my mother on the street and keep us locked up in some miserable hole in the countryside for a week. Why should I help you?"

Össur's head was between the seats and the Baikal was under Tinna Lind's neck.

"You watch your fucking mouth or I'll give you something to think about, you and your boyfriend."

The menace was clear in Össur's voice and drops of spittle had gathered on his lips. Magni brought the car to a skidding halt by the side of the road.

"Put that pop gun away, Össi," he said in a low voice.

"You mind your fucking mouth as well. I should have known better than to trust the bastard hired help."

248

"Yeah. The hired help who got you this far. Without us you'd be in a cell by now, or else Alli and his meatheads would be giving you a hiding you'd never forget. Or get over," he added.

"Fucking pack it in! Shut up!"

Magni switched off the engine and the car was silent. "Have it your own way," he said, winding down the window and taking the key out of the ignition. "I've had enough. Put that pistol away or I'm going to chuck the key away and we can just sit here until the police come and find us."

He could hear Össur's breathing behind him coming in heavy gasps.

"Now, Össi. I'm not joking." Magni's voice dropped to a growl. "Put that thing away."

The answer was a long time coming and Tinna Lind held her breath, listening to the blood pounding at the back of her head.

"All right." The Baikal clicked once and Össur settled back in the seat. "Go on, then. Move."

CHAPTER
SEVEN

Wednesday

"Good morning, Alli."

Gunna breezed into the interview room and sat down facing him with a smile that she forced onto her face. Alli the Cornershop scowled back at her.

"What the fuck am I doing here?"

Gunna sat in silence and took her time leafing through the folder she had brought with her. Eiríkur sat impassive at the end of the table.

"You're an old friend, aren't you?"

"I choose my friends carefully," Alli retorted.

Of course you do. Like this gentleman." She slapped the postmortem picture of Árni Sigurvinsson on the table in front of him. "Now. Tell me what you know." Alli avoided looking at the print where Gunna held it, her finger pinning it to the table in front of him, forcing him to look up and meet her gaze. His eyes were dark pools of anger glaring back at her. "Árni Sigurvinsson was a good friend of yours and now he's dead."

"I'll send his old woman some flowers."

"Let's start with Friday morning, shall we? What did you do on Friday? Talk me through every single moment of your day."

Alli stared at her and wrinkled his nose. "I got up about ten and went out for breakfast."

"Where?"

"The coffee shop in the mall. Ask them. They'll remember me."

"I'm sure they will. Who was with you?"

"Baldvin."

"Ah, Baldvin Ásgeirsson? He's talking to my colleague in the next room and I hope for your sake he's telling the same tale."

A moment of uncertainty could be seen in Alli's eyes. "Baldvin's not bright, you know?"

"We'll find out, won't we? Now let's wind the tape back, shall we? When did you last see Árni?"

"I don't know. Wednesday or Thursday."

"You didn't make a note in the famous little black book?"

"There never was a book." Alli leaned forward and tapped his temple with a forefinger. "It's all in here. Sharp as a knife."

"So was it Wednesday or Thursday?"

"Thursday, I reckon," Alli said. "Thursday afternoon. He stopped by for a coffee and a chat."

"A friendly chat, was it?"

"Of course."

"And how long did he stay?"

"Half an hour. Something like that. He had some job on that he was going to do."

"And after Árni left, what did you do?"

"Stayed in. Watched a movie. Had a couple of cans. Went to bed."

"Before midnight, with a mug of cocoa and an improving book?"

"You took the words right out of my mouth."

"So you slept right through from midnight to ten the next morning?"

Alli scratched his head and sat back in his chair. "Absolutely. Didn't even wake up for a piss."

"And who's going to confirm that? Live alone these days, don't you, Alli?"

"Baldvin was there. He slept on the couch downstairs."

"Would you like to tell me how Baldvin managed to get his teeth punched out? Or did he fall down the stairs on Thursday afternoon?"

Magni prised his eyes open. He saw the pale wood planks of the ceiling and wondered where he was. He lifted his head and looked to one side. He smiled to himself at seeing the top of Tinna Lind's head nestled under his arm.

"Hey," he murmured. "You awake, sweetheart?"

"Hmmm. Yeah. I just don't want to move yet."

Tinna Lind mumbled and wrapped the borrowed duvet around herself as Magni slipped from under it and padded to the chalet's bathroom. The smile on his face was replaced with disappointment when he saw the top of Össur's head protruding from under another duvet on the couch.

He did what he needed to and went quietly back to bed without waking Össur up, gently closing the door

252

behind him. Slipping back under the duvet, he wrapped his arms around Tinna Lind and whispered in her ear.

"Hey. It's daytime. And we need to be out of here before someone notices us."

"I know. Don't remind me." She stretched and snaked an arm under Magni's ribs, pulling him on top of her. "Did you wake Össur up?"

"No, he's snoring."

"Good. We don't know what's going to happen today, do we?"

Magni nuzzled Tinna Lind's neck. "Not yet. Talk about it later."

She shivered as he took an earlobe between his teeth. "It's like living on the edge, isn't it?"

"How do you mean?" Magni asked absently, his knee gently parting her legs.

Tinna Lind buried a hand in the thick hair at the back of his neck and hauled his head back until she could look into his eyes.

"I mean we don't know where we'll be in a few hours, or tonight, or tomorrow."

"Yeah." He grinned. "There's a sort of excitement to it, isn't there?"

She ran her fingers down his face, lingering in the red beard that had thickened during the past week.

"It's exciting and scary. It's like we have to make the most of every second," she whispered. "Any minute could be our last moment together."

"I'd like you to tell me what happened to your face," Helgi suggested.

"Nothing much."

Helgi grunted and, like Gunna in the next interview room, he had spent long enough looking through the file to make his interviewee impatient.

"Baldvin Ásgeirsson," he said finally. "You're aware that you have a current suspended sentence?"

"Yeah. I haven't done anything wrong," Baldvin mumbled. His jaw still ached.

"I didn't say you had. But you have a decent enough track record of being handy with your fists. So who knocked your teeth out?"

"Fell over," Baldvin mumbled eventually. "Pissed," he added after a pause and bridled at Helgi's dubious expression.

"Right. If you say so, but we'll come back to that. You know we don't get many murders in Iceland. One a year, give or take. Some years there are none. But right now we have two. It's unheard of to get two such serious crimes within a day or two of each other."

"Murder? Who's that, then?"

Helgi pushed a copy of the same print that Gunna had shown to Alli across the table and Baldvin stared at it.

"Árni," he said at last.

"Well done, go to the top of the class. Murdered."

"That was an accident, wasn't it?" Baldvin asked, his forehead creased in confusion.

"What would you know about that?"

Baldvin shrugged. "That's what the word is."

"And where did you hear that?"

"Just heard it about."

"We'll start with Thursday. The day you lost your teeth. Talk me through what you did and where you were."

"Is this going to take long?"

Helgi clasped his hands together and put them under his chin, elbows planted on the table. "It'll take as long as it needs."

There was a tap on the door and Eiríkur opened it.

"Helgi, we're needed for a minute," he said.

There wasn't much for breakfast, just a couple of packets of biscuits and a bag of apples and bananas they'd picked up at a late-night kiosk the previous evening, and tea made with tea bags that had been in the chalet's cupboard for a long time. The place was cold. There was no heating, and although there was an iron stove and wood to burn, there was no question of them advertising their presence and waiting for visitors to show up.

Össur was still swaddled in a duvet, hands clasped around a mug of tea. He looked dazed after the exertions of the day before and Magni could see his hands trembling.

"So what now?" Magni asked.

"Don't know." Össur sighed. "I just don't know."

Tinna Lind came in from the bathroom and huddled next to Magni, shaking out the double duvet over their shoulders.

"What's the plan, boys?"

Össur glared at her. "How do we know there are no flights from Akureyri?"

"Because there aren't," she snapped back. "I spent two summers working for a travel company and I know.

It's not difficult to work out. There are flights to Britain, Germany, Denmark and Holland during the summer; June, July and August only. The last flights are always the first week in September. There's no point running flights when there aren't any tourists."

"I thought there were."

Tinna Lind spoke to him as if explaining things to a child. "Look, you can book a flight from Akureyri outside the tourist season if you want to, but it'll land at Keflavík and connect with an overseas flight there."

"The thing is," Magni said, munching a dry biscuit. "If there's a flight from Akureyri and it connects at Keflavík, do we go through passport control, customs and all that at Akureyri where we get on the plane, or at Keflavík, where it connects?"

"Akureyri, I think," Tinna Lind said. "I'm not entirely sure. But in any case, air travel is so tight these days that there are probably checks at both."

"Shit. It's all turned to fucking shit," Össur cursed. "All because that useless fuckwit Árni couldn't get there on time."

"And now he's dead."

"Yeah. And I'm wondering why. That evil bastard Alli the Cornershop must have got to him. It has to be Alli."

"So who's this Alli, then?" Tinna Lind asked, biting into an apple.

"Don't you know?"

"Of course I don't know. Otherwise I wouldn't have asked, would I? Listen, I'm not a criminal like you. I've no idea who these gangsters are."

Össur took a deep breath. "Alli the Cornershop is one of half a dozen people who control most of the dope. He gets some of it brought in by mules who swallow it wrapped in plastic and shit it out, or else they just carry it in their luggage or whatever. Mostly it comes hidden away in shipping containers and things like that. There's all kinds of ways of doing it. He also has a couple of growing operations here and there, and he does girls as well."

"He sounds a fantastic character," Tinna Lind said with distaste. "How do you know all this?"

"Because, prissy miss, I've known Alli for years, doing deals and keeping an eye on a few things for him. He's ruthless, let me tell you."

"And then you decided to pop your fingers in the till and run for it?"

"Yeah. It was all planned out, and if that fuckwit Árni had turned up on the dot, we'd have been home and dry and way out of Alli's reach."

"So I suppose he's not going to welcome you with open arms?" Magni asked.

"You're joking, aren't you? Alli's going to want payback and it's going to hurt."

"Only if he catches us." Magni thought for a moment. "Listen I know it's a stupid question, but what if you gave yourself up? You could grass on him and the court might let you off?"

"What? Murder?"

"Yeah, well. I suppose there is that," Magni admitted. "The coppers tend to take a dim view of that."

"But apart from all that," Tinna Lind broke in. "We need to be on the move soon, so are we going north to Akureyri or back to Reykjavík and try and get a flight from Keflavík?"

"Akureyri's safer for the moment, I guess," Magni said. "Nobody will expect us to go that way."

"Unless your mother spills the beans, and you can bet she's in a police station right now singing her heart out," Össur said bitterly. "I knew we shouldn't have let her out of our sight."

"What's done is done. So do we do a double bluff and go to Reykjavík? It's easier to hide away in a bigger place, but there'll be more people looking for you there," Magni pointed out.

"Looking for us, you mean. If they pick me up, they'll pick you up as well."

"On the whole, I reckon I'd rather meet the law than Alli the Cornershop."

Magni let the Skoda warm up, and by the time they trooped through the puddles of meltwater, their breath steaming in the cool air, the car was cosy and Össur let out a sigh of relief as he sank into the seat behind Magni.

He reversed the car into a turn and let it bump down the track, its underside scraping on the hardened snow.

"Where is it then?" he asked, stopping the car and turning around in his seat. "North or south?"

Össur shrugged and huddled deep into his coat.

Tinna Lind reached down and took a coin from the car's ashtray. She flipped it in the air and they watched it spin until she caught it neatly in the palm of one hand and slapped it on the back of the other, holding her hand over the coin.

"You call," she ordered, looking at Össur.

Össur's brows knitted. "Heads we go north, tails we go south."

Tinna Lind lifted her hand and looked at the coin.

"Reykjavík, here we come," she said, dropping the coin back in the ashtray and Magni wondered if it really had been tails or if it had been her decision.

"I suppose we'd better play safe and go the long way round again," he said.

Erna sat upright in a leather chair in her own living room. The radio burbled in an undertone and a glass of water with a couple of ice cubes and a slice of lime in it stood on the table in front of her.

Bogi Sveinsson sat at the end of the sofa, Erna's hand in his. "Last night. I got a call late last night," he said happily. "So I went and got her."

Eiríkur wondered what had happened. Erna had a poise to her that didn't ring true for someone who'd been held hostage for a week in a remote hotel. Her hair was pristine and her makeup had been artfully applied. He thought he could see lines of fatigue at the corners of her eyes, but not having anything to compare with made it difficult to tell.

"I guess you have quite a story to tell," he said.

Erna's eyes looked blank and she dropped Bogi's hand to reach for the glass of water. She sipped demurely.

"I don't really know."

"How do you mean? I hope you can give me an account of what happened to you over the last week. You disappeared a week ago today."

"I really don't remember very much."

Erna's hand dropped over the arm of the chair and Bogi again cradled it.

"How do you mean?" Eiríkur asked. "You don't recall anything? Do you recall where you were when you met the two men?"

"In Hafnarfjördur. In the car park outside the shopping centre. They got in the car behind us and told us to drive."

"And where did they make you go?"

"I'm not sure. They just gave directions and I went where they said. We went out of the city. I'm not sure where." Erna sighed. "I'm exhausted," she said, "but Bogi said we should call the police."

"I would have thought you would have called last night, especially as your daughter is still missing. Locating her is our main priority, and anything you can tell us is of paramount importance. Have you any idea where she might be?"

Erna shook her head. "Absolutely none."

"All right. The men who abducted you. What can you tell me about them."

"One of them had a gun. I didn't believe it was real and then he fired it. It was deafening," she said with a shudder, and Bogi squeezed her hand. "I was petrified."

"Can you describe them?"

"One of them was quite short and ugly, with grey hair. The other one was a big man, quite a bit younger, I think."

"How old?"

"About your age, probably."

"Did you hear names?"

"The older man's name is Össur, I think. I'm not sure about the younger one."

"You didn't hear them talking?"

"No. The place we were must have been a hotel or a hostel. I stayed upstairs in the room as much as I could."

"And your daughter? Did she stay with you?"

"Yes."

"She was in another room? You were kept apart?"

Erna nodded. "Not exactly kept apart. I chose to keep away from them as much as I could. The men frightened me, especially Össur, the older man, the one with the gun."

"Unfortunately we found the hotel only an hour or two after you must have left. This may sound an odd question," Eiríkur said, "but did you hear them say anything at all about why they were on the run? And why they car-jacked you and decided to hide away in the countryside?"

"I think they had committed some crime — I'm not sure — or else they had been in a fight with someone. I seem to recall someone called Árni being mentioned, but I can't be sure."

Eiríkur nodded, satisfied with an answer for the first time. "Were you mistreated at all? Molested?"

"No. Not really. They were harsh, but they left us alone for the most part."

"But they took your car and your credit card, didn't they? You gave them your security number?"

"I thought it would be best, and it occurred to me that maybe you would be able to trace us when it was used."

Eiríkur smiled. "Exactly. We saw one of the men on CCTV buying fuel twice. Unfortunately he took care, so we couldn't see him clearly enough to identify him. Can you tell me what happened yesterday? How come you managed to get away from the men but your daughter didn't? Do you know where they went or where they were planning to go?"

"We left the hotel in the afternoon when it was still light and we drove a long way. The younger man was driving and I sat in the back with Össur. He had a hand in the pocket where he had the gun the whole time. I was terrified he was going to use it if things went wrong. Anyway, we drove for a long time and I'm not sure where we went, but I recognized the old whaling station, so it must have been Hvalfjórdur, and then we were at Borgarnes."

"And what happened there?"

"They bought fuel again. We were all terribly hungry. It had been a very long day and they had an argument. The younger one said we should all just go to one of those cafeteria places and have something to eat. The older one didn't like the idea, but the young one said it would be fine and nobody would notice them. So he gave in and we went for some food."

262

"And then?"

"While we were eating there was a television on, and there was a report on the news from the hotel, and pictures of myself and Tinna Lind. Össur was either angry or frightened, I couldn't tell which, so he wanted to go. I said I had to go to the bathroom and then I crawled out of a window and hid. When I saw the car drive away with them in it, I went back inside and sat down again."

"I'm wondering why you didn't call the police right away. That way they could have stopped them before they'd gone far."

Erna was silent and put her fingertips to her temples. "I don't know. I think I was in shock. It was only when the place was closing that the waitress asked if I was all right, and I said I wasn't, so she let me call Bogi." She smiled fondly at him. "And he came to rescue me."

"Now tell me," Eiríkur said, "how come your concern for your daughter doesn't extend to informing the police right away?"

Erna's smile vanished.

"It's not as if you can just turn up at the airport and go. They don't let you do that these days," Tinna Lind said. "It's not like a bus. In any case, they'll have your names, won't they?"

Össur scowled, huddled down low in the back seat, and chewed his fingernails as Mosfellsbær rolled past outside and the stream of traffic thickened steadily. It felt uncomfortable and welcoming at the same time to be approaching the city where he felt most at home but in which also lurked all kinds of hidden dangers.

"So if we don't go straight to the airport, where can we go?"

"He's right," Magni said. "We can't just drive around all day."

Tinna Lind rubbed her hands together and thought.

"Passports," she said finally. "I guess you guys have passports, but they won't be any use to you now. You can bet anything you like that if your names show up at immigration, there'll be red lights and alarm bells going off everywhere. So we all need to get passports. You guys are the criminals. Over to you," she said finally.

"Ask him," Magni said, jerking his thumb at Össur in the back seat.

Tinna Lind twisted herself around in her seat. "Ideas, Össur?"

"It's expensive. Alli will sell you a passport if you really need it, but it costs an arm and a leg."

"And Alli is the absolute last person in the world you want to be doing business with right now," Magni said.

"Come on, you guys," Tinna Lind said. "You're the brains here, but I'm the one doing your thinking for you."

"There is a guy we could try, but I'd have to call him," Össur said dubiously. "He's not the kind of guy I'd want to meet anywhere quiet, if you get my meaning." He pulled a battered mobile phone from deep inside a pocket and peered at the little screen. "His number's in this, but the battery's flat."

"So we need a place to crash and somewhere to charge Össur's phone," Magni said. "I think I can do that, but best behaviour from you two, all right? Especially you in the back."

"And internet," Tinna Lind added. "When we have names to travel under, we need to book flights online, and have a card to pay for them. D'you still have my mother's card? Didn't you use it last night to buy fuel?"

"I still have it, but I didn't use it," Magni said. "I used my own card for the fuel because I reckoned your mum's card could be traced, and we daren't use it to buy flights. Don't worry. I'll figure something out. I wonder what your mother has been telling the police?"

Baldvin was sweating hard and looking increasingly uncomfortable as he shifted nervously in the chair opposite Helgi, who read back through his notes.

"You spent all day at Alli's house, as you usually do because you run errands for him. That evening you had a few too many to drink and fell over on the pavement outside, which is when you broke your teeth. You went to A&E that evening as well — my colleague is checking with the hospital records to see if your story balances with what they say," he said. "On Thursday night you were dosed up with painkillers, or so you say, and woke up at midday on Friday, again at Alli's place." Helgi took off his glasses and tapped them against his chin. "It's taken a long time to get there, but is all that correct?"

"Yeah. That's it."

Helgi opened the folder and took out a set of prints that he laid on the table in a pile.

"Right. This is Alli's VW Golf," he said, showing Baldvin the first print. "Last year's model, isn't it? Nice car."

"Yeah."

"These were taken at the N1 filling station at the corner of Lækjargata just after ten on Thursday evening. That's you pumping fuel there," he said and showed Baldvin the second print.

There was a tremor in Baldvin's voice. "Yeah. Alli asked me to take it up there and fill the tank."

"That doesn't look like a man who reckons he was zonked out on painkillers," Helgi said as he placed a third picture in front of Baldvin. "He asked you to fill a can as well?"

Baldvin hung his head as he saw the clear image of himself pumping fuel into a five-litre can.

"I . . ." He stuttered and paused, looking around the room.

Helgi sat back. "Go on," he invited. "I can see from the CCTV that you were buying unleaded for the car and you pumped the same into the can. Unleaded petrol was the accelerant used at the house fire that killed Árni Sigurvinsson. So if we search the place you live in and Alli's house, I'd bet good money we'll find an empty petrol can with a few drops of unleaded in the bottom."

"Alli asked me to buy petrol. I don't know what he wanted it for."

As the realization sank in, Baldvin's face paled to the same washed-out colour as the wall behind him.

"As far as I'm concerned, you're a suspect for the murder of Árni Sigurvinsson. You bought petrol. I reckon there was a dispute between Árni and Alli. You work for Alli as an enforcer. You're not able to account convincingly for your movements from Thursday afternoon until Friday morning. Alli was at home, but that doesn't mean to say you couldn't have gone out quietly and done what you wanted to. Árni's place is five minutes down the hill. You could have been there and back in ten, fifteen minutes."

"So you're keeping me locked up?"

"What would you do? The facts seem pretty much stacked against you, don't they?"

"So what is this place?" Tinna Lind asked, looking around the apartment. It was a light, airy apartment, sparsely but comfortably furnished.

"It belongs to a mate. Used to be married to my ex-wife's sister years ago, so we share having both been married to crazy women."

"And he knows we're here?"

"Of course not," Magni said. "He's an engineer on a seismic ship in Russia and he's away for two months at a time. I reckon it'll be a good while before he's back."

"Not bad." She sank back into one of the deep armchairs. "So this is some kind of bachelor pad?"

"It is now. He had a bit of a fling a year or so ago, so his girlfriend walked out in a huff and hasn't been back."

267

"He doesn't mind you staying here?"

"Well . . ." Magni said. "Y'know, I have a key and so I keep an eye on the place for him while he's away, and we have an understanding that if I need to crash, then that's no problem as long as I leave the place as I find it. Which might be a problem with Össur being such a dirty bastard," he added.

"You mean you can use it as a shag pad if you get lucky?" Tinna Lind asked sweetly.

"Yep." Magni grinned. "That's about it."

"Well, maybe if you play your cards right you could get lucky tonight, I suppose."

Magni rooted through a drawer in the kitchenette in the corner of the long living room and came up with a couple of phone chargers.

"Össi! Phone!"

Össur appeared from the bathroom zipping up his trousers. He fished in his pocket and handed Magni his old-fashioned Nokia.

"Looks like the one," Magni said, comparing the phone with the tangle of wires and plugging one in. "We shall see." He plugged the other end into the wall socket and was rewarded with a signal tone from Össur's phone. "There you go. Give it a minute to start charging and then you can give it a try."

"This is the guy who can sort out passports, is it?" Tinna Lind asked.

Össur grunted in reply.

"Do we get to know who this guy is?"

"You don't want to, believe me," Össur replied, and Magni could sense the fear in his voice.

268

Ívar Laxdal's office was a fairly large one, but it still seemed crowded with Gunna, Helgi and Eiríkur grouped around his desk.

"We have Alli the Cornershop and his latest boneheaded enforcer, Baldvin Asgeirsson, in separate interview rooms, each with a uniformed officer for company. Helgi feels we have enough to hold the bonehead in custody. We're not sure about Alli," Gunna said. "I'd like a search warrant to go through his place. I'm as certain as I can be that Baldvin started the fire, certainly on Alli's instructions. If we can come up with the petrol can, preferably empty, then we'd have something to hold him on."

"And if you don't?"

"We let him go. But knowing the kind of business Alli is in, it seems unlikely we won't come across something that'll let us keep hold of him."

"Unthinkable, I'd say," Helgi put in, while Ívar Laxdal rubbed his chin and listened to the rasp of thumbnail on bristle.

"Don't underestimate Alli the Cornershop," he said finally. "He's been a pain in the neck for years with dope, bootleg booze, handling stolen goods, collecting debts, supplying teenage Russian escorts, and all the rest of it. But we've never been able to make a serious charge stick. Don't forget I remember the bastard of old, before any of you joined the force."

"He's a sly old fox," Helgi agreed. "I'm wondering if we push Baldvin hard enough, will he crack and finger Alli?"

Gunna shook her head. "He might crack, but I doubt he'd implicate Alli. Baldvin's life wouldn't be worth living if he did that, inside prison or out of it. Nobody likes a grass. Baldvin may be dim but he's not that stupid. He wouldn't dare unless he had a cast-iron assurance of a suspended sentence, and he'd never get off that lightly."

Ívar Laxdal nodded slowly. There was a grim look on his heavy face, but Gunna could see a twinkle of glee behind his dark eyes.

"It won't do any harm to push him as hard as you like, Helgi. Go ahead. Pile the pressure on him as hard as his lawyer will let you without complaining too much. Do the same with Alli, and I'll apply for the warrant, which I don't imagine will be a problem. Now, the other side of all this. What's the story there?"

"We don't have a clue where three of the four missing persons are, but one of them turned up safe and sound at home last night, and was considerate enough to call and let us know this morning," Gunna said, and Ívar Laxdal's eyebrows crept upwards in question. "Eiríkur?"

"That's right," Eiríkur said. Ívar Laxdal still made him nervous and he had to force himself not to gabble. "Erna Björg Brandsen's husband called in this morning to say that she had returned last night. Gunna and Helgi were busy, so I went to her home and asked as many questions as I could."

"And?"

"Claims she crawled out of the toilet window at a filling station café in Borgarnes and ran for it. When she saw the others drive away, she went back to the cafe and just sat there until someone asked if she was all right and let her use the phone to call her husband, who went to collect her."

"So the others — the daughter, Össur and the unknown man — are all still on the loose? Did she tell you anything that could lead to them?"

"No," Eiríkur said. "Not really. She claims she was in a daze most of the time. She didn't know the other man's name, didn't notice the number of the car they are travelling in and didn't even recognize the model, other than to say it was a grey estate. There are so many holes in what she's saying that it's hard to know where to start."

"Did she identify Brandur Geirsson's killer?"

"She said Össur had a gun and she saw him fire it at least once, and saw Brandur Geirsson collapse."

"Good. We have a witness," Ívar Laxdal said. "Is she stringing us along, or just being selective?"

"I'd say she's definitely not telling us everything. No question. Plus she seems oddly unconcerned about her daughter. That's the part I can't get my head around. If it was my child, I'd be frantic."

The fingers of one of Ívar Laxdal's meaty hands drummed the table. "My approach would be to arrest Baldvin and let him stew in a cell, and for you to push Alli as hard as you can, Gunnhildur, and leave these two gentlemen to have a serious talk with the lady, preferably without her husband being present. Don't be rough on her, but just go through every tiny detail until she slips up. If she hasn't had a medical examination after a week of being held hostage, then she ought to, and a psychiatric examination may be in order, too." He looked up and surveyed the team sitting in front of him. "I'll get your warrant as soon as I can. Take a couple of uniformed officers and I'm sure someone from narcotics will be only too happy to take a close look at Alli the Cornershop's house."

"We'll see. I'm not expecting a wily old operator like Alli to leave anything incriminating lying around," Gunna said.

A wintry smile lit up Ívar Laxdal's craggy face. "Maybe not, but we'll see if he's slipped up for once, or if his pal with the broken teeth has."

"If there's anything there, we'll find it." She looked at her watch and scowled. "And right now I have an important appointment that I'm already late for."

"My fault, Gunnhildur. Just say it's my fault."

"I always do," Gunna assured him.

Rafn was starting to feel at home in a suit. Planning officials generally found themselves at a sudden disadvantage presented with a man in a designer suit when they had been expecting a thug in leathers. But it was as well to dispose of the suit once the meetings were over and he had to mix with his own people again. In fact, the suit lived in a shallow wardrobe in the corner of what Rafn called his office, the boardroom at the Undertakers' headquarters.

It had once been an industrial building halfway down a sprawling trading estate, between a busy road and the shoreline that had once been a shipyard. The area was rapidly becoming urbanized as smart rows of terraced houses sprang up. The company that had previously owned the building had moved on and the Undertakers had bought the place, something that a few of them now realized had been a very shrewd move on their part, which was largely down to Rafn's business acumen. The old workshops had come with a surprising amount of ground, according to the deeds, some of which the local authority had encroached on, and which the local government suits had belatedly admitted meant a substantial amount of money was owed in compensation.

Things were looking good for the Undertakers, Rafn felt. He wondered how many of them had figured out that the building and the surrounding land, a strip of which was now being negotiated over with a developer as the surrounding area continued to change from semi-industrial sprawl to chic residential, actually belonged not to the association itself but to a company partly owned by the Undertakers, which was also owned by himself and two or three of the smarter members.

He hung the suit in the shallow cupboard and pulled on his jeans and a T-shirt. Rafn looked in the mirror and untied the band holding his long hair back, letting it fall down his back instead. He felt pleased with himself. The development plans were looking promising, with the Undertakers set for a percentage of the profits instead of a flat purchase price on the line of houses and flats that would be built on the edge of their land. With a few more careful investments, they could find themselves legitimate and still respectably profitable in a few years' time. It would be a relief to dispose of a few of their illegal rackets, although it could be a wrench as there were undoubtedly some that would be worth keeping a discreet hold of.

Rafn's phone buzzed and he answered it just as Jón Egill walked into the office.

"Rafn."

Jón Egill stood in the doorway and Rafn motioned him in to take a seat.

"You see, it's a little sensitive at the moment," Rafn said and winked at Jón Egill. "I reckon your name's pretty toxic right now, Össi," he said, dropping the name and watching Jón Egill spin round from gazing out of the window.

"Össi Oskars?" he mouthed, and Rafn nodded.

"It depends, Össi. It depends on your situation and what you have to negotiate with. I get your meaning and understand perfectly that you're in a difficult position. What I don't quite get is what you're asking for. Are you asking us to do you a favour, purely and simply for the love of it, or do you have something to give us in return for what you're asking?"

Rafn managed to sound businesslike in spite of the grin on his face, which Jón Egill found himself sharing.

"No problem, Össi. Always ready to talk, but business is business, you know? All right, man. Think about it and give me a call back," Rafn said. "Yeah, any time."

He ended the call and sat back in his chair while Jón Egill leaned against the window sill and grinned.

"That was Össi Oskars, was it? He's come out of hiding?"

"It was," Rafn confirmed. "And he's in the shit up to his neck."

"Well?"

Magni stood in the doorway with folded arms as Össur put the phone down. "What did your mate have to say? It doesn't sound like he was all that pleased to hear from you."

Össur's face was even paler than usual. "He's all right, is Rafn. Known him since he was a boy," he said with unconvincing false confidence.

"And now he sells illegal passports?"

"And a few other things as well. But he's a good lad, he'll sort us out."

The corners of Tinna Lind's mouth bowed downwards in distrust. "So who is he?"

"He's a businessman, of sorts," Össur replied, a smile revealing darkened teeth. "He's an Undertaker."

"One of the bikers?"

"What do you think?"

"All right," Magni broke in. "So what did he say? Can he come up with three passports good enough to get us out of the country?"

"Yep . . ."

"There's a catch, I take it?"

"It'll cost something," Össur said. "These guys don't do anything for nothing."

"Then you'd better find out and see if we can afford it. Go on, call him back."

"I'll have to meet him somewhere."

"You mean we'll have to meet him somewhere."

Össur's face twisted in doubt. "I don't know. It'd be best if I meet him. I know this lad."

"I don't think so, Össi. All of us or none of us."

"You don't trust me?" Össur barked.

Magni laughed. "Össi, would you trust you?"

Gunna was distressed to see how tired Gísli looked. He sat at a table with a glass of water in one hand and his phone in the other. As she walked into the café his face lit up with a smile and he stood up to kiss her cheek.

"_Hæ_, sweetheart," she said, sitting down. "I'm sorry I'm late. The Laxdal kept me talking and I couldn't just walk out."

Gísli passed her his menu. "Law and order keeping you busy right now, is it?"

"Just a bit. Have you already decided what you're having?"

"I'll go for the burger with bacon."

"The same for me. And can you get a jug of water?"

Gunna collected her thoughts while Gísli went to the counter. The café was a place only open from seven until around four, serving breakfasts and cheap, solid lunches for a clientele of mostly students and tradesmen. She reflected that sooner or later it would be discovered and would gradually slip upmarket and become more expensive while its original customers would, a few at a time, find somewhere else to chat or read the paper while they ate.

276

"Five minutes," Gísli said, placing a jug of iced water and another glass on the table.

"You know the story that's been in the papers about the two women who disappeared?"

"Yeah. I've seen that."

"That's what I'm working on and it's at the top of the priority list at the moment."

"Fair enough. In that case I'd better not ask anything. I know you're not supposed to talk about work."

"I'm always ready to not talk about work. But it does mean I can't hang around for long," Gunna said, shaking off her coat and hanging it over the back of her chair. "Oh, and I have to go and search someone's house this afternoon."

"One of . . .?"

"No, not one of them. But don't ask."

The burgers arrived, fragrant and reassuringly solid, with a vast bowl of chips.

"I thought we could share these," Gísli said.

"I think you'd better eat all of those chips, otherwise I'll have to be shopping for new trousers on the way home. How's your . . ." She hesitated as she sliced into the burger. "How's Thorvaldur?"

"He's not great, Mum. He doesn't have long to go." Gísli's face twisted in discomfort. "You really didn't want me to contact him, did you?"

"No. Not really. He had a zero track record of wanting to be your dad, so I couldn't figure out why you wanted to meet him."

"Curiosity, Mum. Remember that?"

"Curiosity killed the cat," Gunna reminded him, taking a chip, dipping it in mayonnaise and pointing it at him before eating it.

"That's good, coming from a detective." Gísli grinned. "Your whole work revolves around digging into other people's business."

"True. I get to poke my nose into all sorts and get paid for it. All right. I wasn't happy that you wanted to see your dad," she said, skewering a forkful of salad as misplaced penance for the chips. "I can understand it, but I didn't feel the time was right. I thought you were spreading yourself too thin. Two small children, the two girls, and then there was Naomi," she added and her voice tailed off. "So what's troubling Thorvaldur? Has a life of excess caught up with him?"

"You could say that. The woman he'd been living with for a long time died last year and it hit him hard. It was after that that he seemed ready to talk to me, as if she had been the one who didn't want his children sniffing around."

"Thorvaldur and his many women . . ." Gunna said, trying to keep the chagrin out of her voice.

"Anyway," Gísli said, "he has bowel cancer. It was already far advanced before he got round to going to the doctor to find out what was wrong with him and he doesn't have long."

"How long?" Gunna asked, feeling a sudden chill and not wanting to hear the answer.

"Days, probably. He could still get about until a few days ago, but he was admitted to hospital on Sunday night and the only way he's coming out is feet first. So

278

now I feel I did the right thing in making contact with him before it was too late."

"You're right," Gunna said. "You were right and I was wrong."

Eiríkur sat with a bewildered Bogi Sveinsson in the overstuffed living room while Erna rigidly sat opposite Helgi in the television lounge of the sprawling house, tears threatening to flow at any moment. Helgi was tired and making an effort not to be irritable, while Erna's hands were starting to tremble.

"You understand that we are doing everything we can to locate these two men and your daughter, so anything you can tell me would be a help. Even a minor detail could lead us to the person we're looking for," he said, taking a deep breath and preparing to go over the same ground a second time. "Your daughter, Tinna Lind, I'm trying to get a handle on how she interacted with the two criminals. There was no hostility there?"

"There was with Össur, not with the other man."

"You're saying they didn't get on badly?"

Erna shrugged. "I think so."

"They got on well enough? There were no arguments with the younger man? You've given us a description, but it doesn't tie in with anyone in particular in our files. Had you ever seen this man before?"

Erna shook her head.

"You were together in that hotel for almost a week, so there must have been some conversation, surely? You didn't hear the man's name mentioned even once?"

"Össur?"

"The other man, the younger one."

"Well, I suppose I did hear him called Markús or Magnús or something like that a few times."

"Did you get the feeling that Tinna Lind and this man might have known each other?"

"I don't know . . ." Erna said. "They did seem quite friendly after a while."

"Friendly? How friendly?"

"They did the cooking and things like that and they spent quite a lot of time together."

"In the downstairs part of the hotel, or together alone somewhere?"

Erna looked down at the table and Helgi could see an internal battle going on.

"She's always been damned headstrong," Erna suddenly burst out. "Ever since she could walk she's done everything her own way and never listened to a single word I've said to her. She could have had a decent job if she'd managed to stick at something, instead of going from here to there and running off abroad every five minutes."

Erna took a deep breath and expelled it through her nose as she sat back in her chair.

"Is that what you wanted to hear? Am I supposed to be happy that my daughter crawled into bed with the gangster who kidnapped us? Of course not. But I can't stop her doing anything. When she was fourteen she was out all night with all kinds of weird and dangerous men. I tried to keep her in, I tried to stop her. I took her to hospital for Aids tests and . . ." she gulped.

280

"Once for an abortion. But it's like water off a duck's back. She takes no notice of me or anyone else."

"But she takes notice of this Markús or Magnús?" Helgi asked.

"Yes. A criminal." Erna took a gulp of air that was released as a sob. "She seems to take notice of him."

Rafn appeared from the afternoon gloom, glanced both ways and crossed the road as if he expected the traffic to stop for him, raising a hand in acknowledgement without looking at the car that slowed for the figure in the long leather coat with a blond ponytail hanging down his back.

"That's him," Össur said. "Quick. You two go and sit at another table so he doesn't think we're together."

Magni and Tinna Lind moved to sit two tables down, heads together in murmured conversation as Rafn opened the door and nodded to Össur before going to the counter.

"So, Össi. What's new?" Rafn asked.

Magni heard with disquiet the Baikal's safety catch click off-on-off-on deep in Össur's pocket.

"I hear you're famous," Rafn said, taking a seat opposite him. "On the TV and everything."

"Yeah. I'm keeping out of sight for the moment."

Össur hunched deeper into his seat in the corner of the café, discreet but still with a view of the door and the street outside.

"Coming here in daylight isn't exactly keeping out of sight, surely?"

"Needs must, Rafn."

"What are you after?"

"Three passports."

"Going on holiday?"

"Yeah. Probably a long holiday somewhere far away. Three of us. Two guys, one my age and one around thirty, and one chick, mid-twenties. Preferably legal, but as long as they work, I don't care."

Rafn sat back and surveyed Össur coolly, taking in the fatigue lines around his eyes, which had a hopeless look about them.

"Not asking for a lot, are you?"

"Can you do it?"

"Sure. But we don't give away favours."

"How much?"

"A million." Rafn delicately sipped his coffee. "Each."

Sitting two tables away with their heads together, Tinna Lind looked over Magni's shoulder and saw Össur shudder at Rafn's words.

"That's your best price?"

Rafn laughed. "We're not running a junk stall at Kolaport. We don't have a best price, Össi. There's just the price."

"Fuck. A million each." Össur shook his head. "That's steep. Too steep."

"Take it or leave it. Passports aren't the kind of thing we normally play around with, and they don't grow on trees."

"Come on, Rafn. Old time's sake and all that."

"That's as cheap as I can do them. Practically cost price, my friend."

"What if . . .?"

If there was a look of satisfaction on Rafn's face, then it didn't show. "Ah. What if, what?"

"If there was some way of doing each other a favour on this?"

"That could be a possibility. But I take it you're not coming back?"

"Well . . . when the heat dies down, maybe."

"Össi, you're facing a murder charge. Didn't you know that? There was a man shot dead at Hotel Hraun and the word is that you did the business. The heat's never going to die down as far as you're concerned. That's fourteen to sixteen years, and you'd serve eight or ten. You'd be pushing sixty by the time you get out of Litla Hraun. If you know what's good for you, you need to disappear, my friend." Rafn emptied his coffee cup and placed it precisely on its saucer, the handle at an exact right angle to the line of the table's edge. "That's assuming Alli doesn't catch up with you first," he added and Össur blanched.

Alli sat quietly on a hard kitchen chair by the door. He seemed calm, but Gunna could see the twitching of a tic below his left eye as two uniformed officers and a detective from the narcotics squad systematically went through every cupboard and drawer, opening, examining and replacing everything.

"You're not going to go through the rubbish as well, are you?" Alli asked in disbelief as Dísa, the narcotics officer, emptied the contents of the bin onto a plastic sheet and picked through the contents with gloved hands.

"Especially the bin, Alli," Gunna told him, watching his expression carefully. "You never know what goodies have been thrown away."

Dísa picked up and bagged the remnants of some joints. "The rest of this room's clear, is it?"

"Looks like it," one of the uniformed officers confirmed. "Living room next?"

The front room with its window onto the street outside and its blank-screened television in one corner served as Alli's living space, dining room, office and the place where he received visitors. Gunna saw with distaste that the carpet was thick with grime and that there were cobwebs in the corners. She brought the kitchen chair and placed it by the door.

"Sit there," she instructed and put down a stool for herself to perch on.

"I know what you're after," Alli hissed at her.

"Really? Tell me, then. That way we won't have to turn your place upside-down."

"You're looking for anything you can that's going to get me banged up, and if you don't find it, you'll plant it. I know how you bastards work."

The uniformed officers opened and emptied the drawers of a bookcase that took up most of one wall, not that there were many books on the shelves other than an old phone book and a couple of catalogues.

"And I know just how you work as well, Alli. Threats, blackmail, broken fingers, all the rest of it," Gunna said in an undertone.

284

"You won't find anything here."

There was barely controlled fury in Alli's voice.

"You mean you stash your gear somewhere else, do you? Of course you do. You may be an evil bastard, but you're not stupid."

Alli subsided into angry silence, his eyes following the three officers as they searched everything, pulling out the stained blue sofa and checking both the floor and the back of the sofa for hiding places. The two thin armchairs got the same treatment, but there was nothing to be found but empty bottles dropped behind them.

"No joy, Dísa?"

She shook her head. "I'd guess there are residues everywhere," she said, looking around at the nicotine-stained walls.

"Bedroom next? Or bathroom?"

Dísa sighed. "The bathroom's going to be fun."

One of the uniformed officers coughed and grimaced. "This is weird," he said, holding out one of the empty bottles with a minute amount of fluid at the bottom of it.

Gunna's gaze shifted quickly to Alli and she saw him swallow hard.

"What is it?"

"It's not booze. Smells more like petrol."

"Interesting," Gunna said, watching the alarm on Alli's face. "You'd best bag it and we'll dust it for prints."

"You heard all that?"

"Yep. Do you reckon we're being watched or followed?"

Össur shook his head. "I haven't a fucking clue. There might be an Undertaker behind us right now." He sat with his shoulders hunched protectively around his neck and his chin sunk below the collar of his fleece jacket. "Take the scenic route and see if there's anyone keeping up with us, will you?"

Magni drove at a steady pace through the city centre, his eyes on the mirrors. Twice he changed lanes abruptly, and once indicated for a turn and then carried straight on. When a roundabout appeared ahead of them, he checked the mirrors and signalled left. He made a slow circuit of the roundabout, watching for anyone who had been drawn to follow, and then took a second circuit, oblivious to the furious glares of drivers wanting to get on the roundabout, before making an abrupt exit and taking the car at a smart pace through a residential area.

At the far end he congratulated himself on having lost any tail they might have had, but failed to notice a step-through scooter approaching along the road he had waited to turn onto. The scooter's driver glanced briefly at the Skoda with satisfaction as he passed. He had waited at the roundabout in the shadow of a van while Magni took his double circuit, and he had managed to second-guess him as the Skoda turned through the residential district, knowing that there was only one exit and he could beat them to it.

Magni gunned the Skoda along the main road and each time they slowed or stopped for lights, the scooter approached, pop-popping doggedly up the slopes until Magni turned off and the scooter's driver hesitated and

286

followed, reasoning that it was dark enough for him to be less noticeable. He followed at a distance and watched as the car turned into a cul-de-sac between two blocks of modern flats. He killed the lights and watched the three occupants get out, leave the car and go up a stairwell, and a minute later lights flickering on told him which flat they had gone to.

The scooter hummed into life again and the driver went back up the long curving slope and on to the main road again. Two sets of lights later he turned off and drove past a couple of half-built houses, a row of steel-framed workshops and finally straight into the open garage door at the side of a black-painted building.

"Well? How did it go?" Rafn asked as the driver pulled off his helmet.

"Couldn't be easier," Jón Egill said. "Three of them, two men and a woman. They're in one of the flats down by the shore, about a mile back towards town."

The picture of the big man at the filling station who had bought fuel with Erna Brandsen's card was pinned to the wall and they all stared at it.

"What's this?" Helgi asked. "It's not the clearest picture I've seen. What's it about, Eiríkur?"

"It's a one-year-old grey Skoda estate, four-wheel drive," he said, reading out the registration number. "I had this from traffic this afternoon. There's a car rental off Dalvegur in Kópavogur called PK Cars, run by a guy called Páll Karlsson, hence the name."

Gunna nodded, willing Eiríkur to get to the point. "Yes, and . . .?"

"Páll Karlsson doesn't do a lot of business during the winter and anyway, he was away on holiday in Greece. He got back last night, went to check on business this morning and found he'd been burgled. One car stolen, a grey Skoda. Whoever broke in took the keys and one car." He tapped the picture. "This guy. No dabs at the scene, but this has to be the mystery man from the hotel. It's the only reported stolen car anywhere that matches."

"Of course," Gunna breathed. "And Dalvegur is walking distance from the Digranes church where he dumped Erna's Explorer." She glanced up. "That's fantastic, Eiríkur. We have the registration of the car he's driving and I suppose you have an alert out?"

"Did that right away."

"Good. Let's hope he hasn't unscrewed the plates and put some other ones on instead." Gunna turned to Helgi. "Any progress with Erna Brandsen?"

"She's nuts, I reckon." Helgi grunted. "And there's something very odd about the relationship she has with her daughter."

Gunna looked at her watch. "I have to go soon, so give me the bones of it, will you?"

"All right. Erna and Tinna Lind have had a fairly rocky relationship over the past few years; they don't agree on a lot, and it's clear that Erna is deeply frustrated by her daughter's attitude to practically everything, especially stuff like getting a proper job,

288

settling down and all the stuff that young people are expected to do once they turn twenty."

"I'm not sure it's still like it was when we were young, Helgi, but fair enough. I get the picture."

"So that's the shape of it. They get on well on a fairly superficial day-to-day level, but beyond that pretty much everything turns into an argument."

"That sounds familiar," Gunna said and hoped Helgi hadn't noticed. "Go on. Anything on the other man we don't have a name for?"

"Markús or Magnús, something like that. She says she's not sure."

"A week together in the same place and she doesn't know his name?"

"I'm damned sure she does. She's a very strange lady. She's not giving me bullshit, but there's a whole lot she's leaving out."

"Such as?"

"Tinna Lind and Markús, or Magnús, whichever he turns out to be. They're screwing, apparently — it took a while to get that out of her — and she's not happy about it."

"Which is maybe how Erna came to run for it alone?"

"That's what I'm thinking," Helgi said. "Some kind of Stockholm syndrome thing going on here?"

"Which is why this guy's identity would be so useful. His prints aren't on file anywhere, so we can assume he's either very smart or else he's not your usual criminal type."

"Someone who got caught up in this by accident, maybe?"

"Either that or someone very desperate."

The table was spread with foil cartons. Tinna Lind handled chopsticks effortlessly, and by the time they had eaten their fill, Magni's skill with them had improved enough for him to finish his chow mein. Össur stuck with a spoon.

Magni belched. "That was good. Maybe we should head for China?"

Tinna Lind shook her head. "No, China's not a great idea. They're too organized and we'd stand out too much. Thailand or Vietnam would be better. They're both pretty chaotic and there are enough white faces that nobody would bother us much. Thai food's nicer than Vietnamese, though," she added.

"Sounds good to me. How about you, Össi? Where are you headed for?"

"Not sure yet," Össur said, licking the unfamiliar flavours from his lips. "Spain, I guess."

"You've been there before, haven't you?"

"Of course."

"I hear North Korea's lovely," Tinna Lind said.

"Where's that?" Össur asked.

"Next to South Korea."

"Duh."

"So what's happening with this Rafn character, then?" Magni broke in, sensing Össur's rising irritation and frowning at Tinna Lind. "Is he going to fix us up with passports?"

"I reckon so. He said to call at eight and he'd tell me then how long it takes."

"More to the point," Tinna Lind said, picking a few stray noodles up with her chopsticks. "Can we trust him?"

"Rafn?" Össur asked, as if the thought hadn't occurred to him. "I don't know."

"What's this Rafn's relationship with the old guy you two robbed? Are they mates? Will he hand you over to the old man — after he's taken your money, of course?"

"It's a good question, Össi," Magni said.

"They hate each other like poison, if you must know."

"They're rivals?" Tinna Lind asked. "How deep does that rivalry go? Rafn might be happy to make a bit of a profit from three passports and do the old man a bad turn at the same time. But how much would Alli have to offer Rafn for him to turn us all over to him? I mean," she said, putting down her chopsticks, "there must be a price on your head, Össur. But how much is that price?"

Magni looked from Össur to Tinna Lind and back. "She's right, Össi. How much are you worth to Alli?"

"Fuck knows. But it's getting on for eight, so I'd better give Rafn a call."

The sound of the door creaking open and the light by the door clicking on woke her up. A moment's alarm subsided when Gunna realized that the double thump was Steini's boots being dropped.

"You all right, old man?" she asked, craning her neck to look around and see his face, which was more lined than usual under its thatch of windblown hair. "Good day?"

"That depends on your definition of good," he said, padding across the kitchen, his feet leaving damp prints on the tiles. "Let's just say it's been a busy day and leave it at that."

"You weren't diving, were you?"

"In this weather? Not a hope. I spent the afternoon helping Jens with that old bulldozer of his. It seems to be running now, but it'll need a gearbox sooner or later."

"Hungry?"

"Starving. I could eat a fairly respectable-sized horse and still ask for seconds."

Gunna got to her feet and stretched, feeling guilty for having dozed off in front of the television.

"Go and get yourself cleaned up, then. I'm hungry as well, but I was waiting for you."

"You're going to cook?" Steini asked, a smile playing at the corners of his eyes. "You're sure?"

"I haven't quite forgotten how the grill works. Now get away with you, but be quick about it."

Four pork chops, a bowl of pasta and a large tomato salad greeted Steini as he returned from the shower.

"Anyone would think you're after something," he said.

"It works often enough for you, so I thought I'd give the same strategy a try."

"You will let me know if it works, won't you?" Steini hid a yawn. "Where's Laufey? Not home alone, are we?"

"Laufey's babysitting for Gísli and Drífa for a few hours. Gísli said he'd bring her home around eleven."

"How's the lad? Are you friends again?"

"I hope so," Gunna said with a sigh. "We've never been at loggerheads over anything for this long before and it's starting to hurt."

Steini shrugged. "He's a big lad now, time to make his own decisions. I'm sure your parents didn't approve of everything you got up to when you were a good bit younger than Gísli."

"Ach, you're right. He's asked me if I'll go to the hospital with him and see the old guy."

"What? Thorvaldur? How come?"

Gunna scowled. "He says Thorvaldur asked for me to come and see him. It's at least twenty-five years since we last had a civil word to say to each other, and now he wants to be friends. I don't get it." Gunna corrected herself. "That's not quite right. I get it, I think. But I don't like it."

"Maybe it's more for Gísli's sake than for his?" Steini suggested gently. "If he really is on the way out, then perhaps he wants to make some kind of peace after all these years. It won't do any harm to find out, will it?"

"We'll see. Anyway, I have an early start tomorrow. I'm going to Selfoss first thing to interview a witness who phoned in a lead I need to follow up. Then back to town from there, so we'll see how much energy I have left after all that."

CHAPTER
EIGHT

Thursday

Tinna Lind let herself drop forward to fold her hands on Magni's chest, resting her chin on them.

"Still excited?" she asked.

"You need to ask? Looking forward to being on our own somewhere there's less chance of getting our collars felt any minute."

Tinna Lind giggled. "That's part of the fun. Don't you find it exciting?"

"It is," Magni admitted. "What I find less exciting is the prospect of a few years in Litla Hraun."

"They allow conjugal visits there, don't they?"

"Yeah, I think so. But I think you have to be properly married to get those."

Magni ran his hands down her back until they cupped Tinna Lind's buttocks and he rocked her gently back and forward.

"I'm sure that could be arranged if things come to that," she purred. "If you're asking, that is?"

"That depends if you're offering, doesn't it?"

The wind-swept spray from the tops of the waves and the grey water of the harbour had an iron quality in the first of the daylight. Rafn shoved open the door of the harbour cafe and looked around at the tables occupied by men in blue or grey overalls talking in low voices or nipping through dog-eared newspapers.

He picked up a mug of coffee and a pastry and went over to the far corner, where Jón Egill hunched over the previous day's paper.

"G'day," he said as Rafn sat down and sipped his coffee. "Speak to Össi last night, did you?"

"I did."

"And?"

"I offered three passports for a million each. Legal and above board, complete with real names and ID numbers of people living somewhere on the east coast. Össi asked how much for one passport," he put down his coffee and cut his pastry into strips.

Jón Egill raised an eyebrow. "Meaning?"

Rafn shrugged. "Meaning I reckon he's planning on dumping the other guy and the girl and going his own way."

Jón Egill nodded and frowned. "You wouldn't expect anything less of Össur Oskarsson, would you? Can we trust him? Should we have anything to do with this business, or would we be better off leaving them to sort out their own shit?"

"You prefer to keep out of sight on this?"

"I've had the law sniffing around once already and I'd prefer to keep my nose clean, but I can check on them discreetly. I can deal with Össi, although I could do with someone there to do the leg work."

"Beggi, I reckon," Rafn said. "Bergthór Stefánsson. He's a smart character, and he's not too young or too keen to show off. We'll get him to keep a discreet eye on them, just in case."

"He'll do. I'll have a word. He's a good guy and he's clean."

"For the moment," Rafn grinned, and dropped his voice and his head lower, closer to Jón Egill's face. "Listen. Alli was arrested yesterday, and so was Baldvin."

"For Árni Sigurvinsson's murder?" Jón Egill grunted. "That pair of amateurs should have known better. It stirs up the law and makes life difficult for everyone."

"You realize that if Alli goes away for a decent stretch, then the Undertakers have an opportunity to pick up most of his business?"

Jón Egill scratched his chin. "Yes," he said slowly. "The thought had occurred to me."

"So it seems to me we have a bunch of choices here. We can make a couple of million out of the passports easily enough, but that's no great shakes." He tapped the table with a forefinger. "Alli comes to us and says he's been rolled by Össur. That's no big surprise. Össur's practically pond life. It was always going to happen sooner or later."

"Go on," Jón Egill said, and looked up at a young man in blue overalls who made to sit at the far end of the same table. "Seat's taken, pal," he said.

"But there's nobody there," the man protested.

"I said, the seat's taken," Jón Egill repeated, and caught the eye of a thickset man with a fluorescent jacket over his overalls, who stood up, patted the young man on the shoulder and pointed to another table. He winked at Jón Egill, who nodded back almost imperceptibly. "You were saying?" he said.

"Alli told me he'd been rolled for a hundred thousand."

"Euros or dollars?"

"Euros. But if he's saying a hundred thousand, I'd bet the real figure is at least three times that. You need more than a hundred thousand for white powder business on Alli's scale. And that cash is out there somewhere."

"A hundred thousand Euros is fifteen million krónur, and it's more than likely in that flat in Gardabær."

"Exactly. So we have a choice," Rafn mused. "We can bump Össi and his pals easily enough, grab the cash and either hang on to it or take a slice before we hand it back to Alli: Then we leave them to either Alli or the law to deal with, and whichever way that goes it'll be messy. Or . . ."

"Or, what?" Jón Egill asked.

"We have an opportunity to figure out what sort of outcome would suit us best. The other option would be to help them on their way, make sure they leave the country and that headcase Össi isn't cluttering things up here. We supply three passports at a million each and watch them disappear out of the country with a stack of Alli's working capital."

"Which leaves Alli up to his neck in the shit while we quietly move in and take over where he left off, you mean?"

"Still asleep is he?" Tinna Lind murmured as Magni returned from the shower, towelling his hair and beard dry.

"Unless he can snore while he's awake."

"When are we going to get rid of him?

Magni looked through the door into the little apartment's living room, where Össur's feet in their grey socks protruded from under the duvet.

"We're going to have to be very careful," he said, slipping back under the bedclothes. "I'd bet you anything that he's thinking how to do just the same to us. But for the moment we're safe enough."

"Because he still needs us?"

Magni snaked an arm under Tinna Lind's back and gave her a squeeze that made her gasp.

"Until we have passports, we're OK. We need him so we can get passports. He needs us to get around, because the police are looking for him and Össi doesn't drive."

"So once we have the passports, we'll have to watch our step?"

"That's the way I see it," Magni said. "And that loaded pistol in his pocket makes the whole thing a lot more awkward."

The streets of Selfoss were awash with meltwater as the warm south wind and the constant rain showers it

298

brought with it took off the layers of dirty snow to reveal the hardened older ice beneath, which seemed more reluctant to disappear down the town's drains and swell the river that was in flood, bloated with milky water from high in the hills.

Gunna checked the address and parked outside the newish wood-framed house on the town's outskirts. The grass in the garden could be seen peeking out through gaps in the snow cover and the place was littered with the junk left by active children encouraged to play outside, although on a day like this she had no doubt they would all be indoors.

She was right. Svava Jónasdóttir ushered her into the kitchen, bypassing the living room, where a group of pre-school children were ignoring the television and playing with an excited puppy.

"Busy day?"

"Just a bit. If it's dry, I can send them outside to play for a few hours and that tires them out. But that's not going to happen today."

"I know just how you feel, although that's something of a distant memory these days," Gunna said. "I'm Gunnhildur Gísladóttir and I'm with CID in Reykjavík. Lárus Erlendsson said I ought to talk to you."

Svava pursed her lips and fiddled with a strand of hair. She looked through the door to check on the children, as if hoping to be interrupted.

"Yeah. It's about the people you're searching for from that hotel up near the lake at Apavatn," she said in a slow voice, unsure of herself.

Gunna nodded, taking a sheaf of pictures from her folder. "Go on," she said.

"Well, it was something about the car those people had been travelling in, you see."

"This one?" Gunna said, rooting in her folder and placing a picture on the kitchen worktop showing Erna's Ford Explorer where it had been found in the church parking lot in Kópavogur.

"I think so."

"You've seen the vehicle, or the driver?"

Svava nodded and chewed her lip before she answered. "It was either Friday or Saturday, I'm not sure which, but it was in the car park outside Samkaup. I go there a few times a week, and normally I just run round fast and get what I need, but there was someone there I hadn't seen for a long time and it was such a surprise to see him there, in Samkaup in Selfoss of all places."

"And who is this character?"

"His name's Magni. Magni Sighvatsson. I saw him drive away in that car, or one just like it," she said, pointing a finger at the photograph in Gunna's hand.

"You're certain? You spoke to him?"

"We had a chat in the shop. Of course I'm certain."

"I mean you know this man well enough to be in no doubt about this? That's what I'm driving at. I need to be sure there's no mistaken identity here."

Svava's head nodded miserably. "I wish there could be," she said with a long sigh. "But it's definitely him. I've known Magni since we were teenagers. Magni's from the Westmann Islands originally, but we were at

300

school together in Thorlákshöfn after his parents moved to the mainland. I seem to remember that his mother wasn't from the islands and she never felt at home over there. Anyway, we grew up together. He lived with my sister a long time ago."

"Magni has a family?"

"Not really. That relationship didn't last, I'm afraid. I get on all right with Hjalti, my ex, and Hjalti's still good friends with Magni. But it's a different story with Magni and Ína. I don't think he sees his kids very often, if at all."

"You know where he lives?"

Svava shook her head.

"What did you talk about?"

"You know. Ex-partners, children, that kind of stuff."

"Did he say anything about where he was going or why he was in Selfoss?"

"Yeah, sort of. I was surprised to see him because last I heard of him was in the summer and he was working on a factory trawler called *Hafthór* and earning good money. I didn't realize the ship had been sold and he'd lost his job. He said he was going east to Vík and had stopped here to get a bunch of groceries for the weekend — I assumed he was planning on staying for a while because his trolley was piled high."

"Vík?" Gunna wondered out loud. "As someone who knows him; did that sound convincing to you?"

"Well," Svava said and thought for a moment, "I don't know. I got the impression there was someone waiting for him in Vík for a long weekend on their own, and it wouldn't be a surprise. Magni's a really lovely

301

guy and ladies' clothes tend to fall off when he's about."

Baldvin looked even less happy than he had the day before. His face was still a mess, although he'd been escorted to hospital by two uniformed officers where a dentist made a manful attempt at fixing the damage to his remaining teeth. His lawyer, a young woman with severe glasses and an even more severe expression on her face, tapped a pen on a pad and prepared to make notes.

"Let's go over it again, shall we?" Helgi said with patience. "We have all the time in the world to get this sorted out, you know."

"All right," Baldvin said, sucking at his empty tooth sockets and whistling as he spoke.

"You last saw Árni Sigurvinsson on Thursday last week. We've established that he was seen driving down the street towards Alli's place and that his car was parked outside. People saw it there and we have witness statements to that effect, including one from the person whose space it was parked in."

Baldvin nodded.

"Talk me through it again, will you?"

"They just had a chat. Alli was a bit upset, but I don't know what it was that had pissed him off."

"This is where it gets interesting. Let's backtrack a little, and you tell me just what Össur Oskarsson was doing at Alli's place that afternoon, before Árni turned up?"

Baldvin looked pleadingly sideways at the lawyer, who lifted one eyebrow in return.

"Unfortunately Árni is no longer here to give his side of the story," Helgi continued in a patient tone of voice, as if the lawyer wasn't there. "Why did he stay so long? Because he was held there against his will?"

"All right. Árni came along the street. He stopped outside and just sat in the car like he was waiting for someone. Alli saw him and went berserk. He went outside and hauled Árni out of the car and took him indoors."

"And you didn't take part in this?"

"No, not me," Baldvin whistled.

"Árni was ten years younger than Alli and a head taller, yet Alli was able to drag him inside? I find that hard to believe? You must have had something to do with it."

"My client has already stated that he had nothing to do with this, officer," the lawyer broke in. "Can we please move on?"

"Had a gun," Baldvin mumbled after a long pause.

"Össur? A handgun? Or Alli?"

"Össi." Baldvin sighed in despair, giving up to the realization that he was outgunned. "Him and the big guy."

"That's who smacked your teeth out?" Helgi asked. Baldvin nodded again and sighed, and Helgi sensed that he was about to give up. "There was an argument, or a fight? Over what?"

"Cash. A load of cash."

"Go on. Tell me more."

"Össi knew Alli had cash in the house, so he took it. Him and the big guy, they ran off."

"How much cash?"

"Fucking loads. Foreign money. In a bag."

"And then Árni turned up?"

"Yeah. Looking for Össi."

Össur's phone buzzed. Magni looked at it and wondered if he should answer, but instead he picked it up and went into the living room to give Össur a shake.

"Hey, mate," he said, planting the buzzing mobile in Össur's hand. "Phone."

Magni stayed while Össur answered, knowing that there was probably only one person who could be calling.

"Yeah?" Össur answered, stabbing at the green button.

There followed a conversation that Magni was only able to follow half of before Össur killed the connection and dropped the phone on the floor.

"Well?"

"Tonight. Rafn says we can have the passports tonight."

"Three million krónur?"

Össur's teeth were exposed in rare triumph.

"A million each. That makes eight thousand euros each. Just as well I'm travelling alone, I reckon," he said and closed his eyes, his hand once again clasping the comforting butt of the Baikal in his pocket.

Gunna took the stairs two at a time. Eiríkur looked up in alarm as Gunna appeared and went straight to her desk and began rattling her keyboard, punching the keys harder than necessary as she muttered to herself.

"His name's Magni Sighvatsson," she said in answer to Eiríkur's unasked question. "Our mystery man in person," she added, sitting back and looking at the

304

driving licence photo on the screen. Eiríkur stood by her shoulder and studied the beefy face that looked as if it were suppressing laughter just as the cheap photo-booth picture had been taken.

"Magni Klemens Sighvatsson, born twenty-ninth of May 1986 in the Westmann Islands," Eiríkur said. "That's our mystery man?"

"That's him," Gunna said, eyes on the screen as she keyed in the name again. "No criminal record, so it's no surprise his prints didn't show up anywhere."

"He's a big lad as well," Eiríkur said, back at his own desk and tapping at his own computer.

"How do you know that?"

"Google. He was a weightlifting champion when he was twenty."

"So we might be looking at something of a handful," she brooded, looking at the friendly face in the photo, the twinkling eyes topped by a carrot mop and surrounded by ginger stubble. "I wonder what's going on here? Why's someone of that age with no record getting involved with deadbeats like Össur Óskarsson and Alli the Cornershop. It doesn't make sense, unless there's something we've missed."

"Or something we just don't know about?"

"More than likely. At any rate, it seems Magni lost his job not long ago, so maybe he was getting desperate. Eiríkur, find out what you can about this guy while I go and speak to the Laxdal, will you?" Gunna said, scribbling names and ID numbers on a sheet of paper and passing it across. "See if you can find contact details for these people as well while I'm talking to the big man," she added, taking a couple of sheets of paper from the printer and sweeping from the room.

Ívar Laxdal sat with his chin in one hand and the other tapping at a laptop on his desk. Only his eyes moved as Gunna knocked and pushed the door open without waiting for a reply.

"News, Gunnhildur?"

Gunna put the printout of Magni's passport photo on the desk. "Our mystery man is called Magni Klemens Sighvatsson."

"How did you figure that out?"

"Someone who knows him identified him as driving Erna Björg Brandsen's car in Selfoss a week ago, and spoke to him in the shop there."

"No doubt about it? No mistaken identity?"

"No. No doubt about this guy."

"What are you after?"

"A search warrant for a flat at Hólabraut 70 in Gardabær. It's his legal address, although I don't think he actually lives there. According to the national register, the occupiers are a couple called Hjalti Traustason and Kamilla Oddsdóttir, and Magni Sighvatsson's registered domicile is also there. According to my witness, Magni and Hjalti are old friends, each was best man for the other, although I'm given to understand that both those relationships have long since broken up."

"So this Kamilla is Hjalti's new wife?"

"That's what I need to check. Eiríkur's looking for contact numbers right now."

"What do you want me to do?"

"I'm not sure I want this guy's face in the papers and on TV yet. If we find them, then we're going to need the Special Unit to flush them out. Össur's armed, so I'm not inclined to take chances."

"Quite right, Gunnhildur. Let me know when you need them."

There was a tap at the door and Ívar Laxdal looked up, frowning as the door opened.

"Chief?" Eiríkur said, hastily jotted notes in his hand. "I've spoken to Kamilla Oddsdóttir. She's a big cheese at some pharmaceuticals company and it wasn't easy to prise her out of a meeting."

"But you did. So?"

"She and Hjalti are married but separated, and they're still joint owners of the apartment. She moved in with her parents when the two of them fell out and Hjalti still lives there."

"She confirmed that Magni Sighvatsson's legal residence is registered there?"

"She said she has no idea whether he has a key to the apartment, but that it wouldn't be a surprise if he did."

"Sounds promising, doesn't it?" Gunna looked at Ívar Laxdal and back to Eiríkur.

"She also said that Hjalti definitely isn't there, as he's an engineer on a Norwegian oil survey ship and is away for two months at a time. So if there's anyone in the place, it's not going to be one of the two owners as she has no reason to go there. Then she got quite angry and wanted to know what the hell this was all about?"

"You told her?" Ívar Laxdal asked.

"Of course not. I just said it was a very serious investigation and that she should keep away from the place and keep quiet about what we had talked about, and that I'd be in touch to let her know what the situation is."

"You're a diplomat, Eiríkur," Ívar Laxdal said, and Eiríkur glowed at the compliment. "But on the downside, I'm afraid we're going to have to let one of your bad boys go."

"What?"

"Baldvin has confessed to starting the fire and procuring the petrol, and his prints were on the can, so he's staying put. That means that Alli's lawyer can convincingly argue that he should be released."

"Hell. I was hoping it would be the other way around."

"Sit the fuck down, will you? Take it easy."

It was Össur who was edgy and nervous. He had spent much of the day asleep on the smaller sofa in the borrowed apartment's living room, while Magni and Tinna Lind lay entwined on the larger sofa, she with a paperback and he watching the TV with the sound turned down low.

"I don't like it. There's something wrong. I can feel it."

Össur stood at the end of the living-room window, where he could see past the next block of flats to the road outside.

"What's your problem? Anything suspicious?"

"Now you come to mention it, yes."

"Like what?"

"A scooter has passed by a few times too many, and he's sure as hell not delivering pizzas."

"You're sure?" Tinna Lind asked, marking her place in the book with an envelope and putting it aside.

"If I wasn't sure, I wouldn't be telling you, would I?"

"What time are we meeting Rafn?"

"Eight."

"And what's the time now?"

Magni yawned. "It's almost four. Where are we meeting him?"

"Don't know yet. We'll sort out a place at the last moment," Össur said, stretching and craning his neck to see past the next building. "I really, really don't like this. We're rats in a trap in this place, with only one way out."

"Where else can we go?" Tinna Lind asked.

"Between now and eight? I suppose we could drive around a bit and find ourselves something to eat. We could drive out of town, go around Grindavík or Keflavík."

"Yeah, but are we going to be safe coming back here?"

"Who knows?" Magni said. "But Össi has a nose like a bloodhound, so I guess if he thinks things aren't right, then we'd be best off getting out of here for a while." The snick of the Baikal in Össur's pocket made his mind up. "Come on, let's get out for an hour or two. We can drive around, meet Rafn and then come back here and see if the place looks like anyone's been in? What do you reckon?"

"Take all your stuff with you," Össur said, teeth bared as he snarled at the sight of the scooter again. "We might not be coming back here at all."

Thorvaldur Hauksson's eyes followed her as she walked in. Gunna saw straight away that the bright blue eyes that had once had such a captivating intensity to them had turned watery as his illness had taken its implacable hold. His laboured breathing filled the room and he lifted a hand a few inches off the bedspread before dropping it back.

"Gísli, you all right?" Gunna murmured as she sat next to him and Thorvaldur turned his head to one side to look at her. She could see the effort it cost him to do just that.

"Yeah, Mum. I'm fine."

The man in the bed had always been slim, but now he was painfully thin, his hair wolf-grey and his hands blotched with spots while the bones could be seen through skin as thin as paper. He whispered something and Gísli leaned forward, his face close to the old man's to hear what he was saying.

"What's that, Valdi?" he asked gently and Gunna offered up a prayer of thanks that Gísli had not called him dad. "Yeah, that's my mum," he said and listened as he whispered a reply.

"He wants to talk to you, Mum," Gísli said, sitting back up straight, and Gunna froze for a moment.

Thorvaldur's hand fidgeted and found hers as she leaned towards him, forcing herself not to snatch it back.

"Thorvaldur," she said.

"Little Gunna," he wheezed. "He's a fine boy, my Gísli. A lovely boy," he repeated and closed his eyes. For a long moment Gunna wondered if he had fallen asleep as the heart monitor continued its sweep across the screen by his bed, but then his eyes opened with a vestige of that old intensity behind them. "You did a good job with the boy," he whispered. His eyes closed again and the grip on her hand relaxed.

"That's it for the moment," Gísli said with a sigh. "He'll sleep for half an hour at least now."

Gunna took a deep breath and let it out slowly.

"Right."

Gísli flashed a glance sideways at her with a worried look on his face.

"All right, Mum?"

"Give me a minute. I will be."

Outside in the corridor Gunna told herself that twenty years' worth of anger could now be consigned to history as she leaned against the wall and craved a cigarette for the first time in years. She wanted to punch the wall in frustration.

"'Your Gísli'?" she whispered savagely to herself. "My Gísli, you mean. You had nothing to do with him, Thorvaldur Hauksson, not a single thing."

She collected herself as the door swung silently open and Gísli stepped out to join her.

"Sorry, Mum. But he really wanted to see you. I'm glad you came," he added.

"I'm not sure if I should have."

"I'm glad you did," Gísli said. "For my sake, if not for his."

"I'm sorry, Gísli. I can't help being angry at him. It's not the things he did," she said with a gulp. "It's all the stuff he didn't do that's made me furious all these years. All those years of no Christmas presents, no birthday cards and precious little maintenance when I was struggling to make ends meet."

"I know, Mum."

"Gísli. You're some kind of a saint, you know that? Where are all his other kids?"

"One in the States, one in Norway, two in Kópavogur and one in Ósvík, who's three months older than I am," Gísli counted. "I never knew I had so many half-siblings."

"Neither did I, and I'd guess there might be a few more about that aren't on the list," Gunna said. "And you're the only one of the tribe here to see the old scoundrel off."

"It's a second floor flat," Helgi said and the group of four men in black uniforms looked up briefly from the plan in front of them. "Two bedrooms accessible from the living room, one kitchen, one bathroom."

"What can we expect?" asked the raw-boned man in charge of the group, an experienced officer who had often worked with Helgi and Gunna before.

"Two men, one woman. One of the two men is probably armed."

"You know who these jokers are?"

312

Gunna placed the driving licence pictures on top of the plan of the block of flats and Steingrímur's eyes flickered with recognition.

"Össi Oskars?"

"That's him, a record a mile long," she confirmed. "These two are the unknown quantities. Tinna Lind Bogadóttir — she may be a hostage or being held against her will, although that seems unlikely. The big guy is called Magni Klemens Sighvatsson. No record."

"Ah, a new face."

"But he was a powerlifting champion a few years ago, so he's not likely to be a pushover."

Steingrímur nodded and cupped his chin in one hand. "Össi's the one who's armed, I take it? What's the weapon?"

"A 9mm pistol, judging by the slugs Miss Cruz recovered from Brandur Geirsson's body," Helgi said.

"So we don't need to use kid gloves?" Steingrímur asked, his eyes twinkling in anticipation.

"Not with Össur, no. He's killed someone already, so don't take any chances."

"That suits us. How do you want to go about this? Do we know if they're in there?"

"No. We're going to have to wait for someone to show up."

Össur tapped his phone on his knee in the back and fidgeted, but Magni was just happy not to hear the clicking of the pistol's safety catch behind him. They cruised into town at a speed that wouldn't attract attention just as the rain started to come down again, slowing the traffic. Magni tried not to be nervous. The whole thing had turned into a combination of exhilaration and disaster, he thought. A girl like Tinna Lind, with a mind of her own and demands he was only too happy to meet, doesn't come along every five minutes, but neither does the threat of a longish prison sentence, and he had no doubt in his mind that if the police were to catch up with them then Össur would be going away for a very long time. His own sentence would hardly be a short one, and it seemed unlikely that Tinna Lind would wait patiently while he sweated out a year or two locked up in Litla Hraun.

Behind him Össur's phone buzzed.

"Hey. Text from Rafn. He wants us to suggest a place. He says he's easy."

"What? Tell him the car park at Smáralind, the big car park at the top. And ask what car he's driving."

He could hear Össur breathing heavily behind him as he texted back. A moment later the phone buzzed again.

"What's he say?"

"He says no. Too many cameras at Smáralind. Any ideas?"

Magni racked his brains for somewhere suitably public but without CCTV cameras covering it.

"Hell, let me think a minute, will you?" He leaned towards Tinna Lind. "Any ideas? Somewhere with no cameras? Somewhere busy?"

"A trading estate?" she suggested. "Plenty of people about in those places."

"Össur, what do you reckon?" Magni asked.

314

"Suits me."

"All right, tell him Skútuvogur, fifteen minutes. We'll text him with an exact place when we get there."

Össur grunted again in the back seat and Magni imagined him mouthing the words to himself as he painstakingly tapped them into his old-fashioned mobile.

Traffic swept past them in the rain, throwing up sheets of water behind them as Magni kept the Skoda just below the speed limit.

"Not a great night for it," he said.

"It's fine," Tinna Lind said, and he heard a hard edge of determination in her voice. "Everyone will be in a hurry and nobody's going to look twice in this kind of weather."

"I hope you're right. The cash is ready, isn't it?"

"Yep. Counted out and ready to go."

They sat in nervous silence as Magni took the Skoda through the intersection with Miklabraut and edged it into the right-hand lane, ready for the turn-off, and pulled up at the lights.

"Did Rafn say what car he's driving?"

"No."

"You asked, right?"

"Yeah. But he didn't reply to that."

"Did you tell him what we're driving?"

"I just said a grey car."

"Fair enough," Magni said, and pulled away as the lights went green, checking in the mirror that there was nothing behind them and taking a turn onto a long, well-lit road lined with warehouses and square discount stores. "We're on Skútuvogur. You'd best call Rafn and see where he is."

In the mirror he could see Össur with the phone at his ear.

"Where are you?" he heard Össur ask without preamble.

"Tell him the car park outside Bonus," Magni instructed. "And ask what he's driving."

Össur relayed the message and Magni drove as slowly as he dared past the supermarket with its sparsely populated car park, peering at the cars parked there and the few people hurrying through the rain for the doors.

"He's in a black van," Össur relayed.

"Then where is he?"

"Where are you?" Össur snapped into the phone.

Magni turned into the deserted car park outside a closed plumbing supplies warehouse and tapped the wheel impatiently.

"He says he's there," Össur muttered, leaning forward.

"Let's go, then."

The black van was parked at the end of the car park, in view of the road, but far enough away that nobody was likely to come close. Magni pulled up, leaving two clear spaces between the cars, and wound down the window. The black van's tinted window opened halfway and Rafn looked out.

"Suspicious, Össi?" he called across.

"Always, Rafn. Never take a chance, me."

"Come on then."

Rafn opened the door of the van and stepped out, placing a wide-brimmed leather hat on his head as he did so.

Magni turned his collar up, squeezed Tinna Lind's hand and got out of the car, following Össur, who was walking towards Rafn with his hands ostentatiously out of his pockets. Rain was already flattening his sparse grey hair to his scalp.

"What do we have?" Össur asked.

"What you wanted. Three passports."

"Icelandic?"

"Yep. D'you have the cash?"

"Of course."

"Alli's cash." Rafn smiled.

"Yeah, I guess he's not a happy bunny right now."

"Alli's not at all a happy man, but not for the reasons you might think."

Össur looked sharply at Rafn. "Why? How so?"

"Alli's sidekick is on remand."

"Árni?"

Rafn nodded and his voice was soft. "Alli's lawyer got him released this afternoon. Baldvin confessed that he'd set fire to Árni's flat. It was on the news earlier. No names, but it's easy enough to join the dots. They'll put him away for years."

"Shit. I didn't know. And Alli gets away with it?"

"Alli may be a bastard but he's no fool. The law's probably keeping quiet about it while they're still looking for you."

"Could be. They're going to be looking for a long time."

"We'll see." Rafn grinned. "Good luck."

"Passports?"

Rafn reached into an inside pocket and took out three blue passports. Össur jerked his head at Magni. "Check them."

"Hands, Össi," Magni reminded him softly as he saw a hand straying towards a jacket pocket.

Magni flicked through the three passports. All were valid and looked genuine. The older man looked enough like Össur to pass in a crowd. The young woman was older than Tinna Lind.

"Glasses. Get glasses, both of you," Rafn said, as if reading his thoughts.

The younger man's passport was of a clean-shaven character with long hair and Magni wondered if he could pass muster with his sprouting beard and short hair.

"What's the score with these? How did you get valid passports? I mean, these haven't been reported stolen or anything, have they?"

"They're valid and they'll get you though a passport check," Rafn said, passing him a sheet of paper. "Just to help you on your way, here's all the information you need on these people: addresses, ID numbers, workplaces. Just in case there's a question or two."

"You're being very helpful." Össur said.

"The Undertakers take their business seriously. We don't want you singing like a bird in a cell at Keflavík. We want you off our patch."

"You sly bastard. You're after Alli's territory."

318

"No comment, Össi. No comment."

Magni took a wad of notes from his pocket. "Fifteen thousand euros, as agreed for two passports."

The cash vanished as if by magic and Rafn looked expectantly at Össur, who hesitated.

"Don't fuck about, Össi," Magni snapped. "Give the man his money."

Össur grudgingly handed over a thinner stack of notes. "No tricks, eh, Rafn?"

"Össi, what do you think we are?"

"I know what you are."

"Shut up, will you, Össi?" Magni said. "Listen, how's this done? How can we be sure these passports aren't reported and will flag up alerts at the check-in desk?"

Rafn sighed. "All right," he said after a moment's thought. "The guy there." He pointed at the open passport in Magni's hand. "He's been naughty and he owes people more money than is healthy. Understand? The other two passports belong to his father and sister. They don't travel and won't miss them for months. That way we get passports that have a lifetime of let's say three months, or maybe more, before the owners notice they're gone, and the naughty boy gets his debt cleared. Until the next time . . ." Rafn smiled, patted the pocket containing a respectable amount of Alli the Cornershop's euros and opened the door of the van. "Have a good time. Make it a long holiday, Össi."

They were parked far enough up the hill not to attract attention. Gunna and Steingrímur watched the block of flats, waiting for traffic or for lights to be switched on.

"Time?" Gunna asked.

"Almost ten."

"Hell. I'm wondering if our birds have flown the coop?" She clicked her communicator. "Helgi?" she said, forgetting correct procedure.

"Nothing here," Helgi's voice crackled back. "The guys are all about to doze off."

"I didn't hear that," Steingrímur muttered.

"I know, Helgi. The excitement's just overwhelming, isn't it?" She could hear him yawning. "Another hour?"

"I reckon so. We old boys like to be tucked up before midnight, you know."

"Get away with you. Give it an hour and we'll think again."

"Gotcha."

Steingrímur brooded in the passenger seat. The van with Helgi and the three other officers from the Special Unit was parked out of sight on the far side of the building with a view of the entrance, while Gunna and Steingrímur had a view of the road down to the row of blocks of flats.

"Car," Steingrímur said, looking in the mirror and lifting his binoculars as a set of lights swept the rain-soaked street.

The rain had finally stopped and a full moon could be seen between shreds of cloud racing eastwards with a half gale hurrying them on their way.

"Helgi," Gunna said. "We have company."

"Gotcha."

Gunna and Steingrímur sat back in their seats, their faces out of the light, and watched as a black BMW

320

came too fast down the road, grounded on a speed hump and screeched to a halt in a space further down.

"Not them, I think," Gunna said.

"Let's see."

They trained binoculars on the car as both doors opened and a man in a suit leaped from the driver's side while a woman in a short dress got out of the passenger side and strode away with her nose in the air, leaving the door wide open.

"Oops," Steingrímur chuckled. "I think you may be right."

They watched the man close both car doors and hurry after the woman, who had slammed the door of a ground-floor flat behind her. The man hammered on it.

"Sólveig!"

Gunna looked at Steingrímur and smothered a chuckle. "Looks like someone's not going to get lucky tonight?"

"Sólveig!"

"We could do without this," Steingrímur muttered as the door flew open and the woman stood silhouetted in the doorway with her arms crossed.

"What?" she yelled. "Get out! I've seen enough of you. And take your wandering hands with you. Don't think I didn't see you, Sindri. Everyone saw what you were up to!" she yelled and reached behind her, lifting a bag and throwing it down the path. "Now fuck off and don't show your ugly face around me again."

The door slammed shut and the man stood stock still. Eventually he bent down, picked up the bag and slung it over his shoulder as he trudged down the path back to his car, tapping at his phone as he went. A moment later the BMW bumped back over the speed humps and disappeared into the night.

"That's all the excitement we're likely to see tonight, I reckon," Steingrímur yawned.

"We're not going back to that flat," Össur rasped.

"What's got into you?"

"It's wrong. There's something wrong about that place. I can feel it."

They were parked outside a drive-through kiosk, celebrating the arrival of their new passports with greasy burgers and paper cups full of surprisingly good coffee.

Magni screwed up the paper his burger had been wrapped in and dropped it out the window.

"And don't do that," Össur snapped at him from the back seat.

"What the fuck?" Magni growled, putting the car into gear and letting it bump across the car park to the road. "What's got into you? I just dropped some rubbish."

"It attracts attention, and that's what we can do without."

He drove without speaking for the few kilometres through Kópavogur with the street lights shining through the drops of rain collecting on the windscreen, sensing the tension brewing on the back seat. Össur broke the silence.

"Keep away from that flat. You hear me?"

"Come on, Össi. What's the problem? Nobody could know we're using the place, could they?"

Össur's voice cut through the darkness. "You're a proper pair of amateurs, aren't you? There are nosey bastards everywhere poking through other people's business. You've no idea who's seen what."

Magni yawned and glanced at Tinna Lind. "What do you reckon?"

"I don't know. But Össur could be right. Why take chances?"

"See? Even your girlfriend thinks I'm right."

"All right, where are we going tonight, then?" Magni demanded, his temper close to boiling over. "Any smart ideas?"

"It'll be the fucking cop shop on Hverfisgata if you're not careful," Össur snarled from the back seat.

Steingrímur's eyes looked closed but Gunna had no doubt he was awake. She was struggling to keep her eyes open, although the sight of a Subaru coming down the road and parking outside the ground floor flat where Sindri and Sólveig's relationship had come so publicly unstuck had been a diversion. Two women had emerged from the car and been greeted on the doorstep by a tearful Sólveig, a glass of wine in one hand, and opinions on the long-gone Sindri's behaviour, looks, physique, taste and performance in bed had been loudly shared before the trio disappeared inside.

After that everything had gone depressingly quiet again and Gunna wondered to herself if this was a late-night wild goose chase, until her communicator clicked into life.

"We have company," she heard Helgi say from his position in the van on the other side of the building. "A guy on a bike. On his way up the stairs."

"Thanks, Helgi. Nothing so far this side," Gunna said and nudged Steingrímur with her elbow. "Something's happening. There's a light in the apartment up there."

Steingrímur trained his binoculars on the windows. "Nothing to see. No lights on there."

"Not one of the house lights. It looked more like a flashlight inside."

"I think you're right," Steingrímur said with satisfaction. "Fun and games at last."

"Helgi, get ready," Gunna called into her communicator. "Looks like the mystery man is in the flat."

Gunna and Steingrímur silently mounted the stairs up to the broad walkway leading to the row of upper flats with Helgi and another officer bringing up the rear. She listened at the door and shook her head.

"Key, Helgi?" Gunna murmured.

He had the key in his hand, and was about to insert it when the door opened and as much of a face as could be seen between a wool hat pulled low and a scarf pulled up to the chin appeared. For a moment there was silent surprise on both sides before the figure pulled the door back and then slammed it forward, but Steingrímur's boot stopped it short and he shouldered it hard inwards, knocking the man into the wall and onto a small table that collapsed in splinters beneath him as he fell backwards.

324

Steingrímur and Helgi hauled him to his feet.

"Good evening, young man," Gunna said, looking him up and down, and taking in the leathers. "How about we all go down to the station for a chat?"

Magni fretted in the driver's seat while Össur sat still and upright behind him, his gaze fixed on what could be seen of the street through the drizzle.

"Is she going to be long?" he said at last.

"How the hell should I know?"

Magni felt ill at ease, left alone in the car with Össur and the occasional click of the pistol's safety catch.

"Five minutes and then we're out of here."

Magni sat in silence.

"You heard me?" Össur demanded.

"I heard you, and no. We're not going anywhere until she's back."

"If I say go, we go."

The pistol clicked once.

"And if I say no, we don't go anywhere."

"My job. My rules, Magni," Össur said in a quiet voice that was somehow far more sinister than his usual bluster. "Sometimes you just have to cut someone loose. Know what I mean?"

"No, I don't know what you mean, and if you think we're going without her, you can think again," Magni snapped back over his shoulder, expecting to feel the cold barrel of the Baikal at his neck at any moment.

The argument was halted as the passenger door opened and Tinna Lind dropped into the seat.

"And?" Össur asked.

"Go, Magni. Anywhere you like, but let's not hang around here."

He started the engine and the car moved forward as he told himself to keep it slow.

"What happened?"

"Össur was right," she said with a sigh, turning in her seat to catch his eye, while Össur nodded with satisfaction. "There are lights on in the flat and a couple of cars parked outside that weren't there today. And there's some shouting going on, so let's make tracks, shall we?"

The roof of the summer house rattled in the wind that had picked up through the evening. There was a strong tang of the sea in the air and spray from the shoreline a few hundred yards away in the darkness. Although there was nothing to be seen, the roar and crash of waves on the rocks was clear enough. Magni licked his lips and tasted the salt as they hurried from where he had parked the car on the seaward side of the wooden house, out of sight from the road.

Inside he carefully covered the landward windows one by one with squares of black plastic cut from rubbish bags, taping them in place.

"Don't want to attract attention by letting the lights show, do we?"

"What is this place?" Tinna Lind asked, looking around the cabin.

"It belongs to the seamen's union. Members can book it for a week's holiday, but I don't reckon anyone wants it at this time of year."

"Just as well we're not staying long, isn't it?" Össur said, rummaging through the kitchen cupboards. His face lit up as he came up with a bottle of amber fluid. The level was still above the label and he smacked his lips.

"Nightcap, anyone?" he crowed. "I reckon we deserve a drink."

They sat over three glasses of cheap cognac and fingered the three passports.

"They look real enough," Tinna Lind said and caught Össur's eye. "Did Rafn double-cross us on this?"

"Rafn would sell his own grandmother if he could," Össur grunted. "But I don't think he'd screw us over on this. My guess is he wants us out of the way completely, not in a cell."

"Why? Go on, convince me."

"Well," Össur said, "Rafn may be an evil little bastard, and I can say that because I've known him since he was ten years old, shoplifting cardamom drops from Hagkaup and selling them to street drunks. But in the trade the Undertakers have a reputation for straight dealing, and if he screws me over, word will get around, which is bad for business. It's different with you civilians, though," he added and knocked back his cognac. "Besides, if we're caught we could blab to the cops that he sold us stolen passports. That would give them an excuse to shake him down and he wouldn't like that."

"Charming, so there really is some honour among thieves?" Tinna Lind said, sipping her drink and savouring it. "We need to do some shopping tomorrow."

"What for?"

"Hair dye, to start with," she replied, opening the passport. "I need to be blonde if this is supposed to be my photo, and you need to be a lot less grey. Magni should be all right. It just looks like he's cut his hair, grown a beard and lost a bit of weight. And we need to get glasses for both of us. Those cheap ones with heavy frames will do the trick, as long as they're not too strong."

"You reckon so?" Magni asked. "You can do all that stuff with the hair?"

"Duh. Easy enough. It's easier than changing the oil in that car out there. Then we need to get to a computer somewhere."

"What for?" Össur asked.

"Tickets, Össi. We need to get flights."

"I went to a travel agent last time."

"That's fine if you prefer that," Tinna Lind said. "But you might as well put up a notice board outside saying, 'Össur's here', as go to a travel agent in town."

"You can get tickets on the internet?"

"Easy as you like," she assured him. "It takes five minutes. We have a card that's going to work? And we all need to decide who's going where?"

Gunna lay awake for a long time. The memory of Thorvaldur Hauksson close to death refused to leave her and was only replaced by the mental images of him as a younger man in a denim jacket, dark hair in a lion's mane around a chiselled face, and piercing blue eyes through curling cigarette smoke.

After a while she got out of bed silently and ran the tap for a glass of water in the kitchen, where she sat with the day's paper, flicking through the pages without registering much more than the outline of the pictures, although photos of Tinna Lind Bogadóttir and Össur Óskarsson caught her eye and she read the text under the pictures. She wondered if they would ever be found, and then reassured herself that their chances of disappearing entirely were slim. Sooner or later they would show up, probably together, and even more probably with plausible reasons for having been out of touch for so long.

Gunna wondered what had really happened at Hotel Hraun during the days those four people were stranded there together, willingly or not, and decided that most of the truth would probably emerge once all those involved had been through the exhaustive process of investigation and interviews that the law required, assuming Össur, Magni and Tinna Lind did eventually turn up.

"Can't sleep?" Steini asked, a hand landing gently on her shoulder and kneading it for a moment. He yawned and sipped from her glass of water.

"No, give me half an hour and I'll be all right."

"Tough day?"

"A very long day, and there'll be a few more to come before this case comes to some kind of a conclusion."

"That's not what I meant, Gunna." Steini sat opposite her with arms folded. "How's Gísli? It must be bloody tough on him."

"He's not having a great time at the moment," Gunna said with a deep sigh. "I'd hoped he'd stay away from Thorvaldur, but the curiosity was too much for him, I suppose."

"Of course it was. You can't blame him for wanting to find these things out. It's only natural."

"Yeah, you're right. I just hope he comes through it unscathed."

"Gísli will be fine," Steini said, cracking his knuckles and yawning again. "He may have done a few silly things, but he's no fool and he's a survivor. It's you I'm more concerned about."

"Me? Why?"

"Because this all seems to have hit you harder than you like to admit. I've never seen you so shaken up, even when Gísli admitted he'd managed to get both Soffía and Drífa pregnant a couple of weeks apart."

"It's a shock," Gunna admitted. "It's not every day you watch someone about to die, especially someone who was special a long time ago."

"Come on, then. What's the story?" Steini invited. "We've been together for a few years now and it's something you've never told me about."

"You're curious, are you?"

"Sort of. If it helps me understand what's going on in your head, then so much the better, especially if it means you might get back to sleeping normal hours again."

"It was all so long ago," Gunna said, wondering how much she ought to tell him and how much to keep to herself. "Laufey's older now than I was then, but somehow we grew up faster than they do these days. Thorvaldur Hauksson was the handsome art teacher who had aspirations to be an artist himself, but he couldn't keep his dick in his trousers, especially when confronted with a fifteen-year-old with a crush on him."

"He was a teacher? Good grief. He'd be locked up for that these days, wouldn't he?"

"Probably. So there was a secret fling that lasted a couple of mad weeks, and then he had to leave, suddenly."

Steini raised an eyebrow in question.

"He'd also been having an affair with a fisherman's wife, one of my cousins, in fact. Her husband was a big lad and when he found out, it definitely wasn't healthy for Thorvaldur to hang around, so he left in a hurry, packing everything he had into an old Buick he owned and I suppose he drove south and never came back. He did say goodbye to me, very quickly, and that's my memory of him, standing by the gate at home, looking over his shoulder in case Bjössi was on his tail, and me in floods of tears. That's it, in a nutshell," she said and lay in silence, listening to the clock tick.

"And the rest is history?" Steini asked gently.

"Quite. You know the rest of the story. I did see him a few times after that, but he was never interested in Gísli and I suppose he had plenty of other children here and there that he should have been supporting. The last time I saw him he was in a cell at the Hafnarfjördur station, about twenty years ago. He was too drunk to realize who I was and I didn't have the heart to say anything at the time."

"That explains a few things." Steini nodded slowly. "Now are you going to go back to sleep for a few hours?"

Tinna Lind lay with her head on Magni's chest while his arm draped across her, fingertips tracing patterns on the soft skin of her belly.

"You're happy with all this, are you?" she asked, turning onto her side to look along his torso to where he lay propped against a pillow, gazing fondly down at her.

"Yeah. I'm easy with it."

"Sure? Walking away from everything? Friends, family?"

"Yep. Mind's made up. Here we come, new life."

"Good. Just thought I'd check."

"And you?"

"Don't stop," Tinna Lind giggled as Magni trailed his fingers along her side and paused at her hip bone. "I'm ready to go. Fed up with living on this cold rock."

The tips of Magni's fingers travelled along her thigh. "Do you reckon we could ever come back?" he murmured.

"I don't see why not, one day. There are limitations on most crimes, and after a few years I expect it would all be written off."

"Five years? Ten years?"

"More like ten, I expect," Tinna Lind said. "We'll see how good life is in the Mediterranean, shall we?"

"Is that where you want to go?"

"Yeah. I've been there before."

"What are we going to do there?"

"Well, with a hundred thousand euros we should probably be able to buy a decent little bar somewhere near the sea."

"Sounds good."

Her expression hardened and she pulled herself up onto her elbows. "You know, Magni. With two hundred thousand euros we could buy a very nice bar right on the beach."

He grinned. "No change of plan?"

Tinna Lind nodded and let her hair fall over his chest. "I'm just wondering what's the best way to do it."

"You've noticed how much sharper he is now that he's not puffing all the time?"

"Yeah, and I couldn't help seeing how much his hands shake."

"Össi keeps his money in his jacket, which is why I suppose he never takes it off."

"And his gun."

"That's right," Magni agreed. "The fucking gun as well. We need to be rid of that."

"We need to get stuff tomorrow, and I don't imagine he'll let us go without him, do you?"

"Össi? No, he doesn't trust us an inch. It's nothing personal. He just doesn't trust anyone. Have you noticed how he never turns his back on either of us? We're going to have to be very careful between now and parting company with him, because if he can screw us over, he will."

Tinna Lind let herself sink back on her side and Magni's fingertips began a gentle traverse from neck to belly and back.

"We'll see. Maybe Össi will get unlucky and get left behind somewhere tomorrow?" she said in a soft voice. "Preferably without his jacket."

CHAPTER
NINE

Friday

Kamilla Oddsdóttir looked up the moment the lift doors opened and Gunna stepped out.

"Kamilla? I'm Gunnhildur Gísladóttir. Thanks for coming in so early."

"That's all right. My office isn't far from here."

Gunna examined the face that had a flustered look to it and eyes that darted back and forth, declining to meet her gaze as they travelled upwards in the lift. The smart business suit and the stylish hair were at odds with the woman's fingers, which fidgeted with the phone in her hand, and she sighed audibly.

"So what's this all about?" she asked as Gunna closed the interview room door.

"As I told you on the phone, we arrested a man just before midnight in your apartment in Gardabær. It is your apartment, isn't it?"

"In theory, yes. Hjalti and I bought it together, but I moved out a while ago and Hjalti lives there now, when he's in the country."

"He's abroad a lot?"

"He's an engineer on an oil survey ship and works for a company in Norway, so he's not here very much.

Since our relationship came to an end, he doesn't always bother coming back to Iceland between trips."

"But you have joint ownership of the flat and you still have access to it?"

Kamilla rolled her phone over and over between nervous fingers. "Yes," she said, looking up and into Gunna's eyes for the first time. "I still have my legal residence there until I find something more permanent than where I'm living at the moment. I go to the flat every other week or so to make sure everything's all right and to collect any mail for me or Hjalti. It's quite amicable, even though we're not together any more."

"Do you know a gentleman called Magni Klemens Sighvatsson?"

Kamilla shrugged. "Magni's an old friend of Hjalti's. I haven't seen him for a long time. They go back a long way. Magni used to live with a woman called Ína, and Hjalti used to be married to Ína's sister Svava. Not that I know the full story and nor do I want to."

"Does he have access to the flat?"

"I think so. I recall Hjalti gave him a key, and I don't remember it ever being returned. So, yes. It could well be that Magni has access to the flat but you'd have to check with Hjalti, and at the moment he's somewhere in Russia, as far as I know." She paused. "How did this person get into the flat?" she asked, her voice betraying her disquiet.

"He picked the lock. He had a set of picks on him and it's easy enough when you know how."

"Did he take anything?"

"Nothing at all, or so it seems. He had only been there a few minutes when we intercepted him."

"All right," Kamilla said, frowning and looking into space somewhere over Gunna's shoulder. "Nothing stolen and no damage. Is there a problem?"

"I would like you to press charges. The man had entered your property without permission."

"No," Kamilla said, her head shaking so vehemently that her stylish hair shivered. "I'm not pressing charges. I don't see the point. I appreciate what you've done and I'll have the locks changed, but I'm not prepared to get involved beyond that."

"You're sure? This character certainly wasn't up to any good."

"I don't care. It's Hjalti's problem and I don't want to be involved." Kamilla pushed her chair back and stood up. "And now I have to go. I need to get back to work."

They travelled down in the lift in silence. In the entrance lobby Kamilla again avoided Gunna's eyes. She opened her mouth to speak and closed it again as Gunna gently took her arm and steered her out through the doors into the open air.

"Kamilla, there's nobody listening in and nothing being recorded." Gunna looked at her intently, forcing Kamilla to meet her eyes. "I'm guessing you've had a visit?"

"I . . ."

"Or a call? Sometime last night or early this morning?"

Kamilla's frightened eyes told her everything. "A call. At five this morning from a withheld number."

"Telling you to keep your mouth shut?"

"Gunnhildur, my parents are quite elderly. I'm sure you understand?"

337

"I don't like it, but I understand," Gunna said. "I don't imagine you'll have any more problems with this man. Go and get the locks changed. But if you want the place to be more secure, don't go for the cheapest option."

It was a quiet street of old houses built at odd angles, just as Magni remembered it when he and Össur had jogged down the hill with a bag of money, wondering where Árni had got to.

"Here. Stop here."

The house where Alli the Cornershop lived could be seen a hundred metres away up the gradual slope, an innocuous-looking building with its long blanked-out shop windows that had once displayed ironmongery and groceries thick with a quarter of a century of dust.

"Cool down, will you?" Magni said. "Look, Össi, this is dangerous for all of us, and it's not just about you. Think, will you?"

Össur brooded in silence in the back seat, the Baikal in his hand behind the seat and trained on Tinna Lind. Magni weighed up how easily he would be able to make a grab for the weapon and decided it would be hopeless. Össur would be able to fire far more quickly than he would be able to get a hand through the gap between the seats, and even then the gun could still be out of reach.

"We can be out of here tonight, somewhere in Europe with a pocketful of cash," Magni said. "D'you want to risk that?"

"We can still get out of here, Össi," Tinna Lind said. Magni looked sideways at her and could see the tension on her face. "We can get tickets for flights this evening easily enough."

"Yeah? How? Walk into a travel agent?"

"I can do it on my phone."

"You have a phone?" Össur demanded. "You told me you didn't have one, you lying bitch."

"Fuck you, Össur," Tinna Lind spat back, her temper boiling over. "You think you're the only one who can tell lies when it suits them?"

She yelped as Össur jammed the muzzle of the Baikal hard into her side and Magni again wondered how easily he could snatch the pistol.

"Where's this phone?"

Tinna Lind delved into an inside pocket of her coat and pulled out a smartphone. From another pocket she extracted the charger cable she had bought an hour earlier and plugged it into the lighter socket.

"The battery died days ago, and in any case, there was no signal up at that hotel place," she said. "I can book flights easily enough using this if I can connect to wifi somewhere." She switched the phone on and watched the screen power up in front of her.

Össur sat back and took a couple of deep breaths. "All right. But we still get even with Alli."

"You have a hundred and something thousand euros of Alli's cash. Isn't that enough? You still want to go and settle a score?"

They sat in the car parked on a suburban street at the far end of the town. It was just close enough for Tinna

Lind to log into the nearby golf club's wifi and she peered at her phone screen.

"Card?" she asked.

"Is this Össi's flight or ours?"

"His," Tinna Lind said without looking up. "Just read out the numbers. Whose card is it?"

"Mine. I hope there's enough credit on it," he said, twisting around in his seat. "Cash, Össi. How much is it, Tinna?"

"Nineteen thousand." She thought for a second. "Call it a hundred and fifty euros."

Once Össur had peeled off a couple of notes and handed them over, Magni read out the sixteen digits on his card and Tinna Lind punched them in while Magni crossed his fingers and held his breath.

"Expiry?"

"Ten eighteen."

"Security? The three numbers on the back?"

"One zero six."

"OK, wait a moment," she said, eyes on the screen. "It's gone through. Congratulations, Össur, as far as the airline is concerned you're Einar Pálmi Jakobsson and you're on the afternoon flight to Alicante. So you need to be at the airport at three."

Össur grinned to himself in the back seat. "And when are you two lovebirds flying?"

"Checking now," Tinna Lind said, eyes on the phone and scrolling back. "Hell, it's a pain in the neck doing it on this tiny screen," she complained. "OK, we seem to be in now." She typed rapidly, using both thumbs to fill in the boxes while Össur and Magni sat in silence.

"Right. We're Ásta Maria Einarsdóttir and Jóhann Einarsson, and we're flying at eight tonight. Card, Magni? Read the numbers out again, will you?"

"Where are you two going with your loot, then?" Össur asked. With his flight booked, he seemed immediately less tense, relaxed and happier than Tinna Lind had seen him.

"We're going to Zurich," she said, switching the phone off and dropping it into her pocket. "From there we can decide where to go next."

"Chief!" Eiríkur came bounding down the stairs, his face alight with excitement. "Gunna!"

"What's the matter?

"Comms called just now. Tinna Lind's phone popped up."

"Shit . . . where?"

"Hafnarfjördur. It was live for a few minutes, no calls or texts, then went offline again."

"Get every car and motorcycle you can find out there right now, but no sirens, and get the best fix you can on that phone right away," Gunna snapped. "I'll be back in two minutes, be by the door in a car."

"Will do, chief. I've already had an alert out and diverted everyone we can find to look out for a grey Skoda, and comms are working on a position," he said, but Gunna had already disappeared. She was back well within the two minutes and strode outside to find Eiríkur waiting for her in an unmarked Golf.

"This thing has lights and bells, doesn't it?"

"It does."

"Use them. Hafnarfjördur, right now, if you please."

"Ninety-five-fifty, comms," Gunna heard a few minutes later with the morning traffic parting unwillingly for them along Kringlumýrarbraut as her communicator buzzed in her ear.

"Siggi, what do you have for me?"

"The number was somewhere in the old part of Hafnarfjördur to start with when it logged on, then seems to have shifted south towards the back end of town between the port area and the golf club before it was switched off."

"But on the town side of Reykjanesbraut?"

"Looks like it, and moving fast enough for it to have to be in a car."

"Can you pinpoint any better where it was when it first showed up and where it was switched off?"

"I'd say it was switched on around Lækjargata, Austurgata, Hamarshraun — that sort of patch. And switched off somewhere on the other side of town."

"Good stuff, thanks Siggi, Let me know right away if it pops up again, would you?"

The wail of a siren jerked Össur out of his silence in the back of the car. "Where the fuck's that copper going?"

"Relax, Össi, it's probably an ambulance."

But the sight of a speeding patrol car decelerating off the main road and towards the town had Magni stepping on the brake and he made a squealing U-turn back up the hill.

"Shit. We'd best keep out of sight, I reckon."

He accelerated and the Skoda surged up the slope, until Magni again trod hard on the brakes, turned into a side street and let the car roll gently to the end, where he shot across the intersection into a deserted residential cul-de-sac. Magni swung the car neatly into a space between two others.

"Maybe they're not looking for us?" Tinna Lind said. "Maybe it's something completely different?"

"Could be, but we'd best not take a chance." Magni gnawed a knuckle and tapped at the wheel with his fingertips. "We can't stick around here for long."

"Why not?" Össur demanded.

"For fuck's sake, Össi. Look around you. Smart houses, kids on bikes. This is curtain-twitching territory. We're going to get noticed by the Neighbourhood Watch here, and I'll bet you there's half a dozen local busybodies already writing the car registration on their kitchen whiteboards. I'm wondering how we can get back to the main road and go and hide out at the union place for a few hours until it's time to go without being spotted. We'd have been clear if you hadn't had to fuck about, Össi," he said angrily, turning round in his seat to face him.

"You watch your mouth, boy," Össur snarled back. "And don't you forget there's a job to do before we leave."

"Before you leave, you mean. Do your own dirty work. I've done enough of that shit already."

"Boys, please. Keep it for later, will you?" Tinna Lind said in a sharp voice that took them both by surprise, "Look, go back up the road towards the golf club.

There's an underpass under the main road that will bring us out on the other side."

"Can we get onto Reykjanesbraut there?"

"No, but we can double back on the quiet side and get to the slip road that way instead of having to go back through town this side. Make sense?"

Magni grinned. "My criminal mastermind," he muttered, and started the car.

They went through the underpass and Tinna Lind turned around in her seat. "Össi, you'd best duck down."

"Why the hell should I?"

"Because if they're looking for us, they'll be looking for a car with three people in it, not two."

With bad grace, Össur grunted and agreed that she was right as he lay down on the seat, clasping the Baikal hard against his chest. "No tricks, you two," he rasped.

Eiríkur cruised through the streets of Hafnarfjördur while Gunna followed the traffic on her communicator. The three available motorcycle officers had stationed themselves at intersections around the town while two patrol cars combed the streets looking for the grey Skoda. Eiríkur took the unmarked Golf through the narrow streets of the old town and passed Alli the Cornershop's house a couple of times, where Alli's own Golf and a black van were parked next to each other. The second time Gunna had him stop outside while she inspected the place, her fingers rattling a tattoo on the dashboard as she wondered whether or not to knock and ask if there had been any visitors.

344

The fact that Alli would undoubtedly tell her a lie that would be difficult to disprove was enough for her to decide not to bother and they continued to criss-cross the town,

"If you wanted to hide a car, where would you go, Eiríkur?"

"In Hafnarfjördur? I wouldn't bother. The place is too small. Unless you have a garage where you can park it out of sight, it's not going to be all that easy."

"Yeah, but where would you go?"

"One of the quiet streets up the top there, or else around the harbour, I reckon, but you'd still struggle to hide it away somewhere."

"Either they've been lucky and slipped past, or else we've missed them," Gunna decided.

Eiríkur looked glum. "You're probably right. They could have gone along the coast road to Álftanes and gone towards Reykjavík that way, or they might have gone up Flatarhraun and got on to Reykjanesbraut. Or they might be driving around right behind us. But they probably aren't aware that we tumbled them so quickly."

"What I'm wondering is why Tinna Lind's phone popped up for such a short time. It was fourteen minutes from being logged on to being switched off, but no calls or texts."

"Internet? Checking email?"

"Checking something. But what?"

"And was it Tinna Lind or someone else using her phone?"

"Exactly. If there had been a call or a text we'd at least have something to go on. Instead, all we know is that Tinna Lind's phone was in Hafnarfjördur half an hour ago, with or without her. Brilliant."

"Gunna?" Eiríkur said. "Have you noticed how many bikers there are about?"

"Are you feeling suspicious, Eiríkur?" Gunna asked. "You reckon we're not the only ones looking for Össur?"

Magni laughed uncontrollably as he pulled the Skoda off the main road and onto the winding side road leading to the summer house. He was sweating and could feel his heart pound as he parked the car in the shadow of the chalet. He lay back in his seat as he switched off the engine. Tinna Lind put a hand on his arm and patted it.

"It's all right. A few hours to kill and we're out of here," she said in a soft voice.

"Pull yourself together will you?" Össur snapped, sitting still in the back seat and taking care not to get out of the car until Tinna Lind swung her door open and stepped out.

Össur sat on a hard chair by the kitchen table and flicked his zippo to light a cigarette. Tinna Lind watched him and noticed that since the passports had been handed over the night before, Össur had been nervously on his guard, watching them both and taking care to keep something between himself and Magni.

Magni filled the coffee maker, switched it on and collapsed on the sofa with his eyes closed. He took deep breaths and tried to think of something relaxing and far away. A vision of the sun glittering on the water of the harbour at Heimaey came vividly to mind, small boys with their first fishing rods laughing and triumphant with a small pollock wriggling on the end of a line.

"All right?" Tinna Lind sat next to him and he put an arm around her as she nestled against him. Össur blew moody smoke towards the ceiling. Normally Magni would have told him to go outside, but it seemed more trouble than it was worth to start another argument that would never be resolved. "Nervous?"

"You're not?"

"Maybe I don't show it," she said with a fond smile. "We have a couple of hours to kill, so I'm going to have a shower and get myself fixed up. Do you want to go and shut your eyes for an hour? It's going to be a long day."

Magni opened his eyes, rubbed them and wondered if the blonde goddess wrapped in a towel and smiling at him were real or part of a dream he hadn't woken up from. It took him a moment to remember that he was in the bedroom of the Seamen's Union's chalet and the goddess was Tinna Lind with newly dyed hair.

"You like it?"

"Wow. Just a bit."

She towelled her hair gently. "It's a little darker than I wanted it to be, but it'll wash out in a couple of weeks."

"I think you should keep it like that," he said. "For a while, anyway."

"Maybe. We'll see."

Magni yawned and sat up. "What's Össur doing?"

"He was outside just now, probably just having a spliff and planning how to spend all his money."

"We're going to have to be careful."

"You don't trust him?"

"Not an inch."

A sly smile ran around Tinna Lind's face. "And I don't suppose he trusts us either."

"Probably not. It's hardly in his nature."

She sat on the bed next to him, leaned forward to let her hair fall forward and then swung her head up and back to send it in a blonde arc back over her shoulders.

"How long have I been asleep?"

"About an hour."

"So what's the time?"

"About eleven." She shrugged the towel off and swung her legs onto the bed to lie next to him. "We have a good half hour, if that's what you're thinking."

"That's good, because that's exactly what I was thinking."

"They say gentlemen prefer blondes, so you can tell me afterwards if it makes any difference. I've never been blonde before, so it'll be a new experience."

Their half hour together had been intense, tender and raw by turns.

Össur was nowhere to be seen when Magni pushed opened the bedroom door and went to the bathroom to

348

splash his face with cold water. He looked out of the window and checked the car was still there, although he knew the key was still in the pocket of his jeans on the bedroom floor, where Tinna Lind had dropped them after pulling them off him.

Back in the bedroom he found Tinna Lind pulling a shirt over her head, her newly blonde locks dropping a couple of inches below the collarline and contrasting with the black fabric.

"I can't see Össur anywhere."

"He can't have gone far," she said, pulling a hooded sweater over the black shirt and shaking her still damp hair out over it.

"I hope he hasn't run for it."

"Where could he have run to? It's a long walk to anywhere from here."

Magni opened the door and looked out over the couple of hundred metres of lava overgrown with patches of heather between the chalet and the sea.

"You've finished then?" Össur asked and Magni saw him sitting at a picnic table with a cigarette between his fingers. A carrier bag with its plastic handles tied together had been placed on the table.

"What have you got there?"

"Never you mind. Something I need to drop off to a friend before my flight."

"What? You should have said something before. We need to be out of here pretty soon if you're going to catch your flight."

"Then maybe you should have kept your dick in your trousers," Össur snapped. "Anyone would think you'd never seen pussy before the way you've been at it." He ground out the stub of his cigarette on one of the planks of the table. "Come on, then. If we need to be going, we'd best be off."

"Where do you want to drop that off?" Magni asked suspiciously.

"Don't worry, it's only in Hafnarfjördur. Ten minutes there and ten minutes back. Now get on with it, will you?"

"We really shouldn't be going back to Hafnarfjördur if half the police force is looking for us," Tinna Lind said as Magni took the Skoda nervously down the slope towards the town centre. There was plenty of traffic and the place was busy.

"That way," Össur ordered, pointing to a side street. Off the main road the place appeared deserted. There was no traffic here and with a steady drizzle coming down, there was nobody to be seen on foot.

"Where are we going?" Magni asked.

"That way." There was a harsh determination in Össur's voice.

"You're not going to Alli's place again, are you?"

"Got it in one, clever boy," Össur said and Magni saw his brown teeth appear in the mirror in a humourless smile.

"For fuck's sake, Össi? Are you out of your tiny mind?"

"Don't argue. I know what I'm doing."

Össur took the Baikal from his pocket and clicked the safety catch. Tinna Lind expected him to jam it into her ribs between the seats again, but instead he lifted the pistol and held it to Magni's neck.

"Not another word. Understand?" he hissed. "Drive slowly long the street and stop outside Alli's cornershop."

With the muzzle of the pistol pressed against the back of his head, Magni felt his fingertips going numb. He brought the car to a gentle halt outside Alli's place.

"Look," he croaked, nodding at a black van squatting on the other side of the street. "That's Rafn's truck, isn't it?"

"So much the better. Leave the engine running because we're going to have to be out of here sharpish. Now get out of the car, both of you, and walk towards Alli's place."

"Össi, come on. We can be out of here right now and no harm done."

The impact of the Baikal's barrel on the back of his head was sharp enough to make his eyes water instantly and he held his breath, waiting for the crack of the shot that would be the last thing he would hear.

"Do as I say or one of you gets it," Össur said in a low voice, heavy with a determination that was more chilling than his usual angry tone.

They got slowly out of the car, Össur first with the pistol in his hand, which was now dropped down to his waist. He leaned into the car and retrieved the carrier bag.

"In front of me," he said, and handed the bag to Tinna Lind. "You can take that."

In the middle of the deserted street, with rain dripping down his face, Magni wondered what was happening as Össur dug into his other pocket and pulled out his lighter.

"Open the bag, darling," he ordered. "Carefully," he added as Tinna Lind put it down and untied the handles.

"What . . .?"

The reek of petrol from the two bottles was unmistakeable, not least as the rags stuffed into the top of each one had also been soaked in it. He handed her the lighter, then transferred the pistol to his left hand.

"Keep back, Magni. Don't try to do anything stupid. I can shoot with either hand easily enough," Össur warned.

"Give me a light, girl," Össur ordered and Tinna Lind watched in fascination as the petrol-soaked rag in the top of the bottle caught and burned fiercely. Össur threw the bottle in a long arc towards the black van and it hit the ground by the driver's door. The sudden rush of heat as the glass broke and the fuel caught fire was more than Tinna Lind had expected and she instinctively cowered down while Magni watched in dismay as the flames licked at the van's sides.

"Again," Össur yelled, pointing the pistol at her. "Come on you stupid bitch, pick that one up and light it!"

Tinna Lind felt the scorching heat of the fire as the van was practically engulfed and stared at the second bottle of petrol.

352

"There," Össur shouted at her over the roar of the burning van, the pistol back in his good hand, aiming it at the pink house. Tinna Lind sensed the double crack of the pistol as a window at the front of the house disintegrated. "Throw it. That window there. Now!"

She picked up the bottle with shaking hands and glanced at Magni, catching his eye.

"Hey, Össi," she called to him, tossing the bottle of petrol high in the air towards him. "Catch."

Össur stared at her in a moment's furious astonishment, which turned to a roar of fury as he fumbled to catch the bottle as it fell towards him, his attention diverted and the pistol forgotten in his hand. Just as the bottle slipped through his fingers and shattered on the ground, Magni lunged at Össur. Magni's shoulder drove into Össur's back and sent him flying, leaving him lying with his legs in the spreading pool of petrol. The Baikal dropped from his hand and Magni kicked it hard, watching it skitter across the road, bounce off the kerb and come to rest in a puddle of grey water.

Magni watched in shock as Tinna Lind dropped the still flaming lighter into the petrol on the road and it ignited with a rush, the flames snatching at Össur's legs. He screeched with fear and rolled away, beating at his trousers. Magni vaguely registered people in the distance as if they were in slow motion. As Össur slapped at the flames, Tinna Lind snatched at the jacket that Össur had left unzipped, ripping one arm free.

"Quick, pull it off him," Tinna Lind gasped, tugging at Össur's jacket as he screeched and rolled over again on the wet road, trying to extinguish the flames. The black jacket came away in Magni's hands and he was surprised at how heavy it felt. "Go," Tinna Lind gasped, snatching at his arm, and looking over her shoulder to see Rafn and an older man appear with fury and disbelief on their faces.

"But Össi?"

"Fuck him," Tinna Lind swore as a distant siren wailed. She glared at Össur lying on the ground in front of her and aimed a deliberate sharp kick that connected with his groin. Össur rolled over with a howl, his hands reaching for his testicles, and Magni took Tinna Lind's arm. "That's for Erna," she snarled at him as Magni pulled her away before she could deliver a second kick.

"Tinna, come on."

"Fuck him, he was going to rip us off anyway. Let's get out of here."

The search for the mysterious grey car had been stood down. Gunna and Eiríkur held a quick debrief over coffee and doughnuts, which she knew she should really avoid, at the Hafnarfjördur police station, a few hundred yards from where one of the motorcycle officers had spent an hour in the rain hoping to identify three people in a stolen Skoda. Gunna was on her second much-needed cup of coffee when the F1 call buzzed over her communicator, but it was the address that had her sprinting for the door, with Eiríkur at her heels and the two motorcycle officers pulling on their helmets.

354

Outside the rain had faded away to a slow drizzle, as if the air was so saturated with water that it had started to ooze from the atmosphere. Eiríkur's long legs quickly outstripped her and he already had the Golf started by the time she jumped into the passenger seat, and it was moving before she'd pulled the door shut.

The wail of a siren could already be heard and the smell of burning was borne on the wind.

"Control, ninety-five-fifty," Gunna said in a curt voice into her communicator. "What's the story?"

"Ninety-five-fifty, control. Reports of a vehicle on fire and at least two gunshots."

"Any casualties?"

"One reported. There's a car ahead of you and the Special Unit has been alerted."

"Any fatalities?"

"None confirmed."

"Thanks, control."

The scene that greeted her was one of barely contained chaos, and she immediately thought a war zone had unfolded in suburban Hafnarfjördur as she scanned the scene and recognized Alli standing by the door of his house, his face showing shocked disbelief. Eiríkur firmly but insistently pushed the gathering crowd of bystanders back, and the first motorcycle officer parked his bike with its lights flashing to block the road.

An ambulance rolled to a halt and three green-overalled medics jumped out, one taking in the scene as a whole and two going directly to where a figure sat in the middle of the road with its head slumped down

355

over its chest. Gunna crouched by the figure with the two medics and recognized Össur's face as he lifted it to look at them, a dazed expression on his face. She could see that much of his hair had been singed down to the scalp.

"Who are you?" he slurred, his eyes blank and jaw slack.

"Don't worry, pal, we're here to look after you," one of the medics said. "What's your name?"

"Össi."

"OK, Össi. I'm Lóa. Now just sit still there and you'll be fine," she said, putting a blanket around him.

"Lóa," Össur repeated. "That's a lovely name," he said and closed his eyes as he took shuddering breaths.

"Badly hurt?" Gunna asked.

"Not good, but he'll live," the medic replied, looking up. "Some burns but mostly shock. Any other casualties?"

"It doesn't look like it," Gunna said, getting to her feet and looking around to see that in a matter of minutes the street had been cleared and sealed off.

The Skoda bounced down the street that Magni realized he and Össur had run down only a few days before with Alli the Cornershop's money. At the intersection at the bottom he stopped and waited patiently as a police car turned up the road and shot towards the scene. His fingers were still numb with excitement and he wanted to laugh and cry at the same time.

"Go that way," Tinna Lind ordered, going through the pockets of Össur's jacket as she ripped the lining inside out. The wad of notes was surprisingly modest when she found it wrapped in a fat envelope. She patted the jacket, exploring it for tell-tale bulges, and clawed at the lining on the other side. She whooped as she extracted a second bundle of smaller notes.

"Got it, Magni. The whole lot. A quarter of a million euros!"

"All of it?"

"Didn't you see Össur was constantly patting his pockets? Why do you think he never took his jacket off?"

Two more police cars sped along the road towards them and swept past in a blaze of flashing lights and sirens, an ambulance following behind them.

"You reckon Össur will be all right?" Magni said.

"Why are you asking? He was going to do the same to us." She opened the window and bundled the ragged remains of Össur's jacket through it, watching it twist briefly in the car's slipstream before it hit the road. "I'd bet you anything you like he was going to rob us before he got to the airport."

"Won't there be an alarm when he doesn't turn up for his flight?"

"Don't worry about it. People miss flights all the time. In any case, I didn't book his flight."

"What?" Magni looked sideways at her in amazement. "You had this planned?"

"Of course not. How could I have planned anything like this? But I knew something was going to happen," she said. "Listen, we need to drop out of sight and lose this car. We daren't turn up at the airport in it."

"OK. What's your plan?"

Tinna Lind smiled and tapped her nose. "We're going to be tourists," she said, holding up the passport that Össur had bought. "We ought to get rid of this as well, but it's probably not a great idea to drop it out of the window."

Alli was back in his own armchair, his face the colour of chalk. His lips trembled slightly as he took a sip from a mug cradled in his hands. Eiríkur stood up from the stool he had been perched on in front of the old man.

"What's the score here, Eiríkur?" Gunna murmured.

"One window shot out. There'll be a bullet stuck in a wall somewhere, I expect. The van outside is burnt right out."

"Any connection?"

"It's registered to Rafn Sigmarsson."

"Interesting. And where's Rafn now?"

"No idea. No sign of him anywhere. It's the same guy you're thinking of?"

Gunna nodded and sat herself in front of Alli on the stool Eiríkur had vacated. "Alli, you all right?"

Alli looked up and glared at her with watery blue eyes. "I've had a bit of a shock, but since when have the law been worried about my health?"

"What happened? No bullshit. Just tell me."

Alli sipped again from the mug and put it down on the wooden arm of the chair. "Össi Oskars. I guess you've got the little bastard outside, have you?"

"I want to hear it from you."

"There was a big old bang outside and when I had a look that van in the street was going up like a firecracker. Then that mad bastard Össi was there with a gun in his hand and a couple of other people with him."

"Who were they?"

"A man and a woman. Never seen them before. As soon as I saw what Össi had in his hand I shut the door quick." He gulped air and snarled. "Then that window came crashing in, there was a lot of shouting outside and then you lot showed up. That's it, officer. That's all I saw."

"And where's Rafn?"

Alli's eyes had resumed their usual flinty look.

"Who's this Rafn?"

Magni noticed as he drove into the quiet one-way street that the sign said Fjölnisvegur. He parked the Skoda neatly between two other cars and got out. He patted the roof as he said goodbye to it. The car had served them well, he decided, and it deserved better than to be abandoned in a side street. He shut the door, locked the car and posted the key through the letterbox of the nearest house.

Tinna Lind stood up and sent him a smile.

"Ready?"

"As ready as I'll ever be."

They walked down the street hand in hand, Tinna Lind trailing behind her the little suitcase she had bought that morning, its wheels bumping over the rutted pavement. The bare branches of the stunted trees arched over their heads as they took it easy, only breaking into a run once they had left the sleepy residential area behind them and had to cross the main road at a smart pace.

Tinna Lind bought two tickets for the airport shuttle bus, asking for them in English and paying with euros, before they took a seat in the restaurant.

"We could have just driven to the airport, you know," Magni said.

"We could have," Tinna Lind agreed, "but don't you think we've taken enough chances already?"

"You're right, I suppose."

"We had better be careful now. That old man that Össur hates so much. That was the guy you two robbed?"

"Alli. Yeah, that's him."

"With that fire and the gunshots and everything, you can bet anything you like the police will be crawling all over the place. What do you think Alli or Össur will tell them?"

"I don't reckon Alli would say a word, but it's hard to tell with Össur. He might spill the beans if he reckons he's facing a stretch," Magni said. "Whatever happens, they'll be searching for a couple, so maybe we should look as if we're both travelling on our own."

"Then meet up at the far end?"

"That's it."

"It's not a long flight. I chose Edinburgh because it's about the shortest flight you can get, so if there's anyone looking for us then hopefully we'll be long

360

gone," Tinna Lind said. "And I told Össur we were flying to Zurich. Do you think he'd remember that?"

"Who knows?" Magni said. "Good thinking. If we had a flight to Switzerland or Italy or somewhere, there's more time in the air for them to try and identify us."

"Then we can get a train to Glasgow and fly wherever we want to from there."

"Which puts anyone looking for us off the scent? Sounds good to me." He looked up. "Is that our bus?"

Tinna Lind glanced at her watch. "Let's get the next one. We don't want to be too early. Let's get something to eat while we're here, shall we?"

The little boy's eyes were wide with a mixture of excitement and trepidation. He swung his legs under the chair that was too high for him while his mother fussed making coffee.

"Tell the lady what you saw, Nonni," she said. "It's all right. You're not in trouble."

"Are you really a policeman?" he asked and corrected himself. "A police lady, I mean?"

"I am," Gunna assured him. "I'm a real-life detective."

"Who solves crimes and catches bad people?"

"Sort of. That's only part of what I have to do, and most of it isn't all that exciting."

"Do you have a gun?" Nonni asked, eyes wide.

"No, we don't carry guns," Gunna said, and his disappointment was immediately visible.

"So what do you do if you meet someone bad who has a gun?"

"I don't know. It hasn't happened yet. So I don't know what I'd do," Gunna said and picked up the mug of coffee that had appeared in front of her, while Nonni got a glass of squash and a slice of cake, which he bit into.

"What would you have done if you had seen the man I saw today?" he asked in a serious voice. "He had a gun and I saw him shoot it. Would you have been frightened?"

"I expect so," Gunna said. "Guns are very dangerous things. Were you frightened, Nonni?"

He thought as he chewed his cake and washed it down with squash.

"I wasn't at the time, but I was afterwards," he decided. "But he didn't see us, so we were all right."

"Where were you when you saw this?"

"We were in Thröstur's garden."

"That's next door," Nonni's mother broke in. "They play together all the time."

"So can you tell me what you saw? Take your time and think carefully."

"There was a car that came up the street and it stopped and a man got out and a lady and another man, a big man. Bigger than my dad."

"Good, and what did they do?"

"The man gave the lady a bag and she opened it and got a bottle out."

"Good," Gunna said. "This was the big man or the smaller one?"

"The little man."

"And what happened then?"

362

"He set fire to the bottle and threw it and there was a huge explosion," he said, spreading his arms in an arc to demonstrate just how huge it had been.

"Wow! So what did you do?"

"Thröstur went inside because he was frightened but I watched through the fence."

"You saw the black car catch fire? What happened after that?"

They started shouting at each other and the little man was really angry. He fired his gun and broke a window and the man who lives there came out, and another man."

"We know who lives there," Nonni's mother said darkly. "We'd never have bought this place if we'd known at the time."

"Now, Nonni. The two men who came out, have you seen them before?"

"Only the ugly old man who lives there."

"What about the other one?"

"He's weird," Nonni said with conviction. "He had hair like a girl, like mummy's." He looked at his mother with her blonde ponytail hanging down her back.

"As long as your mummy's hair?"

"Longer."

"Did you notice what he was wearing?"

"No, just . . . clothes," he said finally.

"You're doing really well, Nonni. Just a few more questions and then we're done. The two men who came out, what did they do?"

"They went to hide indoors because they were frightened of the man with the gun."

"All right, then what did the other men and the lady do?"

"They were shouting at each other, like Thröstur's mummy and daddy do sometimes, but louder," Nonni said, and his mother looked awkward. "And then the lady had a bottle and she threw it at the man."

"The big man or the small man?"

"She threw the bottle at the little man and it broke on the ground and then he caught fire and he was rolling around and screaming like a girl and they pulled his coat off because it was burning and then they drove away really fast in a car," he said in a single rushed breath and then looked at his mother who patted his back. "And then the police came and I ran home in case I got into trouble."

Magni's nerves were raw as he fidgeted on the bus. Tinna Lind had wanted to suggest that they should sit apart on the way as well as check in separately for their flight, but he was so jumpy that she relented and they sat hand in hand in the half-empty coach as it swept through the black countryside towards Keflavík and the airport beyond it.

There was nothing untoward to see as it passed Hafnarfjördur and she assumed that the fuss had long since died down. As the bus left the town and the street lights along Reykjanesbraut behind, Tinna Lind peered into the twilight towards the chalet where she and Magni had been engrossed in each other only a few hours before while their shared awareness of the risks they were about to take added a spice to their eagerness. She squeezed his hand in the gathering darkness and rested her head on his shoulder.

"You'll be all right, won't you?"

"Yeah. I'm just not as used to travelling as you are."

"What's your name, big boy?"

He grinned. "I'm Jóhann Einarsson."

"And why are you going to Scotland?"

"Just for a weekend break to drink a few beers and watch some football."

"You'll be fine."

"I know. It's the waiting that's the hard part. Once I'm off the bus I'll be fine."

She patted his hand again and he squeezed hers back, hard enough to make her wince, although his strength also made her tingle with a moment's excitement.

"Hey, before we get off, you'd better give me some cash so I can get a beer while I'm waiting for the flight."

Tinna Lind rummaged in her shoulder bag and pulled out a wad of notes that Magni stuffed into his pocket. "Don't spend it all at once," she whispered.

"I won't," he assured her as the coach pulled up at the terminal.

"You go first and check yourself in. I'll go to the bathroom and then follow you through," she whispered. "It's best if we're not seen together now, but I'll be watching out for you," she said, pulling him to her for a lingering kiss and getting a hug that practically squeezed the breath out of her in return.

It had to be something important for Ívar Laxdal to make a personal appearance, Gunna thought as she saw the bulky figure in his thick pea coat — non-uniform of the kind that only he could get away with — and the black beret he had brought with him from the Coast Guard all those years ago and refused to part with. He watched as two of the forensic personnel in their white suits and four of the Special Unit crew, who had been disappointed to find the excitement all over by the time they arrived, combed the street inch by inch, while Eiríkur lifted the blue tape for him to duck under.

"Sitrep, please, Gunnhildur?"

"Two molotov cocktails. Two gunshots. One 9mm Baikal pistol. One casualty, Össur Óskarsson, being treated at the National Hospital, and Helgi's there waiting for him to be fit for questioning," she rattled off. "Also, one very pissed off and frightened dope dealer, plus a couple of mysterious disappearances from the scene, either four people, or three, or just two, depending on witnesses. Whatever happened here took place very quickly. We were at the station just up the road at Flatarhraun when the F1 went up, so we were here within three minutes, and by then it was all over."

"Your version of events?"

"From what I've seen, Össur turned up here expecting to settle a score. He set fire to the van there, which belongs to Rafn Sigmarsson."

"Who we've been keeping a careful eye on, assuming it's the same Rafn Sigmarsson?"

"It is. The Undertaker. It seems that Össur also shot out Alli's window, and there was a second gunshot as well, although that may have been accidental."

"Motive?"

"Who knows? We'll maybe find out when he's capable of answering questions. But I'd guess simple revenge for the death of Árni Sigurvinsson," Gunna said and paused.

"But?"

"How did he get here? There's no car, and I don't imagine for a moment he walked here with two molotov cocktails in a shopping bag."

"You're thinking the other two who were at Hotel Hraun?"

"Exactly. What was their part in all this, and where are they now?"

Tinna Lind joined the back of the check-in queue. She had changed in the toilet into smart clean jeans and brushed her hair, anchoring it in a glossy ponytail high on the back of her head, and put on a pair of virtually zero magnification glasses. She could see Magni in the queue ahead of her, a head taller than anyone else in the line for the desks.

She saw him present his passport and glance towards her with a grin as he thanked the girl at the desk and set off towards the stairs leading to departures. A few minutes later Tinna Lind approached the desk and proffered her stolen passport.

"Baggage to check in?"

"No, just hand luggage."

"Can I see?"

Tinna Lind lifted the little case easily in one hand and the girl nodded, took a brief glance at the passport again and handed over a boarding pass.

"Boarding at seven-fifty, watch the screens for the departure gate. Have a good flight."

Upstairs she looked around discreetly for Magni's copper-gold head, but couldn't see him anywhere. Her passport and boarding pass were given the briefest glance and she held her breath as the little black case disappeared into the X-ray machine, closely followed by her boots. A search at this point, revealing the wads of illegal euros placed between paperbacks and magazines lifted from the Seamen's Union summerhouse, would be a disaster and would undoubtedly lead to a further search and the discovery in her coat pockets of yet more of Alli the Cornershop's working capital, finding its tax-free way out of the country.

She smiled at the customs officer, who nodded at her to put her boots back on, and she made an effort not to hurry zipping them up before placing the case back on its wheels and making for the duty-free area.

The flight was on time, according to the screens, and she went to the café for an espresso and a sandwich, spying Magni's head in the cafeteria restaurant in the distance as she buried her head in a magazine and tried to keep her mind clear.

Össur looked like a man defeated by life. Much of his thin hair had been burned off, giving him a blackened, lopsided look, but his eyes blazed with hatred as he looked from Gunna to Helgi and back.

"You have a tale to tell, don't you, Össi?" Helgi said.

Össur jerked his chin towards Gunna. "Who's the chick?"

"This lady, Össur, is my boss, detective sergeant Gunnhildur Gísladóttir, and you'd be well advised not to upset her."

"Get fucked," Össur spat and Gunna laughed, making his eyes burn with an even more intense loathing.

"Össur Oskarsson, you're under arrest for the murder of Brandur Geirsson. You don't have to say anything, but you have an obligation to tell the truth. You have the right to a lawyer at every stage of proceedings," she said, reeling off the words as Össur's eyes bulged. "There are a few other things we can throw in there as well, aggravated theft, abduction, possession of an illegal firearm, but that'll do for the moment."

"It wasn't me . . ." he said. "It was . . ."

"Ah. Now we're getting somewhere, are we?" Gunna said, swinging a chair under her and sitting close to Össur's bedside, pushing the stand with the drip attached to his arm out of the way. "So if it wasn't you, who was it?"

Össur sat in obstinate silence for a moment.

"I want a lawyer. I'm not saying anything until I have a lawyer."

"Helgi, would you organize a lawyer for the gentleman?"

When Helgi had left the room to make the call, Gunna moved closer to Össur and looked at the scalp visible through the singed remains of his hair.

"Listen, Össi. I'm not going to fuck about here," she said and saw him look at her sharply, knowing that the word had grabbed his attention. "This is your one and

369

only chance to tell me anything off the record. After my officer comes back, everything you say is taped and can be used in court. Understand?"

"Yeah?"

"Yeah. You and Magni bumped Alli the Cornershop. How much did you get out of it?"

Össur sighed. "A quarter of a million."

"Pounds? Dollars?"

"Euros. More or less."

"And where's the cash now?"

Gunna thought she could see a tear forming in Össur's eye, until his face hardened into an expressionless mask.

"I don't know."

"So who has it? Magni or Tinna Lind?"

"I don't know what you're talking about."

"You and Magni Sighvatsson rolled Alli the Cornershop, which is why he and his friends have been on the hunt for you, and why you've been keeping out of sight."

Össur looked at the door, as if expecting Helgi to reappear with a lawyer in tow.

"Nothing to say."

"Come on, Össi. Where have Magni and Tinna Lind gone? Akureyri? Somewhere up-country? Still in Reykjavík somewhere? Don't worry, they'll show up soon enough," Gunna said, and was rewarded with a momentary sideways glance at her. "Believe me, I don't care a jot about Cornershop Alli's money. If dope dealers want to rob and kill each other, then that's

370

absolutely fine by me, so long as there aren't any civilians in the way."

Össur stared at the wall in front of him. Gunna could see the inner turmoil taking place and feel the misery within him.

"Last chance, Össi. Once Helgi comes through that door, everything's on the record. We have a cast-iron case against you. We have the weapon that killed Brandur Geirsson up at Hotel Hraun a week ago and your dabs are all over it. We have a witness. Open and shut."

"Nothing to do with me."

"So make it easy for yourself and come clean. No?"

The door squeaked open and Helgi returned. He looked expectantly at Gunna, who gave him a slight shake of the head.

"The lawyer will be here in half an hour," he said.

"Good. You'd better get the recording kit ready. I need to have a chat with the doctor and find out if this character can be transferred to Litla Hraun tomorrow," Gunna said and she saw the tear finally detach itself from the corner of Össur's eye and roll down his cheek at the mention of the prison's name.

Magni ordered a second beer. He had gone straight through passport control. The officer who checked him through looked tired as he glanced quickly over the top of Jóhann Einarsson's passport at the man in front of him.

The departure area was crowded with passengers for a delayed flight to somewhere in North America, asleep here and there among their baggage, while he could see a queue starting to form at the departure gate for the Edinburgh flight. He looked at his ticket and saw that his seat would be near the front of the aircraft. Hell, he thought, he didn't need to stand in a queue when the bar was a far more comfortable place. He could be the last one on, he decided, and laughed to himself at the thought that he might find himself sitting next to Tinna Lind, even though they had taken care to keep away from each other.

He made his beer last, savouring it as he waited and watched the queue start to move. He couldn't help looking out for Tinna Lind and decided she must have been at the front of the line.

Magni downed the last of his beer, put his glass down and smiled at the barmaid before sauntering to the back of the queue, feeling awkward as the only person in the place without any hand baggage. His passport and boarding pass were checked yet again and, as he boarded the plane and found his seat, he looked around for the blonde head and saw several among the rows of seats behind him, before settling himself back and closing his eyes.

Gunna's phone buzzed. She looked at it quickly to see if anyone important might be sending her a message, and was surprised to see Gísli's name there.

Hæ Mum. I'm at the hospital. Th's not well. Can you come by today sometime?

She found herself wondering what she could say, irritated by the distraction from the day's frenetic activity and at the same time brought down to earth.

372

OK, I'll give you a call when I'm off duty. How long will you be there? she thumbed back into her phone and stabbed the send button.

The answer came back after a few seconds. *As long as it takes. Call when you can. xx,* she read, and found herself overwhelmed by sadness at her son's situation and her own powerlessness to help him. She sent back the shortest message she could. *Will do. xx* and put her phone away as Ívar Laxdal arrived, driving thoughts of anything other than work from her mind.

"What do we have, Gunnhildur?"

"We have Össur in bed at the National Hospital, and he's going nowhere other than custody at Litla Hraun."

"He's your suspect?"

"He is," Gunna confirmed. "There's no doubt in my mind that he murdered Brandur Geirsson and was the instigator of the kidnapping of Erna Brandsen and Tinna Lind Bogadóttir. I'm confident forensics will confirm the pistol is his and that it's the one he used to shoot Brandur."

Ívar Laxdal stood up and gazed outside. Gunna wondered if he was admiring his beloved black Volvo in the car park below, even though it was dark and the rain had started to pelt the building again, rattling the windows.

"Press conference time, I think?" he said with a smile, knowing the effect it would have.

"Again?" Gunna's heart sank. "Can't you do it?"

"You're the investigating officer. You're in charge of the unit. It's your police work that's put Össur in a cell."

For a moment Gunna toyed with the idea of telling Ívar Laxdal that she had been two steps behind from the start.

"All right. If I must. But we ought to wait until tomorrow when we have the results."

"We need to speak to the press tonight, I'm afraid, and it has to be in time for the evening bulletin."

Gunna groaned. "In half an hour, then?"

"Shirt, tie and polished shoes?"

"I'd prefer sweatshirt, jeans and trainers, but I don't think that'd go down well upstairs."

"Upstairs are happy, Gunnhildur," he assured her. "But we need to look the part for the gentlemen of the press."

"That's good to know. Now, if you'll excuse me, I need to go and slip into something a lot less comfortable."

A few flashes popped and Gunna tried not to blink as she read out her statement while Ívar Laxdal sat next to her. He wasn't smiling, but there was an aura of satisfaction about him.

"I can confirm that we have a suspect in custody," she intoned slowly and clearly, aware that her words were being recorded and trying not to sound anything other than as bland as possible. "The suspect is linked to the death of Brandur Geirsson and the suspect's name is not being released as yet." She took a deep breath as several hands shot up. "We are actively continuing the search for Magni Klemens Sighvatsson and Tinna Lind Brandsen Bogadóttir, and we are

374

treating this primarily as a missing persons inquiry. They are wanted for questioning in connection with the death of Brandur Geirsson, but we are not at present treating them as suspects. Pictures of both individuals are available on request."

She looked around the room.

"Any questions?" Ívar Laxdal rumbled.

"Are these people involved in the kidnapping a few days ago?"

"We believe so. That's why we need to speak to them," Ívar Laxdal said, scanning the dozen faces opposite them. "Next? Skúli?" he said, pointing towards a fresh-faced young man.

"Is there speculation that Tinna Lind Bogadóttir could have been abducted?"

"It's a possibility we can't rule out," Gunna said.

"Or are you looking at some kind of Stockholm syndrome scenario?"

"That's another possibility. As I said, we need to speak to them. That's why the search is being pursued vigorously."

"One more question," Ívar Laxdal decided, pointing at a young woman in the group of journalists.

"Is there any truth in the rumours that the disappearance of these two persons is linked to organized crime?" she asked, and there was an immediate hush in the room.

Gunna looked at Ívar Laxdal. He gestured to her to answer and she grimaced.

"That's a question we're not in a position to answer at the moment," she said.

"So you're not ruling out an organized crime link?"

"The investigation is at an early stage, and at the moment I'm not ruling anything out," Gunna said in a sharp voice. "But I can tell you that we have no indication so far of any links with anyone outside Iceland." She paused, coughed and cleared her throat.

"Inspector . . .?"

"That's all I can say now. You will, of course, be kept informed, and there will be a press call again at the same time tomorrow."

Ívar Laxdal turned to Gunna as the journalists straggled from the room. "Now, before we go, what about the others, Össur Oskarsson's accomplices?"

"That's the big question," she said in an undertone. "Össur won't say anything, probably from force of habit as much as anything. But the money, assuming it ever existed, is nowhere to be seen. My opinion is that Magni Sighvatsson and Tinna Lind Bogadóttir have whatever money there is, but we don't have a crime. Alli the Cornershop hasn't made a formal complaint and he isn't likely to. I'd very much like to question both of them, but as far as I'm concerned, I'm happy just to have Össur waiting for me to throw the book at him."

"The other two are accessories to several crimes."

"They are, as well as being witnesses, which is the more important reason I'd like to have them here, as well as to simply explain what the hell they've been up to."

"So where are they?" he asked. "We need to know."

"I've alerted every airport in the country that has international flights, which is Keflavík and the airport in town that has a flight to the Faroes a couple of days a week. I've already checked and there are no flights overseas from Akureyri or anywhere else at this time of year. We've already been through the passenger lists and there's no Magni Sighvatsson or Tinna Lind Bogadóttir booked on anything, but we've alerted the airlines and the ferry to Hirtshals in case there's a last-minute booking."

"They could be travelling under other names, couldn't they, assuming they are trying to leave the country?"

"We've circulated their photos, along with all the others, and we'll have a look through the airport CCTV footage when we have time." Gunna shrugged. "I'd hazard a guess that both Alli the Cornershop and the Undertakers will be looking for them, and it's not as if you can stay out of sight for long in a country like this. If they want to stay healthy, then they have to get out of the country, and my gut feeling is that they'll want to lay low somewhere quiet until the hue and cry dies down. But I could be wrong," she said. "It wouldn't be the first time. Anyhow, I have my hands full with Össur at the moment, and Helgi and Eiríkur will be paying Rafn Sigmarsson a visit this evening to find out why someone might want to set fire to his van, and why it happened to be parked outside Alli's place, Then we need to ask Alli a lot more questions as well. Not that he'll tell us anything, but it's worth it just to watch the old bastard squirm."

"As long as he doesn't complain about police brutality, then you can make him squirm as much as you like, Gunnhildur," Ívar Laxdal said, jangling his keys. "Do your worst. With your villain in custody and a solid case, plus the opportunity of applying pressure to the Undertakers, I'm not complaining."

Magni's flight landed early, and he took it as a positive omen. It looked like being a cool evening on the other side of the airport's plate glass windows as he followed the crowd towards passport control, looking from side to side. Gradually the group of Icelanders from his flight became diluted with arrivals on other flights, and by the time he was at the passport desk, he could no longer hear any familiar voices around him.

His passport was checked and he was sent on his way with a nod and a curt "thank you", and with no baggage, he was soon outside in the arrivals area, leaning on the metal barrier with the taxi drivers holding up their placards marked with odd — to his eyes at least — names. One by one the drivers peeled off as their passengers came through the gate, scanning the crowd for their own names, and the drivers were replaced with new ones.

After half an hour Magni went to the arrivals area café and bought himself a coffee, paying with euros and getting some change in pounds. Once his coffee had been finished and he crushed the empty cup in his hands, he had to admit to himself that Tinna Lind wasn't coming. He couldn't have missed her as he had been one of the first off the flight. Had she been stopped at Keflavík, maybe at the passport desk, where her new blonde hair hadn't been enough to convince the officer on duty that she was Ásta Maria Einarsdóttir?

He realized that he had no way of contacting her. He didn't have the number of Tinna Lind's phone, and his own cheap pay-as-you-go mobile probably wouldn't work outside Iceland. He could find Erna's phone number, but that would lead nowhere, and he knew nobody who might be able to help him contact her. He stood despondent, leaning on the polished rail with strange voices chattering around him, wondering what had become of her. Finally he retreated to the café and huddled in his coat, trying to figure out what to do. He emptied his pockets and counted the bundle of euros Tinna Lind had handed him before they'd left the bus. Eleven hundred and sixty euros might seem a lot, he reflected, but it wouldn't keep him for long in a foreign city where he knew nobody and had nowhere to go.

Gunna stood for a long time with her hand on Gísli's shoulder. Gísli sat stone-faced, staring into space with Thorvaldur Hauksson's withered hand in his. There was silence in the room and Gunna slowly became aware that the sound of laboured breathing had stopped. The heart monitor's screen displayed a single unbroken line.

"He's gone, Mum," Gísli said in a flat matter-of-fact tone, and gently laid the hand on the bed.

Gunna pulled up a chair and sat next to Gísli, fumbling for his hand and putting her other arm around his hunched shoulders.

"Thanks, Mum. I'm glad you came."

Gunna thought to herself that she would rather be practically anywhere else in the world, but said nothing as Gísli sniffed and stifled a gulp before it became a sob.

"I'm so sorry, Gísli. Truly I am. It's not fair on you that he should be taken away just as you'd got to know him."

"Yeah, Mum. It's a bit shit, isn't it? Still, I know you had your misgivings about him, so I appreciate your showing up."

Tinna Lind crunched through crisp snow as she walked to the hotel from the airport. It was a refreshing short walk under a clear sky with a semi-circle of ivory moon high above. She shivered, but reminded herself that another flight tomorrow would take her somewhere much warmer.

The hotel was welcoming in the frigid way that only airport hotels where nobody stays longer than one night can be. At the desk she ordered a wake-up call, ignored the young desk clerk's subtle invitation that she could call anytime if there were anything she might need, and retired to a large room on the fourth floor with a view of the terminal building.

She spent a long time under the hot water of the shower, swathed herself in a towel as thick as a bearskin and examined the still unfamiliar blonde of her hair, deciding that she might let it stay that way.

She poured a drink from the mini bar, put the television on and emptied her case onto the bed. She counted notes into piles, keeping a tally as she went, and grinned with satisfaction when she'd finished. Tinna Lind looked in the mirror opposite the bed and raised her glass to herself before she stowed the cash back in the case and lay back on the stack of pillows to watch the television news in a language she only half-understood.

Later that evening she dropped the card from her phone into the toilet and watched it disappear. Her phone hummed into life and she plugged it in to charge before connecting to the hotel's wifi network and keying in a message to an email address she knew off by heart.

Hæ Mum. This is TL. Don't worry, I'm alive & well, having a great time in the sun. I'll be in touch again in a week or two. xxx.

She watched the screen as the message was flagged up as having been delivered, and then she switched off the phone, unwound the towel and crawled under the bedclothes. She turned off the light and stretched out in the huge crisp bed. Tomorrow would be another long day, and after that there would be business to be done.

Acknowledgements

With grateful thanks to all those patient people who answered many questions.

Other titles published by Ulverscroft:

COLD STEAL

Quentin Bates

A successful housebreaker who leaves no traces and no clues as he strips Reykjavík homes of their valuables has been a thorn in the police's side for months. But when one night the thief breaks into the wrong house, he finds himself caught in a trap, and the stakes are raised far beyond anything he could have imagined. Gunnhildur Gisladóttir of the Reykjavík police finds herself frustrated at every turn as she searches for a victim who has vanished from the scene of the crime, and wonders if it could be linked to the murders of two businessmen with dubious reputations that her bosses are warning her to keep clear of.

CHILLED TO THE BONE

Quentin Bates

When an elderly shipowner is found dead, tied to a bed in one of Reykjavík's smartest hotels, Sergeant Gunnhildur Gisladóttir of the city police force sees no evidence of foul play, but still suspects that things may not be as simple as they appear. As she investigates the shipowner's untimely and embarrassing demise, she stumbles across a discreet bondage ring whose existence she never suspected, and which someone is exploiting as a blackmail tool to extract cash from the most unlikely people. What begins as a straightforward case for Gunna escalates into a dangerous investigation uncovering secrets that ruthless people are ready to go to violent extremes to keep.